THE GREEN WAVE

THE GREEN WAVE

An Australian colonial steampunk story

Cassandra Kelly

 A catalogue record for this book is available from the National Library of Australia

First edition: 2019

In memory of William Bland (1789-1868): Surgeon, duellist, convict, politician, philanthropist and airship designer.

THE GREEN WAVE

PRELIMINARY OBSERVATIONS

The airship circling the harbour turned towards the town, its engine spluttering. The vessel began to descend. The observer's gaze switched from the airship to the two well-dressed men watching it, laughing. One of them slapped the other on the back and shook his hand. The posture of the men indicated a military background, or perhaps that of cultured gentlemen of the upper classes. Less than half an hour ago the observer had seen one of the men disembark from the wet ship at the dock. The other must have come to meet him. It wasn't much but it was worth reporting.

CASSANDRA KELLY

1

THE SEMINARY

"When your head is in the clouds your feet don't touch the ground." The words couldn't compete with the world outside the window where the yellow summer sun flashed on the green balloon of an airship as it passed over Canterbury. To Rosalyn the awe-inspiring sight rivalled the cathedral itself. The noise of the engine drifted down to her, the pigeons on the roof falling silent as the airship's shadow covered them. She stared wistfully from the small, stone window of her college room, vaguely aware of a voice behind her. She turned her attention from the movement and colour back to the dull, wood-panelled room that had been her home for the last two years.

"Did you say something?"

"Are you sure you're back?" said Lorena, from her perch on the edge of Rosalyn's desk.

"Yes. I'm back. What were you saying?"

"I said I've just returned from Maud's study."

"You've got it? Your posting?"

Lorena grinned. "Yes."

"Where? Where are you going?" Rosalyn grasped Lorena's hands and looked into her sparkling eyes.

"Dublin."

Rosalyn pulled Lorena close and gave her a hug. "That's wonderful. You wanted Dublin."

"Yes. All those old manuscripts—the Book of Kells. I'll be able to see it every day."

The door opened and another woman entered. Her dark ringlets curled around her pale face. She smiled smugly.

"Hullo Constance. I notice you didn't knock. You're looking quite satisfied."

"And well I should. I've been given a plum position in London. I knew I would be. The Church wants to keep the best where we can do the most for our own people, I imagine. I'm so relieved I won't have to deal with any foreigners."

"The Church also likes to receive donations from rich fathers," said Rosalyn.

"I don't know what you're implying and I don't care for an explanation."

"I suppose you're wondering where I'm going," said Lorena.

Constance stared at her. "No. Whatever gave you that idea? Never mind, I don't really want to know that either. Ta-ta. I must go and pack." She turned, walked to the door, paused, and looked back over her shoulder. "By the way, Rosie, the Dean will see you now."

"My name is Rosalyn." She pushed the door shut the instant Constance was on the other side of it. "Cow. I hate her coming into my room."

"She's so annoying."

"With any luck we'll never see her again."

"Aren't you going to go?"

"Go? Oh! Yes, my turn. I'm so excited."

The students' rooms let out into a long corridor and stairways were built into two turrets along its length. Rosalyn walked down the stairs, stepped out into the cloisters and looked along the passageway. Her gaze drifted along the tiled floor and up the interior wall to the oak ceiling before passing back down over the medieval-styled cloister windows. The dormitories, newly constructed, had been built to match the older parts of the seminary. The entire complex had fallen into ruin until rescued by the rise of the new Enlightenment Church. It had purchased the site and restored it for the training of clergy. After two years studying here Rosalyn felt an overwhelming feeling of confinement. She walked out into the fresh, free air of the quadrangle.

Looking up at the sky she hoped to catch another glimpse of the airship. It was nowhere in sight. In spite of her eagerness to learn where she'd be assigned, she dawdled across the grass to the centre of the quadrangle where stood the monument to Saint Augustine. On top of the stone plinth sat a wooden cross with a brass cog in the centre. The first-term students kept the cog to a high shine. Opposite the dormitories, on the other side of the quadrangle, workers laboured to construct another building to house male students. Largely due to Queen Victoria supporting the expansion of the Church, work had progressed rapidly. Scheduled to open in 1840, the work would now be completed next year, an entire year ahead of schedule.

In the corner of the quadrangle, workers toiled at the restoration of Ethelbert's Tower—a relic of the medieval abbey and in danger of collapsing. Rumour had it a platform would be built on the top of the tower to provide landing space for small airships. This intrigued Rosalyn, but she knew completion of the work was still some years off and as yet the number of airships in the Church fleet could be counted on one hand.

Rosalyn had one last look at the sky above. Apart from a few fluffy white clouds and a passing crow it remained empty. She continued to the Dean's office, pausing before the imposing door with her fingertips resting on the handle, itself in the form of a brass cog. The cog—symbol of creation, industry, and science—almost as important to the Church as the crucifix. Still, Rosalyn found herself wondering if sticking cogs on everything laboured the point.

She swallowed hard and took a deep breath. She was certain she'd be given a good position, perhaps in Paris. London was considered better but familiar with London, and knowing Constance had gained a position there, she had lost enthusiasm for the idea. Paris would give her greater access to the delights of the continent. Perhaps she might get sent further afield, somewhere like Moscow. That would be an adventure but a little too remote. No, she was sure it would be Paris, or one of the other great European cities. There she could work her way up through the clerical ranks and into her own position teaching at the seminary. With one hand still resting on the handle she gave a loud knock with the other.

"Enter," came the voice of Maud Hunt, the Dean. Rosalyn took another deep breath, and now suitably inflated, put on her most confident air to show herself to be well up to the task of a responsible European posting. She walked in briskly and stood, chest out and chin up in front of the large, carved-oak desk and remained still as Maud studied her in silence. Rosalyn began to feel uncomfortable under Maud's gaze. She lowered her head and stared at the floor. Eventually Maud spoke. "How do you think you went, Rosie?" Rosalyn stiffened and gritted her teeth.

"I think I did splendidly. I'm well versed in Church doctrine and I accepted the new ideas of the Enlightenment readily. I showed great ingenuity and intelligence coupled with an ability to demonstrate fresh and astounding ways of explaining the scriptures to the barely Enlightened of the working class."

"If you're referring to the time you put the iron bar into the mechanism of the Solar Orbitron then you are right. It certainly was astonishing and did demonstrate effectively the value of every tooth of every cog in the workings of our Lord's creation. However it also caused forty seven pounds, two shillings and threepence worth of damage—as you know." Maud's voice was cold and her hard, brown eyes glared at her. Rosalyn wondered if things were going to go as well as she had hoped.

The Dean continued, her voice stern. "You have also demonstrated an ability to disobey simple instructions and you've failed to conform to the rules of this grand, new institution of which you're a part. You have consistently endeavoured to find other ways of carrying out tasks for which the regulations have already made a path abundantly clear." Rosalyn wondered if she was being praised or condemned and stared out the window. "You have an astounding inability to pay attention, you live in a world of your own, wandering off on your flights of fancy and taking far more of your Technician's time than you ought." Rosalyn drew her attention from a dove which had landed on the window sill back to the Dean, wondering if she'd missed something important.

Maud paused, continuing to stare at Rosalyn who now felt rather uneasy. "Rosie, in spite of this you are going to be graduating, but I can assure you that like the earliest morning sun you have barely crept over the horizon and we will be watching you carefully. Consider your new title of Reverend to be probationary."

Rosalyn started to tremble. "Probationary?"

Maud ignored Rosalyn's question. "That's a little misleading—your title is to be Reverend Missionary. We're sending you to Sydney."

Rosalyn looked up at the ceiling trying to place Sydney on the map of Europe when the penny dropped with such force it drew an exclamation from her. "The Antipodes? You're sending me to Sydney? It's miles away and there's nothing there. You can count the number of people in that town on your fingers and toes."

"Yes, the Antipodes. Her Majesty The Queen's colony of New South Wales—and Sydney is quite a large town now. We could think of none better suited for the work we have in mind." She added, "And although you are going to Sydney that is merely your arrival point in the Great South Land. Once there you will be going inland to bring Enlightenment to the heathens."

Without asking, Rosalyn flopped in a big leather arm chair, her legs spread wide to prop up her elbows which in turn, with hands clenched together, propped up her bowed head. She stared at the floor. Maud gave her a little time to compose herself as Rosalyn muttered, "Sydney? There must be some mistake. It's got to be a mistake." Maud poured two glasses of whisky from a crystal decanter on her desk and rose from her seat. She walked over to Rosalyn and sat on the arm of the chair, handing one of the glasses to the dejected girl.

"There's no mistake, Rosie. We discussed this at great length at a Cogboard meeting. Some on the Council didn't want to pass you. I argued vehemently that you pass, that the Church could find a use for someone of your temperament. You're fortunate that this is a time of rapid expansion for the Church and we need everyone we can get. The Council made a compromise and lowered its standards for you. See this as a chance to prove yourself. Some Missionaries rise to the challenge and make quite a name for themselves."

Rosalyn gave Maud's words a few second's thought. "And there are many who reach an unfortunate end at the hands of the heathens, if they don't die of some horrible disease." She paused and stated, "The Antipodes. I know nothing about the Antipodes. It's filled with ignorant, murdering savages who care nothing for the Colonial authority—and there are the blacks to contend with as well." Rosalyn shook her head in despair. "They're convicts, the worst we have are down there." Tears welled up in her eyes as the thoughts of such a harsh exile flooded her mind. "I'm being transported aren't I? Am I going to get seven years or fourteen?" she spat out in despair.

Maud ignored her outburst and tenderly stroked Rosalyn's hair, tucking a loose strand behind her ear. "You're wrong about them being the worst. We hang the worst of them. However it is to the frontier and the Aboriginal people to whom you'll be taking Enlightenment. You'll be well supported by the Church, and on the plus side," Maud paused for effect. "You will have your own airship." This last point took its time sinking in and when it did Rosalyn looked up, wide-eyed.

"My own airship? Seriously? I'll have full command of it?"

"You will, but don't get too excited, it's not a big ship and it's one of the early models. It's a light carrier, designed to take up to three people plus baggage. It should be more than enough for the Mission."

"My own airship!" Rosalyn stood. "When do I leave?"

Maud smiled at the girl's new found enthusiasm. "Do you know Queen Victoria herself has asked for a greater emphasis on Missionary work in her Empire?"

"Uh, yes. I remember when she came to the throne last year, she caused a flutter by giving her support to our Church. It was mentioned in one of our lectures."

"King William was a supporter but it was hoped by many that the new Queen would fall back to the Old Church. It was a great disappointment to those who oppose us."

"I was never much interested in the politics."

"I can see that on your academic record, along with the other subjects you weren't much interested in." Maud sipped her drink as she looked into Rosalyn's blue-green eyes. She went on. "Missionary work can be dangerous and we don't have enough volunteers for all the positions we have planned. As the work is voluntary you can decline the Orders, but in your position the Church has no other place for you. Do you understand?"

"Yes. I'm volunteering to go. I'll accept the Orders—and the airship."

Maud smiled. "I knew you would and I have every confidence in you." She went to her desk and picked up an envelope. "In here are your documents for travel and introduction. You will be sailing from Southampton on the ship Iris. And Rosie, don't go mentioning to anyone that you are getting an airship; it would only incite jealousy and soon every Missionary would be clamouring for one. In this other envelope are your Mission Orders. Keep them safe."

Maud handed the Orders to Rosalyn and spoke in a more formal tone, "Colonial Missionary Reverend Rosalyn Flynn, your ship departs in a little under four weeks."

Rosalyn looked up at the Dean. "Four weeks? That will give me a good amount of time to see my parents before I go."

"They're in Lewes, aren't they?"

"Yes. It's on the way to Southampton, more or less."

Maud stared directly into her eyes. "You won't have much time for them, I'm sorry. Before you sail you're required to attend the Royal College of Airship Aviation at Salisbury Plain. You didn't think we were going to send you off with an expensive airship and no training? We're confident you'll pass the flying course. If you fail the course your career with this Church ends."

"Fail at flying? I won't fail, you know I won't fail. I love flying."

"I know you'll do splendidly. Do you have any questions?"

Rosalyn sipped her whisky and stared thoughtfully at the wall opposite. "Yes, I do. Aren't Colonial Missionaries supposed to have three years training?"

"Yes, they are, but due to the rapid expansion we've had to send some out with less than that. When our new student accommodation opens we'll be returning to three years of training."

"Why am I being sent as a Missionary to a colony? I thought only the men were sent on Missions to the frontiers."

"The quick growth of the Church has also left us in need of Ministers and so we're opening the Colonial Missionary field to women. However, you won't be alone as we're sending you a Guardian. When you arrive in Sydney you'll go to our Church there and see the parson. He'll look after your travel arrangements to Bathurst where you'll meet the Guardian. Bathurst will be your departure point for the frontier."

"I've never heard of Bathurst. I'll still be in charge of the airship won't I?"

"Yes, Rosie, you will. The Guardian has had no airship training. That will be compulsory for them in future but for now you have nothing to be concerned about."

"Do we only have the one Church in Sydney?"

"Yes, there is just the one, but we will have more Ministers sailing soon and establishing new Churches. There'll be a second one in Sydney and we'll be building one in Bathurst. Others will follow."

Rosalyn studied the envelope. "And everything I need to know about the Mission is in here?"

"It is. I must stress that you keep those documents to yourself and don't open them until your ship has sailed. Congratulations, Rosie. I wish you all the best."

Rosalyn's enthusiasm was only slightly tempered by the sadness at the news she would have little time for farewells to her family. She stared at the wall and pictured herself on the airship flying through the soft, blue sky. "Thank you, Dean." Impulsively, she hugged Maud and kissed her on the cheek. She rushed out the door, mumbling, "My own airship, my own airship."

Rosalyn returned to the dormitory and marched straight to Lorena's room to break the news to her. Lorena gave her a big smile. "Sydney is on the other side of the globe but to be in command of your own balloon... You must be so excited."

"Airship, Lorena, it's an airship. You see the balloon is the part above the boat and..." Lorena threw a pillow at her.

They spent a good hour chatting about all the possibilities their lives now had in front of them and promised to write, care of the Seminary. The packing done, they said their last farewells and left each other's company. As Rosalyn's buggy passed out through the Seminary gatehouse she turned back for one last look. A tear rolled down her cheek, carrying with it the joy-filled memories of her days within those walls.

Maud left the Seminary and made her way to the Cathedral where she took a position in a pew in the rear. A well-dressed man who had been admiring the stained glass sat down next to her.

"Did she accept?"

"Yes, of course. Her acceptance was never in doubt."

"Are you sure she'll pass her course?"

"She has a burning passion to fly. She'll pass. She may only scrape through but she won't let herself fail it. When she's flying she'll do anything she's told so she can keep flying."

"She knows to keep her Mission secret?"

"I stressed that to her. She'll visit our parson in Sydney and then go on to Bathurst."

The man smiled. "We'll have our own person in the airship with her."

"Does anyone else know of our plans?"

"If they do we should have heard of it. We have an agent in place in the Royal Scientific Society for the Exploration of the Antipodes. They and your Church have the only other expeditions and we will be in on all three. I don't see how we can fail."

"What we're looking for may not be there."

"We're sure it is. It's too great a coincidence for it to be otherwise."

Maud looked up at the ceiling. "And the girl—will she live?"

"I do hope you're not descending into sentimentality. We have no room for that, especially with the stakes this high. She will be killed, if necessary."

Maud nodded. "I'd best return to the Seminary. I have to report to the Church Council that Reverend Flynn has accepted the Mission."

The man studied the interior of his hat. "You did well to get the Council to pass the girl. That can have been no easy feat given what you've told me about her attitude."

"She's not a stupid girl but her mind is on other things. She's naive, and she lacks confidence in herself. She's embraced Church doctrine and will be easily manipulated. Those are the qualities you told me to look for."

The man nodded. "Yes, although I would have preferred her to be stupid, too."

"I hope we haven't underestimated her." Maud stood, smoothed her skirts, glanced around the Cathedral and departed.

2

THE GHOST OF STONEHENGE

Rosalyn alighted from the buggy at Boscombe Down and found herself once more staring into the sky. A large airship hovered low over the fields and several smaller ones could be seen moving about at various altitudes. The memory of her one and only airship flight came back to her. A friend of her father who had acquired a small cargo vessel had taken the family up for a ride. On the brief flight Rosalyn's mother became terribly sick and refused to get up from the deck. Rosalyn remembered how she herself had grinned from ear to ear for the entire trip as the wind shook through her long dark hair. A voice from behind her brought her back to earth.

"Reverend, is everything all right?"

Rosalyn looked around at the young man with the buggy. "Yes, everything is fine."

"Nice vessels aren't they, Reverend? Are you going to go flying in one?"

"They are magnificent. And yes, I'll be going up."

"You're not scared at all? I think I'd be frightened going up so high."

"I'm not at all scared. If I could afford it I'd buy my own. Sadly I won't get one on Church wages."

"I've heard they cost a penny or two. I don't see why—it's just a boat with a balloon attached and a steam engine thrown in."

"The lift is created by a substance called blue ascension—it creates the special steam that fills the balloon. It's made from a mould discovered by the Mysterious Captain Hivetree—I'm sure you've heard of him. The mould needs careful cultivation and is disinclined even to a moderate rate of growth. That's where the cost lies."

The young man nodded and looked up at the airship. "I won't get to fly in one even if I want to. I can barely afford to feed myself."

"But you have a horse and buggy."

"Not mine. I drive for Mr Castleton and I get a cut of the fare."

Rosalyn looked at him. "What's your name?"

"Tommy Sweetwater."

"Tommy, you're thruppence richer if you'll get my bags in."

Rosalyn stood in front of the main doors as Tommy struggled past with her baggage. The building was red brick and only a few years old. Ivy had started working its way up the brickwork and the perimeter had been planted with roses. No grand reception awaited her but being the only woman on her training course Rosalyn had her own private quarters.

The training was carried out as a joint civilian and military venture. The military pilots, on passing the course, would be joining the Royal Aviation Corps and going on to further training. The civilians would follow their own respective pathways after qualifying.

The students assembled that evening to be introduced to the school's Commander, Major Horbuckle, who had left the cavalry when airships first took to the skies. He scanned the line-up and his eyes came to rest on Rosalyn.

"You're not the first woman who has been through the course. I should warn you that the failure rate of our women is higher than for the men. With no disrespect meant, Reverend, I cannot give you any special considerations in training. If you can't understand any of the theory, or if you show in any way a failure to control the craft in the air, I will have to fail you."

Rosalyn took a deep breath and replied, "I expect no special considerations, and I might add that I will not fail this course."

Major Horbuckle hmphed as he fiddled with his fob watch. He continued his walk along the row of trainees. "And look what we have here—a Chinaman." Major Horbuckle raised his voice and spoke slowly. "How well do you speak English?"

"Quite well thank you, but have much work to do on accent."

The Major took a step back, eyebrows raised. "Yes, you do speak it surprisingly well but I'll be making no allowances for you either. Where are you from—Shanghai?"

"Chengdu, but have much business in Canton. Live there most of time."

"And what is your name?"

"Wang Bo." He gave a slight bow to the Major who found himself bowing in return.

The Major turned away from him and faced the trainees. "You, or the organisations which have sent you here, have paid a considerable amount of money for you to do this course. We will not, however, pass you on the basis of that. The Royal College of Airship Aviation is building a reputation for producing the finest pilots and crew in the realm. In fact, it is one of only three such schools in Britain at this point in time. We are the best and will continue to be the best even when the number of schools increases, and trust me, they will increase—airships are the future. Don't fail."

Theory took up the first day and in the evening the trainees retired to the lounge. The men treated Rosalyn politely but for the most part she found herself omitted from their discussions. A small library occupied the far wall although, with airship aviation still in its infancy, there were few books on airships. The current textbook was the most interesting of them all so she curled up in a chair and as dry as the subject may have been to an outsider, she soon became absorbed in it. She looked up only briefly to see Bo, ensconced in a leather armchair, nearby. He nodded politely to her and quietly read for a while until Rosalyn became aware that he was staring at her.

"Yes?" she asked, perhaps a little too curtly.

"You worship sun?"

"What?"

Bo made an arc with his arm over his head. "Sun, you religion?"

Rosalyn laughed. "No. Not at all. When our Church first began it was called the Church of the Sun Cog. The name gave people the wrong idea so the name was changed to the Enlightenment Church. People didn't understand that 'The Church of the Sun Cog' was a symbolic name."

"Symbolic?"

"Yes. The sun is not a cog but it stands in for the way machines work with their cogs, great and small. You see the solar system is like a big machine, as is the rest of the universe. And we know now that all systems operate like machines and are well-ordered. The goal of our church is to marry modern scientific principles, industry and Enlightenment ideas with the social and high moral nature of humankind."

"You give sermon?"

"What? Yes, I'll be giving sermons as part of my church duties, of course."

"What is humankind?"

"Us. People—we are humans."

"And humans are machines?"

"No, we're like machines. Well... not us of course, but the systems we operate to keep society ordered and functional are machine-like."

"Who makes machine run?"

"We see that as one of the roles of our Church. That is, we make sure everyone finds their place in the machine."

"Ah." And at that, Bo went back to reading his book.

Captain Nathaniel Drake, dubious about taking on his first female trainee, approached his task with a high degree of professionalism and gave Rosalyn the same direct attention that he gave the other trainees. They had been divided into groups to be instructed on small craft. Rosalyn found herself, by default, in a group with Bo, another merchant gentleman, and an amiable young man of good breeding who held the rank of Lieutenant in the Royal Marines.

The men paid close attention to her when she took the wheel for the first time but such was her excitement that Rosalyn paid them no mind. The wood of the wheel beneath her fingers felt magical and the grin she wore on her first time aloft came back to her in full flower. Her turn at the helm was all too brief. "You said you've never flown an airship before but you have, haven't you, Reverend?" asked Nathaniel.

"No. Really, Captain Drake, this is my first time and I love it. I could fly all day—and night, too."

Nathaniel smiled. "I'm impressed, Reverend Flynn. You have a refreshing affinity for the air."

Rosalyn watched and listened closely when each of the other trainees took their turn at the wheel, noting every piece of new information. Every aspect of flying appealed to her, from the creaking of the timbers, the swaying of the boat and the strange acrid smell of the blue ascension. It wasn't so appealing to Ajax Young, the lieutenant, and Gideon Brook, the merchant, both of whom wasted their breakfast over the side shortly after they went aloft.

Ajax became quite friendly to her and curious about the details of her theological training and Mission to the heathens, interrogated her on the details. "You don't know where you're going when you get there?"

"Yes. When I arrive in Sydney I go and meet the parson of our Church."

"Is that the Old Church or the Church of the Sun Cog?"

"It's called the Enlightenment Church and from what I understand both are present in the colony along with the other Protestant churches and the Catholics. Our Church wants to establish itself there as the primary denomination. In that way as the colony grows it becomes a centre from which the Church can spread the Enlightenment to surrounding regions."

"Doesn't the Church give you more guidance than that? I mean, sending you to Sydney with an airship and only a few weeks training—that's such short notice. Surely they must have told you something else."

"No, they did give me Orders but I'm not to open them until I'm on board the ship out."

Ajax gave her a mischievous grin. "I'd be opening them now. The Church wouldn't know. Do you have them with you?"

Rosalyn avoided his question and replied, "I can't disobey Church instructions. If I make any mistakes on this…" She let her voice trail off and then changed the tone. "What about you? Why are you on this course? You're Army not Royal Aviation Corps."

Ajax laughed, "The Royal Marines are part of the Navy, not the Army. When I pass the course I'll be automatically transferred from the Marines to the Corps. I wholeheartedly concur with Major Horbuckle that airships are the future, and whoever controls the skies will control the battlefields. I believe that in the future politics will flow from the cannons of the airships."

"When Enlightenment comes to all there will be no more need for wars."

"That's an optimistic view, Reverend. I share your views on creating a more Enlightened society but I don't think it will be coming quickly. Tell me," said Ajax changing the subject, "when does your ship sail?"

"I believe it's scheduled for two days after the course finishes."

"That soon?" He looked disappointed. "What ship do you sail on?"

"It's called the Iris. It's a wet ship of course. Have you lost interest in sailing the seas?"

"I enjoyed my life as a marine aboard the ocean-going wet ships, but it's now airships for me. There is something especially thrilling about flying around so far above the ground, looking down on everyone. It gives one a fresh perspective."

"Yes, it's certainly quite something." Rosalyn studied the young man, finding in his enthusiasm a kindred spirit.

Nathaniel pointed out to them that Stonehenge would be appearing off the port side and he directed Bo to fly lower to give them all a good look. They stared at it in wonder. "It was built by druids," said Ajax.

"It's haunted, too," said Nathaniel.

"Haunted? I hadn't heard that." Gideon leaned over and gave the stones a closer look.

"Have you seen a ghost there, Nathaniel?" asked Rosalyn.

"No, but I was told a story when I arrived here. It happened about twenty years back. I'm not sure exactly when but it wasn't long before airships were invented. An early morning mist shrouded the countryside and some travellers saw a spectral figure, as white as snow, and tall, almost as tall as two men, with eyes of ice, and it was walking into the circle. The mists swirled around and it vanished."

"Do you believe it?"

Nathaniel breathed in deeply and shook his head. "Early morning and mist? I believe it's a tale from a tired or imaginative mind."

Ajax added, "And given the early hour possibly the mind of someone returning home drunk."

That evening Ajax joined the other military trainees who were naturally drawn together as a clique, along with a couple of civilians who had gravitated into their circle. Gideon joined Rosalyn and Bo in the leather armchairs at the library-end of the common room. "Whisky, Reverend? It's from Ireland, quite superior to Scotch but don't tell any of the Macs I said that."

Gideon poured the whisky for her and Bo. "We're starting a new enterprise Reverend— a toast." He raised his glass and Bo and Rosalyn followed suit.

"What is the enterprise?"

"We're going to fly opium from India across the mountains to

China and bring back silk on the return journeys."

"That sounds like it will be quite profitable but I thought I heard the Chinese court is trying to stop the import of opium."

Gideon laughed. "It will never happen; there are too many people making money from it. The East India Company won't allow anything to interfere with their free trade, and if they can trade, so can we." He patted his large round belly. "Of course I'll have to lose some of this so we can carry more cargo."

Rosalyn smiled at him. "It sounds like a worthy endeavour, Mr Brook. Good luck to you both."

Bo spoke quietly without moving his head. "I see people look at you. See them often look here at you, Reverend."

Rosalyn looked up and saw Ajax and the men in his company looking her way. Gideon raised his glass to them across the room and they raised their glasses in return. "Hardly surprising," said Gideon. "You're the only woman here and I think the young man likes you, Reverend."

"I think perhaps he does. He wants to know everything about me."

"Not interest like that," said Bo who had been sitting quietly observing.

"I should think not," said Rosalyn. "You're old enough to be my father." Bo winced, shook his head, drained his glass and made his leave.

"Funny Chinaman." Rosalyn stared after him as she nursed her drink. She resumed the conversation, speculating on the views Gideon would be afforded as he crossed the mountains from India to China, and some of the intricacies of setting up business in a foreign land. After a second whisky she said good night to Gideon and gave Ajax a nod as she left the lounge.

A cool breeze blew down the corridor towards her from the open door of her room. She crept towards it and as she neared, the door slammed shut. Pushing it carefully back open she peered inside and by the light of the lamp she could see her clothes scattered over the floor. Her papers and books were strewn across her desk and the curtains were flapping in the wind blowing through the open window. Rosalyn looked out but could see no sign of anyone in the darkness. She closed the window, drew the curtains and set about tidying up the mess. She folded her clothes and restored them to the trunk. Apart from the lining of the trunk, which had been ripped apart, nothing appeared to be missing or damaged. There being no lock on the door she pushed a chair against it before going to bed.

She cocooned herself under the blankets. Although warm and comfortable, sleep didn't come easily. She tossed and turned until the sheets and blankets were twisted and tangled. It wasn't only the ransacking of her room which left her unsettled, it was also her exclusion by the men on her course. It was a subtle thing and she told herself that of course men would prefer their own company. She tried not to let it bother her. As she lay in the dark she thought of the good times she'd had at the Seminary, the companionship of Lorena, and her other friends. A tear rolled down her cheek. She turned her thoughts to flying and imagined herself at the wheel of an airship drifting through the clouds. She slept.

Rosalyn reported the ransacking of her room to the administration who were lacklustre in their response. They did, however, promise to have the room watched and to have one of the servants always close by. Rosalyn took it up further with Nathaniel when they were out flying that morning.

"You say nothing was missing so robbery would hardly be a motive. I hate to admit it, Reverend, but there are many who are completely opposed to women being the pilots of airships. I'm sure you being a woman of the cloth and sanctioned by the Queen has prevented worse excesses. Many of the women who attempt the course fail to complete it because of the hostile attitude of their male counterparts. Unfortunately, there are even some staff here who would rather women were excluded. I can readily believe that it was the efforts of one of those men who stand in opposition who was trying to deter you from completing the course."

Rosalyn scowled. "I'm every bit as good at flying as anyone else and I certainly will not be deterred from my endeavour. If I find out who did it I shall have harsh words for them."

Ajax, who was standing nearby, interjected. "I'll do more than that if we find out who did it, I can assure you."

"Thank you, Ajax. I know I can count on your support."

Unnoticed, Bo stood frowning as he watched from the rear of the vessel.

Nathaniel was more than pleased with Rosalyn's progress but it was in the basic elements of navigation that Rosalyn floundered. The rest of her classroom theory was sound and fortunately the lack of navigation skills was not a determinant for passing the course. Of airship terminology Rosalyn had an advantage over most of the course as they were familiar with only wet ship sailing. Rosalyn, with nothing to unlearn, was a blank slate.

"What is called the gunwale on a wet ship is known as a skyrail on an airship. Going to ground, or grounding, if you are on a wet ship," continued Major Horbuckle, "you would be in a bit of a pickle. However, if it's an airship it means you are bringing your airship back to the ground. When you get there you don't anchor, you hook."

"It's still a form of sailing, isn't it, Major? The hooks are still anchors," asked a young man from the back of the room.

"We like to distinguish ourselves from the wets. There are similarities as airship terminology has borrowed a few items from our aquatic friends, but do not assume airships are the same as sailing ships or you will find yourself in a frightful mess. The reason we are creating a new terminology is to get it out of the heads of people that this is not wet sailing—that flying is a new venture. If you have been a sailor you don't want to react in the air as you would on a water-borne vessel."

"I hear what you're saying, sir, yes."

"In time it won't matter so much but as things are, most of those coming to us have nautical experience either as passengers or crew. When airships become as common as sailing vessels the people who come to us won't be coming to us from a background of sailing—they'll be people like the Reverend here, people who passionately want to fly. When you're up there in the clouds, the boat swaying, the breezes blowing and the view of creation spread out below you, there you will find an exhilarating sense of freedom unknown to the flats."

"The flats?"

"Those people who are confined to moving only on the surface. We, as flyers, have an experience like no others. Being a pilot is not merely a career, It's a way of being in the world, and when you feel it deep inside, you will never want to ground again." The Major's eyes blazed as he imagined himself at the wheel and a thousand feet up. Rosalyn closed her eyes and imagined the same.

"Airships are quite limited in their abilities, aren't they, Major?" asked another student.

"They are, but they are improving all the time. Even as we speak, developments are being made in the field of metallurgy. We now have Gravitationally Ignorant Brass."

"That is next to useless other than as a parlour amusement," said Gideon.

"That's true. It's either too brittle and snaps at the slightest bit of pressure, or even breeze, or it's far too soft and breaks up into little bubbles. If It's perfected we can expect to see airships made from it, and much larger airships."

"What is it?" asked Rosalyn.

"It's brass that if placed in the air will remain where It's placed. It will neither fall to the ground nor rise up in the air."

"How is that so?"

"I don't know the science behind it but it has to do with the alloy of bronze and copper being able to retain something of the blue ascension; something that doesn't work at all with other metals."

"It sounds like quite a remarkable substance. An airship made of

23

brass would present a dazzling spectacle, I would imagine."

For the last few days Rosalyn trained in a light freighter which had a crew of three. More than once, Nathaniel had to instruct Rosalyn to speak up and give her commands clearly. As the pilot, it fell on her to instruct the other crew members in the setting of the side sails and other tasks unmanageable from her position at the wheel. Other than that, Rosalyn managed the transition from the small craft to the larger vessel with ease. On the afternoon of the second last day of the course Major Horbuckle assembled the trainees and instructors.

"It's time to announce the position of lead pilot. As you know, this is a great honour and is an automatic graduation with the rank of Airship Pilot. The man who takes first place in the course also gets the privilege of piloting the Imperial Air Cruiser *Pegasus* which you have seen flying around here."

The assembled students waited expectantly and Rosalyn looked around the room wondering who the lucky man would be. Major Horbuckle opened the large and important-looking brown envelope and drew out the certificate on which was inscribed the name of the recipient. He paused, frowned and twitched his nose. "I am pleased to announce that the dux of this course is Reverend Rosalyn Flynn. If you could please step forward."

If the room was quiet while waiting for the recipient to be announced it was even more silent now. Some of the faces were marked with disgust and it was Ajax, Gideon and Bo who commenced clapping. The others slowly joined in, and Rosalyn, recovering from the shock, walked to the front and stood before Major Horbuckle. Nathaniel joined him there and handed the Major a small box. The Major took from it a brass badge in the form of a pair of wings with enamel inlay in rainbow colours, and affixed it to Rosalyn's tunic. "Airship Pilot Reverend Rosalyn Flynn, congratulations. You are not only dux of the course but you are the first woman to achieve this distinction thereby setting a high standard for any others who might follow." He handed her the certificate and after studying it she returned it to the envelope and placed it in her satchel beside her Mission Orders and the Enlightened Bible.

"Thank you Major Horbuckle." She turned to Captain Drake. "And thank you, too. You're a first-rate instructor." Rosalyn had a smile from ear to ear and as she returned to her friends she did not see those men who were not so happy at her success.

Rosalyn rose early the next day for her flight in the *Pegasus*. The smartly turned-out crew looked at her with curiosity. News had travelled that the lead pilot was a woman and everyone wanted to see for themselves what such a woman looked like. The Captain of the *Pegasus* welcomed her aboard and instructed her in unhooking procedures for the large craft. He stood close by as Rosalyn brought the ship up into the air and guided her in some of the finer points of piloting a bigger vessel. Rosalyn had a full hour at the wheel but the flight continued all day as other novice pilots took their turn at the helm.

She walked around the deck, poking her nose into everything, watching the crew at their tasks and asking questions about their roles. At other times she stood near the helm to learn as the other pilots underwent instruction. Below were the rich green fields and hedgerows of the countryside, dotted with farms and villages. She wondered when she might next see it all. The *Pegasus* passed over Salisbury Cathedral which was still under the control of the Old Church. It would only be a matter of time, she thought, when it too, would belong to the Enlightenment Church.

Rosalyn said her farewells the same night as she needed to leave early for Southampton where she would board her ship to Sydney. Gideon shook her hand enthusiastically as he wished her on her way and Bo gave her a bow and a warning to beware of bad men. Rosalyn smiled at his concern and accepted the advice gracefully. Ajax took her trunk and loaded it onto Tommy's buggy. "You take care out in the colony and I'm sure one day I'll see you again. Good turnings, Reverend."

3

BOUND FOR BOTANY BAY

The Voyage. Part one. The Docks.

Rosalyn's carriage dropped her off at the docks where the *Iris* lay at berth. As she stood, bewildered by all the activity, a man approached her. He was a grubby, unshaven fellow with a scruffy, ancient tricorn on his head and a weathered, tatty, blue military jacket that appeared so old it may once have seen service in the wars against Napoleon—but then so did the man. He leaned in close and spoke to her with a breath of stale beer and bad teeth.

"Pardon me, Ma'am, would you be the Reverend Flynn?"

Rosalyn stepped back to avoid the man's vapours and did her best to not look offended by his presence. "Yes, I am."

"Ah..." The man peered into her eyes in an unsettling way. "And what ship are you sailin' on, Reverend?"

"The Iris."

"You are, yes. You see, I've been sent by the Captain of the Iris to find you and direct you aboard." He turned, and with a bent and shabby finger, pointed. "It's that one there, Reverend, the big one, the barque. You go and let the Captain know you're here and to send someone for your trunk. I'll watch it, you see. That's my job. Watchin' baggage, that's what I does."

"Well," said Rosalyn, uncertainly. "All right. A man should be here soon, I expect." After walking a few steps Rosalyn glanced back over her shoulder to see the man sitting on her trunk. He smiled at her and tipped his hat and Rosalyn hurried on.

Lifting her skirt and watching her footing, she made her way up the weathered, timber gang plank. If the men loading the ship noticed her, they did not show it. As the labourers pushed past her she stood on the deck, staring. Her gaze travelled up to the mast tops, the furled sails and rigging. As she took in the details, excitement flooded through her, and she imagined herself soaring through the southern skies. A passing crewman brought her back to earth by treading on her foot as he stumbled past under the weight of a large sack. "Sorry lady. You might want to move out of the way. If you've just come aboard you'll need to see the Cap'n. He's over there." The man indicated with a tilt of his head.

The Captain's smart appearance and blood-red jacket contrasted with the dull and shabby clothing of the workers moving around him. Rosalyn approached him.

"You must be Reverend Flynn. How do you do? I'm Captain Spat. That's Rufus Spat."

"I'm delighted to meet you, Captain Spat. It's ever so exciting to be aboard at last. There's so much activity."

"It will be a pleasure to have your company for the voyage, Reverend Flynn. Where is your baggage?"

"Your man is over there, watching my trunk. If you could be so kind as to have someone collect it and bring it to my quarters I would be appreciative."

"What man is that?"

"That unshaven, old fellow with the tricorn and blue jacket." Rosalyn looked back to where she had left the man but couldn't see him. "That's peculiar. I left him with it about where that fashionably-dressed young woman is standing."

"He was no man of mine, Reverend. Come, I'll take a man and we'll have a look. You might find he's scampered and taken your trunk with him."

They picked their way through the crowd to the woman, who watched them approach. Rosalyn breathed a sigh of relief to find the trunk where she had left it. She turned to the woman to be immediately entranced by her beauty. Wisps of long blonde hair, having escaped from the confines of her bonnet, were blowing about her face. Her blue-grey eyes contrasted with full, red lips that any young man would have risked death for a chance to kiss. Rosalyn's captivated appreciation was curtailed when the lips started moving.

"Good afternoon. I'm Miss Cecilia Spotswood, and I'm certain this is your trunk." The woman smiled as she spoke.

"Yes, it is. I left a man to watch it. Did you see him?"

"I did. I was watching you from down the way there and saw you leave it with him. As soon as you were out of sight the devil started making off with it but fortunately I intercepted him in time."

"That was courageous of you."

"Not really. I threatened to scream and there are so many people around who would have come to my rescue that he fled rather hurriedly."

"I suppose I must thank you. I'm Reverend Rosalyn Flynn, and this is Captain Spat of the Iris. I'm sailing with him tomorrow."

"Hullo, Captain Spat. It's a pleasure to meet you." Cecilia turned to Rosalyn. "I'm also sailing on the Iris." Cecilia extended her hand and Rosalyn gave it a gentle shake. The two women looked each other in the eyes as though they might find there some further information as to the character of their travelling companion.

"In fact, Reverend, you and Miss Spotswood will be sharing a cabin. I apologise for the small quarters but your bookings were rushed and a shared cabin is all that could be managed. Why don't you go back to the Iris now? This man will take your trunk and I'll accompany Miss Spotswood to arrange for her luggage to be brought aboard. I expect you'll both want to have a good chat and get to know each other."

The man heaved the trunk onto his back and Rosalyn followed him onto the *Iris*. She let him take the trunk below and decided to wait on deck for Cecilia before going to see the cabin. From the stern of the ship she stood looking out over the dock and the rows of old grey buildings. At some distance from her, at the corner of one of the buildings, she spied the fellow who had tried to make off with her trunk. He was in conversation with another man who was standing in the shadow of the building. The ship was the attention of their focus but on noticing Rosalyn staring their way, they disappeared around the corner.

As she watched to see if they might reappear, she saw, coming around the same corner of the building, a large number of women escorted by a small company of red-coated soldiers. As they drew closer she could see the women were manacled. With horror Rosalyn realised these unfortunate creatures were being brought aboard. She was on a convict ship!

The clinking of the chains and shuffling of the feet grew louder as the convicts were led up the gangway onto the deck. Rosalyn turned as they were led below. Some of the women saw her watching and waved, calling greetings to her with their gutter tongues. Others walked with heads bowed in silence or loudly sobbed, but all of them allowed themselves to be led below without resistance. Rosalyn stood silently, clutching at the folds of her dress as the grim parade passed by. When they had disappeared from view Rosalyn turned her attention once more to the activity on the wharf but her mind was now puzzling over the man in the tricorn. Absorbed in thought a light touch on her elbow brought her back to the world and she turned to see Cecilia.

"Hullo, Reverend. Fascinated by the activity?"

"Yes," said Rosalyn. "That is... I didn't know this was a convict ship."

"They didn't tell you when you made your travel arrangements?"

"No, the Church took care of all the details for me. You knew?"

"Yes I did. Daddy made the arrangements with the Society and they assured me that travelling on this ship would be quite safe."

"The Society?"

"Yes, the Royal Scientific Society for the Exploration of the Antipodes."

"You're an explorer?"

"No, I'm an entomologist."

"I've heard that word before, I'm sure. What's an entomologist?"

"I study insects—beetles and butterflies—that sort of thing."

"Oh, a naturalist. Sounds fascinating." Rosalyn hoped her voice carried some enthusiasm and that her expression matched her words but they didn't.

Cecilia laughed. "You're too kind. I know it's not for everyone but I love the little creatures."

"They're all part of God's great machine and every one of them plays a part."

"Yes, exactly, and my job is to identify the things and the part they play." Cecilia paused and looked at Rosalyn intently. "Perhaps you could show me the cabin."

"I haven't seen it myself yet. I was waiting for you."

The two found a sailor to guide them to their quarters. Rosalyn stood looking through the doorway. "It's rather cramped but I suppose we shall be spending much of our time on deck."

Rather cramped was something of an understatement. Rosalyn ducked her head under the lintel and stepped inside. Two small beds left room for luggage at the foot of each one. Between the beds a hatch window gave something of a view and access to fresh air. By the door were built-in cupboards and some drawers topped by an enamel wash bowl. "I'll have some fresh water brought for you." The sailor disappeared and left them to settle in.

While engaged staring out from the little window a crewman knocked on the door. It wasn't the water being delivered but a small packing chest for Rosalyn from the Church. The man fetched a prise bar, forced the lid off and took his leave.

On the top of a pile of wrapped objects rested an envelope addressed to 'The Reverend Missionary, Airship Pilot, Rosalyn Flynn'. She tore the envelope open and found a short letter from Maud.

'Dear Reverend Flynn,

Congratulations on your most successful passing of the airship pilot course.

Although you have not been an outstanding pupil in your theological studies at this college we are pleased that you have brought great credit to the Church in your achievement at the Royal College of Airship Aviation. Indeed, you are the youngest member of the Church to achieve this distinction and you have managed this in substantially less time than any of the other Church aviators. In recognition of this feat we, the Church College Council, have put together at no small expense, a few items which you may find necessary on your Mission. You will also find other items contained herein that are standard issue to all Church Missionaries on their departure. Unfortunately time does not permit us of the more formal departure ceremony.

Wishing you the best of luck and we expect to see you again after the successful completion of your Mission, whenever that may be.

May your Cogs turn freely.
Maud Hunt,
Dean, Canterbury Seminary.'

"Good news?"

"Only a note wishing me well." She tucked the letter back into the envelope, put it in her satchel and looked at the contents of the chest. The first item she withdrew was long and heavy and wrapped in an old piece of cloth. The item was a carbine. Rosalyn stared at it wide-eyed as she held it. The reality of the dangers of her Mission were now all too apparent.

"Have you fired a carbine before?" asked Cecilia, who was watching the unpacking with curiosity.

"A what?" asked Rosalyn as she put the weapon aside.

"I see. Daddy has many weapons and bores me to tears with their details, so I've come to know the names of them. The weapon you're holding is a carbine."

"No. I've never fired any weapon before. The Church does run a weapons course for Guardians and Missionaries but I never went to it. There wasn't time."

"Guardians?"

"Yes. They act as armed guards and assistants for the higher rank-ing clergy of the Enlightenment Church. Sometimes they're also sent to accompany Missionaries. They're ex-military men and re-ceive all sorts of training in weapons, riding, swimming and such."

"And you received no weapons training and you have no Guardian?"

"Not yet. As I'm sure you're aware, the Enlightenment Church expanded rapidly when King William was crowned. With his coro-nation and with Enlightenment becoming the official religion of the realm there has been no end to our expansion and unfortunately the training hasn't been able to keep pace. When I arrive in Sydney I have to call on our parson and he'll arrange for my meeting with my Guardian. I don't know much more as I haven't read my Mission Orders yet."

"That sounds terribly exciting. When do you read them?"

"Oh, I can read them at any time now. I have them right here." Rosalyn patted the satchel. "I'll leave it until later, there's no great hurry. It will be a long voyage."

Cecilia looked at the leather satchel Rosalyn carried and turned her attention back to the trunk. "What else do you have there?"

Rosalyn took up another cloth-wrapped object and this one turned out to be a flintlock pistol.

"It looks like you're going to be well-armed. I can only suppose you're going somewhere exciting and dangerous."

"Yes. I'm going to the frontier to bring Enlightenment to the heathens," said Rosalyn. "I don't have any idea how to use these weapons and I hope I never have to."

"There are soldiers on board. I'm certain that you could prevail upon one of the officers to teach you during the voyage."

"That's an excellent idea, Cecilia. I'll do that."

Rosalyn moved to the next item. Thick, brown paper tied with string contained something soft. She tore it open like a Christmas present to reveal two Missionary uniforms. Each consisted of a skirt, a long, brown tunic with brass buttons and a high leather collar. A brass cog and cross was fixed to the front of each collar. Rosalyn touched it reverently. Also contained in the package was a brown leather corset which fitted over the tunic.

"That looks splendid. I can't wait to see you in it. I think you're going to look the absolute image of the Enlightenment Missionary."

A box was next to be opened. It contained a pair of knee-high, brown, lace-up boots with brass buckles for the top straps and sensible heels. She studied the leather, smelled and stroked it. She'd never owned footwear as expensive as this. The parcel contained something else of leather, which at first Rosalyn took to be a large satchel. It unfolded into a coat in a military style. It was of the type that had found favour with airship pilots. Rosalyn stood and held the coat by the shoulders at arm's length as she studied its details.

"The Church certainly looks after you. Those boots and coat are of a superior quality."

"They aren't Church issue. These have been included as a gift."

"Then someone holds you in high regard."

Rosalyn smiled, "I think it was the Dean. It was her who ensured that I come on this Mission."

"I see," said Cecilia as she felt the leather of the sleeve. "You must have really impressed her with your studies."

Rosalyn blushed. "I suppose so." She put the coat on. "How does it look?"

"Quite appealing. The leather becomes you and the military cut of the coat lends you an air of authority. I might add that it shows off your figure to perfection." Cecilia's look was one of admiration and Rosalyn smiled as she tried to see herself, stretching out her arms to look at the leather. "Perhaps the Captain has a mirror in which you might admire yourself."

"I suppose he might, but it can wait." She took the coat off and looked at the last few items.

She found a purple, woollen scarf which would come in useful in the chill of flying, and a pair of fingerless, brown, leather gloves. A small cardboard box from the famous expedition outfitter and manufacturer Professor Staughbort contained a pair of cheap and ordinary aviator goggles. Constructed from brass and leather they came with tinted filters, which left Rosalyn supposing that it must be quite bright in New South Wales.

"What are the goggles for?" asked Cecilia.

"For flying. The wind up there can be dreadful when it's blowing into your eyes."

"Flying?"

Rosalyn nodded. "I'm an airship pilot and the Church has supplied me with an airship for my Mission."

Cecilia's eyes widened and sparkled. "An airship? You'll have your own airship?"

"Yes. I didn't want to do Mission work in the Antipodes but when the Church told me I would have my own airship and were sending me on a pilot's course I changed my mind ever so quickly. Have you been up in an airship?"

Cecilia's excitement faded and she paused, lowering her eyes before answering quietly, "No, I haven't. It looks so scary—exciting yes, but scary."

"I love it. I feel at home in the air, so free."

There were some other items in the chest; a small telescope which appeared to be well-used and had no doubt seen service on wet vessels, and the Church Missionary journals which every Missionary was expected to keep up to date.

"That's it. Please, could you do me a favour and help me change into my Missionary uniform? I can manage it but the corset I'll need some extra help with."

"Of course." Cecilia helped Rosalyn out of her acolyte uniform and into the mission browns. "You have such a splendid figure already, Reverend. Do you like your corset tight?"

"Rosalyn. Please call me Rosalyn. And quite firm but not too tight."

Cecilia gave the laces a tug. "Your airship—is it large?"

"I haven't seen it but I believe it's adequate for my purpose."

"I'm hoping to make a name for myself in the science of entomology. I wanted to be an actress but Daddy said actresses are whores and I should learn something else. Insects fascinate me so I became a naturalist instead—an entomologist. There aren't many women entomologists at all and no famous ones, at least not since Maria Merian and no one has heard of her."

"Oh?" Rosalyn tried to glance out the window as Cecilia tightened the corset.

"Yes. You see, in the Antipodes so much is still unknown. There must be so many new species awaiting discovery, naming and description."

"I'm sure there are." Rosalyn gave up on the window and instead studied the wood grain pattern in the oak planks of the ceiling, grunting softly with each pull on the corset laces.

"Undoubtedly. Do you know what my favourite insect is?"

"No, I have no way of knowing."

"The praying mantis. It sits so still, like a stick, and the other insects don't notice it. Then, when it sees its moment, it strikes. And dragonflies. I love dragonflies—the way they dart about and the brilliant flashes of colour as they catch the sunlight. I love butterflies too, although I suppose everyone does, and there are some interesting beetles, as well." Cecilia tied off the laces. "There, all done."

"Thank you. I suppose there is much to learn in the thrilling world of colonial entomology. Why the Antipodes? Aren't there closer lands? I've heard a great many naturalists are drawn to South America."

"I'm sure the Upper Orinoco is positively overflowing with young women from Europe armed with butterfly nets. I doubt there are any insects left there at all."

Rosalyn laughed. "I suppose the Australian colonies aren't as attractive a proposition."

"There's some interest. The fact that it's so remote and a haven for convicts deters quite a few naturalists, however, it's still so unexplored that many exciting six-legged discoveries are yet to be made. I've been given a book by the Society of the known Antipodean butterfly species and another covering beetles, but I want to produce a fully illustrated book of my own finds. It will give great impetus to furthering the cause of women in science—and my own career of course. I'm so happy that you're interested. You know, most of the scientific community are operating around the settlements which is where Daddy said I had to stay, although there have been some explorations further afield. Most of the unknown species are going to be on the frontier or beyond." Cecilia paused to see if Rosalyn would bite. She didn't. "You're going to the frontier aren't you?"

Rosalyn answered cautiously. "Yes, I am."

Cecilia threw her cards on the table, her words coming out in a rush. "I wouldn't take up much space. It would be nice for you to have company and I could be of assistance."

"I'm sorry, but the Church strictly forbids the carrying of passengers in airships on Church Missions." Rosalyn had no idea of Church doctrine on the unscheduled carrying of passengers in Church airships. The benefits of company may be outweighed by the burden of it, and after a long voyage cooped up in a cabin with the woman, Rosalyn thought she may not wish to be confined in an airship with her as well.

"I see." Cecilia sat down on the bunk, her enthusiasm dampened. "If you do see a way in which I might join you I would be most grateful."

"I'll put my mind to it. According to my travel documents my airship is to be transported on this ship. It's a small airship and will require some assembly when I arrive in Sydney."

"You couldn't fly it to Sydney? It would be quicker wouldn't it?" Cecilia asked.

Rosalyn laughed. "No, it wouldn't. Airships can't carry much weight so they have to ground regularly to take on water and food. Also, they aren't stable and in heavy winds are difficult to fly. If they hit a storm it's the end of them. It's far too dangerous by air."

"Has anyone attempted it?"

"I've read of several attempts. One of them made it as far as Persia, and another came apart over the Mediterranean, somewhere near Crete. Its crew perished."

"Oh, I see." Cecilia dropped the subject and insisted on showing Rosalyn her collection of glass jars, books, journals and watercolour paints and brushes. Her talk drifted to the intricacies of some of the lesser known species of English water beetles. While Rosalyn supposed that Cecilia would prove to be a tolerable cabin mate, her constant talk of insects had her feeling like sticking a pin through Cecilia's thorax and fastening her to the ship's main mast.

With everything stowed away the women returned to the deck and stayed until sunset watching the last of the cargo being loaded. They were asleep in their bunks when the *Iris* sailed with the morning tide.

The Voyage. Part 2. The North Atlantic

"Now, raise that arm up more, standing side on, yes, like that, you're a smaller target from the side. Right side to the foe, your heart is on your left, protect it. Don't be scared of your weapon. Hold it firmly, it will jump. Now, pull."

The pistol let out a loud crack, a flash of fire erupted from the barrel and smoke shrouded her briefly before dissipating in the sea breeze. Rosalyn let the barrel drop and turned to Sergeant Hopson. "How did I do?"

"You handled the weapon well enough. The target is safe but we can work on accuracy later. Fire a few more rounds and try to relax as you do."

Cecilia watched from the railing as Rosalyn loaded and fired again under the watchful eye of the sergeant. The first lesson was chiefly about loading, firing and cleaning the weapon. The target was a straw dummy wrapped in an old shirt and affixed to the stern railing. As the voyage progressed so did Rosalyn's proficiency with the firearms, although her aim remained altogether mediocre.

Captain Spat took Rosalyn under his wing to teach her navigation. Cecilia also took an interest in the subject, professing a love for maps. Together they learned to read a chart and use a compass and sextant. The two dined in the evening at the Captain's table where Rosalyn found a new duty in saying grace.

"And what do you think of our convicts, Reverend? Is there hope of redemption?" asked Captain Spat, as he stuffed a forkful of potato and peas into his mouth.

"I've barely spoken to any of them as yet, but it's the Church's position that there is a place, however small, for everyone in the Great Machine. The convicts have to realise that and when they do…"

"The cogs of the machine will turn smoothly and God's creation will reach perfection."

"You know the Church teachings well."

"I've had many a long voyage and ample opportunity to hear the views of a great many people. What you have told me is the Church doctrine. What do you personally think of the convicts?"

Rosalyn was surprised by the question and thought carefully before answering. "My views are the same as those of the Church. There must be order and everyone has a place in that order. Some have a place to govern and others to be governed."

"I see. And you, Miss Spotswood?"

"Me? My interest is in the realm of those creatures possessed of six legs, not two."

"You must have an opinion."

"I was seldom asked for one at Daddy's table but I find myself partially in agreeance with the Reverend." Cecilia paused in thought and her expression changed. "Although I did find myself talking to one of the convict women yesterday. She was being transported for seven years for stealing three silk handkerchiefs. It's a trifle harsh."

"But, Cecilia," said Rosalyn, "if she stole handkerchiefs she has no one to blame but herself for her misfortune. She is a loose cog and must be brought into place."

"A loose cog perhaps, but she stole them to sell so she might buy something to feed herself."

"You see, that is the way of the lazy among the working class. If the woman had taken on some gainful employment she would have been able to feed herself without causing distress to others through stealing."

"She said she'd tried to find work but had no money and no food. I felt myself feeling quite sorry for her."

"They will play on your sympathies, Miss Spotswood," said Captain Spat, as he reached for his wine. "Show any weakness and they will take every advantage. We must be strict with them."

Rosalyn nodded her agreement. "Discipline is essential."

"I suppose you're right. I think perhaps I best stick to my insect collecting rather than espouse my views regarding the complexities of social policy."

Captain Spat laughed. "I did ask for your views and they are much as expected from one of the fairer sex. You're altogether too soft and caring. Now Reverend Flynn here," continued Captain Spat, waving his potato-clad fork in the general direction of Rosalyn, "has grasped the teachings of the new Church and the need for discipline and order."

"I'm sure seven years in the colony will see them find their way back into civilised society and the Church will be there to assist them."

Cecilia gave a curt nod and put an end to the conversation by adding, "Amen."

The Voyage. Part 3. The South Atlantic

Rosalyn sat on her trunk polishing the brass cog on her cross.

"Didn't you do that an hour ago?"

"Yes, I like polishing it. It keeps me busy. There's little else to do."

"Can't you go and preach to the convicts again?"

"I don't think they like me. They said I was boring and they'd rather be flogged."

"They're an incorrigible lot. I hope your blacks will be more receptive."

"Captain Spat said he'd flog the women for me if I wished. I declined. I don't want to see the poor wretches suffer further. Mind you I'm so bored myself I could almost watch a flogging for the sheer excitement of it."

Cecilia, who had been lying on her bunk, put down her book and sat up. "Come now, that's no way for a member of the clergy to talk. I have some paints, pencils and some paper if you'd like to try your hand at drawing."

"I have no talent for that. Perhaps I could look at your butterfly book."

"My butterfly book?"

"Yes, if you don't mind of course; the book the society gave you with the pictures of colonial butterflies."

"Colonial? Oh, the Antipodean butterflies. Yes, of course, it's in one of the drawers here with my other books." Cecilia fished in a draw, pulled out the crudely bound book and handed it to Rosalyn.

Rosalyn rested it on her knees and read the title aloud. "A Preliminary Survey of the Lepidoptera of New South Wales."

"Lepidoptera are butterflies and moths," Cecilia explained. She sat watching as Rosalyn opened the cover and leafed through the first few pages. "It hasn't been published yet. The book is a collection of copies and originals of notes and illustrations made by different naturalists who have been to the colony. I'm to fill in any blanks in the knowledge."

"What sort of blanks?"

"Well, for instance, perhaps a caterpillar has been found but not the butterfly. I have to try to find the caterpillar and watch to see what it becomes."

"Sounds frightfully boring."

"Yes, it must sound mundane to others but not to an entomologist like me. I think it's the most exciting thing in the world and I see parallels."

"What on earth do you mean?" Rosalyn asked as she stared engrossed at an exquisitely detailed illustration of a Banksia Moth in its different life stages.

"Imagine us as caterpillars..."

"Really, Cecilia, and wriggle up the masts I suppose?"

"No silly. Imagine us as caterpillars making our cocoons, but we are yet to become butterflies, our childhoods now behind us and everything that lies in front of us is yet to come."

"I prefer to think I've left the larval stage and am a butterfly already."

"You're pretty but you're not flying yet."

Rosalyn laughed. "I do love your enthusiasm. I'll be flying when I reach New South Wales."

Cecilia went back to her book and left Rosalyn to browse the notes and pictures. Many of the butterflies were quite attractive but more interesting to Rosalyn were the notes. Some of them were original jottings and here and there she could glean some minor insight into the land awaiting her. A substantial number of the examples were missing information and questions were written in the margins in ink or pencil. The last page was almost entirely blank. It contained a brief description of the peculiar behaviour of a swarm of butterflies. No illustration graced the page and a single handsomely written line in black ink at the bottom said, 'The Green Wave.' In pencil after it had been added, 'as referenced by Dr Phatts.'

"It was interesting thank you, Cecilia. Perhaps tomorrow I'll look at your beetle book."

"You may look at it now if you wish."

"That's quite all right. I can't take too much excitement in a single day."

"Beastly girl! Go polish your cross."

The Voyage. Part 4. The Indian Ocean

Rosalyn sighed, closed the window, and sat on her bunk. "I've never been to Durham. Have you always lived there Cecilia?"

"Most of my life, yes. I went to boarding school in France and later to Edinburgh University."

"University? Were there many women in attendance?"

"Not a great many, and mostly in the Arts. Women need to have higher marks to gain entry to the Sciences—or a rich father with good connections."

"Having wealthy parents to open doors is the height of fashion. Is your father not concerned to have you travelling alone all the way to Sydney?"

"No. There are other Society members in Sydney and I have letters of introduction."

"So the Society is funding your work. I know they're quite Enlightened but as you have pointed out there's still a strong element among the Scientific Societies who oppose the participation of women in the sciences."

"Yes, I'm only too aware of such opposition. I was quite fortunate actually. The decision to fund a person of science to travel to the Antipodes was a hurried one. They had initially chosen another person, a geologist, but unfortunately for him he was unable to travel."

"That must have been disappointing for him. Do you know what happened?"

Cecilia stood, opened the window, and stared out at the grey ocean. "I heard he fell sick."

"That's unfortunate for him and lucky for you—and even luckier that you have such a supportive father."

"He did have to pull some strings with his friends in the Society."

"Who is your father?"

"Lord Oswald Spotswood. Have you heard of him?"

"No, I'm sorry, I don't move in those levels of society."

Cecilia, who had caught her breath, let out a sigh. "That's all right. It's not like he's magnificently famous outside his own circles."

"Father or not, I'm sure you'll distinguish yourself in the colony. You do know your subject quite intimately."

"Oh, I do. Have I told you about the life cycle of the Northern Emerald Dragonfly?"

"Several times."

4

The Emu's Footprint

Lying languidly on their bunks, a knock on the door brought the women to attention. Cecilia answered the knock. A crewman stood there. "Sydney, Ma'am. The Captain thought you'd like to know."

Rosalyn slid off her bed and followed Cecilia onto the deck where they took positions at the railing near the bow. Off the port side a towering cliff was topped by a lighthouse but they could see no sign of a town. About three quarters of a mile north of it rose another cliff, equally bare of settlement. As they looked about puzzled the captain came up beside them. "We're coming through Sydney Heads and into the harbour—and a fine harbour it is indeed. Sydney town will be on the port side. We'll be docking at the place where the convicts of the First Fleet were landed fifty years back. I thought you might like to be on deck as we came in."

The Captain excused himself, leaving the women looking wide-eyed at every new thing. Thin plumes of smoke rose up from the headlands and small boats could be seen on the harbour. "Look," said Rosalyn pointing, "There are blacks in those boats with the white men. It looks like they're fishing." Rosalyn and Cecilia held each other's hands as they stood at the railing, grinning with excitement.

"They don't look so wild do they?"

"No, I can see they're quite tame. I expect they'll be easy to convert to the ways of the Lord. I'll explain to them all the marvels of mechanisation and their own place in God's universe. They'll be like fruit ripe for the picking."

Cecilia leaned over the rails as she gazed at the sights. "I hope you're right."

"What are you going to do first?" asked Rosalyn.

"You know, with all that time we've spent on board ship I haven't given it much consideration. All my thoughts have been about what exciting creatures I might find in the interior but not at all about what my first move is to be. I suppose I'll have to find lodgings for the night and tomorrow seek out the Society members for whom I have the letters of introduction. What will you do?"

"I'll go first to meet the parson here and see what advice or assistance he can render. You know, I forgot entirely about my orders. I was supposed to read them on the ship. Really, I'm such an ass sometimes."

"You could read them now."

"And miss the excitement of coming into the harbour? I think I'll wait. Perhaps we could find lodgings together for the night and go to our respective contacts tomorrow."

"That would be lovely. I'd like that." Cecilia looked out at the town as the ship drew closer. "It's so much bigger than I thought it might be."

"Yes, I imagined it would be crude huts, but look, there are forts here and the houses look quite substantial. It might not be such a terrible place after all. It's not as green as England and it's warmer, but it does look to be of an English flavour. I don't mind the warmth but the trees, they look grey and sickly. It's something I'll have to get used to."

"I think I'll like those sickly trees. Can you imagine all the little insects that must live on a single tree?"

"I suppose I could if I put my mind to it. Do you think we'll be safe from the convicts? Sergeant Hopson said they let them roam around loose."

"Did I hear my name mentioned?"

"We were wondering how safe it is with the convicts wandering around."

"Don't worry, Reverend, they keep the worst in irons or in cells so you'll be safe as houses." Sergeant Hopson tapped his foot on the deck." We'll be taking this lot off in chains."

"Where will they take them?"

"Up to the female factory and put to work. Husbands will be found for them and they can try to make something of themselves."

"That sounds beneficial to all concerned." Rosalyn's smile faded when she saw Cecilia's frown.

"What's the matter, Cecilia?"

Cecilia looked at them both and replied, "The women are convicts, so marrying may be a means of escaping the harshness of penal servitude."

"Why is that a concern?"

"They may feel compelled to take that path and marry some wretch unsuited to them."

"Come, Miss Spotswood, it isn't like that." said Sergeant Hopson. "The women do get a say in who they go with."

"Choice is a form of freedom, although it would be a poor choice between a convict life or as the wife of a man of low character."

"They're convicts, Miss Spotswood. They're all low character."

At the dock they stood looking over the side at the activity on the wharf. A crowd of people had gathered around to hawk their wares to the new arrivals or to seek news of home. Fresh fruit and vegetables were the main items proffered up for sale, but they had few buyers from the convict ship.

Sergeant Hopson, cradling a hatful of peaches in his arm, gave them a cheery wave from the dock. The convicts he escorted looked around at their new surroundings, bewildered and curious. A detachment of soldiers marched onto the docks to assist in their escort. Captain Spat, satisfied all was in order, approached his passengers. "I'd have thought you ladies would be anxious to get ashore. You look to have made a home on the railing."

"Making plans, Captain Spat, but we'll disembark soon. Now what about our baggage?"

"I'll have someone unload it to the dock but you'll have to find a carrier from there—as you can see there are plenty about."

"And my airship?"

"It will be delivered to the bonded warehouse. You'll be able to arrange delivery with the overseer there."

The women continued to watch the scene in silence. Captain Spat leaned on the gunwale smoking his pipe. When the activity had died down they took their leave of him and made their way onto the dock. Rosalyn's attention was captured by a young lad of about twelve years who was nudging her elbow. "You want a paper? Read the latest 'ave yer?" Rosalyn took a step towards him and sensing a sale the boy directed all his attention at her. "I sees yer of the God botherin' clan. Bit in 'ere about Missionaries. Yer might find it to yer likin'."

"How much," asked Rosalyn.

"Frippence for a woman of the cloff," said the boy.

Rosalyn fished around in her coin purse, found a threepenny bit and handed it over as she asked, "And how much is it for everyone else?"

"Frippence," replied the boy, in a tone which suggested stupidity on Rosalyn's part for even asking. As the boy had intimated his knowledge of printed English, Rosalyn enquired as to whether the boy was literate. "Of course I can bloody read but I ain't readin' it to yer."

Taken aback by the lack of charm in the young man's manners, Rosalyn, on recovering, asked, "And who taught you?"

Before he could answer, another voice entered the conversation. "I did."

Rosalyn, a little taller than the average woman, turned to see a fresh-faced youth of about her own height—a height enhanced by a stylish hat, tilted back on his head. He wore tattered, sun-faded clothing. The pants, too long, were folded up at the cuffs. A baggy blue and white striped shirt was tucked neatly into the trousers. An unbuttoned waistcoat, half black and half canary-yellow, sported an upside-down government arrow on the yellow half. A diagonal leather strap crossed the chest and supported a long wooden case.

"I'm Fey." The young 'man' introduced herself with a theatrical bow, removing her hat in the process. Her head was revealed to be shaven at the sides leaving a strip of long hair running from the forehead to the stern. "Can I help you fine ladies? In need of lodgings, food, something to wet your palate? Nice ale or something? You both look a bit dry. I know some good watering holes where mollies are welcome."

Rosalyn stood stunned. With her mouth gaping open she made a rapid mental repositioning of Fey as female. In addition to the young woman revealing her strange hair style, when she bowed she also revealed a remarkable cleavage.

"You'll catch flies with your mouth open like that," said Fey drily.

"But you're a woman," said Rosalyn.

Cecilia took two steps closer and examined Fey as though she were an insect. "So she is."

Fey stood her ground under the women's curious gaze. "It happens that there's plenty of space here in New South Wales, and yet you sail all the way around the world to inhabit mine. Can you back off just a wee bit so I can have room to expand my lungs. I'm fair near suffocating under your attention—not that your attention is undesirable itself—it's the proximity of it."

"That's contemptible," said Rosalyn.

"You might stand huddled together like penguins in that cold, crowded little island you come from, but here it's contemptible to be up in someone's phiz."

"I mean you. You're an abomination. Why are you in men's attire?"

"Save your judgements for the pulpit, cog turner. I'm not interested in them." Fey, in a casual fashion, opened the box on the strap, pulled out a long clay pipe and packed it with tobacco from a pouch on her belt.

"For your edification I wear these here rags so as I don't get aggravated by every passing Tom, Dick or Harry who might otherwise insist on some horizontal dancing. Men don't give me half an eyeball when I tog up like this—they think I'm a feller like themselves. Makes it easier for me to traverse the roads of the township without being accosted. And," she added, "they're a lot more bloody practical than the garments of good ladies. I like my togs." Fey struck a match on the box and lit her pipe.

Rosalyn coughed and stepped back. "I see. Yes... I understand... still... it's not like at home."

"You're a long way from home, cog turner." Fey grinned. "Welcome to Sydney town. You can expect things to be a bit different here, but we all speak the same language."

"I'm not so sure," said Cecilia. "Some of your words are strange to my ears."

"You look a bright sort, love. There's a colonial touch to the Queen's English here, but pay attention and you'll catch on." Fey stood up straight and pushed her chest out, hands gripping the edges of her waistcoat, her pipe clenched between her teeth. "Now's there anything I can do for you?"

Rosalyn appeared not to have heard the question. "But those arrows, aren't they government arrows? Doesn't that mean you're a convict?"

Fey laughed. "Yeah, convicts wear the emu's footprint. It's a way to shame them and make them stand out if they bolt. However, ladies, I'm not a convict and never have been but I'll wear the emu anyway."

"The emu?"

"I just said, the emu's footprint. Try to keep up. For a cog turner your cogs turn slowly.

Rosalyn ignored the slight. "And your father, who is he?"

"What's my bloody pedigree got to do with me offering my services? For all I know my father was a ship's captain or a convict."

"He's a convict?"

Fey's voice took on a slight edge. "I don't know who my father is, all right? I don't know who he is or where he is and I don't think my mother knew who he was either. Can we skip over the genealogical background? I'm trying to earn a bob or two here."

"I see." Rosalyn stepped back awkwardly. "And I see the Church has much work to do here."

Fey's brow lost its frown and she grinned. "Yeah, go for it. You'll be flat out bringing us lot into order."

Rosalyn and Cecilia looked at each other, gathered themselves, and turned back to Fey. "I think I stepped off on the wrong foot with you. I do apologise. I beg let me begin over. This is Miss Cecilia Spotswood of the Royal Scientific Society for the Exploration of the Antipodes, and I'm Colonial Missionary Reverend Rosalyn Flynn of the Enlightenment Church, on my way to the frontier to bring Enlightenment to the heathens. And the answer to your question is yes."

"My question?" asked Fey.

"Yes," said Rosalyn. "You asked if we needed help with anything. We need rooms. Nothing too shabby but nothing too expensive either."

"Yeah, I can fit you up for a room. Do you want one room or two?" Fey gave them an inquisitive look.

"We've been in one room on the ship, but two rooms would be nice."

Fey's eyes sparkled in the bright sun. "I took you to be close enough to have one room."

"I suppose that's from spending so much time in each other's company; having shared a cabin on the voyage out. We've become good friends, haven't we, Cecilia?" Cecilia smiled and nodded.

Fey turned away as she rolled her eyes. "I know a square crib which will suit. You got baggage?"

"Do you mean, 'Do you have any baggage'?"

"No. I don't mean that. I mean have you got baggage?"

"I was correcting your speech."

"I know what you was doing and I don't want you to correct my speech. I'm trying to earn a living here, not learn grammar or take elocution lessons. What are you going to do next, teach me deportment? Have me parade up and down the dock with a book on my head?" Fey took a newspaper from the boy, placed it on her head and walked a few exaggerated steps before returning. "Now, have you got baggage?"

Cecilia giggled, Rosalyn felt her face flush and started giggling too. "It's over there—that pile." Rosalyn turned and pointed. As she did so, she saw two men looking at her. Upon noticing her attention, the men looked away. Rosalyn recognised one of them as a crewman from the *Iris* but the other she didn't know.

"What did you say your name was?" asked Rosalyn.

"Fey, Miss Fey Grey. You can forget the Miss and the Grey. Fey sits fine."

Rosalyn nodded. "Fey, who is that man over there, the one with the tall hat?"

"Like I know every bloody person in Sydney. I dunno, I've never seen him around. Why do you ask?"

"I thought they were talking about me."

"They probably are. As you've just got off the boat and you're dressed in them Cog Church togs, I'd be asking too. People get curious." Fey discreetly looked at the two men. The one with the tall hat, she remembered, had only arrived in the colony a week back—she had observed him as he walked along the pier. He had been met by another well-dressed man. Her efforts to ascertain their business proved almost futile but she did manage to garner the information that they were connected with a small shipping company which owned a shipyard in Blackwattle Bay, further west along the harbour.

Rosalyn nodded. She supposed it was quite innocent, but something about them reminded her of the gentleman in the shadows who had been talking to the grubby man with the tricorn hat when she was on the docks in England.

Fey hailed two porters waiting next to the ship for work and gave them instructions as to where to take the baggage. Turning to the women she asked, "Are you ready, ladies?"

Cecilia turned to Rosalyn. "Don't you want to know where your Church is?"

"It can wait."

"The cog turner's church is one street back that way and up the far end," Fey gestured with her pipe. "I'll show you tomorrow."

The rough, narrow lane they followed led into a wider street, although as far as streets went this one needed work to bring it to the dignity of the classification. The houses were built of sandstone, most with wooden shingle roofs, but a scarce few with slate. Cages containing brightly coloured rosellas, cockatoos and lorikeets hung from some of the verandas. The women remarked on the brilliance of the plumage and Fey showed off her knowledge by telling them the names of each species.

The porters, on arriving at the lodgings with the baggage, demanded the sum of three shillings each for their short labour. "That's a bit steep," said Rosalyn.

"So was the road," said Fey. "It's three shillings, my loves, three shillings. The thing you have to understand here is that everything costs more in this place—this isn't London. What, with transport of goods around the world and all, people have to pay more to live." Fey ceased her explanation and looked at the two women. Dipping into their purses they paid the porters their fees.

As the porters left Fey called after them. "Don't spend my cut." She turned to her charges. "Now if I was you I would be smart and employ me as a guide. Three shillings a day is all I ask. I'll take you wherever you want and help you as you find your feet in the town."

Cecilia said, "Thank you Fey, but I'm sure I at least do not require a guide."

Rosalyn concurred. "Yes, thank you, Fey but we don't need you."

"But I think you do," said Fey. "You're going to get yourself robbed blind if you don't have someone to navigate you proper."

"No, I think we are educated and astute enough to find our own way," said Rosalyn.

"If you was astute you wouldn't have paid those porters any more than a shilling. That's the fair price."

The two women started on Fey together. "But... but you said to pay them three!"

"Yeah, and if you had me employed as a guide I would have saved you four shillings already." Fey paused and then continued, "So three shillings, hey? That's only one and six each." Fey grinned at them. "It's only for a few days—until you set your jib."

Cecilia was swayed and gave Rosalyn a nudge who then decided it might be best if she employed Fey as her guide after all. "Only a shilling a day. Three is too much."

"I do like a woman who tries. Make it a shilling each and you've got me at a hank."

"I have no idea what a hank is, but I suppose it sounds fair," said Cecilia. Satisfied with her successful bargaining Rosalyn concurred and they handed over the coins.

"Now," said Fey, as she pocketed the money, "you should never pay up front on a transaction like this. I could take your coin and bolt to the nearest grog house. You should pay me at the end of each day." Rosalyn stared at her and nodded while Cecilia turned away to hide her smile.

Fey introduced them to Biddy, the owner of the house in which they were staying, and helped take the baggage to their rooms. Rosalyn, on coming into the kitchen for water, saw Fey taking money from Biddy. Fey looked up at Rosalyn and explained without embarrassment, "This is for finding you. I get a little for each customer I bring to her. I'll be here to fetch you in the morning." Fey disappeared out the door.

Rosalyn turned to Biddy, "Is that normal here?"

"What's that?"

"Her. The hair, the clothes."

"For the currency lads and lasses it is."

"The what?"

"The currency..." Biddy saw the confused look on Rosalyn's face. "Currency lads and lasses. It's what we call the ones who was born in the colony. They're a new currency, they aren't pound sterling. They don't know much at all about old mother England, this is the only home they know."

"Oh," said Rosalyn as she stared from the doorway to watch Fey walk up the dusty street. Her clothes were old but she held her head high, and she moved with confidence—as if she owned the town itself. Rosalyn turned back to Biddy. "Do they all dress as convicts?"

Biddy laughed. "No, not all of them, and they're not rightly dressed as convicts. Convicts don't wear a uniform. Some of them did in the early days, and you might still see some around with the government arrow but mostly convicts wear their own clothes. A few of the currency lads and lasses wear clothes made of the black and yellow but they have the government arrow pointing down instead of up."

"Why is that?"

"They call it the 'emu's footprint'." Rosalyn nodded, remembering Fey had used the term earlier. Biddy went on. "It's facing down because they don't come from home, they come from this land down under, so they have the arrow pointing down. That's what I was told. Some others say it's so that it doesn't appear as a government arrow."

Rosalyn listened intently to Biddy's explanation. "Why does that matter?"

"To avoid trouble with the government, I suppose. The ones who wear it, and wear their hair cut like that, they're an unruly lot and don't have much respect for their betters—indeed they accept none as such."

"But they're convicts," said Rosalyn frowning. "Don't they know their place?"

"Not convicts love. Their parents might have been—perhaps still are, but they see themselves as equal to even the finest of the free settlers from the old country and refuse to bend to anyone. Some of them need a good slap around the side of the head—cheeky things they are at times." Biddy smoothed down her apron. "Cup of tea for you both?"

"Not for me, I'm exhausted," said Cecilia.

"Nor me, thank you. I'll be asleep as soon as my head touches the pillow, I'm sure."

"Are you from the Sun Church?"

"The Enlightenment Church. Are you familiar with it? I'm to go and see the parson tomorrow."

"I'm old Church, Reverend. I've had a mind to go and see the new one of yours but haven't been up there yet. I'll show you your rooms. You will have the two rooms to the left at the top of the stairs. Mine is to the right, should you need anything."

To the relief of both of them, the women retired to their separate rooms. It was the first time in months they had had the luxury of being alone. Closing the door behind her, Rosalyn walked around her room, looking at the sparse furnishings and the empty space. Light from the window gave the room a soft glow. Having now arrived in Sydney she found herself thinking of home. She took off her bonnet, took out a handkerchief and dabbed away a tear. Home was half a world away and it might be years before she could return to it.

She moved to the window and looked out into the evening sky.

Taking a deep breath she put away her handkerchief and thoughts of home, instead imagining herself flying high above all earthly concerns, in command of her own airship. This strategy for shaking off the intense feelings of sadness worked every time and her smile grew even as the sun set.

Rosalyn readied herself for bed. Tired, and relieved at her safe arrival, she skipped her prayers and crawled gratefully between the covers. Although fatigued, she tossed and turned, her mind racing with a thousand thoughts. Soon she would be flying—into what? A vast, unknown and dangerous wilderness.

Fey collected sixpence from each of the young porters who had been waiting for her outside. She whistled as she walked up the street, the coins clutched tightly in her hand. She turned once to see Rosalyn staring after her.

Acquaintances greeted her, and although she acknowledged them she entered into no conversation. First, she made her way back to the docks where the *Iris* lay at berth and found one of the sailors. After a brief chat she made her way back up the hill to a small, weathered, whitewashed house of sandstone. In spite of having her own little room tucked away in the attic of the house she knocked softly on the door. Without waiting for an answer she stepped inside. The door creaked as it moved on its rusty hinges. Fey closed it after herself. The interior was dim, illuminated only by light filtering through the gaps around the faded curtains.

"Hullo, Fey, I see by your face that you have some good news."

"Yes, Mother. Here, take this, four shillings—and I'll be getting more."

"Make yourself a cup of tea, it's freshly brewed."

"Would you like one, Mother?"

"I have one. So you have work?"

"A little. There're two English toffs—women—they need a guide."

"Two women travelling without men?"

"Yes Mother, one is a Missionary, the other is a bug catcher." Fey took a chipped china cup from the shelf and poured herself tea from the pot by the stove.

"A bug catcher?"

"Yes. She's here to catch insects for some mob back in the old country." Fey knelt on the floor beside the elderly woman's chair.

Mother Mary stared at the wooden planks of the ceiling and smiled. "Bug catcher? She's an entomologist. That's what naturalists who study insects are called." She sipped her tea. "Well there's no shortage of insects here. She can have as many as she wants; perhaps she'll start with the flies." She looked down at Fey. "Do you have enough money for your own use? You best keep a shilling of this."

"I could use some, Mother, but sixpence is all I need. You keep the rest for your work. I'll be back with another two shillings tomorrow."

Fey rested her cheek against Mother's thigh and the old lady softly stroked the girl's brow with her arthritic fingers. After a few minutes of quiet thought she said, "You be careful, Fey. Do you think these women are trustworthy?"

"Yes, Mother. They're young, about my own age, and I have a notion they don't know much about the world. You'd almost think the Missionary was simple and I'd be surprised if the bug catcher has ever had her hands dirty."

"Nevertheless, you might be able to learn from them. Keep your mind open."

Fey wondered what she might possibly learn from two women who'd never been to the colony before. "I will, Mother."

"And Crayfish said to remind you there's a meeting tonight. It's at the usual place."

"Ta. I'd been thinking about it all day until I met those women. I would have clean forgotten it. I'll wander down there after this cuppa. Do you need anything, Mother?"

"No precious, I have everything I need, and the children are always stopping by. If I need an errand run I'll have one of them do it."

Fey left Mother Mary's house and cut down an alley, working her way to One Hole's house. A young barefoot lad in an oversized hat was sitting on the front step. Fey greeted him. "Hullo, Jim. Am I late?"

"Yeah, they're all inside waitin' for you. You got any fill for me steamer?" Fey paused, pulled a pinch of tobacco from her pouch and gave it to the boy. It was a tax he asked of everyone who entered.

"There you go, don't smoke it all at once. It's good tobacco that."

"You always got good smellin' tobaccer. Where's it from, Fey?"

"Alabama."

"Never 'eard of it."

"It's in America. One of them states the Frenchies sold them."

"'ow do you know all that stuff?"

"From the sailors. You can learn all sorts of stuff about the world from them sailors. They've been everywhere."

"Will you take me to talk with 'em, Fey?"

Fey looked down at the boy and smiled. "Yeah, one day, Jim. Not this day but one day. I have important things to do."

"I got you marked on it, Fey."

"I won't forget." Fey left the boy to his pipe and opened the door. The voices that filled the air became quiet as she entered. She squinted through the pipe smoke into the gloom. "Sorry for keeping you. Did I miss something important?"

One Hole was a middle-aged man who had lost all the hair on the crown of his head, giving him the look of a medieval monk. He carried some extra weight and his voice sounded like the inside of his throat had been sanded. "We're trying to figure a way to get the farmers and merchants on board." He leaned one elbow on the table and drew on his pipe. "I don't think we're going to be able to pull this off, Fey. We've not much to offer. Do you have any news?"

"Not really. I've got a job showing around a couple of English titters who got off the last boat."

"Good for you. What are they doing here?"

"One's a cog turner, the other is a bug catcher."

"A bug catcher?" asked a woman from the other side of the room.

"Yeah. She came out to catch bugs and spiders and write about them for some society back in England."

"Do you think they're all right? Not Government are they?" asked Crayfish.

"I don't think so. The cog turner is a Missionary on her way out west. Strikes me as a bit simple. The other one is togged to the nines and has more wit about her but I don't think she's got anyone behind her except for her society."

"Keep a good eye on them," advised One Hole. "We think the Government has wind of us."

"One thing," said Fey as she took a cup of tea that was offered her. "When these mollies arrived I saw a bloke on the wharf had an interest in them."

"Who was he?"

"He was talking to a sailor from the ship they came in on. Getting intelligence by the looks of how they were. I don't know who he is but I seen him before—he's from the ship works. He was one I reported on a week back when the Bennelong took crook. I think he was asking the sailor about the women."

"Two unaccompanied women are going to attract attention. There's probably nothing in it."

"It was the bloke who made me think something was up. The women were talking to me and that might have been what twigged his own curiosity. I'm wondering if the government has tumbled us and is watching us already. I've seen a few blokes who give me the suspicions."

"You've said that before. Keep your head straight about you, but I think you might be a bit over touchy. We've been looking for anything out of the ordinary but nothing has turned up."

5

THE CHURCH OF THE SUN COG

The sun was still somewhere behind the horizon, the Earth's rotations yet to bring its light to shine on sleeping Sydney town. The woman crept down the stairs, her boots in her hand, and let herself out the front door. Dressed in black she blended into the deep shadows of the veranda. She put her boots on and made her way along the main street, avoiding the few people who were about at this early hour.

The woman walked from the road, past the silent church, to the parsonage next door. No lights showed in the windows. The woman stood at the bottom of the veranda stairs and spent a few minutes preparing herself for the emotional outpouring to come. A tear rolled down her cheek as she thought of the saddest thing she could and then, feeling ready, she walked up the stairs and knocked on the door. She waited, heard nothing, and knocked again. After a few moments, a noise inside indicated the occupant had risen. A lamp light appeared in a window then disappeared. The door opened and the light shone on the woman's veiled face.

"What is it?" asked the parson.

The woman's voice trembled as she spoke. "I'm so sorry to trouble you at this early hour. I couldn't sleep. My husband, you see... The voyage..."

"Yes, I do see. I'm so sorry for your loss. That is terribly tragic, and sadly all too common. When did you arrive?"

"Only yesterday. He... He's still onboard." The woman cried softly, her head bowed. "Please, may I come in? I have no-one."

The parson, dressed only in a gown, opened the door wider and stood aside. "Of course, of course. Come in. I'll make tea."

The parson led the woman into the sitting room where he lit some candles. Glancing at the clock on the wall, he went into the kitchen and set out the cups and saucers. At the stove he stoked the embers of the fire. Standing, he turned to see the woman in the doorway behind him. He stepped back, startled.

"I'm sorry," the woman whispered. "I didn't want to be alone, I think I'm going to faint." She staggered and the parson rushed to support her lest she fell. The woman put her arm around the parson's shoulder and the dagger concealed in her hand slashed across his throat. Blood sprayed around the kitchen and the parson dropped to the stone floor.

Avoiding the blood on the floor, the woman picked up the lamp and went back to the sitting room. Moving quickly she searched through the desk in the parson's study and found what she was looking for. She tucked the letter into her corset, extinguished the lamp and made her way back, creeping up the stairs before the first greying of the dawn appeared on the horizon.

After a light breakfast, Rosalyn and Cecilia stepped out onto the veranda to find Fey waiting for them. "G'morning ladies. Ready for today's perils?"

"Yes, quite," said Rosalyn, shouldering her satchel and stepping down the stairs.

"What's your first port of call?" asked Fey, as she followed.

"I need to call on the parson at the Enlightenment Church to introduce myself. Cecilia has to find her Society friends so we'll need to do that, too."

"Might surprise you but I know where a few churches are. Yours is on Brickfield Hill at the south end of town. It will stretch your legs to get there, but I can point out some places on the way. Stay close and keep your hand on your purse—place is full of thieves and convicts." Fey smiled to herself, stepped past Rosalyn, and led the women away.

Dirt-faced children played on the dry, unpaved street. On seeing the women they ran to them, drawn by their curiosity to Rosalyn's Missionary attire. Rosalyn smiled indulgently and answered their endless questions as they walked. When they started asking for money Fey shooed them away.

"Here you go. This is your Church, Rev'."

Rosalyn stood in the street looking at it. The Church was small and constructed of sandstone with a slate roof. A spire supported a wooden cross with a brass cog in its centre.

"See, it's been built up here facing east so the rays of your Sun God can come blazing forth in the morning to illuminate the congregation and fill their heads with radiance and Enlightenment."

Rosalyn stared at the ground and shook her head. "We don't worship the sun. The sun has simply been chosen as a symbol of the mechanical way in which the universe operates as laid down by God's law. The sun represents the social and industrial machinery, and also the new clockwork mechanisms of our time, which are a product of Enlightened scientific knowledge. You see..."

"Are you going in or giving a sermon?"

Sighing deeply Rosalyn entered the Church with Cecilia and Fey following. It was silent inside and Rosalyn called out a greeting. Receiving no answer she walked to the far end and knocked on the door of a small room to the side of the altar. Fey came, opened the door and peered inside.

"He isn't here. He has a house next door."

"That would be the parsonage. Do you know the parson?"

"Nope."

"Let's try there. He may still be at breakfast."

A veranda surrounded three sides of the wooden house and a brick chimney rose above the roof top at the rear. Rosalyn knocked on the front door and waited, listening for some sound of life. Nothing stirred. She tried again with no more response than before. "I suppose he's gone on some errand." Rosalyn looked up and down the street in the hope of catching sight of someone who looked like they might belong in a pulpit.

Fey followed the veranda around the corner of the house, looking into every window. She stopped at one, peering intently, her hand covering her brow to cut out any reflections.

"Fey!"

Fey looked around at Rosalyn who was standing at the corner. "What?"

"Do you have to stare into his house like that? You should respect people's privacy."

Fey straightened up and turned to her. "Yeah, you're right. Listen, I've a spark in my brain to where he might be. Why don't you and Ses go and wait in the Church and I'll fetch him back here. Won't take me long." Rosalyn and Cecilia allowed themselves to be ushered back into the church by Fey who then set off down the street at a quick pace.

"Ses? Did she call me Ses?"

"I suppose that's her way of saying Cecilia."

"I'll let it pass. Her manners are abysmal, but she's so gay isn't she? Do you think we can trust her?"

"I don't know. I'll give you that she's full of life, but she's a colonial of the serving class. I wouldn't expect too much of her."

Cecilia sat quietly in one of the rear pews while Rosalyn paced the aisle. Frustrated at the time taken by Fey to return to them she stood and waited outside. She spied Fey further down the street, in the company of a gentleman, and called out to Cecilia who joined her at the door.

"He doesn't look much like a parson," said Cecilia.

"He's not dressed like one but he's carrying a big staff. That must be him."

Fey and the man walked up to them. "Roz, Ses, this is Luke O'Riley. He's a constable." Luke raised his hat.

"I'm pleased to meet you, Mr O'Riley, but I was expecting the parson."

"I'm told there's trouble of sorts," said Luke, with a strong Irish accent.

"Trouble?" asked Rosalyn. "What sort of trouble? There's no trouble here."

"In the house there," said Fey.

"What's in the house? What's going on, Fey?"

Luke answered, "I'll find that out presently, Reverend. It might be best if you ladies wait here."

Luke went over to the house with Fey following close behind. He tried the handle, the door was unlocked and they entered.

"In the kitchen, Luke."

The body of the parson lay on its side, the red gash of the knife cut visible to the observers. The floor was crimson with blood and blood splatters covered the walls.

"Looks fresh," said Luke.

"Feel him, is he cold?"

"I'm not feeling him! You feel him yourself if you want the poor gentleman felt."

Fey knelt beside the body and touched the face and chest. "He's not too cold."

"Aye, well, the gentleman is still in his night gown too, so he must have met his end in the night."

Fey looked up at Luke. "You're a clever feller aren't you?"

"It's true. I am. I'll be in charge of the whole Sydney police force one day."

The arrival of Rosalyn and Cecilia in the kitchen doorway cut off Fey's unflattering response. Rosalyn let out a horrified gasp. Luke turned around. "You shouldn't be seeing this. You ladies go back."

Cecilia backed away down the hallway but Rosalyn stood speechless, her eyes transfixed to the bloody scene before her.

"I didn't want you to see this, Roz. I saw him through the window when we came calling and had to get the constable."

Rosalyn's voice came back. "Who did this?"

"How the devil would I know. I just got here meself," said Luke.

"Might have been a robbery gone wrong, Roz. Your parson might have interrupted a sneaksman."

Rosalyn continued staring at the body of the parson. "We didn't see any sign of a break in."

"There was none—the front door was unlocked," said Luke.

"Look," said Rosalyn, as her initial shock subsided. "That ghastly spray of blood is over that wall and around the stove. Whoever attacked him must have come up behind him."

Luke looked around the room and then down at the stove. He felt the kettle and lifted it up. "It's warm but empty. It's boiled dry."

Rosalyn folded her arms across her chest. "The poor fellow was making a cup of tea for himself and was struck down. This is awful."

"Maybe it wasn't just himself he was making tea for."

"What do you mean, Fey?" asked Luke.

"Look there on the table, two cups. The parson had a visitor, someone he knew and trusted."

"And someone he wasn't expecting," added Luke. "The gentleman would have dressed if he was expecting a visitor. Someone came to him early in the morning, he let them in, put the kettle on and was done in."

"Yeah, that's it in an oyster shell, Luke. You better get this reported."

"Aye, I will, Fey. But first," said Luke, as he turned to Rosalyn. "What was your business with the parson?"

"I was to meet him. I arrived here yesterday aboard the Iris. He was going to assist me in my Mission to bring Enlightenment to the heathens on the frontier."

"You're from the Sun Cog Church?"

"The Enlightenment Church, yes."

"You don't know if the parson had any enemies?"

"As I said, I have only recently arrived in the colony and hadn't met the parson yet. He may have had enemies—our Church certainly does."

"What do you mean?"

"Our Church is growing quickly, taking worshippers away from the old churches. There is resentment towards us. Instead of being seen as the salvation for a new era we're seen in some quarters as an evil enemy." Rosalyn paused and added, "This particular Church is the first of ours in the colony, so I suppose it's possible that someone here may have wanted to try to stop its influence."

"But to kill a parson? Would they resort to murder?"

Before Rosalyn could answer, Fey spoke. "Religion makes people act in a real peculiar way, Luke."

Rosalyn turned on Fey. "Religion brings comfort and salvation to us and shows the way forward."

"Forward to what?" asked Fey.

Luke stepped between them. "We can discuss the philosophy later. I've seen enough of religious squabbles back in my old country. Now, I think you women should wait outside while I get some assistance up here."

Rosalyn sat on a bench on the veranda and stared out across the town. "This is terrible." Cecilia sat beside her, placing a comforting arm around Rosalyn's shoulders. Fey watched Luke as he hurried down the street. She let the women sit with their thoughts and feelings before speaking.

"I'm sorry for getting sharp back there. It was a bit upsetting fixing my eyes on that slaughter. What do you need to do, Roz? How can I help?"

"I suppose I had best send a letter to the Church explaining what's happened here. I'll have to stay for the funeral, but the parson must have had an assistant who can take care of Church affairs until a new minister is appointed."

Cecilia looked at Fey. "We can leave visiting the Society today. I don't think it would be appropriate."

Rosalyn's face was grim. "I have to see about my cargo. I'll need a decent sized store house and a yard until I can get organised."

"That must be some cargo. I'll find you a trusted pair of eyes to keep a watch on it if you're going to leave it unguarded."

Rosalyn and Cecilia exchanged glances. "I'm sure that won't be necessary."

"Follow me then and we'll find your cargo. It will help you take your mind off this other bloody business." The three of them walked back downhill to the wharves and Fey guided them to a warehouse. She disappeared into the interior gloom where she hailed someone with whom she was obviously well acquainted. After a lively discussion between them, Fey returned. "I have some good news and I have some bad news," she announced. "Cecilia, your trunks await you. You'll have to arrange with the cove as to where you want them delivered." She paused and turned to Rosalyn.

"And?"

"And," continued Fey, "your cargo is on its way to Moreton Bay."

Rosalyn stood speechless and then managed to utter, "What? Where is Moreton Bay? How—"

"You didn't plan to continue to Moreton Bay?"

"I've never heard of Moreton Bay. I'm supposed to fly from here to Bathurst and the frontier," she said with a touch of frantic despair.

Fey's eyes widened. "Fly? Like... in an airship?"

"No, I was going to flap my arms and fly like a bird. Of course I mean in an airship! That's the cargo—the cargo which is apparently now on its way to Moreton Bay, wherever on earth that is." Rosalyn clenched her fists as her eyes reddened.

"You're not going to punch me, are you?" asked Fey.

Rosalyn stared at Fey and then looked down at her fists. She unclenched them and said in tones much softer. "No, no of course I'm not. I'm sorry. This has all gone horribly wrong. It's my first day here and the parson has been murdered and my airship is missing."

"Do you want some laudanum? I can fetch you some."

"No I don't want any laudanum"

"Opium? Gin?"

"No! I need to think. I need a clear head."

Fey pondered while Cecilia looked at Rosalyn and remained silent. Unnoticed, some distance away, another pair of eyes watched the scene. Fey spoke, "Well, your cargo sailed this morning. Moreton Bay is a convict settlement some distance up the north coast."

"That's no good to me. How can we get that ship to turn around?"

"I suppose we could run after it and ask it to stop."

Rosalyn snapped again. "Please don't be flippant—I need that airship. How do I get to Moreton Bay?"

"Sorry, Roz, but that's not going to happen. It's a convict settlement and you can't go waltzing in there. It's a restricted area. You'll need to get permission—or you can send a letter to the Commandant at Moreton Bay asking him to have your cargo shipped back."

Rosalyn buried her face in her hands and said at last. "I'll go to Moreton Bay. Who do I need to see to get the permissions and arrange the transport?"

Fey squatted and picked up a pebble, playing with it as she talked. "Even if you do get permission there won't be another ship sailing north for some time. The thing is, Roz, because you'll have a bit of a wait to go north, your cargo will be sitting up there. If word gets out what it is you're going to find that it's been commandeered. Everyone wants an airship. See how they're all flying around here?"

"No."

"That's because aside from the Bennelong there aren't any."

"The Bennelong?"

"Yes. The colony's only airship. It was named after an Aboriginal cove who was best mates with the first governor. See that fort across the bay?" Fey stood and threw the pebble in the direction of the fort. Rosalyn nodded and Fey continued. "Well that bit of land the fort is on is called Bennelong Point, after where the black feller used to live. The fort—that is Fort Macquarie. What I'm steering at is that an airship is something desired by everyone. If the Commandant at Moreton Bay gets it you'll have a devil of a time getting it back."

Fey watched Rosalyn's face carefully to see if the seeds of fear she had planted had taken root. A single tear trickled down Rosalyn's cheek and Fey laid out the next part of her plan.

"There is a solution to your predicament." Fey stated flatly as she looked deep into Roslyn's eyes—eyes that looked back hopefully.

"Yes? What? What solution?"

"I know a bloke who has a wet ship. Nothing fancy like, but big enough to do the trick."

"What are you suggesting? Nothing illegal, surely?"

"No, not like going to crack a crib or nothing. I'm suggesting you charter the ship to take you to Moreton Bay."

Rosalyn considered the idea only briefly. "I can't. I don't have that kind of money."

At this point Cecilia spoke up. "I do."

Rosalyn and Fey looked at her. Rosalyn, about to ask why Cecilia would cover such an expense, let the words die on her lips. She looked into Cecilia's eyes and nodded her assent. Cecilia smiled. "Wonderful," she said. "Where is this ship?"

Fey stood. "Now there's the rub. If you want my help in this there is another condition." She let her voice trail off and Rosalyn sighed.

"Yes, Fey, what is it? More money?"

"No. Nothing like that. We'll keep to the agreement of two shillings a day, but I come with you."

"To Moreton Bay?"

"And further. I want to fly with you."

"Out of the question!"

"Aw c'mon! I don't take up much space, and besides, you need me."

"Need you? Why would we need you?"

"Because you're a Missionary and Miss Spotswood here is an ent... an ent... a bug catcher. You'll be busy doing your work. Someone has to do the cooking and repairing and other jobs and things."

"How do you know I'm an entomologist?" asked Cecilia.

"I made enquiries, didn't I? I like to know who I'm dealing with." She turned back to Rosalyn as Cecilia studied her suspiciously. "So how about it?"

"No," said Rosalyn, although her voice wasn't so adamant.

"Please? I'll really come in handy. I've had experience and all."

"Experience?"

"Yeah, I was an apprentice steam mechanic. I worked on the Bennelong's engine. Even been up in it a few times and learned how to fly."

"Where is this airship? I haven't seen it."

"It's in the yard for repairs. Something wrong with its engine. I think they're waiting on parts from the old country. So how about it? C'mon, I love flying."

"I'm not so sure it's a good idea."

"I can speak the black's language, too. Useful for all sorts of things I am."

Rosalyn looked at Cecilia who shrugged. "You did say the craft is a three seater."

"There you go," said Fey. "A three seater, and there's three of us. Must be that God of yours turning the cogs so they line up."

Rosalyn sighed and nodded.

Fey threw her hat in the air and let out a whoop. "I better shake a leg and get this ship organised. I'll get you a bloody good price. If you ladies find your way back to your lodgings I'll meet you there when I've got it all sorted."

"Could you show me where the post office is?" asked Cecilia. "I need to write a letter home to my father to let him know I've arrived safely."

"I'd best write to the Church, too," said Rosalyn.

"I won't have time for that," said Fey, as she picked up her hat. "I'll send one of the young ones to Biddy's to take you."

It wasn't until the afternoon that Fey returned to them and by the grin on her face they knew she had been successful. On hearing the figure Cecilia nodded in agreement.

"We sail in the morning. I've arranged for Ses's trunks to be taken aboard and porters will be here first thing to take your luggage. I wouldn't be speaking to anyone about the plans either. Do you ladies have enemies?" They shook their heads. "Well someone has been following me, but I gave them the slip. An airship would be quite a prize here. Think of all them convicts who would love to abscond by soaring aloft—on the wings of an eagle so the song goes. So guard your tongues ladies, something is out of alignment."

Rosalyn was awoken in the dark hours by someone tapping at her window—which was particularly odd as she was in an upstairs room. Moving the curtain aside, she peered out to see Fey, her nose pressed against the glass. She opened the window and whispered, "Fey, what is it?"

"Change of plans, love. We have to leave now," whispered Fey. "You're going to have to be deadly quiet. Get Ses, pack yourselves up quickly—and don't wake Biddy. Come out by the back door. I'll meet you there."

"This is most unusual, sneaking about like thieves in the night."

"Stow it. Do as I says if you want to get to your airship. You clear on that?" Rosalyn nodded. "Good, now real quiet like. I have to get this ladder back."

Rosalyn conveyed the plan to Cecilia who was likewise disturbed by the change in the departure time, but between the two of them they managed to get their trunks downstairs without too much ado. Fey greeted them by the back door and had in her company two men to help cart the luggage. At that moment a voice came out of the darkness from close by. "What do you think you're doing here? Caught you doing a knock have I?"

They looked around and Fey said, "It's a charlie."

"Fey Grey, is that you?" asked the policeman.

"Yes," Fey whispered. "And can you keep your voice down?"

"Why? What are you about?" The policeman spoke softly.

"We have a ship we need to board."

"Don't try to pull the lid over my eyes, Fey. I can see you're doing a robbery, why else the back door? Why the silence? You're all nibbed. I'm taking you in."

Rosalyn stepped forward and stood in front of the man. "I'm the Reverend Missionary Rosalyn Flynn. Whom do I have the pleasure of addressing?"

The policeman looked at her in the gloom and satisfied that Rosalyn's attire was that of the clergy replied, "Olthwaite Lockwood, constable, Ma'am... Reverend, and I need to kno..."

"Olthwaite Lockwood—from London?"

"Yes Ma'am... how did you know?"

"If you could keep your voice low I will explain the manner of the circumstances in which you find us, but first I must pass on the greetings from your parents."

"My parents? How do you know my parents?"

"The cogs turn in mysterious ways. They visited the Church when they heard of a Missionary sailing for Sydney. They asked specifically for me to pass on their love to you if I saw you—and I must confess, I had all but forgotten the encounter until you reminded me by your introduction."

"That sounds a bit queer to me, my father is a drunk and barely spoke a word to me."

"That may have been in the past but he has since found his way in the Church and is now as sober as a judge. They wish you well and ask that you write."

Olthwaite rubbed his chin. "That's good turnings to have brought such news. And my mother, is she in good health? Does she still have that cough?"

"I would like to say otherwise but she does still have the cough."

"Thank you, Reverend. That's the most wonderful circumstance that's brought their words to me—but the back door? Why are you sneaking out? You're not doing a runner on Biddy are you?"

"I'm not sure what you mean, Constable Lockwood. Biddy was quite exhausted last night and fell asleep on the sofa in the front room. As we were leaving early we did not wish to wake her by dragging our luggage out that way and have come out the back way instead."

Olthwaite pondered this. "That's considerate of you, Reverend. You best get a move on if you're to make the tide."

The women bade Olthwaite a good night and they moved on with the porters in tow. Fey lingered and whispered to Olthwaite, "Don't get me pegged as a nose but there's a man been watching Biddy's house. He's across the street from it and down a bit, around the corner. He was there last evening just before dark and now he's there again. He means mischief to Biddy, I'm sure of it."

Olthwaite looked at Fey and nodded, "Don't you worry lovely, I'll see to him." And with that Fey hurried off after the party.

The captain was waiting for them on the wharf and they boarded the brig immediately. Cecilia checked that her trunks had been brought from the warehouse and the crew cast off. They were well outside Sydney Harbour when the light of dawn appeared.

Baker knocked lightly on the door. No light shone from within, and not wishing to draw attention to himself, he declined to knock louder. Instead he set to work and picked open the lock, letting himself into the drawing room of the house. He removed his boots, twirled the ends of his moustache, stretched out on a settee and allowed himself to sleep.

"Trouble?" A tall man in a red robe stood next to him holding a cup of tea. The curtains were still closed but around their edges the morning light found its way into the room.

"Some, but nothing that will interfere with my work. Is that for me?"

"The Missionary?" The man ignored Baker's question.

"She's on her way to Moreton Bay." Baker sat up and pulled on his boots.

"So soon? I'd thought she'd explore other avenues here."

"Regardless of her success or failure in Moreton Bay, I'll have ample time to carry out my next task."

The man sipped his tea. "Did anyone see you come here?"

"No. I saw activity at the house and a policeman came snooping, but I left him behind. The Missionary had sailed by the time I found my way to the docks so I came here to report."

"Do refrain from coming here. We mustn't be seen together again." The man paused. "There is tea in the pot in the kitchen. You can make yourself breakfast but don't let anyone see you leave. We can't trust anyone."

"Much obliged." Baker stepped past the man and made for the teapot.

"And Baker, be ruthless when you have to be. If we are to secure the future then we cannot always afford the luxury of kindness."

"You know I get my work done."

"Yes. It's why we chose you."

6

Moreton Bay

Rosalyn spent most of the voyage standing in the bow, hoping to catch a glimpse of the vessel that carried her precious airship. Moreton Bay was reached without incident. The settlement was located up a river which flowed into the bay, and they navigated slowly along its length.

Rosalyn looked up to a canopy of sky so deep and blue she felt she could reach out and touch it. Tall, white-barked trees reflected in the clear water of the river. A flash of colour caught the eyes of the observers as a kingfisher flew into the light, and a flock of rainbow lorikeets rising into the sky drew cries of delight. Enormous fig trees sent roots dripping earthwards where they sprawled thickly over the ground like wax from candles.

"It's stunning." Cecilia stood at the railing, transfixed by the sights.

"Indeed. God must have been particularly inspired when he created this place," said Rosalyn in response.

"We're about to reach Hell," said Fey who had come up behind them. "Look, there's the settlement." The ship was passing around another bend and evidence of agriculture could be seen on both banks. Buildings stood on the top of a ridge, and on a piece of farmland a line of agricultural labourers toiled on the slopes. "Convicts," said Fey. "Moreton Bay is where they send the hard cases, the ones transported to Sydney from the old country, and who've got themselves nibbed again for something or another. They're made to work here in chains."

The women stared at the line of convicts in silence. The next bend brought them in sight of the settlement proper and the vessel they had hoped to catch lay at anchor. A boat was made ready and the women were rowed ashore. Word of their approach had already preceded them and a small party waited to greet them.

"We had no idea a Missionary was coming," said a gentleman in an important-looking uniform. "I'm Major Sydney Cotton, Commandant here."

"It was an unplanned-for diversion from the course the Church has set me on. I'm the Reverend Missionary Rosalyn Flynn and these are my travelling companions Miss Cecilia Spotswood and Miss Fey Grey."

"And you're a Missionary party to the settlement here are you? But no, you say this is an unplanned diversion. You'd best explain yourself."

A small group of soldiers and convicts had gathered around them to learn what they could of the news so they might be important in its retelling in their respective barracks that evening.

"I'm on a Mission to bring Enlightenment to the heathens on the frontier."

"That's all well and good and I think this qualifies as frontier, but this is not yet a free settlement and we already have a clergyman to see to our spiritual needs. Moreton Bay is a penal station and a restricted area. Do you have your papers from Governor Gipps?"

"Not exactly, that is... No. We don't have papers. I was in pursuit of an important piece of Church property which appears to have been sent by some colonial accident to this settlement from Sydney recently."

"That would be the boat, wouldn't it, and the chests that came with it? Come with me." They followed Major Cotton a short distance to a large, stone storehouse. The boat and its accompanying crates rested on the ground outside it. "Is this what you're looking for?"

Rosalyn walked along the length of the boat and looked about the prow. The painted yellow cog and cross stood out from the wooden hull and identified the vessel as an Enlightenment Church airship. Rosalyn's inquiring gaze then took in the crates and the markings on the side. "Look here, Cecilia, Fey, look." On the side of each crate, artfully stencilled, could be seen:

'Property of the Enlightenment Church
Colony of Sydney, New South Wales
Care of R.M. Rosalyn Flynn'

This had all been clumsily crossed out, and underneath, painted in ill-formed letters, read:

'Redirect to Moreton Bay penal colony
Care of Major Cotton'

The women stared at the words in dismay. Rosalyn turned to Major Cotton. "Yes, this is my cargo. It's Enlightenment Church property."

"Then perhaps you might inform me as to why it has been readdressed to me."

"Major Cotton, I was hoping you could tell me the same thing."

The two looked at each other and then at the airship and then back at each other. Major Cotton spoke, "It's all quite irregular—this cargo being addressed to me and you turning up here with no documentation. We can discuss this over dinner. I insist you..." he looked at Cecilia and Fey, although with Fey his expression lost some of its insistence. "...will join me this evening. In the meantime I'll assign you a guard and have someone find you quarters for this evening."

Sailors unloaded the women's trunks onto the wharf. A guard directed convicts to carry the trunks to the lodgings. Fey's baggage consisted of nothing other than an old flour bag filled with little more than a change of clothes and a blanket. She'd sewn into the open edge a length of rope with a piece in excess tied off to allow for a handle. She threw this over her shoulder and watched the convicts labouring under the weight of the trunks. One of them, a tiny fellow, struggling up the slope, slipped, and dropped the trunk he was carrying. It was Cecilia's, and the smashing of glass could be heard as it crashed to the ground.

The guard in charge spewed forth a torrent of abuse. "Goosey, you bloody little idiot. Why they keep you out of chains is past my understandin'. You'll be damned well flogged for this." For good measure the guard started punching Goosey around the face and head as the convict did his best to shield himself from the blows.

"Soldier! That's enough," said Cecilia. "I'm sure whatever is broken can be replaced."

"He's a layabout and an idler, Ma'am. If I was the Commandant I'd have him in irons." The convict stood with his head bowed, holding his cap in his hands.

"What's going on here?" came a voice from behind them.

The women turned around to see a familiar face.

"Sergeant Hopson, what are you doing here?"

"I arrived yesterday, Reverend. My detachment of the 28th is here, and I'm under the command of Major Cotton. How is it that you're here?"

"We're tracing the fate of my cargo which was sent on to this settlement in error."

"Can I help you with it?"

"No, I don't think that will be necessary. My airship was sent on here by mistake but Major Cotton is looking into it."

Sergeant Hopson looked thoughtful and nodded. "And what's the fuss here?" Sergeant Hopson turned to the soldier.

"Nothing much, Sergeant. This wretch dropped the lady's trunk."

"There's really no need to punish the man," said Cecilia.

Sergeant Hopson turned from the private to the convict. The

convict was a slight, clean-shaven man and had a small silver earring in each ear. He looked the epitome of misery. "Not much to you is there? Take more care with your work." He turned to the soldier. "You'll let it go this time. Move it along now."

They stood and watched as the private led the convicts away. "It's nice to see a friendly face in a place like this. And thank you, Sergeant Hopson for sparing that poor wretch further punishment. The fellow looked like he was about to cry."

"Don't concern yourself about him too much, Reverend, this place will toughen him up. Do you know how long you're staying?"

"We hope to leave as quickly as possible. We're dining with the Major tonight so I expect we will have everything sorted out over dinner and will be away tomorrow."

"If I don't see you again then best of luck to you in your Mission. If you'll excuse me I have things to see to."

They followed the soldier to their lodgings in the rooms of a civilian administrator, now temporarily bunked in with the settlement's doctor. The soldier sat himself on the veranda steps but finding guard duty too onerous for his liking, delegated the task to Joe Goosey. The women rested while Joe sat on the front porch smoking his pipe. A convict came to them with the news that, due to the unfortunate lack of table space, the Major could only entertain two of the three women. As Cecilia and Rosalyn were from England, the Major would like their presence so he might learn of any events there.

"Bullshit," said Fey after the messenger left.

The other two women turned to her. "What do you mean?" asked Rosalyn.

"I mean he doesn't want me at his table. I'm a currency lass. I'm not good enough for his company." Joe, who was listening, nodded in agreement.

"I'm sure you're wrong," said Cecilia.

"If we were in England would you invite me to your table?" The women didn't answer. "Yeah, as I expected. I'm going for a walk. Enjoy your dinner. Bring me back a few scraps from the table will you?" She walked away with a scowl on her face.

Rosalyn watched her go, and when Fey was out of earshot turned to Cecilia. "She forgets that she's our servant, and really, she has no place being at the Major's table anyway."

Cecilia lay back on her bed, saying nothing.

The women returned from dinner to find Fey had put aside her earlier mood. She was waiting on the veranda for them. "I've got some intelligence for you, and it isn't good." Rosalyn and Cecilia drew closer. "That little feller, Joe Goosey, he told me something he heard. Has his beak in all the right places he does. He said that Cotton has no intention of letting go of your airship. He wants it here to keep an eye on the convicts and to do a bit of exploring. This place is being opened to free settlement this year and he means to have that airship available to him. He's going to baulk you until he gets rid of you and he's going to do that tomorrow by sticking us back on the boat we came in on."

Rosalyn clenched her fists and stamped her foot. "He can't do that. That's Church property. He has only just assured us that everything will be taken care of. We have to talk to him."

"Won't do you any good. That airship is as good as his. He's the law here."

"What are we going to do?" asked Cecilia.

"Well," Fey leaned forward conspiratorially. "We're going to fly out of here tonight."

"Tonight?" asked Rosalyn.

"Yes. As you ladies were busy stuffing your faces alongside the refined gentry of Moreton Bay, I was in league with Joe. You've seen the boat sitting in the open, the chests with the balloon next to it. We take it to the water and move with the tide upriver and settle ourselves on the far bank, get the thing assembled and fly off."

"That sounds simple." Cecilia turned to Rosalyn with hope

restored.

"It's not that simple," countered Rosalyn. "How are we three going to manage that? We couldn't even lift the boat together and the chests are heavy. And besides, isn't it breaking the law to do that?" Fey stared at her until Rosalyn added, "I'm sure the Church will understand. How do we do this?"

"Easy," said Fey. "For a few coins Joe has the soldier on guard in his pocket and that Sergeant you're friendly with, he's going to help cover us. I've cleared it with the brig's Captain and he and a few of his crew are going to help us."

"Why would he do that?" asked Rosalyn.

"This is why you're paying me two shillings a day love. While you two were admiring the dolphins and seagulls and the fluffy white clouds on the trip up the coast I was below decks tallying up my winnings at the flats. Those blokes are poor card players for sailors, and are due to settle with me in the morning. I did a deal with them that I'd forget the debt if they helped us out. Major Cotton has no hold on the brig."

"And I thought you were below deck because you were seasick. When do we go?" asked Rosalyn.

"Now. We have two boats waiting, including yours. I'll let Joe know we're ready."

On Fey's word, Joe left his place on the end of the veranda where he'd been resting and disappeared into the darkness, returning with two men from the ship.

"I fear sneaking out of houses is becoming something of a habit." Rosalyn closed the door after her, quietly following the others to the landing point. The soldier on sentry duty was clearly nervous and in a hurry to get them away. Rosalyn paid him a small amount and Joe took him aside, keeping his level of agitation down by talking softly with him. The women were able to give Joe only the briefest of goodbyes and their thanks.

The incoming tide helped the boats in the journey up the river and having rounded a bend, they pulled into the mouth of a small creek. Here they found an area free from mangroves and pulled the boats into it. The crates were unloaded, the sailors gave a few curt farewells, returned to their boat and headed back down the river.

7

MAJOR COTTON'S CORROBOREE

Rosalyn held up a lamp and stared at the crates. "I have no idea how this thing goes together; I only know how to fly it."

"Don't look to me," said Cecilia. "I'm familiar with the mechanics of dragonfly flight and the fluttering of butterflies, but the operation of airships is quite beyond me."

Both of them turned to look at Fey. "This is your field," said Rosalyn.

"It's like this—when I said I'd worked on airship engines what I meant was that I watched some of the men working on them." Silence followed Fey's admission and the darkness hid the scornful looks of her companions. "But," she hastily added before either of them could speak, "I reckon I can get it together if you'll follow my instructions." Cecilia sighed and Rosalyn told Fey to go ahead. Fey lit another lamp. It cast a dim light around the area, creating eerie shadows in the surrounding trees.

Fey used a pry bar from the boat's tool compartment to break open the long crate containing the balloon. With Rosalyn's help they unfolded it, and laid it along the length of the boat. The two spars for the side sails were folded against the hull, kept in place by brass hinges. They were extended by the use of a winding handle and Fey got to work extending the port side. "Roz, you take the starboard. We want these at full extension or the ship will tip over when we fix the balloon up. Ses, you open the other boxes. We'll need to get that engine mounted, so you'll have to search through the storage compartment to find the right tools."

The boat still leaned to one side when the side spars were extended but in no danger of falling over. "All right, we need to put up the mast into that bracket there. Ses, you bolt it in place when we have it up. There're holes in the bottom of it. Slide the bolts through." The mast was short and not too heavy and Fey held it as she continued to give instructions. Roz, you need to get those two 'V' struts up fore and aft of the mast. They're folded together there. You'll have to open them up like a pair of dividers and slot the base into the holes."

A long, folded strip of wood, hinged in the middle, was the next part to be attached. They opened it up. It ran the length of the boat, about twenty feet. The hinge rested in a groove on a plate on top of the mast. "This holds the base of the balloon, we need to get the balloon onto it now."

The women grunted with the exertion as they took the weight of the balloon on their shoulders. With effort they hauled it into place, ensuring the base of the balloon rested on its long, narrow support. "See these pegs protruding from the reinforced base of the balloon? They align with the holes in the support. Ses, you'll need to find the pins to secure them in place. Roz, we have to start on the engine. It will take a while to fill this balloon."

"I must say, I'm quite impressed with your ability here, Fey. You must have been paying close attention to the men working on that Benning airship."

"The Bennelong, and yeah, I have a bit of a fascination for how things work. It's a matter of observing, seeing how one thing fits with another, and why each bit is there. Everything has a purpose."

"That's one of the teachings of our Church."

"Well, good for that, now give me a hand getting this engine mounted. It's lighter than it looks."

They managed to manoeuvre it into place and while Rosalyn was fastening it to the deck plate Fey fetched water and filled the boiler. "We need the coal bricks and the blue stuff now."

"Blue ascension," said Rosalyn.

"I'll fetch the bricks," said Cecilia. "I found them when I was looking for the tools." She opened a compartment and handed Fey two of the coal bricks. Fey used a splash of spirits in the ignition compartment to get the coal burning and Rosalyn opened the little drawer for the blue ascension.

"Fill the drawer, Cecilia."

Cecilia managed to lift the firkin of blue ascension and open the tap at its base. A thick, oozy liquid drained out of it. "Take care," said Rosalyn. "It's frightfully expensive and we don't want to lose a drop of it."

With the water heating in the boiler, Fey set them to work securing the net over the top of the balloon and roping it to the rings on the skyrail. Ropes were unpacked from another box and Fey went about finding which one went where and fastening them on. That done she attached the piping that fed the blue steam from the engine into the balloon. Rosalyn and Cecilia secured their trunks onboard, testing the tautness of the ropes to ensure they wouldn't shift in flight.

"What about the rudder and propeller, Fey?" asked Rosalyn.

"I'll get working on them now. If you two aren't doing anything you can get out those side sails and start attaching them to the spars. Make sure you get them the right way up and on the proper sides."

The women set to work threading the rope through the eyelets. Fey paused to take stock of their progress. Crouching down next to Rosalyn she said in a low voice, "The propeller is in, I'll do this, you see to the engine. I think the water is boiling and you need to start getting the balloon filled."

"Is dawn approaching?"

"No, but there are blacks watching us from the trees over there."

Rosalyn looked around but saw nothing in the darkness. "Are we in danger?"

"Dunno, we might be. They're in spear range but it's got me curious why they're awake at this time of night. We must've been making a bit of noise. We'll keep an eye on them but we need to keep working if we're going to be above the trees before dawn."

Rosalyn climbed into the boat and looked at the controls. She pushed a lever and heard the whoosh of steam as it fed into the mixing chamber. Above it was a valve and she turned the handle until the dial on the gauge showed maximum. With little to do now but wait, she opened her trunk, taking out her coat, scarf and goggles. She laid them out next to the wheel.

With everything in place the women sat back in the boat and looked about in the dull light of the lantern. Two fixed seats at the bow faced each other and gave the only comfort to passengers. The raised deck of the boat left some extra storage space underneath, accessible by hatches set at intervals along its length. About four feet back from the bow a semi-circle of wood extended from port to starboard. This provided the support for a canvas covering to give extra protection from the weather should it be needed.

The space along the sides of the boat consisted of storage compartments and at the square stern a small cabin gave privacy when ablutions were required. Fishing net had been tailored to fasten to the securing lines of the balloon net to add extra height to the sides. The space forward of the mast between the seats held the women's travel chests leaving little room to move about. Barely inches above their heads, the balloon also acted as an umbrella, shielding the boat's occupants from sun and rain.

"Looks like a ship's launch or a fishing boat," said Fey.

"It's an airship," said Rosalyn.

"Yeah, I know, but look, the thing is built with a 'V' shaped cross section. Why would you? See how it leaned to one side as we put the balloon on? We had to put the side spars out to keep it upright.

You wouldn't design an airship like this, and all this wood is adding weight."

"You could do better, I suppose?" asked Cecilia.

"Yeah, I reckon I could."

"It's a first generation airship, Fey. These first airships were wet boats converted for use. This appears to be one of them so I suppose you're right. This was once a fishing boat or some such vessel."

"It wasn't designed for the air. Anyone with a half-formed brain box can see that."

"Wet ship builders constructed the second generation of airships," Rosalyn went on. "Their skills were much the same as those needed for airships but the builders and designers still had their heads—brain boxes as you call them—in the sea. It's the airships being designed now that will show a greater leap into the skies."

"Do you know what this was used for before your Sun God gave it to you for your Mission?"

"We don't worship the Sun God."

"Whatever, but he's making his appearance now; the sky is lightening."

"I notice your balloon is filling fast," said Cecilia, "but is it going to be inflated before Major Cotton discovers we've stolen the airship?"

"We didn't steal it, Cecilia. This airship belongs to the Enlightenment Church and I am the captain."

"Captain or not, Ses is right. We need to be aloft before the Major gets his daylights onto us."

Birds were already starting to stir, the kookaburras being the first to call out to the coming day and the warbling of magpies joined the dawn chorus. The Aboriginal people who had been watching them disappeared back amongst the trees and scrub from which they'd appeared. Roots of a nearby Moreton Bay fig tree snaked down from the trunk and branches, covering the ground. The falling tide exposed the upright roots of the mangroves and small crabs scuttled about. The women fell into silence as the dawn light revealed the new details of their surroundings. The boat gave a shudder as the blue ascension reached lifting point.

At that moment a shout caught their attention. The three of them turned as one and looked out between the trees, in the direction of the river. A boatload of soldiers rowed towards them, with Major Cotton in command. He shouted something but the foliage muffled his words. Rosalyn turned to Fey, "What did he say?"

"I think he said you're clear to cast off."

"I think you're quite right. It did sound like that to me. Pull in the hooks and sit down, we're going up." Rosalyn pushed a lever and a fan started that gave an extra shot of blue ascension into the pipe. The airship gave a jolt as the balloon took the full weight of the boat and it left the ground. A cloud of smoke filled the air around them and they started rising.

The soldiers paddled frantically against the tide and current and reached the bank. Their boots squelched as they stepped into the mud. As they made their way between the mangroves, the airship approached treetop height.

Branches brushed against the balloon, some of the smaller ones catching in the netting and snapping, causing erratic movements of the boat, sending down a shower of twigs and leaves. The airship rose further, above the tallest of the trees, the horizontal rays of the sun hitting the side of the boat. Rosalyn grinned as Fey and Cecilia clung to the netting, peering over the side.

Below them, Major Cotton jumped up and down, yelling at them to return, his feet sinking further into the mud with each effort. He barked an order at one of the soldiers, a single shot was fired and it whistled past the balloon. Rosalyn, hands on the wheel, ignored it. The sounds of the shouting faded away as they ascended steadily to a height of six hundred feet. Rosalyn, still grinning, pushed a lever, engaging the propeller, and she turned the wheel so the nose of the airship pointed upriver. The engine chugged and the airship moved forward.

If they'd looked back they would have seen the spreading convict settlement receding behind them but they didn't do that. Cecilia, who had been most afraid when they first rose into the sky, had managed to calm herself quite well. The three of them looked at each other, their faces flushed with success. "Where are we going?" asked Cecilia.

"The frontier," replied Rosalyn, who had forgotten for the moment her Mission, enraptured as she was in the sheer joy of flying.

"I hate to be a wet blanket and all but in our haste to depart we left without food and with little water. Most of what water we have we'll need for the engine. We're going to have to stop somewhere soon to stock up," said Fey.

"Where do you suggest? Are there towns hereabouts?" asked Rosalyn.

Fey looked at her as though she were simple. "Towns? Sure, there are towns dotted all over the landscape. Have a look over the side and you'll see them. We can put down, slip into a shop, buy what we want and continue on our way." Cecilia and Rosalyn looked over the side.

"I can't see any towns." Cecilia peered into the distance. "Nothing but little wisps of smoke here and there. Perhaps they're farms and we can procure what we need from them."

Fey buried her face in her palms as she shook her head. "Those little plumes of smoke are fires from the blacks. There're no towns between here and Sydney—and that's weeks away. We were already at the frontier, now we're sailing past it."

"Are we going to Sydney?" Cecilia looked at Rosalyn.

"No, we are not going back to Sydney. Fey, you speak the black's language. If we put down we might be able to trade with them. See what we've got here that we might exchange."

Fey gave them a sheepish look. "When I said I could speak their language I meant I could speak a few words of it."

Rosalyn winced. "All right, we need ideas. Is there anything at all on board that we can eat?" Fey ventured forth some biscuits, cheese and bread. It wasn't much. "If we split this three ways it should keep us going for a day."

"I've heard that kangaroos can be eaten. Can't we just catch one of them?" Cecilia looked at Fey wide-eyed as a tone of desperation entered her voice.

"We'll have to take stock of our situation," said Rosalyn. "We have no choice but to try to make contact with the blacks and barter for food. We also need to know where we're going." It was then that Rosalyn remembered her sealed orders from the Church. "Fey, take the wheel. I have some reading to do." Fey gave her a peculiar look. "You can fly, can't you, Fey? You said you could fly."

Fey's eyes fixed on some distant spot on the horizon. "When I said I could fly what I meant was, I'd seen the Bennelong flying and I reckon I could fly one." Rosalyn pursed her lips, grabbed Fey by the wrist and pulled her roughly to the wheel. "Your duplicity astounds me, and the worst thing is, you have no shame."

"Don't go hard on me, Roz. How's a person with no experience supposed to get work? I had to rub the truth a little."

"A little?" said Cecilia. "You lied about speaking the black's language, about your mechanical abilities and your airship skills."

"Don't interrupt, Ses, I was talking to Captain Flynn."

Rosalyn stared icily at Fey, who turned her attention to the dials on the engine. A brief and rudimentary course in airship piloting ensued and Rosalyn left Fey to it.

"It's a bit slow isn't it?" stated Fey as she took to the 'on the job' training.

"It's an airship and it actually goes quite fast relative to how quickly you could travel if you were walking."

"I'm not walking."

"You will be if you complain about my airship."

"I'll button my lips. What do you call this airship anyway?"

"I don't know. I don't think it has a name. What would you like to call it?"

"As it goes so bloody fast I think we should call it Lightning."

Rosalyn shook her head and turned away to hide a smile. "All right, Lightning it is." She opened her satchel and took out the Mission envelope. As she sat down to open it she looked at the seal and saw it was broken. Dismissing it as an accidental breakage, Rosalyn removed the Orders from the envelope. Cecilia watched her from across the boat and observed the frowns on Rosalyn's face as she read.

'Reverend Missionary Rosalyn Flynn,

You are to proceed on arrival in Sydney to the Enlightenment Church and make contact with Reverend Barnes, the parson, who will assist you in the provisioning of the airship. He will give you letters to take to the person named on such and whom you will find in Bathurst. This person will accompany you on your Mission, and it is imperative they do.

Your Mission is threefold:

Firstly, you are to locate the missing explorer, Doctor Norman Phatts, and if he has survived, return with him to the Church in Sydney along with any notes and journals which are still extant.

Secondly, you are to find a desirable location for a Mission settlement.

Thirdly, bring Enlightenment to the heathens at every opportunity and usher them into the Church fold.

May the cogs turn with you,
Bishop of the Cog
Bartholomew Roberts'

"Bad news?"

"I don't quite know what to make of it. The parson, this Reverend Barnes in Sydney, was going to give me letters to take to someone in this place called Bathurst. And this is strange—I'm supposed to be looking for a lost explorer by the name of Norman Phatts. It adds that I'm also to bring Enlightenment to the heathens." Rosalyn studied the letter again and discovered another line, hidden by a fold in the paper.

'PS It is essential that you tell no one and trust no one.'

"Oops, and there's another bit at the bottom that says I'm not to tell anyone." Rosalyn omitted the part about trusting no one.

Cecilia looked at Fey. "No, no of course we won't tell anyone. Who would we tell? We're all here in an airship with no one else around."

Rosalyn continued staring at her orders hoping some sense would come of them. "The name is strangely familiar but I know nothing of a Doctor Phatts. Where would I even begin looking?"

"You might try Bathurst. Your letter mentions someone who is important. I reckon they might have all the intelligence you need."

"I don't know who we're looking for. How big is Bathurst?"

"I've never been as far west as Bathurst but I know it isn't a big town. You fly in on this and the person you're looking for will find you."

"I do suppose you're right, Fey. And I recall Maud saying that the person is an Enlightenment Church Guardian. I'm a bit concerned though that by the time we get there news will be out that we've taken back the airship—the Lightning, and we will once again be held."

"There's another thing," said Cecilia. "One of us will have to sit out. How will you fit four people in here with the extra food and water that will be required?"

"She'd have to leave you behind, Ses. She needs me. I'm crew, you're a passenger."

"I will not be left behind. You're a colonial. I paid for our passage to Moreton Bay to fetch the Lightning."

"Good on you, and you'll get a place in heaven for your good deed, I'm sure. I reckon Roz will even say a prayer for you, but you're dead weight on this trip."

"I'm not dead weight. You're the one who lied to us about your qualifications to gain a position on board." Cecilia's face reddened.

"Yeah, you kindly pointed that out earlier, but I learn fast and I can already fly an airship like an expert."

Rosalyn listened to the argument as she folded the letter back into the envelope and stuffed it in her satchel. "It's quite possible that if I find this person, both of you will be left behind, and if you continue to behave like this I don't think it's altogether such a bad idea." Fey and Cecilia exchanged glances and fell into a sullen silence. "We need to go to Bathurst. Fey, where is it?"

"West from Sydney. We might want to head southwest from here." Fey stood at the wheel, her mood sour.

"Have you heard of this Doctor Phatts?" asked Rosalyn.

"Yeah. He took an expedition out into the interior and never came back."

"How long has he been gone?"

"About three or four years."

"Three or four years? How on earth does the Church expect me to find someone who has been missing for so long? He must surely be dead."

"Maybe, Roz, but the feller back in Moreton Bay who helped us, the convict with the pretty earrings, Joe Goosey, I was chatting to him about the place. He says that some of the convicts who managed to escape lived with the blacks further north for years before returning to the settlement."

"That's a possibility," said Cecilia.

"I still have this nagging feeling I've heard the name before. Do you know of him, Cecilia?"

"I can't say I've heard of him, but it's possible our paths crossed at some point, or that I may have read one of his scientific papers, if indeed he had anything published."

They flew on in silence and Rosalyn noticed Fey grinning. "What is it, Fey?"

"Back there, as we were lifting off up through the trees, did you see Major Cotton?"

"I had a brief glimpse over the side but I was at the helm. What about him?"

"He was jumping up and down and running about like the blacks do when they're dancing. I think he's gone native."

Rosalyn smiled. "I think he'd like to have us in chains like his convicts if he could catch us."

"Not much chance of that, Roz, there's not another airship between here and Sydney."

Rosalyn took the helm from Fey who stood at her elbow watching everything she did. Cecilia busied herself, going through her various books and notes. "Look here." She waved a piece of paper. "I found this in the papers the Society gave me. I expect it will be useful."

"What is it?"

"A map with some figures. Look, there's a latitude." She pointed at a line on the map.

"A map of what? You're not making sense."

"It's a map of Doctor Phatts' journey. It has the latitude he intended following. We can fly to that latitude and pursue the course of your Doctor. Now at least we have somewhere to start." She laid out the map in the bottom of the boat. Sydney was marked but the penal settlement at Moreton Bay was not. "Look, there's Bathurst. You were to leave from there and if you had taken this bearing here you would pick up the latitude. As we are north of Bathurst we could simply continue on a line to intersect with Doctor Phatts' latitude, and that is our starting point."

"However, I have to go to Bathurst to try to find the person I'm supposed to meet."

Cecilia and Fey looked at each other and Fey stated, "But there's no room."

"What?"

"There's no room. This craft is crowded now. If you took a fourth we'd be falling over the sides."

"We've already discussed that. The Lightning is Church property,

I'm on a Church Mission and I do have to follow Church Orders."

"No you don't."

"What do you mean?"

"I mean, you don't have to follow Church Orders. What are they going to do, send someone out here to scold you? Besides, you don't even know who you're looking for—man or woman, young or old."

"Fey has a point."

"You said they would find me if I flew into Bathurst on this airship. I could at least ask around."

"You'd be wasting time. Those two ships were leaving Moreton Bay today and when they're back in Sydney the report will go out that you stole this airship, and if news does somehow manage to reach Bathurst before we get there, they'll seize the airship. We'll be sent as convicts back to Moreton Bay."

"They'll be travelling on the ground. News would never get there before we could. We'll be gone long before then."

"Not if the Bennelong is up and flying, and I'm sure it will be by the time we get to Bathurst. It's a long, long way to the south."

Cecilia added, "You had to meet this man to get your directions, and to provide you with protection. Thanks to this map you have the directions now, and Fey is proving capable and does learn quickly."

From her position behind Rosalyn, Fey gave Cecilia a thumbs up and said, "It would be a shocker to fly all that way only to have the Lightning seized again, and us all in chains."

"And it's good being the captain of the airship isn't it? You don't really want to risk this chance by having your ship confiscated again do you?"

"I know what you're doing." Rosalyn pursed her lips as her friends tensed and awaited the decision. "Very well, we won't go to Bathurst. We'll continue on until we reach the latitude we want and then head west to find this Phatts fellow." After checking the compass Rosalyn turned the bow more to starboard and fixed the course. Cecilia and Fey exhaled and relaxed.

"Fey, take the wheel. Cecilia, that book of colonial butterflies, may I see it again."

"What brought on this sudden interest in Lepidoptera?"

"I'll tell you when you show me the book."

Cecilia rummaged through one of her trunks and brought out the volume. Rosalyn took it from her and turned to the last page. "I thought so. Look. See here?"

"It's an empty page."

"No, down the bottom, it says, 'The Green Wave'."

"And?"

Rosalyn tapped her finger on the page. "Look. Next to that—in pencil—it says, 'as referenced by Dr Phatts'."

"So it does."

"You didn't know this was in here?"

"I didn't even know I had the map until a short time ago. May I have my book back now please?"

"Yes... Wait. Look—on the page opposite—the lines running along the edge. It's faint but I can read it: 'Important. Find it.' What do you suppose that means?"

"I don't know. That could have been written on the paper before it was included in the book."

Rosalyn examined the writing, "I don't think so. Study it closely—it's the same hand writing that wrote 'as referenced by Dr Phatts'."

"Well, I had no idea. I suppose I should focus my observations in regard to this butterfly and so keep the Society happy by ascertaining its whereabouts, but there's not even an illustration."

Fey, who had been listening to the exchange, asked, "Why would a butterfly be important?"

"I don't know. I can only guess that it's some kind of rare and exotic species. It may be worth quite a bit of money to a collector."

Rosalyn closed the book and handed it back to Cecilia. "It seems we both have reason to find Dr Phatts."

8

The Flight Of The *Lightning*

Rosalyn's hands relaxed on the wheel as she listened to the poetry of the creaking ropes and timbers. She altered the altitude to make best use of the winds, instructing Fey to extend the side sails. A simple system of cogs enabled a single operator to wind out the spars, independently or together. The sails were square and their position could be altered to suit the conditions. Wind filled them the moment they unfurled, with an immediate effect on the airship's speed. In spite of being an old, cumbersome model, the sails gave the small airship an elegant appearance.

Only the steady chugging sound of the engine disturbed the tranquillity of the clear, blue day. A mountain range lay before them and Rosalyn worked the airship up the heavily-timbered slopes, the keel, at times, brushing the tops of the trees. Cecilia knelt on her seat peering over the side. Fey stood as far forward as she could, holding tightly to the netting, watching the dense, green foliage pass beneath her. The sounds of birds reached them from the trees. Parrots flew from them in fear, their bright, jewel colours blazing in the sunlight. Cresting the range, and shaded from the bright sun by the balloon, Rosalyn took the opportunity to look over the side. She could see the courses of waterways marked by the dense lines of trees. In the distance clouds of smoke covered large areas of the ground. As the airship flew closer she could see the scrubland burning. "What's caused the fires?" she asked Fey.

"The blacks do it. They burn the grass to hunt out animals and the new growth brings more animals back to graze."

On one occasion, due to adverse higher altitude winds, they had to fly low and their course took them into the smoke of such a fire. They could see the Aborigines below, who at first didn't notice the airship passing overhead. When they caught sight of the strange flying thing, individuals reacted in different ways—some running away and some hurling spears. None of the missiles had any chance of hitting the *Lightning* as it was well out of spear range and soon the airship was past the smoke, the scene disappearing behind them.

Many such groups of blacks were encountered, some of whom noticed them and some who did not. The reaction from those who saw them pass was always the same: shouting and running or displays of aggression. The women, safe in their boat, remained detached from such scenes, observers of the landscape but not part of it. Rosalyn took the time to fill in her Missionary journal, including the manner of her late night departures from Sydney and Moreton Bay and her reasons for doing so. Cecilia took out her insect net, extending it outside the boat from time to time in the hope of catching passing bugs. She had no success. The Antipodean insects preferred to remain closer to the ground.

When evening came they watched in rapt attention the setting of the sun. Flocks of white birds, in great numbers, screeched below them, their white wings turning to gold in the long rays of the last light. The women continued the sunset vigil in silence until the final glimmer of light had gone.

They ate what little food they had with them and sailed into the night, their hunger not quite sated. Rosalyn and Fey continued taking turns at the wheel and they slept curled up in the bottom of the boat, not entirely comfortable but safe above the earth.

The dawn light found Rosalyn at the wheel, the airship at an altitude where it caught the sun while the ground below still lay in darkness. The others woke, rising from the wooden bed and stiff from their cramped sleeping positions. As dawn progressed it revealed the landscape they sailed over. Monotonous in its sameness, Rosalyn found herself intrigued by its difference from the familiar, cultured, green landscapes of England.

A gurgling in her belly interrupted her musings. Hunger was making its presence felt. She asked her companions for ideas. Cecilia suggested catching passing birds in her insect net.

"It will be just like fishing." She waved her net about, almost hitting Fey in the head.

Fey pushed the net aside. "And how many birds have you seen flying close enough to be nabbed?"

Cecilia pouted, turned away and stared out at the white clouds on the horizon.

"I'll take us down closer to the ground and we can look for game," said Rosalyn. "We might find something we can shoot from the airship. Fey, you take the carbine. You can shoot can't you?"

"Yeah, I can shoot."

"That's surprising," said Cecilia. "You're lacking in every other skill you claim."

"I got out us out of Moreton Bay, didn't I?"

"Yes, I suppose I can grant you that. You do have your uses."

Rosalyn stamped her foot, the sound of leather on wood reverberating through the decking. "Enough!" Her companions fell silent.

Flying the *Lightning* down low over the grasslands, and avoiding the few trees scattered about, Fey and Cecilia leaned over the sides trying to spot their breakfast. Fey saw a mob of kangaroos in the distance, but Rosalyn, unable to turn the airship around fast enough, could only watch as they disappeared from view.

Cecilia gave a shout which brought Fey over.

"What have you got, Ses?"

Cecilia pointed. "There, look. I think those are emus."

"Yes, almost below us. Keep the course, Roz, and come down a bit."

The airship descended and Fey moved to the bow, carbine loaded and ready. The birds dodged and weaved in panic as the large, noisy object flew towards them. Some of them ran directly below the bow and Fey fired a shot. One of the birds stumbled and fell before getting up again. "Ammo'!" Fey kept her eyes fixed on the injured bird and handed Cecilia the carbine. She reloaded it and handed it back.

Rosalyn watched Fey and Cecilia closely and steered the airship in whichever way they were looking. It was sluggish to operate and she had trouble keeping up with the twists and turns of the panicked bird. They followed it some distance and eventually the emu started to tire. Fey indicated with her hand to slow down and Rosalyn eased the power to the propeller. She watched as Fey aimed at a point almost directly below them and squeezed off the shot. "Yes!" Fey shouted as the bird tumbled down. "Stop the boat, we got breakfast."

Rosalyn shut down the engine and vented the balloon as Fey cast out a hook. Keeping a watch to the sides, and sensitive to the breeze, Rosalyn eased the airship to ground level. Fey stepped out over the side and used the other hook to securely fasten the airship to a grey and weathered fallen tree. The emu lay thirty yards back and they walked over for a closer inspection. It was the first time Rosalyn and Cecilia had seen one close up. Cecilia was filled with scientific curiosity, for her interests, while directed more specifically to six-legged creatures, encompassed all of the natural world. Immediately she took out her note book and pencil and started writing.

"How do we do this?" asked Rosalyn.

"I'll give it a go. I've slaughtered a few waterfowl in my time. We'll have to get it back to the Lightning, though. We can hang it up from the boat to bleed it."

The bird was heavy and Rosalyn and Cecilia helped to heave it onto Fey's shoulders. She staggered under the weight but managed to get it to the boat where they strung it up by its feet from the stern. Fey slit its throat, "We can rest up for a bit now. That will take a while to bleed. What we really need now is more water. Did anyone notice anything from the air while we were chasing the emus?"

"Yes, I saw some over that way. It looked like a dry creek but there were some pools of water in it." Cecilia, to make herself useful, took two water bags and wandered off to fill them. Rosalyn and Fey waited in the shade of the airship where Rosalyn fell asleep. Cecilia meandered her way through the grass to the creek bed and followed it along until she came to a pool of the clear liquid. She pushed the bags under the surface, weighted them with rocks and sat back to observe the dragonflies as they darted around. Their wings sparkled in the light, the brilliant red colour of their bodies rivalling the plumage of the parrots in intensity.

Her eyes followed one in particular as it landed on the sand nearby. She observed the venation of its wings, its eyes, every minutia. And then she observed the footprint the dragonfly was resting in. "That's most peculiar," muttered Cecilia to herself, "I'm wearing shoes." She scanned her surroundings but saw no one. Looking at the sand again she could discern the footprints of several individuals. Reaching into the pool she took out the waterbags and made her way back to the ship, looking around constantly for the local residents.

"What is it, Ses? You look agitated."

"We're not alone. I saw footprints down at the creek bed and they looked recent." Fey rose to her feet, took the water bags and put them in the boat. She did a slow circumnavigation of the vessel, studying the landscape from every angle. "Anything?" asked Cecilia.

"No. I don't think we need be alarmed. There are blacks everywhere. Those prints you saw most likely have naught to do with us, and we didn't see any blacks from the balloon. Besides, the ones that we have seen up to now are so frightened they tend to run away."

"Oh." said Cecilia.

"But nicely spotted, Ses, you've got a good pair of daylights there.

Still, I don't think we should hang about here too long. I'll get this bird cooking and we'll get on our way. Why don't you take Rosalyn's telescope and keep watch while I go about our breakfast?"

Fey scraped out a shallow fire pit at a safe distance from the balloon. With much in the way of trial and error she managed to relieve the bird of its skin and put the dismembered parts on the glowing coals. The process was well under way by the time Rosalyn woke from her slumber. Fey and Cecilia told her about the footprints.

Rosalyn splashed water on her face. "We're going to have to make contact with the blacks eventually if we're going to find Doctor Phatts."

"How far are we from your latitude?" asked Fey.

"Hmm. At our current rate of progress I would imagine we'll be somewhere in the vicinity of the required latitude in about a week, but really I can't be sure."

Fey cut the meat up and passed it around. "We're in a spot of trouble, you know. We really need to stock up on supplies if we're going further out. Dunno what your Church and your Society was thinking, sending you out this far."

"The parson was supposed to help by giving me the information I needed for continuing the Mission, which I presume included provisioning the airship. Him being murdered and us having to escape from the penal settlement were not in the Church plans. Regardless, we have managed ourselves to this point. We have food and water and a means of transportation."

"And not a clue," added Fey drily.

"We'll find clues," said Rosalyn, who missed Fey's point entirely. "We'll make friends with some of the savages and they'll tell us about the Green Wave—and Doctor Phatts of course."

"Here's your chance," said Fey as she crouched down and dragged an emu leg from the fire. "Look."

A hundred yards away stood four Aboriginal men. They carried wooden shields decorated with ochre designs, and held long spears. Apart from those items they were naked. "Don't do anything rash now. Be calm but get ready to fly." Fey put the meat into the boat and unhooked.

"We're not going to befriend them?" asked Rosalyn.

"Even if they're the friendly kind it would be a waste of time. We need to cosy up with the blacks further along."

"Why won't these chaps do?"

"They don't speak the same language as they do where we're going."

"How do you know that," asked Rosalyn.

"Because there are dozens of different languages here. There might be at least a dozen of them spoke between here and where we're headed."

"Oh, I see," said Cecilia. "So when you said you could speak a few words of their language you meant a few words of the language of the Sydney blacks."

Fey glared at her. "Yeah, Ses, that's exactly what I meant."

The men in the distance moved closer and Rosalyn made the decision to lift off. She gave an extra burst of blue ascension into the steam chamber and smoke filled the air. When she started the propeller the Aborigines took fright at the sound and ran off.

As the airship rose, Rosalyn added more power to the propeller and checked the heading against the compass. Fey sat in the bottom of the boat cutting up the meat and handing it out until they'd had their fill. Cecilia dabbed her lips with a handkerchief and engaged herself on the bow with Rosalyn's telescope.

Several hours had passed when Cecilia became excited about something she'd spied in the landscape. "Look there!"

Rosalyn and Fey looked and down below, off the port bow was gathered a mass of Aborigines. "There must be over a thousand of them. Look, young ones as well." Cecilia watched, fascinated.

"I would put it at more than that. There must be three thousand at least."

"At least. I've never seen a mob that big around Sydney," said Fey.

"Perhaps there's more food out here," said Rosalyn.

"Dunno. I heard from the old lags that plenty more lived around Sydney in the old days but a lot of them got sick and died."

"Do you think they moved over here away from the settlement?"

"Maybe, but they like being on their own land."

"Own land? I thought they were nomads," said Cecilia.

"Yeah, sort of. Can't say I understand them much. I only know the ones at Sydney."

The women watched fascinated as the people below ran about like ants whose nest had been disturbed. The gathering of Aboriginals passed away behind them and Fey took the wheel as Rosalyn and Cecilia sat writing in their journals

"May I see the map?" asked Cecilia. Rosalyn passed it to her. Cecilia took it but grasped it too lightly. The wind blew it out of her hand and it sailed away on a course all of its own. "Oops." Cecilia bit her fingertip, and cheeks flushed, looked across at Rosalyn's scowling face.

Fey noticed the consternation of her comrades. "What's up?"

"We lost our map." Rosalyn gave Cecilia a despairing look. Cecilia bowed her head, putting her fingertip aside and biting her lip instead.

"Not to worry loves. It didn't look much of one, nothing we can't remember. How about we keep heading this way for a week and then put down and try chumming up to some of the local personalities? We'll be right." Rosalyn and Cecilia were buoyed by Fey's positive attitude and no further word was said about the loss of the map.

The water bags needed to be filled every two or three days and more water brought for the steam engine. This was carried out without incident and during one such filling Fey managed to catch some freshwater crayfish. The emu meat continued to be eaten as breakfast, lunch and dinner until it was gone. Fey cooked the last of the rancid meat by boiling it in a pot on the engine's hot plate.

Inevitably, they ran out of food; the hunt for more meat being nowhere near as successful as on the first occasion. For nearly two days they went without any food at all.

The hours aloft became routine, with little to do other than stare at the clouds or the ground. Cecilia sat reading and Fey, out of sheer boredom, sat next to her and began reading too. She softly sounded out the words in Cecilia's ear as she read until Cecilia snapped and pulled the book away. "Do you mind?"

"No. Put the book back. I was up to an exciting bit about how the beetle eats leaves."

"I can lend you a book."

"I don't want a loan one, I want to read what you're reading."

"You do not, you're trying to annoy me."

"No I'm not, I'm reading. I'm keeping you company."

"I don't want your company. You've no manners at all. Go away."

"I don't think I will."

Rosalyn, who had been listening to the exchange, stamped her foot. "Fey, go and sit on the other side of the boat."

"Aw, Roz, I was just having a read."

"You were not."

Before Fey could respond, Cecilia grabbed Fey's hat. "Sit over there." She threw the hat at Fey's seat opposite but failed to take the wind into account. The hat sailed up over the netting and disappeared into the firmament. "Oops."

Fey watched in horror and reacted quickly. She took Cecilia's book and threw it after the hat.

"My book!" Cecilia leaped up and grabbed hold of the netting to witness her book plummeting earthward.

"Both of you, sit down. You're rocking the boat. I should never have brought you."

"She started it," said Cecilia.

"You chucked my hat over the side."

"It was an accident. You threw my best beetle book away." Cecilia curled up with her head on her knees.

Fey watched her in silence for some minutes. "I'm sorry, Ses. I dunno why I acted like that. I'll buy you a new one when we get back to Sydney."

"They don't sell it in Sydney."

"They might. They have book shops—I've seen them. And if it isn't there I'll get it from England. I know plenty of sailing blokes who I can ask to get it for me." Fey turned to Rosalyn. "Sorry Roz, it were my fault. I got bored. I feel bad. Sorry."

Rosalyn stared at her. "Shut up and take the wheel for a while. I need a rest. I don't want to hear any more talking from either of you before sunset."

9

HEAD-HUNTERS

Cecilia, continuing in her role as lookout, brought their attention to another oddity in the landscape. "Look. There are houses down there."

"Here, let me have a squiz." Fey peered though the telescope. "She's right. There are houses down there."

"Yes, Fey. I know what houses are."

Rosalyn wanted to see for herself, and satisfied that there were indeed houses, she steered to them.

"That has me fair perplexed," Fey said. "Settlement hasn't reached this far so I don't know what houses they could be."

"Could it be the blacks? Perhaps it's a village."

"I don't think so, Ses, I never seen the blacks build anything bigger than a small, round shelter you can't even stand up in, but I wouldn't put a shilling on it. Maybe out here they make bigger houses."

"Do you think it's Bathurst?"

"No, Roz, it's not Bathurst. Bathurst is more than a few huts."

Rosalyn brought the craft down low over the collection of houses. The 'village' turned out to be three huts arranged in a 'U' shape, made of wooden slabs with bark roofs. The roofs were held down by branches in the manner of so many of the crude huts around the outskirts of the growing Sydney colony. Only one of the huts had a chimney and a pale, ghostly wisp of smoke rose from it.

Away from the huts a short distance, a flock of sheep grazed and a small herd of cattle stood in a bare yard. A bullock wagon sat empty nearby. A pack of dogs heard the sound of the approaching engine and barked furiously. The women saw a man emerge from the door of the larger hut with a musket in hand. He looked around and seeing the dogs barking at the sky, spotted the airship and stared up at them, his forearm shielding his eyes against the glare.

Rosalyn, by now quite adept at handling the airship, brought the craft down with great precision between the buildings to ground in the yard. Fey threw out a hook to the man who wrapped it around a stump. She jumped over the side as Rosalyn cut the engine. "Nice place you have here, Mister."

"Thank you." The man stared past her at the balloon and turned to Rosalyn who was climbing over the skyrail. "You must be Reverend Flynn."

Rosalyn looked at him surprised. "How on earth did you know that?"

"Ah, a little bird told me—or rather, a tall man. A gentleman passed this way not two days ago, asking if I had seen a Missionary in an airship. I don't get too many Missionaries in airships out this way—you in fact being the first of either."

"What sort of gentleman? Do you know his business?"

"A lot of questions and I have my own." The dogs jumped around barking. Fey knelt to pat and stroke them and with the addition of a stern command of 'quiet' from their master, they settled down. "Come in out of the sun, we'll have a cup of tea and get some talking done." The man, tanned and solidly built, appeared to be in his early forties, unshaven and sported a large, well-groomed moustache. His clothes were dusty and his faded, floral-pattern waistcoat missed a couple of buttons. They followed him into a dwelling only mildly less crude inside as it was without.

Skins of kangaroos and wallabies took the place of carpets on a floor formed from packed earth. Bones the dogs had gnawed littered the floor. Old newspapers and prints hung haphazardly from the walls in a manner which added nothing to the aesthetic appeal of the hut, but must have brought some comfortable reminder of home to the occupant. Crumpled sheets and blankets covered a bed of sorts, half-hidden by a dusty mosquito net suspended from the ceiling. Chairs surrounded a small, well-made table in the centre of the room, and crockery-lined shelves constructed from a packing crate filled the end wall.

"The name is Maxwell, Maxwell Lake. You can call me Max. Now, while I get tea together tell me who I have here and what brings you to this remote place."

Rosalyn introduced Cecilia and Fey and gave her explanation of the journey thus far. She omitted the part about stealing back the airship at Moreton Bay, saying instead that in the excitement of getting away they had simply forgotten their provisions. "And we're looking for an explorer, one who went missing."

"Hmph, a few of them have done that but I assume you are talking of Doctor Phatts," said Max as he set up the cups and saucers.

"Yes, that's him. Do you know of him?"

"I do. It was his trail I followed to come to this piece of land. He argued with his men over direction and leadership and half his party turned back. On the advice of one such of those gentleman, as to the quality of good grazing land here, I came with two assigned convicts, settling here last year. It hasn't been easy but I think I can make a go of it."

"Two convicts? Where are they now?"

"One returned to Bathurst for supplies and the other is out tending sheep. I've asked for more government men—I could use a dozen. I'm so far outside the limits of settlement that I don't think they'll send me any."

"The limits of settlement?" asked Rosalyn.

"Yes, the government likes to control the spread of settlement. I lacked the inclination to wait for official approval. There's plenty of good land here lying empty—I took it on myself to settle it."

"Where exactly is here? You see we lost our map." Rosalyn looked at Cecilia who at that moment found something interesting to stare at through the doorway.

Max poured the tea. "Here, let me show you." He went to a battered bureau tucked in an unlit corner of the hut, pulling from it a large roll of paper. He spread it out on the table and weighted down the curling edges with the tea cups. The women leaned forward to study it. "Here; this is the coast with Sydney, here is the mountain range, and this is the road to Bathurst over here."

Rosalyn followed as he traced the route with his spoon handle and noticed his elegant handwriting. His refined accent and the way he articulated his words, indicated to Rosalyn a man in possession of a high degree of education.

"So where are we?" asked Rosalyn. Max traced a dotted red line with his finger to a position some distance northwest of Bathurst. "About here, I think. Where I've marked this 'X' in pencil."

"You think?"

"I'm no surveyor but it's a fair estimate. I've drawn this map myself from the government maps, and from the information I received from the returned members of Doctor Phatts' expedition. To this I've added my own observations. All in all I think it's a tidy piece of cartography. You'll see here there is a Mission station which once was a convict outpost. I know I'm some distance past that." Max stood back and admired his work.

"We're much farther to the east than I'd estimated. What is this other Mission?"

"Germans. They aren't doing well and I can't really see their Mission lasting."

"They can't be of my Church or I would already know of it. Can you tell me which way Doctor Phatts went from here?"

"We think he went west, northwest. One of my men, when out on a brief scout around, found a tree with a 'P' carved into it and an arrow. It could only have been him."

"I see. And this gentleman who was here, who was he?"

"I can't remember his name, Samuel something. Yes, that's it, Samuel Bluerose. He said he was from your Church and showed concern for your whereabouts."

"Oh dear. That must have been the fellow I was supposed to meet in Bathurst. He's almost certainly the person mentioned in my orders. Did he give any indication of why he was seeking me out?"

Max shook his head. "He was worried for your safety and said something about the dangers being more than you realise." At this point Max mused a little. With his hand on his chin he spoke to the ceiling, or rather the rough canopy of fabric which had been fixed to the rafters to prevent the unwelcome descent of spiders and insects. "Or did he say 'they realised'? I suppose he was talking about your Church. The man himself was quite odd."

"In what way?" asked Rosalyn.

Max, who had leaned back over the map, stood erect, and in order to undertake some advanced pondering on the oddity of his previous visitor, held his chin betwixt his thumb and forefinger. "He was a tallish sort of chap with largish sideburns and a fine moustache. I thought he was a trifle elderly to be out here alone, however he was possessed of a confidence which invited no questioning on that account."

"How was he dressed?"

"In a peculiar fashion, with a smart, black, military jacket and a black hat. He carried equipment unfamiliar to me—a strange musket-like thing hanging on a leather sling over his shoulder—one of those new-clockwork devices. When I asked its purpose he told me it was an experimental style of surveying telescope, although in spite of my interest he was not friendly to further investigations on the topic."

"What else can you tell me of him?" Rosalyn leaned forward over the map.

"The gentleman also had a couple of braces of pistols and a cavalry sword. He didn't talk much and at times was quite unfocussed.

I put it down to the fatigue of his travels, but I think the most peculiar thing was the brevity of his visit. He didn't even stay for a cup of tea. Can you imagine? To my mind that is odd. I wouldn't want to get on the wrong side of him for I could see an unhinged look about him. Truth be told, when I first saw him I took him to be a bushranger." Max looked at Rosalyn. "Do you know him? Do you think it was this man you were supposed to meet?"

"I've never met him but I can't think who else it might be. It must have been him and from your account it sounds like he's a Guardian which is wonderful." Fey saw that even as Rosalyn expressed her pleasure she sported a worried look. Glancing at Cecilia, she noticed she was smiling and when she saw Fey looking at her the smile passed from her lips.

"What's a Guardian?" asked Max.

"A Guardian is an agent of the Enlightenment Church. Their purpose is to travel around visiting the Missionaries or be assigned to us to ensure we are safe. They help control the savages if the Missionaries require it. They also act as bodyguards to the Church elite. Some of the old religions, and even the post-Schism religions, use methods which are most unsavoury to spread their version of God's word. It was necessary to create this order of Guardians. Only the best are chosen and they're trained in a range of skills."

"Rather tough chaps, then, hmm?"

Cecilia interrupted at that point. "Mister Lake, do you mind terribly if I make a copy of your map? You see, as I lost our one I feel quite awful about it."

"By all means, yes, of course." Cecilia left the hut, walked to the boat and retrieved her drawing tools. The map, being so large, would have to be copied across several pages of her sketch book.

Max turned to Fey. "Now, young man, while the young lady is at her pens perhaps you'll show me this airship of yours. I've seen the one in Sydney but only from a distance. Magnificent thing it is. Flying! Whatever will they think of next?"

Rosalyn turned to him. "The airship is actually mine, Mister

Lake—or rather the Church's, but I am its pilot and custodian."

"I see. This new Enlightenment thinking has left me behind, I fear. An airship with a woman pilot who is also a Missionary? I can't say I agree with it but I'm not standing in the way. Science, industry, the new clockwork, this Sun Church of yours—it's all changing so fast I can't keep up. Life is much simpler out here."

"I'd be tickled to show you the ship anyway, Max, that's if Roz don't mind." Rosalyn nodded her assent. Max gave a nod of thanks and offered Fey some tobacco—also offering it as an afterthought to Rosalyn, who declined. The serious business of packing and lighting their pipes out of the way, they moved over to the *Lightning*. Rosalyn followed and stood aside as Fey took delight in showing Max the engine controls. Rosalyn was surprised at the amount of knowledge Fey had acquired in the short amount of time they'd been travelling. She even explained things about the working of the engine which Rosalyn herself had not known.

"See here," said Fey, as she lifted the lid of a built-in compartment next to the engine. "These black bricks are special compressed coal, made to some scientific formula which is a bit beyond my learnings, and we have two of these compartments full. The thing is, with the blue steam we don't need much coal to go a long way. We have enough coal bricks here to circumnavigate Australia—maybe." Fey paused. "I see a puzzled look on your visage. The blue steam is created from this." She opened a panel on the engine. "See that thick, blue, gooey liquid? They call that... Hey Roz, what's the blue liquid called? You had a name for it."

"It's called 'blue ascension'."

"Yeah, blue ascension, and this little knob here, this is the 'blue aether injector'. It takes the blue ascension and pushes it into the steam chamber here, which shoots it up into the balloon—and that's what gets us up to the clouds. This valve here controls the rate by increasing the amount of steam or extracting it to get us down lower. There's a fan which can be engaged that gives it a quick push for a sudden, short lift. That lever there controls the propeller which gets us moving—a bit slowly, but." Fey glanced at Rosalyn and hastily added, "But much faster than walking."

"Amazing." Max looked impressed as he ran his eye around the airship.

"Yeah, that's about it. There's a touch more to it but that's the bare bones of the machine."

"What is equally amazing is that you're not a man at all. You're a woman in men's clothing." Max's tone had changed. "You don't fool me. What's your game?"

Fey sighed and went into her explanation for wearing male attire—an explanation which, although it satisfied Max, also reaffirmed his view that the world was changing too fast for him.

Rosalyn, curious as to her surrounds, wandered off. Her gaze alighted on some foul-smelling objects on the ends of stakes. Set back from the huts, the things buzzed with flies. She looked closer and screamed. Fey came running, and Cecilia, alarmed, rushed to the door of the hut to learn the cause of the fearful sound. Rosalyn and Fey stood staring at three heads affixed to the posts. They were in various states of decay, empty eye sockets turned to the scrub beyond the huts, their white teeth fully exposed. Max wandered over.

"No need to worry about them, Reverend, they're long since dead. When the blacks come too close I shoot them and mount their heads on the posts to deter others."

Rosalyn, wide-eyed with the horror of it, gazed fixedly on the maggoty spectacle of the rotting heads. "But... but that's barbaric."

"Not at all, Reverend. You have to remember the blacks here aren't fully human. They're little better than animals and just as savage—more so. I wouldn't trust any of them so I shoot them whenever I can."

Rosalyn turned, fleeing back to the hut where she explained what she'd seen to Cecilia, who was equally mortified. Fey and Max joined them. "I'm sorry you had to see that, Reverend, but it's a different world out here on the frontier. It's brutal and sometimes one has to be equally brutal to survive."

Rosalyn's hands trembled as she sat silently, watching as Cecilia finished off the details on the map. Max poured her a whisky. "Drink this. It will help." He watched her as she drank. "If I'd known a company of ladies was descending on me I would have put those things away. Let me make amends. You told me you left without provisions. I can fix you up with a few things from my stores. Nothing fancy but there's some salted pork, biscuits, tea, sugar, flour and rice, dried and tinned fruit, and I'll even put in some tins of jam and beef to make up for the fright I gave you."

Rosalyn accepted the provisions gratefully and she and Cecilia spent the night sleeping in the convicts' bunks. Fey stretched out on the floor. The angry barking of the dogs and the bellowing of cattle woke them early in the morning. The sun shone through cracks between the upright, wooden slabs of the wall. As they emerged from the hut Max ran past, musket in hand and pistols tucked into his belt. "They're spearing the bloody cattle!"

The cattle shoved each other about in a panic, throwing up thick clouds of dust and roaring in fright. Max fired off a shot and in return two spears thudded into the ground next to him. He drew his pistols from his belt, aiming at one fellow who had ventured closer than the rest. The lead ball hit the man's shield but failed to penetrate it and his other shot whistled past the native's head. The man raised another spear to strike at Max when Cecilia pushed past him and fired a shot from the carbine. A spray of blood erupted from the man's shoulder. He dropped his spear and ran. The natives retired rapidly, scattering into the grass.

Max turned to Cecilia and looked at the smoking gun in her hands. "Well done, young lady. Where did you learn to shoot?"

"Yeah," said Fey. "Where did you learn that?"

Cecilia lowered the weapon as smoke drifted out of the barrel. "I...I really don't know how to shoot. Daddy had weapons and I watched on the ship when Rosalyn was learning. I picked up the gun from the boat without thinking about it. I was scared and acted in haste."

"I'm damned glad you paid close attention to the Reverend's lessons. You might not have killed him but you winged the beggar and scared them all off."

"Yeah, for someone who doesn't shoot, you shoot bloody well." Fey took the carbine as Cecilia handed it to her and watched her as she returned to the hut and her cartography.

With the skirmish over, Max assured himself that the Aboriginal warriors had retreated and went to check on his cattle. One of them was lying on its side bellowing in pain with two spears buried in its side. Another limped around the yard, a spear sticking from its rump. Musket reloaded, Max shot the one lying down, ending its miseries. The other he pulled the spear from and after calming the beast, inspected its wound. "It'll live. I'll keep an eye on it." He returned his gaze to the dead steer and looked at the women. "If you ladies care to stay another night you can have as much fresh meat as you want. There's plenty here."

Rosalyn looked at Fey, who nodded. "Yes, thank you, we will. Max, why were the blacks spearing the cattle? I can't see that they would have been able to stay and butcher them with you so close by."

Max, sitting now on the dead beast, looked up at Rosalyn. "They're trying to drive me out."

"How is spearing your cattle going to do that?"

"They're cunning creatures and learn quickly. They've realised if I've got no cattle or sheep there's no point me staying here."

"Are they likely to attack you?"

"They've already tried—and maybe that attack was to draw me out, or perhaps they saw your balloon and came close out of curiosity and the attack was opportunistic. Bloody vermin they are." Max tapped the dead steer with the musket butt. "Fey, can you give me a hand here? I need to get this thing butchered, and call me sentimental but I don't like the cattle to see it happening. I'll have to move them to the other yard." Fey helped Max move the cattle and to bleed and butcher the steer. For the most part they worked in silence. Max's dogs ate well.

Rosalyn returned to the hut to sit with Cecilia, updating her journal. Cecilia made another pot of tea and sat down with Rosalyn. "Tell me now, Rosalyn, the man who came here, the one you said was most likely the man you were supposed to meet, what is it that had you worried?"

"It fits that he was a Church man, a Guardian, coming to look for me. What's concerning is the outfit Max described, it would be more of what I would expect of someone from the Divine Order of Mechanics. That doesn't make sense though. Why would one of the Mechanical Order be looking for me?"

"Perhaps your Church has enlisted his services."

Rosalyn shook her head. "The Church will have no truck with the Mechanical Order. Their philosophy is dangerous and their methods questionable."

"I've heard that said before. Well, whoever he is, the man is looking to protect you and that can't be a bad thing. I shouldn't be too worried." Cecilia smiled reassuringly and sipped her tea.

"I'm not entirely sure it's nothing but as this land is so big it's unlikely we'll ever run into him to find out." They sat in silence for a while before Rosalyn added, "Mister Lake worries me, too. Putting the heads of the blacks on sticks, leaving them to rot like that— it's disgusting." Cecilia nodded in agreement, leaving Rosalyn the space to continue.

"This is the frontier, this is where I thought I was coming to, where I could bring the Enlightenment to those same people who Mister Lake is impaling. How is it possible to win over the blacks if he's doing that?" She sighed. "And now I learn I'm supposed to go on this fool's errand to find some dead explorer."

10

SAMUEL BLUEROSE

The man stroked his fingers down each of his grey sideburns as he gazed up the street. The military barracks were on his right. He'd been told the post office was opposite them so he crossed the street, muttering to himself, and found his way to his goal.

"Do I have any mail?" he asked the clerk behind the counter.

"And what name would I be looking for?" replied the clerk. The man paused, stroked his sideburns again and looked to be deep in thought. "Sir?"

"Yes? Ah, yes. Bluerose. S. Bluerose—the 'S' being for Samuel."

The clerk turned to the rows of pigeon holes and searched through a small stack of letters, drawing one out from the pile. "Yes, sir. There is one here for you."

"Thank you, thank you." Staring at the envelope, Samuel fished a sixpence from his pocket and without looking at the clerk laid it on the counter. He tore the envelope open as he left the post office and unfolded the single sheet of paper. The letter was written in a delicate, cursive and familiar hand. 'My business in Sydney has been taken care of. To conduct your business you must go inland over the ranges to a town called Bathurst. The gentleman you will need to talk to is Ellis Claxton.' The letter was unsigned.

Samuel strode off to one of the shops along the street and picked up a few things he might need for his travel inland. After making some enquiries he found himself two horses, whereupon he returned to his lodgings to pick up his belongings. "You're not staying in Sydney, Mister Bluerose?" asked the landlady.

"No, Ma'am. I want to go and survey the land out west."

"Are you taking up a property?"

"Property? Why, yes. Yes, that's what I'll do. I'll take up some property. A good day to you."

A few days later he reached Bathurst and secured a room at an inn. The inn displayed every element of vernacular architecture—vertical timber slabs supported roughly-sawn beams capped by a wood-shingle roof. More effort had gone into the interior furnishings. Tasteful wallpaper from England, hand-coloured, framed prints and shelves of crockery gave a more civilised touch than the rough exterior suggested. The stone fireplace added to the warm, welcoming feel.

Samuel stood on the veranda, gazing in through the doorway as he played with his whiskers.

"New in the colony?" asked the innkeeper, loudly.

Samuel turned to face the man. "New? That's refreshing, people keep telling me I look old." He walked inside and stood at the bar. "Oh... I see your meaning. Yes, recently arrived. Gin please."

"Looking to take up land?" The innkeeper took a bottle from the shelf behind him, made a show of polishing a glass, and poured the gin.

"Land? Yes, I am. How did you know?"

"You look like you might be. Why else would you come to a town like this?"

"I'm supposed to meet a... a business partner here. I've heard he's already in town. Name of Claxton."

"Claxton, Claxton. Name rings a bell. He's not that Church person is he? The one from the new Church. What's it called now?

119

The Intelligence Church. No, that can't be it."

"The Enlightenment Church?"

"Yes, that's the one."

"That would be him. Do you know where I might find him?"

"Not here. I think he's been staying in a house on the north side, out of town a short way. I can give you the directions. It's not hard to find. There's not much to the town but it's filling up quickly."

"Thank you. That would be helpful, so would a room."

With the accommodation for himself and his horses taken care of, Samuel returned to the bar and ordered another gin.

"Are you looking for land for your Church?"

Samuel stared vacantly at the innkeeper. "Church? Yes, I suppose a Church will be built here."

"He's a popular fellow."

"Who?"

"This man you're looking for. I remember now where I heard the name. Another gentleman was in here earlier this morning looking for him."

Samuel swallowed his gin without hesitation and after getting the directions retired to his room without a further word. He inserted a key into the padlock of one of his bags and took out two pistols, which he carefully loaded. He strapped a leather gun belt around his waist, put the pistols in and threw on an overcoat. "Damnation," he muttered to himself as he exited by the back door to the stable. Jumping on his horse he set off at a trot to the current residence of Ellis Claxton.

The house was easy to find and not much more than a shack, the bark roof held in place by thick branches. The floor was raised a couple of feet on hardwood stumps and extended to form a veranda. A bench made from old timber provided somewhere to sit and smoke. The rough, stone chimney gave the dwelling an appearance of substance.

Samuel left the track as he drew closer to the house and dismounted down the hill at a hundred yards distance. Tying his horse loosely to the branches of a wattle tree he approached the rest of the way on foot. As he turned the handle of the front door a shot rang out from inside. A second followed and Samuel recoiled as the wood of the door splintered, a lead ball grazing the flesh of his shoulder.

Standing back he raised his foot and kicked at the door, and held only by a wooden latch, it splintered inwards with a crash. He stepped inside with pistols raised. Someone was exiting by a rear window. The person fired again, this time missing his target altogether, as he dropped outside the window. Samuel fired his pistols and the room in front of him filled with smoke. He reloaded a pistol and dashed to the window to see the assailant swinging himself into the saddle of a horse. Samuel fired again and missed. The gunman rode off in haste, the horse's hooves thudding heavily on the dry ground, raising clouds of dust.

Samuel loaded both pistols and turned his attention back to the interior. The house consisted of two rooms, with little in the way of furniture. A writing bureau had had all its drawers removed and the papers were scattered on the floor. More apparent was the chair with a man tied to it. In the man's forehead, a small, round hole oozed blood, the crimson trickle running into his dull, open eyes. A fly buzzed around the man's bruised and bloody face. Naked from the waist up, his body was covered with small cuts.

Samuel crouched down to glance over the papers when he heard shouting from the track out the front. Through the doorway he could see three armed men running towards the house. They stopped at the edge of the veranda when they saw Samuel standing inside. For a few seconds no one spoke. Samuel stared at them and they at him, and then they saw the bloody body tied to the chair, and the guns in Samuel's hands.

"He's done him in," said one.

Another raised his musket as he said to the third, "Go fetch the troopers, tell 'em we 'ave a bushranger. We'll 'old 'im. 'urry now." The third man turned and sprinted away.

"You gentlemen..." began Samuel.

"Put the guns down, you murderin' bastard."

Samuel looked at the guns in his hands but didn't want to waste any time with long explanations. He needed to catch up with the killer and he had no particular desire to succumb to any police interrogation of his reasons for being in Bathurst—or New South Wales for that matter. He raised his guns and the two men leaped out of his line of fire. Not wasting any time, Samuel ran the few steps to the window and hurled himself through, grunting as he landed on the ground outside. Without looking back he ran around the side of the house and down to his horse. The two men cautiously peered in through the front door while Samuel galloped off over the crest of the hill into the distant scrub. He took a circuitous route back to the Inn.

"Innkeeper, I've been invited to stay with Mr Claxton so I won't be needing the room after all, but please take this for your trouble." Samuel fished around in his purse and handed over a pound note. The innkeeper examined the note, weakly professing that no payment was necessary even as he dropped the money into his apron pocket. Samuel dragged his luggage out the back door. By way of gratitude, the innkeeper followed him out and helped strap the bags to the pack horse. Samuel gave him a nod of thanks and put the spurs to his horse.

The killer had fled north from Bathurst but Samuel headed northeast from the Inn. As the day turned to evening he changed direction, taking a course he hoped would intercept the killer's tracks. He would have to be careful as the killer was well-versed in his business. To add to his concerns the mounted troopers would be out scouring the countryside for him. He stroked his sideburns as he looked around for a camping spot for the night.

11

A Fascination With Anatomy

Max declined an offer of a short flight around his holdings and stood, arms folded and shaking his head, as he watched the women board the airship and take to the skies. The trio were glad to be aloft and in the breeze again. Rosalyn held the wheel firmly, raised her chin, took a theatrical stance and said, "My comrades, we are now beyond the frontier."

Cecilia leaned on the skyrail as she watched the landscape pass underneath, her map book and pencil at the ready. "You know, only explorers have been further than we have and I think we're the first ones to travel this far in an airship."

"That makes us explorers too now, Ses. We were lucky you spotted Max's station, but that will be the last one we see. We're on our own now."

They stayed aloft for three days, zigzagging across the sky as Rosalyn played the winds. It became necessary to ground and take on water. Cecilia, who in her self-appointed role as ship's lookout, had her eye glued constantly to the telescope. She spotted a dried-up river, directing Rosalyn as they followed its course in the hope of finding a waterhole along its length.

The river wended its way between two low cliffs. "There," Cecilia pointed. "In that gorge—there's a large pool of water. Bring her down." Rosalyn took the *Lightning* into a spiralling descent as the other two kept a lookout for blacks. She managed to find a spot between the rocks and trees on a sandy shore, and they disembarked. Glad of the chance to stretch her legs on solid ground, Rosalyn stared out over the water hole. Her body still felt as if it were swaying with the motion of the airship.

Rosalyn held her hands up to look at the grime under her nails, walked to the edge of the large pool and glanced around for any watchful eyes. She undressed and folded her clothing neatly, placing it on a rock on the river bank. Putting a toe in the water to test the temperature, and surprised at its coldness on such a warm day, she remained undeterred and entered the pool. The water was fresh and clear and she watched the way the sunlight sparkled on the ripples she was creating. Submerging herself she took up handfuls of sand from the river bed and scrubbed herself lightly, holding her hands up again to see the jewel drops of water twinkling on her clean skin.

Fey, having taken care of the water bags, watched Rosalyn closely. Rosalyn turned and saw her and called out, "Are you coming in? The water is cold but it's delightfully refreshing."

Fey, not having slept well in the air, looked from the soft sand to Rosalyn. She stumbled as she walked to the water's edge, picked herself up and called back. "Aye, I could use a tub." She undressed, leaving her clothes scattered on the sand. Rosalyn watched her, realised she was staring, and turned away. She swam to a rock projecting from the water. Fey joined her and they lay there, their bodies half submerged. They didn't talk, resting instead and losing themselves in the peace of the moment.

Rosalyn looked at Fey, who was lying on her back with a faint smile on her face.

Fey turned to her. "What?"

"Nothing really. I was wondering what you're thinking about that makes you smile so."

Fey responded, "The calmness of the day and the pleasing company."

Rosalyn smiled in return and looked up at the sky. The smile disappeared as she remembered the rest of the company. "Where's Cecilia?"

"Dunno. She took her butterfly net and went bush." They looked around for her in vain. Not the slightest breeze disturbed the grasses and treetops, and not a sound could be heard. Bright red dragonflies darted about around the water's edge. Out of this silence and into their gaze came Cecilia, her skirts gathered up in one hand, her butterfly net in the other, and an expression on her face as though all the spectres of Hell were after her. Oblivious to Rosalyn and Fey as they stood pale and naked in the water, she climbed straight into the boat, disappearing beneath the sides as she huddled out of view.

"Queer behaviour," said Fey, without moving.

"Quite. I think something may be chasing her. We..." Rosalyn's attention focussed on the bank near the gorge entrance. Several Aboriginal women, all of them naked and carrying baskets and sticks, stood looking at the airship. "Don't move, Fey. We don't want to alarm them."

"No, I'd hate for them to run off screaming. It would disturb the tranquillity of the moment."

Rosalyn looked at her, not knowing for certain whether Fey spoke in jest or with serious intention. The Aboriginal women saw Rosalyn and Fey in the water and the two parties of women stood looking at each other. For the Aborigines, the airship remained the object of much of their attention and like all the natives they had encountered thus far, were in awe of it. "Stay here, Fey—and get ready to make for the Lightning if something goes awry. I'm going to try something."

Rosalyn waded out of the water towards the women, and Fey, rather than watch the Aboriginal women for hostile intent, found her eyes drawn to the pale, wet form of Rosalyn's back as she emerged from the water.

The Aboriginal women made no sign of moving either away or towards Rosalyn as she approached them. Having reached a distance of ten feet she stopped and looked at them with as much curiosity as they did at her. One of the older ones moved forward and held out her long, solid stick by one end, prodding Rosalyn a couple of times in the stomach. Rosalyn stood her ground as the women watched for her reaction. The old woman stepped back and spoke with her comrades. This set up an excited discourse amongst them that Rosalyn couldn't even begin to guess the meaning of.

When they had quietened down Rosalyn stepped towards them a pace. One of the younger ones reached out to touch her, but the older one pushed the exploring arm away, speaking to the girl sharply. Thinking how to proceed, Rosalyn decided to try food. Turning side on she indicated the airship. "I'm going to get food— don't go away, I'll get food," and she gestured with her fingers to her mouth before backing away a few paces, turning and walking to the airship. Fey splashed through the water and met her at the boat. She looked down into it. "It's okay Ses, they're friendly. If they were hostile Roz would have a big dent in her brain box right now."

"I don't care. I'm staying right here." Cecilia's voice carried no quavering of fear and Fey stared at her until Cecilia looked away.

Fey mumbled, "Quite the actress aren't you?" Cecilia feigned to have not heard her.

The brief exchange went unnoticed by Rosalyn who put a few things in an empty bag. Fey followed her back to the group of Aboriginal women. Rosalyn knelt down and opened the bag, taking out some biscuits. She offered one to the older woman who stared at her without moving.

Rosalyn took a bite of the biscuit and chewed it. She tried again to give one of the biscuits to the woman and again the woman ignored her. From behind the old woman a hand darted out and snatched the biscuit. The young woman who had seized it stuffed it into her mouth and chewed. The women watched silently as the biscuit was devoured and waited the critic's verdict. Lively discussion resulted in a myriad of hands reaching out for biscuits, which Rosalyn was happy to give. The women relaxed and they sat down and ate them together, talking with each other as they did so.

With the biscuits consumed, Rosalyn produced some sugar. The older woman allowed Rosalyn to take her hand and pour a quantity onto it. The woman sniffed it, took a peck and tasted it and then turned to the other woman, saying something before licking the remaining sugar from her palm. All of them now had to have a taste and with the sugar devoured, the Aboriginal women were of a friendlier disposition.

"Now what, Roz?" asked Fey, as they sat naked and surrounded by their new acquaintances.

"We have to find this explorer so we're going to have to learn the language of these people or teach them ours."

"You're pulling your lid over your eyes aren't you? It's going to take a long time to learn the language."

"I don't see any other way forward," said Rosalyn.

The Aboriginal women had lost some of their previous fear of the airship and moved closer, looking at different parts of it and discussing it with each other. Cecilia too, had warmed to the idea that the Aborigines weren't going to spear her, and sat in the boat doing sketches of the meeting. Other women had started touching Rosalyn's and Fey's skin; stroking, pinching and pulling it, playing with their hair and exhibiting every form of curiosity.

Rosalyn held her breath as her breasts were squeezed and her hair pulled, while Fey responded in kind to the touch of the women. She ran her hand along their scars and her fingers through their hair, showing as much interest in them as they did in her. "Have you seen how they're missing a front tooth, Roz? All of them except the youngest ones."

Fey touched her finger to her teeth and then to the absent tooth on each of the women. This sent them into a discussion before they turned to Fey again with futile explanation.

"I think they're telling you it's an initiation thing, Fey."

"Well thanks for explaining it to me, Roz. I'd be lost without you." At that, Rosalyn made to say something and thinking better of it turned her attention elsewhere. Fey rose to her feet and attempted to use gestures and signs to ask the women something. One of the women spoke to the others and this resulted in tones of agreement. Fey was taken by the wrist and led away, most of the other women following.

"Fey, where are you going? I don't think..." Rosalyn's voice trailed off as she watched Fey walking away. Looking once behind her to see that Cecilia was safe, she followed along after Fey. The women led them deep into the gorge and up a narrow side branch. Ferns grew here and water ran down from a crack high in the rock. The air was cool and still. They came to a gallery of images painted with ochres on the chasm wall. Many of the paintings were stencilled hands, but Rosalyn noticed there were other things too; axes and throwing sticks and figures, which to her were strange and mysterious.

The women drew their attention to one particular painting and it appeared to them to be a figure wearing a hat and riding a horse. Fey and Rosalyn looked at each other. "Doctor Phatts," they said in unison. They tried to ascertain how long ago this person had passed but no amount of pantomime was able to elicit an intelligible answer. The women did, however, take them back into the gorge proper, and with various actions the white women understood that the figure on the horse had gone 'somewhere that way'—the direction in which they had been travelling.

They walked back to the airship accompanied by their hosts to find Cecilia in a flustered state. A handful of the women had stayed behind and were trying to look at all the objects in the boat. This examination included taking anything portable out of the boat, with a view to obtaining possession of the items for further study. Cecilia's skirts were not exempt from scrutiny and exploring hands kept trying to raise them. Rosalyn laughed as a red-faced Cecilia cried out, "Make them stop!"

"They only want to see if you're like the both of us, Ses. If you get your clothes off they can make an assessment and you'll be all right after that."

"I will not take my clothes off in front of all these people."

"Don't be like that, Ses. You're just a little shy is all. Give them a peek and you'll be left alone."

Cecilia relented. She stood in the boat, and with the women gathered around, raised her skirts to show the assembled group that she too was a woman like Fey and Rosalyn. Fey clapped. "That's the spirit. The way you raised your skirts was just like raising the curtain at the theatre."

Cecilia blushed furiously. "There was no need for you to look."

Fey laughed. "Uncharted territory, that."

Cecilia lowered her skirts and glared at her. "Uncouth colonial! Fey, you're a beast."

"Cheer up, Ses. We have some intelligence for you. We're headed the right way to find your butterfly."

Cecilia instantly forgot about her indecent exposure. "Where?"

"That way. Over there," said Rosalyn pointing. "We don't know how far, but we're on the track of Doctor Phatts."

"There's a real nice painting, like in your books, but on the cliff wall. A man wearing a hat, on horseback. Has to be him."

"That's good, wonderful," said Cecilia excitedly. She stopped as a thought struck her. "But he may have passed this way three years ago. The Green Wave might be around here." She pulled out her journal and opened to a blank page, rapidly sketching out a butterfly and splashing on some green paint.

Forgetting the previous fear she'd displayed, she stepped out of the boat and held the picture up to the Aborigines. "Have you seen this? Any of you?" She looked dismayed at the blank faces staring at her until the older woman spoke again, waving with her hand in a westerly direction. Cecilia's face lit up. "Thank you. Thank you." She turned to Fey and Rosalyn. "Yes, our course is correct and it means that the homing balloon Doctor Phatts sent was not sent before he reached this spot. We must push on!"

"I dunno how you figured all that. The old woman could have been waving about anything."

"I'm positive she understood."

"Wishful thinking," said Fey.

Such was her satisfaction at having made friendly contact with the Aborigines, Rosalyn only now remembered her nakedness. Something Eden-like had been at play—the innocence of the nudity, the clear water and the laughing women.

For a brief time civilisation had been washed from her and she felt transported to some other world entirely. Now her civilisation came creeping back and she felt the shame of nakedness which Eve must have felt when she was expelled from the Garden. She found her clothes and dressed as the Aboriginal women watched, fascinated. Fey also watched, fascinated, but then feeling self-conscious at being the only one of their party still wandering around naked, also dressed, albeit reluctantly.

They stayed the rest of the day by the water, deciding to spend the night on the ground in order to further build trust. The afternoon sun created a rich, warm glow on the rock walls of the gorge and the white stands of the eucalypts. Rosalyn watched entranced as the women bathed in the water, laughing and splashing. She looked at the clothes she was wearing, and now, instead of feeling ashamed at having been naked in the presence of others, felt strangely ashamed at being clothed.

Before the sun faded, the Aboriginal women indicated they were leaving and although disappointed, Rosalyn gave them some of the precious sugar supplies and a blanket as a parting gesture. Rosalyn, Fey and Cecilia looked on in silence as the Aboriginal women walked along the gorge in single file. "I really hoped they'd stay the night," said Rosalyn, as the last of the women disappeared from view.

With the late afternoon being so serene, they decided to stay on the ground for the night anyway. Sitting on the sand drinking tea, they watched the last light of the sun touching the top of the cliffs. Rosalyn remarked on the peace of it all only seconds before a flock of black cockatoos took flight from further along the river bed. The birds soared past them, screeching to one another as they went.

A look of alarm crossed Cecilia's features. "What's that?" A strange rhythmic noise could be heard in the distance. As they listened it grew louder.

"I'll tell you what that is—that's another bloody airship!"

"Here?" asked Rosalyn.

"Yeah, here."

"It must be the Bennelong—that government airship from Sydney. They're searching for us for taking back the Lightning." Rosalyn stood and gazed up at the sky.

"It might be, but if it is, it's got a different sound to it now. Must have got the engine replaced."

They were all standing now, looking at the sky as the sound drew ever closer. The airship passed to their east, the rays of the sun picking up the craft as it flew on by. "That's not the Bennelong. The Bennelong doesn't have a red balloon and is smaller besides. I don't have the foggiest notion what ship that is."

Cecilia had put her eye to the telescope. "It's a red balloon with a white circle on the side with a black cog in the centre. Rosalyn, isn't that the symbol of..."

"The Divine Order of Mechanics. What are they doing here?"

"At a guess I'd say they're looking for you, Roz. You're a popular woman."

"Why though? This doesn't make sense. Could it be they are also looking for Doctor Phatts?" She walked over to the airship and perched herself on the skyrail to think. The others joined her and to assist in the thought process Fey smoked her pipe. "Perhaps..." said Rosalyn as she coughed, "...perhaps Doctor Phatts found something."

"Yes, of course he did. He found the Green Wave," said Cecilia.

"No. Something more important."

"What could be more important than a rare and exotic butterfly?"

"The Order wouldn't send an airship all this way to find a butterfly—I don't care how exotic a species it is. It can't be worth more than the cost of an airship expedition. Fey, can you think of anything else you know about Doctor Phatts?"

Fey took a pull on her pipe and furrowed her brow. "Nope."

"What about you, Cecilia? Is there nothing else, nothing in your journals and books? Why don't we look?"

"There's nothing else. I searched through them all after you brought the Green Wave to my attention."

"Did any of them people from your society tell you anything more about your expedition other than you're on an heroic quest to hunt and kill the ferocious Green Wave butterfly?"

"No. I'm to fill in the blanks on known species, to document new species, and to collect specimens—and apparently find the Green Wave."

"It's queer to me that if this butterfly is so important they didn't talk to you about it before you left."

"My part in the expedition was rushed and I'm sure the information was simply overlooked in the haste to prepare. As I explained to Rosalyn, I wasn't even supposed to come. The Society originally intended to finance a geological expedition and had selected a chap to go. Unfortunately he died in the most unfortunate of circumstances, which threw the Society into something of a quandary. The Society considered a botanist instead, but Daddy knew how much I wanted to go and make a name for myself. He managed to use his influence to secure me the position."

Fey and Rosalyn looked at each other and then back at Cecilia. Fey asked, "Cecilia, this geologist feller, how did he meet his end?"

"Apparently he was examining the rocks along the top of a cliff when he fell over."

"Was anyone with him?"

"No, I don't think so. I don't really know. Why?"

"You told me he fell sick," said Rosalyn.

"No, I said he fell—although I do suppose he was quite sick by the time he reached the bottom of the cliff. The poor man died."

"I don't know, Ses. Something is funny about all this. How did you come to be on the ship out to the colony with Roz?"

"What? Oh, I was supposed to sail on the ship the unfortunate geologist was booked on, but the Captain of the vessel, on hearing the news of the man's demise, booked the cabin to someone else. Daddy managed to get me on another ship—the Iris."

"So neither of you know anything else about this expedition of Dr Phatts, or why you're sent to find him or this butterfly?"

"As far as I knew I was to go to the frontier to bring Enlightenment to the heathens. I assume Max's station would be at the limits of the frontier and it would have been to that sort of situation where I'd have set up my Mission. I had no idea I was to travel further into the interior until I opened my orders. I suppose that explains the airship. I was so excited about being given one that I never really thought to question why a Missionary would need it."

"There's something fogging my brain box," said Fey. "You're both connected by this same man and now we not only have another man on horseback looking for you, but also a huge bloody airship. There's something bigger here than a butterfly or a lost explorer. There's something else that's odd too. The geologist is killed but your society thought he could be replaced by a flower squasher or a bug catcher. I may not have your learning, but I don't see how a bug catcher can replace a rock breaker."

"I didn't think to question them about that. The Society has a variety of scientific fields they wish to expand their knowledge in, and while their first preference may have been in the field of geology there are also the fields of entomology, botany, biology, palaeontology, ichthyology, temporology, astr... "

"Yeah, I get the picture you're building. So they sent a bug catcher."

"Yes," said Cecilia, through pursed lips, "a bug catcher."

"Now we're thinking on these things, it strikes me as more than a little odd the way the Church rushed me out here. Normally a

Missionary has to undertake and pass an extensive course of study before being sent on a Mission to heathens in uncivilised parts of the world. I was rushed off for three weeks of airship training and sailed for Sydney. I really don't know what the Church's interest in this explorer is."

"That brings us to this Doctor Phatts who hasn't been heard of in three years."

"We'll find him. We know he passed this way. We do have to go on."

Darkness had crept up on them, and letting the questions pass from their minds, they curled up on the sand by the boat and slept.

The next morning Rosalyn said, "We'll fly for another three days, put down for water again, and see if we can contact more blacks," For want of a better plan, Fey and Cecilia agreed.

When the wind came up from behind them they cut the engine and extended the side sails. During such times the silent sky held a special enchantment and the airship drifted through it like a dream. Cecilia kept diligent observation as they continued westward, updating her map as they travelled. Fey took first turn at the wheel, keeping their altitude low, although they didn't really expect to learn much from their position aloft. After three days of flying, during which time they saw no sign of the Mechanical Order's airship, they set down next to a waterhole.

12

BAKER COVENTRY

Baker drew his horses in under a large ghost gum overlooking a creek and dismounted. For some minutes he stood silently, listening. Hearing no sounds which might indicate danger, he checked his weapons and continued to the water's edge. His horses drank thirstily and he did the same, splashing the cool liquid over his face. He'd been riding all day and had no idea how far behind him his pursuer might be or if he was being pursued at all. The arrival of the old man at Bathurst had been as unexpected as the man's attire, and only Baker's quick reflexes saved him from a pistol ball tearing into his flesh.

Intelligence informing him the Church was sending another Guardian hadn't reached him. The one he'd spoken to was frustratingly resilient, giving him no useful information other than he was waiting for someone. Baker had assumed that person to be the Missionary and he had no idea where she might be now, other than somewhere on the coast. He would speak to Sir Rothwell about it when he caught up with him. The horses were tired and the sun was setting. He didn't want to abandon his horses this early in his travels so he put them to rest tethered to a small tree. With his back against the smooth, white bark of the gum tree, he allowed himself to doze off.

Next morning he set off at first light, keeping a more leisurely pace, and headed west, the dry eucalypt leaves crunching under the hoofs of his horses. With the distance travelled on the previous day he should be close to the road to the German Mission in Wellington Valley. Although the Mission had nothing to do with the Enlightenment Church he had no desire to see anyone there—or more importantly to be seen at all. Caution too, had to be taken with squatters who had pushed outwards and illegally taken up land beyond the limits of settlement. He reached the track, crossed over, checked his compass and turned to the northwest. He needed to pick up the last known heading of Doctor Phatts and make contact with Sir Rothwell.

After travelling for days through the scrub, seeing nothing more interesting than wallabies and brightly-coloured birds, Baker changed his course to ascend the highest point in the landscape— which happened to be a low hill. From his pack horse he unstrapped a long, leather case and extracted the brass object from within.

With the three legs extended, and a tube screwed in place on top, the item looked similar to a telescope. Using the compass built into the tube he aligned it to the north. The side of the device housed a chamber, accessed by a small screw-top lid. Into this Baker poured the tiniest amount of blue ascension. He next wound a handle quickly, watching a dial that would indicate the temperature generated, and that the device had enough air pressure built up for its purpose.

Satisfied, he stood back, expecting no result this far from the latitude he was aiming for, but wanting to try the device out in the field. To his surprise the tube spun slowly to the northwest. He packed and lit his pipe, had a good long pull on it and sat on a rock to stare out into the dull, faded landscape. The device, the 'atmotic vessel directional indicator' was secret, the plans having been bought by the Divine Order of Mechanics. They'd obtained them from someone who claimed to have been on intimate terms with the Mysterious Captain Hivetree, the machine's inventor.

Somewhere to the northwest, and closer than the estimated range of the directional indicator's maximum of thirty miles, was an airship. He didn't think it would be Sir Rothwell—his course should have taken him south of Baker's position. He knew it couldn't be the *Bennelong*, not after the damage he'd done to the engine and other vital parts—they couldn't possibly have repaired it so quickly. The only other airship known to be in the colony was the Sun Cog's vessel, and he'd sent that to Moreton Bay. The Missionary should have been tied up in red tape for weeks trying to recover her airship. Perhaps Sir Rothwell had changed his route, or the Missionary had been able to manipulate Major Cotton into releasing the airship to her. He'd continue on and do position readings morning, noon and night.

The spear struck him with a thud in the side of his thigh as he rose from his position on the rock. He grunted, and with the spear still sticking from his thigh, fell behind the rock. He had a pistol drawn the instant he was in cover. Wincing from the pain, he wriggled further around the rock to see an Aboriginal warrior approaching, armed with a wooden club. His shot hit the man in the left eye and the fellow dropped dead instantly. Taking out another pistol he lay still, listening for the sounds of more assailants. He could hear nothing but the sound of his own laboured breathing.

Blood ran down his leg. He gripped the spear shaft to prevent it from falling sideways and tearing his flesh. He put down his pistol and drew a third. Another black might be creeping up on the far side of the rock. He fired again, this time at the spear shaft a few inches above the entry point. The wood splintered and the long shaft fell to the ground. Baker put away his spent pistols, picked up his loaded pistol and looked about. With the aid of the broken spear shaft he forced himself upright, sweat forming on his brow. Hobbling around the other side of the rock he satisfied himself that there were no other attackers.

The spear tip wasn't embedded deeply, but had a cruel barb. Using his knife, he cut back the cloth of his trousers. He took his neckerchief and rolled it into a tight wad, stuffed it into his mouth and bit down. Gripping the stump of the shaft he wriggled the spear head one way and the other, trying to free it from the wound without tearing at the flesh. The barb came free. He looked at the blood dripping from it and tossed it aside.

Baker took a few minutes to collect himself. Tears from the pain rolled down his dusty cheeks as he struggled to push himself back against the rock. He passed out. No other blacks had come to investigate the sounds of the gunshots and he remained unmolested. Regaining consciousness and standing again, he hobbled to his horse, took out a bottle and had a good swig of gin. He poured more on the wound, gritting his teeth as he did so. The neckerchief he now used to bandage the wound. With difficulty he reloaded his pistols, packed up the directional indicator and remounted his horse.

Baker kept moving for another few days, stopping only for brief periods for his horses to feed and recover. The inflammation in his thigh gave cause for him to at last stop and rest up. A sandy stretch in the shade next to a billabong became his camping ground. The flesh around the wound was raw and inflamed. In his fever he struggled to rid himself of his clothes. He slid into the cool water, lying with the sandy bank as his pillow, his wet neckerchief across his forehead.

In the late afternoon he woke up, his head foggy. He knew he'd passed out. He splashed the cool water over his face and drank thirstily before crawling up the bank. His senses were recovering and he looked around. His horses were close by and so were two Aboriginal men. He recoiled, keeping his eyes fixed on them. On seeing their posture, he relaxed. They were sitting cross-legged in the sand a few yards away, staring at him silently. Scars ran horizontally along their chests and shoulders. Neither appeared to be much older than thirty five, about the same age as himself.

Baker lay observing them for many minutes before attempting to stand. The soaking of his wound and body in the cold waters had helped in his recovery. The warriors didn't move as he limped to his pack horse and swabbed the wound with gin. Still as naked as the warriors, and having now recovered from the deep sleep he was in, he sat down opposite the men. He noticed one of them had helped himself to Baker's axe and the other had his knife. The ground in front of him had been disturbed and he could feel the heat coming up from it.

One of the men, on seeing Baker's gaze, scooped back the sand to reveal a layer of charcoal. Using the end of his throwing stick the man pushed the coals aside and revealed a large lizard, well-cooked. The men started eating, indicating to Baker that he do the same. Neither of the men had spoken. Baker stuffed chunks of the reptile's flesh into his mouth, its fat running down his chin. Having eaten, he made his way back to the water to drink again. On returning to the cooking pit one of the men spoke to him. Baker had no idea what the man said. It may have been a query.

The evening was coming on and the two Aboriginal men watched fascinated as Baker dressed. He pulled his boots on, lacing them firmly. The men turned to each other, passing comments, grinning and laughing at the strange performance of the pale man. Baker checked his pistols to ensure that all four were loaded. Taking one in each hand he walked over to the men, looked down at them and shot them both in their foreheads. He picked up his axe and his knife.

13

THE DUSTY OUTBACK

Dry, shallow, water courses cut through the land around the waterhole. Rocks lay strewn across the surface, exposed by centuries of floods and wind. In the hard earth between them, pale-leafed, stunted bushes found purchase. The flies swarming about were the only things moving in the hot, still air. As Rosalyn and Fey filled up the water bags and boiler, Cecilia took her net and left in search of other insects.

Pushing through the scrub, her attention was drawn by a murder of crows. She saw they were circling and feeding off a carcass. She walked over to take a closer look at what beast had become unfortunate, sending the birds cawing into the deep blue sky. As her mind made sense of the scene before her, she stepped back in horror. The birds were feasting on the remains of a person.

Bones of the skull showed through and the eye sockets had been pecked empty. The lips, eaten away, left the teeth in a frightening death-grin. The stench of rotting flesh sickened her as much as the sight. Cecilia put her handkerchief to her nose, trying not to vomit as she looked around. Other corpses lay scattered about in a state of decay. The ground around them was littered with spears, shields, digging sticks and other bits and pieces. She backed away, turned, lifted her skirts and ran back to the airship.

"There are bodies," she gasped out.

Rosalyn and Fey followed her to where the bloated corpses rotted on the red earth. After taking in the spectacle before them, the three women moved forward to make a closer examination.

"Look," said Rosalyn, crouching next to a body. "This one has a small round hole in its forehead. What do you suppose caused that?"

Fey squatted, pinching her nose, her palm covering her mouth, and said, "They've been shot."

"Shot? There's no one here to shoot them." She paused. "That airship? You think they did this?"

"Who else could have done it?"

Cecilia, ashen-faced, looked once more at the carnage and without saying another word, walked away. Rosalyn turned to Fey, "Do you think we should try to bury them?"

Fey waved flies away from her face. "No. Their own will come for them and do it the proper way."

"Proper way?"

"Yeah. They've got their own way of doing things. Let's let them have it."

"I can't leave them like this. I best say some words, at least."

"You do that. I'm sure they'll feel better for it. I'm going back to the boat." Fey walked off after Cecilia, leaving Rosalyn to her prayers for the dead. When she returned, Fey suggested they unhook immediately. "The kinfolk of those unfortunates aren't going to be happy to see us."

"We didn't do it."

"No Roz, we didn't, but do you really think you can explain your innocence to a tribe of angry blacks? They'll have seen the other airship and they'll see us as the same. We need to go."

Cecilia remained huddled in the bow as Fey brought the airship up.

"Why?" asked Rosalyn.

Fey shrugged. "I've no notion. From what I've seen of brutality to the convicts, the savagery of men brings no surprises."

"It's the worst thing to ever happen to me," said Rosalyn, clutching her Enlightenment Book of Understandings.

"To you?" asked Fey.

"Yes. It was hideous. The bloated flesh, the stench, the flies. I've never seen anything of the like before."

Fey scowled and her voice grew hard. "It didn't happen to you. It happened to them."

"I saw it!" Rosalyn's hands trembled as she held the book. "The sight of it happened to me."

"If that's the worst thing that's happened to you, you've led a protected bloody life. What about you, Ses? I suppose it was the worst thing to happen to you, too."

"No," said Cecilia softly. "My mother died giving birth to me."

"That wasn't good," said Fey. "I'm sorry."

Rosalyn waved the book at her. "And what about you, Fey Grey? You think you're so damned worldly. I suppose you've had worse? What could be worse than that carnage?"

"Shut it. If it didn't happen to you, it don't count. Get yourself in front of it. And take the wheel, I need to have a smoke."

The sky remained blue and clear. A gentle tail wind continued into the night. With the passage of time, the ill feelings induced by the horrific scene faded from them. At dawn of the next day, Cecilia called out to her companions, drawing their attention to something on the ground. The red balloon of the Mechanical Order airship contrasted with the stunted green bushes around it. The *Lightning*'s course would take them over the top of it and at no great distance.

"I think we should remain aloof, Roz. I don't trust them bastards at all."

"Neither do I." Rosalyn took the *Lightning* up and they passed over the other airship well beyond musket range. The men on the ground looked up at them, shouting and waving. Someone fired a shot.

"We might need to go a bit faster, Roz. If they come up in pursuit they're certain to overtake us."

"I'll give it more power but I don't think we'll be able to get much more speed out of this old thing."

Cecilia moved to the stern and kept watch for any sign of pursuit. The red balloon of the other airship receded into the distance, making no sign of ascending.

"We've got away, Roz. I would've sworn blue they'd be straight up and after us."

"Perhaps they were taking on water or had a scouting party out. If they're looking for Doctor Phatts and not us they may have other priorities."

"I hope you're right, love. I don't think them coves in that vessel are going to be helpful to us."

The next day Cecilia once more brought their attention to the red balloon of the Mechanical Order airship. It cruised some distance away, on their starboard side and to the rear. "Have they spotted us?" asked Rosalyn.

"I'm unsure—wait—yes, I think they have, they've turned our way," said Cecilia.

"Damnation. We have no way of outrunning them. Is there anything on the ground below? Any gorges to hide in, or forests?"

Cecilia lowered the telescope and stared out over the landscape. "It's desolate country, the same as we've been passing over for miles. I can see nothing that might lend itself to our purpose."

Fey peered into the distance. "If we make it into that cloud up front we might be able to lose them in it."

Cecilia raised the telescope to her eye. "I don't know if we'll reach it in time." She continued staring through the telescope. "It's a strange species of cloud—it's orange."

"Fey, take the wheel please. I need to have a look." Rosalyn took the telescope and peered intently. "That's a fast moving cloud, too, and it reaches to the ground. It's most peculiar."

"Here, take the wheel back, Roz, I want to have another squiz meself." Fey took the telescope and peered through it. "I can tell you why it's a funny-looking cloud. It's because it's dust. We're heading into a dust storm."

"Dust? That's impossible." said Rosalyn.

"It may be impossible love, but so is flying and yet here we are."

Cecilia stared at the cloud. "It's astonishing. It stretches from horizon to horizon. I've never seen anything like it."

"Never mind that, where is the red ship?" asked Rosalyn.

Cecilia turned and looked. "It's closed the gap a bit, but we still have some distance."

"I don't know what to do here. I don't think we can get up over the cloud and if we do manage it, the other airship will, too. If I go down we'll be flying close to the ground and chance wrecking us. I can feel the wind coming against us now and this engine isn't going to carry us forward against it."

"Well you better think of something, Roz; it's approaching fast."

Rosalyn frowned and came to a quick decision. "Here's what we'll do. I'll keep her nose into the dust until we're shrouded, drop down, turn back to the northeast and run diagonally across the storm. Hopefully the Order won't see us as we pass under them and we can give them the slip."

"Aye aye, Cap'n. We better batten down the hatches. Here, Ses, get the loose items and shove them in the trunks. I'll put the cover on. We better tie on, too. I think this is going to get rough." Fey secured the cover over the front end of the boat and buckled the belt around Rosalyn's waist as she stood at the wheel. Rosalyn breathed in deeply as Fey's arms passed around her. Straps were attached to each side of the belt and Fey clipped the ends to rings on the skyrails. She and Cecilia crawled under the bow cover, tying themselves in. "Good luck, Roz."

Rosalyn lowered her goggles and wrapped the scarf around her face, making sure to fasten her leather coat up tight. Frightened by the appearance of the massive clouds of swirling dust in front of her, she felt as if she were flying into Hell itself. She took one last look to the starboard before the storm consumed her. The voluminous orange cloud surrounded the *Lightning* and visibility dropped to no more than a yard. Rosalyn could no longer see the bow of the boat. She flew on blindly.

The wind buffeted the craft. She said a quick prayer while trying to turn the airship. The craft creaked loudly, the balloon and boat twisted out of alignment and the airship began to roll. Rosalyn gritted her teeth, her hands clenched the wheel and she commenced the descent, struggling to keep the airship from capsizing. The *Lightning* screamed with the strain as Rosalyn, inch by painful inch, managed to turn the bow. With no idea of how far they'd dropped she now ran with the wind, back the way they'd come. Oblivious to the wind howling through the ropes and netting around her, she succeeded in returning the *Lightning* to an upright attitude.

The compass and her goggles were caked with dust and the massive amount of the fine powder filling the boat added to the weight of the ship. She wiped her hand across the lenses to try to get a compass reading, cursing as the goggles fell apart at her touch. Doing her best to grip the wheel she lowered her head to the compass face, barely able to make out the needle before the fine particles started coating her eyes. It looked like they were heading in the direction she desired but she couldn't be sure. She kept her eyes squeezed shut as the storm threw her about, the waist belt and her grip on the wheel holding her in position. She could hear Fey yelling something from under the canvas cover but the words were muffled by the noise.

The wind eased and the sky lightened. As if someone had flicked a switch the storm was gone. Rosalyn lifted what was left of her goggles onto her forehead, shook out her scarf and wiped her eyes clean. Clearing the dust from the compass she found they were only a little way off course. She turned the airship to the northwest and called to her companions. "You can come out now. It's over."

Fey emerged from under the canvas and looked around the boat. The powdery dust was ankle deep and every surface was covered with it, giving the airship a uniform orange colour.

"How did we hold up?"

"We seem to be in one piece. Did you hear those frightful sounds? I think the mast may have twisted. I was too busy holding on and I couldn't see anyway, as these cursed goggles fell apart."

Fey looked at her with something in the way of adoration. "I was sure the boat was going to break up. You did a bloody good job, Roz. I'll fly with you any day."

Rosalyn smiled. "Thank you. We'd better get this boat back in order. Why is Cecilia so quiet?"

"She chundered—tossed up everything in her tummy. It wasn't pleasant under the canvas with her. I hope we can find another waterhole soon so I can wash my duds. Myself too could use a scrub after that and I know Cecilia could do with a full watery immersion. Let's have a look at those goggles."

Rosalyn took them off and handed them to Fey who studied them intently. "These look cheap—were they made in some Liverpool sweat shop?"

"I have no idea where they were made. They're from the shop of Professor Staughbort. The Church gave them to me."

"You'd do better to make a pair yourself. I'll try to fix them for you but it don't look like much can be done." Fey tossed them aside. "Where's the other airship?"

In her concentrated struggle with the storm, Rosalyn had forgotten all about the Mechanical Order airship. She looked about the skies but couldn't see it anywhere. "I wonder if they survived it."

Rosalyn continued on the northwest course in the hope of putting further distance between them and their pursuers—if they still had pursuers. Cecilia remained under cover and Fey took the watch, looking over the side for any sign of water.

"Fey," said Rosalyn quietly, "We're losing altitude."

"How bad is it?"

"It's not much; I've got the ascension going at full and we're still descending. And we need to find water soon, for if we come down in the desert here without any..." She didn't need to finish her sentence.

Fey took out the telescope and scanned the landscape near and far, from horizon to horizon. "I never seen a place so dry." Her attention was caught on some distant spot and with the telescope still to her eye she motioned for Rosalyn to bring the craft more to starboard. "I can't see water but there's a green patch there. There's got to be water but it may not be on the surface."

"We daren't pass it up. We're going to have to take the risk. Guide me to it." Rosalyn brought the airship down in a long, gentle descent in front of a low ridge of boulders. Scattered, white-barked trees grew between rocks of a deep red ochre. Rosalyn set the *Lightning* down amongst them. Fey cast out the hooks and the boat came to rest. She peered under the canvas.

"You can come out now, Ses. We're there." Cecilia lost no time in scrambling out from under the cover. Her hair was dishevelled and her face covered with orange powder. "Let's be a bit careful this time. Don't go wandering off, Ses."

14

A Brief Introduction To Herpetology

The women took on a spectral appearance as they shook the dust from themselves. The fine particles lingered around them in clouds. Rosalyn took out the weapons and stripped, cleaned and reloaded them. She kept the carbine and gave the pistol to Fey. Throwing the water bags over their shoulders, and with Cecilia still bleary-eyed and coughing, they set off in search of water. The red-ochre boulders were scattered everywhere, some of them the size of houses, and they scoured around them looking for a spring or a soak. The air was warm and still and the only sounds were their footsteps and the occasional call of a distant bird. A rock overhang jutted out from half way up the ridge and they climbed up to see if it concealed water. The rear wall and parts of the ceiling were covered with strange paintings in red, yellow and white ochres.

"Cecilia, look at this one. It might interest you." Rosalyn pointed out a depiction of a big lizard-like creature into which a stylised figure jabbed a spear. "What do you make of that?"

At that particular moment Cecilia didn't want to make anything of it. Her mouth was dry and her head was ready to explode from a throbbing headache but the image was intriguing. "It looks like a black person spearing a large lizard. I can't stand them."

"The blacks?"

"No, lizards—and snakes. Horrible, slithery, scaly things they are."

"But what do you make of this painting? The lizard in the picture is the size of a horse compared to the figure. Do you think there are any large lizards like this here?"

Cecilia studied the figures. "Some of the European cave paintings have great antiquity and depict animals which have become extinct in the distant past. This painting is almost certainly quite ancient and as it shows, the blacks are hunting the lizards—if lizards are what they are. I daresay these larger creatures are also long since extinct. After all, there have been no reports of any large lizards around Sydney have there?" They both looked at Fey.

"Nope, not that large anyway. Some of them goannas get on the big side but not that big."

"I daresay you're right, Cecilia, the blacks must have hunted them to extinction. The paintings may have religious connotations or something to do with hunting magic." Rosalyn had one last look and turned away. "We really need to keep looking for water."

Continuing on they came to a glade. Here the boulders came down from the ridge in two rough lines leaving a space between them. This had been colonised by a stand of ghost gums with lush green grasses growing around them. In between the boulders a pool of fresh clear water reflected the sky.

After slaking their thirsts Fey took it on herself to take water back to the airship and fill the boiler. She returned to her friends who refilled the water bags. Rosalyn looked around, observing the tranquillity of the landscape, while Cecilia had her attention taken by a pair of brilliant blue dragonflies chasing each other around the pool.

"Look at this." Rosalyn, standing with her back to the ridge, stared out past the trees.

"What? I can't see anything," said Cecilia, as she strained to see what Rosalyn was seeing.

"I see it." Fey stood up and Cecilia followed suit, putting her face next to Fey's to try to follow her line of sight.

"Yeah, not too close, Ses, you smell like vomit. Look at the boulders. See how them boulders are scattered. Then there are none in between those two lines of slabs."

Cecilia stepped back. "Yes, I can see there are no boulders there."

"Look at the slabs," said Rosalyn.

The two lines of stone slabs were arranged exactly parallel and each stone in the line was equidistant from the ones beside it. Not only that but the slabs themselves were of a regular shape. A few of them leaned out of place or had toppled, breaking the regularity of the lines.

"Oh! I see it now. They've been put there."

"I wonder why." Rosalyn walked over to the nearest one and ran her hand over it. "It looks like an avenue doesn't it?"

"Yeah, it does. It leads into that ridge." Fey stared back at the jumble of boulders where the edge of the pool was obscured by low growing shrubs overhanging the water. Pushing them aside she made her way past them. "Hoy! Look at this." Her friends followed her past the bushes. The stone under which the pool lay had been artificially shaped.

A large opening revealed a dark space beyond into which the pool of water continued. A narrow walkway either side of the water gave access to the interior. The walls formed a short corridor which led deeper into the rock. "I'll go and get a lantern." Fey returned with it a short time later, also clutching some candles. Rosalyn led the way into the chamber. It opened out inside, going left and right for equal distances; the whole area being about forty feet square. The walkway around the pool was wider inside the chamber.

"The walls! Look." Cecilia brought their attention to the relief carvings that covered the surfaces. The carvings were abstract depictions of people and animals. They continued walking around the pool looking at the artwork. On the far side, two recessed areas, the walls blackened around them, must once have been small fire pits. On closer examination they found what appeared to be chimneys, although these had long since been blocked with rubble and dirt. In between the two fireplaces a trickle of water ran out from the wall. The wall at this point hadn't been carved, the water issuing from a cleft in the natural rock. The women came back to their starting point. "Who could have created this?"

"I don't know, Cecilia. There must have been some ancient civilisation here."

"I've never seen anything like this around Sydney. Haven't heard anything about it, either."

"We must be the first Europeans to set eyes on the place," Rosalyn said, looking around the chamber. "Perhaps it was built by Egyptians or Babylonians or even one of the lost tribes of the Hebrews."

"I don't think so," said Cecilia. "I'm familiar with the styles of those people and these carvings aren't in the slightest bit similar. It's possible one of the Asian civilisations had an outpost here."

"I don't really care who done it, I'm getting my duds off and going in." Fey put down the lantern and unlaced her boots.

"Do you think it's safe to go in the water?" asked Cecilia.

"I'll find out in a flash, love. It's wet and I have to get this bloody dust off, the stuff has got in everywhere." Fey finished stripping as Rosalyn fixed her candle to the stone.

"Are you also going in, Rosalyn?"

"Yes. I haven't bathed in days and as Fey has said, the dust is everywhere and I need to get these clothes washed."

"Quite," said Cecilia, a little unsure. I suppose I had best do the same." She walked around to the other side of the pool and after fixing her candle to the stone moved to the edge of the light to undertake the lengthy process of undressing.

Fey sat on the edge of the walkway dangling her feet in. "It's bloody cold." She let herself slide slowly in and stood in water that came up to her armpits. Rosalyn followed her in. Cecilia gasped as she too, immersed herself in the cold, clear water. The cold became more bearable the longer they were in and soon they were splashing about in pure enjoyment, delighting in the magic play of reflected light on the chamber ceiling, and for a while the outside world was forgotten.

They washed their clothes as best they could and Cecilia, to make herself useful, took the clothes out into the sun, laying them out on the rocks to dry. Fey and Rosalyn stood in the water, letting it become still, speaking in whispers as though in some sacred place.

Rosalyn noticed Fey staring at her. "What is it?"

"The light. You look so soft and appealing." Fey realised what she'd said and became flustered. "That is, the candle light and all, it... I... well... it shows you..." Her voice trailed off.

It was the first time Rosalyn had seen Fey so uncomposed. She looked at her and said gently, "Thank you, Fey." She continued looking and in an attempt to be soothing said, "I see what you mean about the light. You look rather..." and then it was Rosalyn's turn to become flustered. For the first time she saw Fey as more than a servant. Fey's shaved head with its strip of hair and her tanned skin gave her an exotic look quite unlike the young women of England, and her lithe body gave a feeling of unassuming strength. The smile that had appeared on Fey's face was captivating. "Anyway," said Rosalyn as she tried to look away. "I'm glad of your company. Cecilia..."

"Yeah, Ses is a good one but a little on the shy and frightened side." Rosalyn nodded. Fey paused and asked. "Are you shy and frightened?"

"Me? Why, no." And then she had a glimpse of understanding of Fey's question and became flustered again with a touch of indignation. "That is... No, I'm not, but, yes... that is, I'm..." Rosalyn couldn't answer and instead splashed water at Fey, unsure whether to be angry or to laugh. The issue was not carried further as at that moment came a shriek from outside.

Fey rolled her eyes. "I think she must have seen a goanna."

Cecilia rushed into the chamber, still naked and too panicked to even attempt to cover herself from the sight of her friends. "Lizard!" She ran past them and they started to laugh. "Big lizard." Cecilia added, cowering in the corner near them.

Their attention was taken from Cecilia to the chamber's entrance. The light entering the chamber grew dim as though a dark cloud had come over. Something large was coming in and its size blocked out the light. Rosalyn and Fey moved quietly to the edge of the pool and took up their weapons. "Easy now, Roz." Fey whispered as she brought the pistol up. "Don't fire yet, let's see the thing."

Transfixed, they watched as a big, flickering forked tongue, followed by the beast's scaly head, searched its way into the chamber. The women remained motionless as the giant reptile turned towards them, its tongue darting in and out. Neither woman wanted it to come any closer. They fired in unison, the crashing sound reverberating around the chamber in a most deafening way. The gunsmoke filled the area in front of them and sunlight reflected into the chamber once more. "Reload," said Rosalyn. The women reloaded and waited in silence as Cecilia whimpered in fear in the corner.

"I think it's gone," said Fey. The two women waded to the entrance and looked out but could see nothing.

"Come on out, Cecilia, It's time we left." Rosalyn stood guard with the carbine while Fey and Cecilia dressed, and then put on her own clothes. Fey helped tighten her corset strings and Rosalyn tensed under her touch, aware of every movement of Fey's hands, and she feared that Fey could sense the nervous trembling of her body.

"Scared you, didn't it? I can feel it in you."

"I wasn't scared."

"It scared me. That bloody lizard was the size of a cow."

"I thought you meant... Never mind. I didn't hear you properly, my ears are still ringing from the gunshots in that enclosed space. We need to leave."

Dressed again in freshly cleaned clothes, now almost dry, they checked about lest they had missed some item, took up the water bags and headed to the airship. They made their way back in silence, Rosalyn taking the lead and Fey following behind. The boat was still a mess of dust although a lot of it had been blown away by the breeze after the dust storm had passed. Cecilia came up with the idea of using a tuft of grass as a broom and managed to get the *Lightning* into a cleaner state.

Fey and Rosalyn examined the damage caused to the mast by the storm and found no major damage. The crack from which the blue aether escaped came from a loosening of the pipe to the balloon. It was a simple matter to retighten it. One of the support ropes had snapped and the balloon's cover net had shifted. They repositioned it, securing the ropes and replacing the broken one. Cecilia stood on guard with the pistol lest the giant lizard make a return visit. It didn't and as soon as the engine was fired they unhooked and rose above the tree tops.

Rosalyn bade Fey take the wheel and circle the area. "I want to see if there are any more signs of the civilisation that made the avenue and grotto." Scanning the ground closely she could see nothing and they decided to follow the axis of the avenue, which led them directly west. Rosalyn and Cecilia busied themselves with their respective journals, putting in all the exciting news of the day. Cecilia, being scientifically minded, drew a plan of the avenue and the grotto and then put the location of the grotto on her main map. With a touch of whimsy she added a small picture of the lizard and wrote next to it, 'here be dragons'.

15

AN ASTRONOMICAL ANOMALY

Night approached and Rosalyn took the *Lightning* to a higher altitude in the dark hours lest they drift into a hill or a treetop. High above the ground, the evening light continued shining for a time, giving the airship a golden glow. Specks of campfires showed in the distance, and once, at a time when they were running with a silent engine, they drifted over the top of such a campfire unnoticed. The figures of the Aborigines could be observed, sleeping about their fire.

"They look so peaceful," said Cecilia.

"After we've next grounded for water we're going to look for a tribe to disturb. We need to find information on the whereabouts of Doctor Phatts, or his earthly remains."

For the most part, boredom aloft was something of an issue. Cecilia, ever curious, spent her time jotting down observations and adding to her map. Fey had learned all she could from studying every nut, bolt, rivet and rope on the airship and out of sheer boredom asked if she could read one of Cecilia's books. "I didn't know you could read, Fey."

"Of course I can bloody well read. I was reading your bug book wasn't I?"

"The book of mine you threw away?"

"Yeah, the one some black woman is reading while she wears my hat."

"I didn't know they had schools in Sydney."

"They do—and I told you back in Sydney I could read. And the fact is I didn't do my learning at school; it were Mother Mary taught me to read. She done it from the newspapers and from all the books she has. I read the papers every day they come out. I look at the shipping intelligence, police reports and everything so I know what's up."

"Very well, but scientific books have many words with more than two syllables. You might find them a different proposition. I have a selection here. This one is interesting: 'Journals of Two Expeditions into the Interior of New South Wales by Order of the British Government in the Years 1817-18'."

"Yeah, I can see how that would have your daylights riveted to every page, Ses. What else do you have?"

"How does this one sound? 'The Fine Art of Creative Complication Without Pontification in Enlightened Discourse'."

"Ses, you're putting me to sleep reading out the titles. Here, let me have a squiz at what you've got." Without waiting for Cecilia to respond, Fey leaned over and took a book out of Cecilia's trunk. She studied the title page. "This might be the go: Chamber's 'A Miscellany of Essays and other Works for the Inquisitive Reader.' I'd wager today's shillings that you were waiting at the book shop for this to come out."

"I bought it for the voyage. It might not suit you for a long flight."

"Why is that?"

"They're short works of various descriptions."

"Yeah, I picked up on that from the title, but thanks for the explanation. Between you and Roz I'll be ready to take up a Chair at Oxford."

"Pass it back—you'd be much better to settle into a lengthier tome."

"Nope, I don't think I will. It says 'works for the inquisitive reader' and that's what I am. I'll get me phiz into that." Fey turned to the first page and set to reading. Several hours later Fey looked up and asked Cecilia, "Didn't I hear you say something about the Mysterious Captain Hivetree earlier on in the flight?"

"I really can't remember. Why do you ask, Fey?"

"I'm reading an essay here about him. He's the feller that's responsible for the blue aether and airships."

"I wasn't aware such an essay was in that volume," said Cecilia, "I'm sure there're better works in there for you to read."

"Better or not I'm reading this one."

"I doubt you'll find it compelling."

"I'm finding it particularly fascinating, and you might too when I tell you what's in it." A look of concern passed over Cecilia's face. "Why the worried look, Ses?"

"I'm not worried. I'm feeling sick from the motion of the boat. You know I get airsick."

"What is it, Fey?" asked Rosalyn from the wheel.

"The writer is speculating about whether or not Captain Hivetree did visit another planet and brought back the fungus that makes the blue aether as he claimed, or whether he brought it back from the jungles of Central America as he also claimed, or if he brought it back from a ruin on an island in the East as he claimed on another occasion, or if he did find it under the boiler in the cellar of his house in Wiltshire as others have said."

"And what is so interesting about that?"

"Not so much, but it goes into the different versions of Captain Hivetree's stories, picking to pieces each particular detail of what Captain Hivetree has claimed, assessing each point as to its likelihood."

"Is there a point to this, Fey?"

"Yeah, Ses, there is a point," said Fey, with a touch of ice. "One of the claims the Captain made was about a particular green butterfly, the way it gathered in bunches of its kind and how they'd open and close their wings so the whole mass made a rippling effect like a wave."

Cecilia sat silently and stared at her.

"My goodness. Let me see." Rosalyn locked the wheel and sat next to Fey. She read from a quote in the essay from Captain Hivetree's own writings; "It is found on a particular flower I called the Shellbean Flower, because the flower was growing in an area of fossilised shells and itself took the form of an open bivalve mollusc, each side the shape of a kidney bean. It was in such an area that I found the pretty Aqua Glass which I shall use to power the Universal Instantaneous Geographical Displacement Engine and other cunning machines." Rosalyn stopped reading and looked at Fey. "Do you know what this means?"

"Yeah, I'm not bloody stupid."

"No, of course you're not. Cecilia, were you listening?"

"Yes, I heard. It sounds like the insane ramblings of a deranged mind."

"I don't think so, Cecilia. Without realising it, Doctor Phatts may have discovered a source of this Aqua Glass and that it acts as some sort of power source for some kind of engine."

"Yeah, you got it Roz. It explains why the Society wanted a rock smasher, a flower squasher or a bug catcher—anyone who could figure out the right area."

"But Captain Hivetree made all sorts of nonsensical claims. As you said earlier, Fey, he gave different conflicting accounts of where he found the blue fungus that makes airship travel possible." Cecilia furrowed her brow.

"He did find the blue fungus, Cecilia, therefore that gives him some credibility. If he found something that gives us flight perhaps he did find something that causes instant travel between distant coordinates as he implies. Goodness knows what other sorts of machines he was planning. The Mysterious Captain Hivetree may be of an unsound mind but somewhere in that mind is something of a genius. It's certainly being taken seriously enough for my Church, your Society and for the Mechanical Order to each send out expeditions. And those on the basis of a three year old message from an explorer who was already lost when he found the butterfly. It also explains why the Church rushed me off so quickly."

"It also means," said Fey, "that we done right to avoid the Mechanical Order. If a machine can be built giving a person instant transport between two points it's going to give a big advantage to whoever possesses it, isn't it? Do you think this Hivetree bloke came to New South Wales and found his Aqua Glass here?"

"It's possible, I suppose. This may not be the only place it can be found, although if it is the only place known where it might be found this would be the place to start looking." Rosalyn returned to the helm.

Cecilia peered over the side of the boat. "It's like looking for a needle in a haystack. Worse. I've never seen a haystack this big or unwelcoming. Anyway, I'd like my book back now."

Fey smiled at her and handed the book over. Cecilia took it and flicked through the pages. "Looking for something, Ses?"

"You—you took my notes!"

"You've been hiding something from us, haven't you, Ses?"

Cecilia glared at her.

"What are you talking about, Fey? What's Cecilia been hiding?"

Fey ignored Rosalyn's questions. "Who are you working for, Ses?"

"I told you. I'm here for the Royal Scientific Society for the Exploration of the Antipodes."

"Yet you knew all along about the connection of the Green Wave to this Aqua Glass."

"What's in those notes, Fey?"

"I'll read it to you Roz—interesting letter:

'Cecilia, it is of the utmost imperative you learn of any mention of the Green Wave, if it exists, especially notes of its location. Be aware also of any reporting of the Shellbean Flower. The Royal

Scientific Society for the Exploration of the Antipodes has several members in Sydney who you can talk to on arrival and who may have new information by the time you arrive in Sydney. Interrogate them closely but carefully; do not divulge anything you already know. Our search for the Green Wave must remain a closely guarded secret as there are rivals in its discovery, some of whom, as you know, can be quite ruthless. Take caution with the Sun Cog, their ranks have been infiltrated. Err on the side of mistrust.'"

Rosalyn turned to Cecilia. "You knew all along?"

"Yes," said Cecilia indignantly, "Yes, I knew all along."

"And you didn't see fit to tell me, your friend and Captain?"

"You read what the letter says. I don't know if you're innocent or you too have known all along. I was told to be cautious with you."

"Do you want me to throw her over the side, Roz?"

"No I don't. Cecilia is right not to trust anyone. And what about you? Who do you work for?"

"Yes, Fey, do tell us."

"You can shut your mouth hole, Ses."

"Don't talk to her like that."

"I'm working for you, Roz, that's who I'm working for. I don't know anything about your societies and orders and churches that you bring from England. I'm trying to make a quid—unlike Ses here who's in league with others."

"I am not. I'm..."

"Quiet, the both of you. We'll have no discord on my airship. Now, Cecilia, explain yourself."

"There's little to explain. Yes, I knew of the Green Wave and its connection to this Aqua Glass. The board of the Society sent me but didn't want to make their plans known. It's why they sent no large expedition, no airship, and it's one of the reasons I was able to go instead of them replacing the geologist with another man. It was thought sending a woman would arouse less suspicion."

"Who would be suspicious?" asked Fey.

"Anyone else seeking the Green Wave. If that Aqua Glass exists here it could be used for all sorts of artful and scientific devices, and not all of them for the common good."

"Do you mean the Divine Order of Mechanics?"

"Yes, Rosalyn, they are the first of our rivals who come to mind, but there may be others."

"Others?"

"Foreign governments."

"That does sound credible. It was someone of a foreign government who stole a quantity of blue ascension and destroyed Britain's hopes for atmotic supremacy," said Rosalyn.

"I have to get my brain box outside this. This Green Wave lives on a flower which grows in areas where Aqua Glass is found, but the Green Wave may not even exist?"

"If Doctor Phatts was lying or hallucinating then perhaps it doesn't exist, however his description of the insect matches perfectly that of Captain Hivetree's."

"And it was Phatts' message set all these cogs turning?"

"Yes," said Cecilia. "The message was sent before the book was published. Doctor Phatts would not have read the different accounts of Captain Hivetree and therefore couldn't have been copying him. When the message was received and made public it didn't take long for interested people to discern the parallels between the two descriptions of the butterfly."

"Cecilia," said Rosalyn, "we're not your enemies. I hope in future you'll be more forthcoming."

"I'm sorry, I had to be careful. I couldn't know for sure if you were working for the Mechanics. Fey I don't know at all."

"I'm on the square, Ses, but I'm still not sure if you are."

"Fey, leave it! Take a turn at the helm."

Lost in their own thoughts they continued on. After dark, Cecilia, who'd been observing the stars through the telescope, brought Rosalyn's attention to a strange anomaly in the night sky on their port side. "Look, the stars down near the horizon keep disappearing, and there are some bright stars that seem to be moving. It's most odd. It's an astronomical anomaly and it's keeping pace with us."

"I'm not so sure that's anything to do with astronomy, Cecilia. Is the area where the stars disappear above the moving stars?"

"Why, yes it is. Rosalyn, how did you know that?"

"Because the astronomical anomaly is another airship."

"Oh dear. It's the wretched Divine Order of Mechanics, isn't it?"

"I would assume so. Douse the lights. Fey, take us down and change heading to the north—and Cecilia—good work. Keep watching the anomaly and tell me what it does."

Fey guided the airship down, trying to fly as best she could while peering over the side, attempting to discern the elements of the landscape below. Cecilia remained on watch and reported that the other airship had appeared to remain on its course but she had now lost sight of it.

Rosalyn stared out into the darkness. "Continue on this course, Fey, and stay close to the ground. We need to hide against the background lest they see our own silhouette. They may have been shadowing us for some time, waiting for the dawn."

Close to midnight, as Fey handed over the wheel to Rosalyn, the tranquility of the flight ended abruptly. The *Lightning* connected with something solid, the boat bucked upwards sharply and wood splintered and cracked. Cecilia, asleep in the bow, woke with a loud scream. The mast snapped and Fey and Rosalyn were flung backwards, the side nets preventing them from being flung overboard.

A screech of metal, a hiss of steam and the strong smell of blue aether filled the air as the copper transit pipe came away from its engine mount. The airship dragged past whatever it had hit and bounced up from the obstruction. The propeller still turned but the balloon was coming adrift. The *Lightning* spun around through 360 degrees, bow down, in a rapid descent. They hit the ground with a thud and the airship settled to the sound of escaping steam.

"Is everyone all right?" asked Rosalyn from the darkness.

"All my bits are where they should be," replied Fey.

"Cecilia, are you safe?" Rosalyn listened. "Cecilia?" She spoke into the darkness but no reply came. "Fey, we need to find the lantern or a candle."

Fey fumbled around, found the storage compartment with the candles and passed one to Rosalyn. They lit them from the coal brick that still burned in the furnace, the light from its doorway illuminating the debris in the rear of the boat. Dust and smoke filled the air and it mixed with blue aether escaping from the balloon. The balloon itself had come down next to the boat, still tethered to it by the cover net and ropes. Rosalyn held up her candle and moved to the front of the boat while Fey shut down the engine.

"Fey?" Fey looked over to where Rosalyn stood. In the candlelight she could see the bow of the boat was missing. The planks had shattered and the forward section of the keel, while still present, had been smashed and twisted. Cecilia was nowhere to be seen. The two women walked around the wreckage, searching by candlelight for their missing friend, calling out into the darkness.

"Where could she have got to?"

"I dunno, Roz. I have a horrible feeling about it." Fey held the candle up. "Roz, your head."

"What is it?"

"You've got a nasty gash and you're bleeding. Can't you feel it?"

Rosalyn put her hand to her brow and looked at her blood covered fingers. She turned ash white and collapsed on the sand.

Fey did her best to bathe and dress Rosalyn's wound and sat for a good part of the night with Rosalyn's head pillowed in her lap, stroking her cheeks and hair soothingly whenever she stirred. The sand was soft and warm and Fey lay back exhausted. Some time deep inside the night she fell asleep.

16

THE CIRCLE

Rosalyn opened her eyes and lay still, wondering where she was. Her head was throbbing and a strange woman looked down at her.

"Good morning, Roz. Did you sleep well?"

"Fey?"

"Yeah, it's me, Fey. Can you see?"

Rosalyn blinked a few times and nodded. "What happened?"

"We crashed."

"Crashed?" Rosalyn looked up at Fey. Her memory of the event returned and she sat up, leaving the comfort of Fey's lap. "Cecilia. We have to find her."

"Yeah, we do. I wanted to make sure you were all right first."

"My head hurts but I'm fine otherwise."

"Let me help you up." Fey stood and extended her hand. Rosalyn gripped it firmly and pulled herself to her feet. She looked around. They were in the centre of a circle of massive, grey columns which stood out starkly from the red sand. Huge lintels bridged the uprights and in places some of the stones had fallen, breaking the circle. No breeze was blowing and although the sun had only just risen the day was already hot. Rosalyn looked about in awe at the size of the structure.

"Impressive, isn't it?"

Rosalyn nodded. "It's so quiet, too."

As if on cue a faint moaning came to them and their eyes were drawn to the top of a lintel. A piece of Cecilia's crimson dress draped over the edge of the stone.

"Cecilia!" Rosalyn shouted.

"She's hurt. I'll have to get up there."

"How?"

Fey studied the situation. One of the fallen columns had come to rest against the column that supported Cecilia. "I'll climb up that."

"You still won't be able to reach the top. Fey, it's too dangerous."

"Look, I can use what's left of the mast as a ladder and take rope up with me. I'll lower Ses down and climb down after. We'll need the pilot's harness too." Rosalyn thought about Fey's proposed plan and looking around and not seeing another skerrick of timber anywhere, acquiesced. Fey gathered the tools together and managed to unbolt the top of the mast from the fitting. Together they hauled the mast over to the broken stones. Rosalyn went back for the pilot's harness while Fey dragged the timber up and wedged it in place. With no thought other than to reach her fallen companion, Fey climbed up the mast and onto the flat top of the stone lintel. Cecilia lay groaning to herself, her eyes were closed and dried blood caked her forehead. Around and over her were the splintered timbers of the bow of the *Lightning*.

"Don't you worry, Ses, I'll have you down in a flash. We'll get you looked after no worries—you'll be right." Rosalyn threw her the pilot's harness and Fey strapped Cecilia into it, double checking the engagement of the buckles. With the free end of the rope wrapped tightly around herself, Fey eased Cecilia over the edge of the stone. She played the rope out slowly, perspiration running down her face from the exertion in the hot morning sun. Rosalyn reached up and eased Cecilia down onto the broken stones. Fey climbed back down the mast and together they dragged Cecilia onto the soft sand under the shade of the column. "How is she Roz? Is she going to live?"

"I think so. Fetch me some water." Fey returned with a water bottle and using a piece of cloth torn from Cecilia's petticoat, Rosalyn bathed her forehead. They tilted her head up and trickled some water onto her mouth and were relieved to see Cecilia respond, her tongue searching out the water. Under the tender care of her friends, Cecilia blinked back into consciousness.

"I've got an awful headache." She sat up and held the wet cloth to her temple. "What did we hit?"

"These stones. You're fine. I don't think you have any broken bones, although you're quite bruised and have a few cuts." Rosalyn knelt beside her showing every bit of concern.

"You're injured, too." Cecilia raised a feeble hand to Rosalyn's forehead.

"Yes, I'm afraid we both took a bit of damage."

"The airship?"

"Don't know yet, Ses," said Fey. "The boat is a bit crook and we lost the mast. The transit pipe has come adrift, the bow is firewood and I think the propeller has had it. Nothing too serious though. I'll go and see what I can salvage. You two best rest up for a bit and nurse each other's heads." Fey stood and walked away. Rosalyn watched her as she went.

"She's quite a different kind of woman, isn't she?"

Rosalyn realised that Cecilia had been observing her and turned her attention away from Fey. "Yes, she is. Quite capable. I suppose it comes from the hard life in the colony."

"Yes, I suppose it could be that." Cecilia was still staring at her. "You like her don't you?"

"She can be abrasive and her manner is a trifle uncouth but she's all right. Yes, I suppose I like her."

"I can see that you do."

"You should make more of an effort to like her, too."

"My meaning escaped you."

"You're still a bit dizzy from the injury, I think." Rosalyn dabbed at Cecilia's forehead with the cloth, a little too hard and too quickly.

"You've taken a nasty bump. Your senses haven't yet fully returned. Have you noticed your surroundings?"

Cecilia looked around at the stones. "I see, yes. It looks like Stonehenge, but wider and higher." She strained to sit up a bit more but finding the effort to be too much, slumped down again.

"Please Cecilia, you must rest." Cecilia sat back against the stone. It was only marginally cooler than the air around them.

Fey returned. "We only have the one bag of water. It will do us for a day if we're careful but we need more. There's some left in the boiler too, so we'll have to take that."

"Take it?" asked Rosalyn. "Take it where?"

"Well we can't stay here forever. We'll perish."

"Can the airship be fixed?"

"It can. We need some wood for the mast. We could put netting across the bow. I'm not sure if the propeller can be fixed. I think the shaft twisted when it was churning dirt and that's what was making the screeching noise. The engine wasn't damaged. The transit pipe can be put back in position if I can find something to bind it with. The side sails will need some work, and we'll need more water."

"If we can get the mast fixed and the transit pipe back in place then the loss of the propulsion from the propeller won't be such a heavy cross to bear. I can sail her by the wind to find somewhere more hospitable."

"We might see something from the tops of the stones. Do we still have the telescope?"

"Afraid not, Roz. The thing is bent and the main lens smashed. We'll have to rely on the power of our daylights."

After ensuring Cecilia was comfortable, they climbed up onto the lintel and looked out to the east from whence they'd come. It was all deep blue sky, red sand, faded, olive-coloured bushes and dried tufts of grass. They walked around to the south side of the circle and stared into the landscape.

"Do you see that, Fey?"

"Yeah. Another avenue, a long one. It disappears into the desert down there."

They stood looking at it. "The other avenue, the one at the chamber of the lizard, it ran east-west. This runs north-south. Do you suppose something worthwhile might lie at the lines of intersection?

"I wouldn't know, Roz. My clever interests lie in knowing what ships are arriving in Sydney and when. I make my tin from passengers like you. I don't know anything about stone avenues, but what you're putting out rubs together well. Something might be there."

Cecilia shifted her position to examine the stone against which she was leaning, wondering at its size and how it might have been shaped and moved into position. The stone was smooth to the touch, worn away by years of wind and sand. A rough patch under her palm gave her cause to make further enquiry and on closer examination she could see two inscribed letters and a date. She smiled to herself, glanced around and saw her companions engrossed in the sight of some distant feature.

Kneeling now, Cecilia scooped away the sand under the inscription and with but a little digging was rewarded by the find of a small bottle sealed with wax and a glass stopper. Looking once more to her companions to ensure she wasn't under their gaze, she held the bottle up to the light. Inside, through the green glass, she could see a rolled up piece of paper. She didn't attempt to take the paper from the bottle, instead slipping the vessel under her skirts, securing it away from view. With the precaution taken of filling the hole in the sand she sat back and waited.

Fey and Rosalyn continued walking around the lintels of the circle until the fallen stones interrupted their circumnavigation. Nothing further of interest could be seen apart from what appeared to be a range of blue hills at some far distance to the west. They returned to Cecilia. After telling her about the southern avenue she agreed there might be something at the intersection if the avenues met.

"I found something myself while you were gone." Cecilia moved aside to reveal the initials 'N P' pecked into the rock with the year

'1836'. "He was here."

Rosalyn crouched to inspect the inscription. "1836? That's only two years ago. He was here perhaps a whole year after he sent his message. If he was able to survive out here for such a length of time then it may be he's still out here somewhere,"

"It's still a big haystack. We have little chance of finding him."

"That's the spirit, Ses. Your optimism is fair contagious."

Rosalyn stared at the inscription. "I have a thought, perhaps he left something here, buried."

"Why would he do that?"

"Perhaps he carved his initials and the date to draw attention to his having been present. He may have left a more detailed account for those who follow. Let's dig."

"That's a clever thought, Rosalyn. I'll help."

"You two fill your boots. I'll watch."

Rosalyn knelt down next to Cecilia and together they scooped out a large hole in the sand but found nothing. "Dash it all. I felt sure we'd find something."

Cecilia lay back against the stone. "I don't care. My head hurts, we're out in this awful desert, our airship is broken, we're running out of water and you're still thinking of finding someone who could be anywhere. It's time for you to go home."

"For me to go home?"

"For us, I mean."

"Then you better start walking. If you head east and walk fast you might get there by Christmas," said Fey.

"Stop it. The two of you, just stop." Rosalyn stamped her foot for emphasis and sent up a cloud of dust. "Cecilia, we can't go home. And Fey, stop baiting her. We have a long way to travel yet and if we bicker it will ruin us."

Fey looked at her and then at Cecilia. "Yeah, you're right, we have to hold ourselves together. Sorry, Ses, and you too, Roz. I'll try and keep my tongue in. And Ses, we'll get out of this." Fey returned to the shattered airship and studied how it might be made fit to fly.

Rosalyn followed her over. "Can we fix it?"

Fey shrugged. "The mast snapped and the only section of length is split. The propeller shaft I don't know. I suppose we could take it out and try to hammer it straight. It's going to take a couple of days at least even if we could. We really do need a mast. Both pairs of forward and aft 'V' struts are broken, too." Fey lowered her voice. "I don't need to tell you how much of a fix we're in, Roz. We only have a day or two of water and the food is low. We can't stay here and if we go out there and can't find water, we're done."

Rosalyn looked at her. "We're not done. The Church sent me on a Mission and I will do it. We must have faith. We're going to have to try searching. We can either follow the direction of that avenue south in the hope we find something, or we can head west to those blue hills and pray we find water there."

"Neither is a solid proposition. The hills may be two days away at least and I don't know how far northwest we came from the line of the east-west avenue. That central point may be a week's walk away and we don't even know if there's anything there."

"We'll head west. There's nothing else for it. It has to be west." They walked back over to where Cecilia was still nursing her head and told her of their decision.

"I've been thinking," said Cecilia. "Whoever made this circle must have had quite a large workforce and those labourers would have needed water."

"You're quite right, Ses. These stones though, they're ancient—and look at how dry the desert here is. There might have been water here once but there isn't now. There isn't even anywhere hereabouts where water might be stored or gathered. I reckon they brought it in here with them."

"I think you're wrong," said Cecilia. "Many ancient cultures stored their water underground, in cisterns, just as we still do now." Fey and Rosalyn looked at each other and then back at Cecilia. "It's true. I may be a bug catcher but I have interests in other areas as well. I've read many travellers' accounts."

"Cecilia where would we start looking for such a thing? There is so much ground to explore."

"We could be wasting time. If we don't find water here we'll have wasted what we do have."

"I'm not going out into that beast-filled desert. I have a frightful headache and these shoes are not made for long walks in hot sand."

Fey sighed and picked up a piece of broken planking. She knelt down and started digging through the sand. Rosalyn joined her and soon they were hard at work, sand flying everywhere. After much exertion they'd managed to dig a hole about four feet deep and twice as wide but they were still no closer to finding Cecilia's cistern.

Sitting back and mopping the sweat from their brows they heard a loud, "psst!" from behind them. Cecilia sat, smiling, on one of the broken rocks. "Over here." Puzzled, the two diggers walked over. Cecilia stood up and led them around to the outside of the circle to a gap in the fallen stones. "We can find water in there."

"How on earth do you know that, Cecilia?"

"You can learn a lot from the flight of birds. I was watching as a pretty little finch flew into the rocks here. I thought it may have been chasing an insect but then I realised it couldn't have been after an insect and must have been after something else—water."

"How do you know it wasn't after an insect?"

"Finches don't normally eat insects, they eat seeds. And look here." Cecilia pointed out the numerous tracks where a variety of small marsupials and reptiles had gone into the same area of rock.

"Well done, Ses. I forgive you completely for the loss of my tile." Fey stooped down onto her hands and knees and peered amongst the broken stones. "There's a hole here all right, a little on the squeezy side, but I can make it bigger. Roz, I'll need that bit of plank."

Fey sent up a shower of sand as she dug. Sweat ran in trickles down her face and satisfied with her work she crawled out and sat back. "That should do it, and I bloody well hope there's water in there. After that effort I'll need a gallon of the stuff."

Rosalyn tried peering into the darkness. "I'll need the lantern."

"No lantern love, it was smashed. I'll get candles."

Light in hand, Rosalyn wriggled forward through the passage, removing more sand as she went. Fey and Cecilia, waiting anxiously at the entrance, heard a cry and then a splash. "Roz? What happened? Are you all right in there?"

Rosalyn's voice came up to them. "Yes. I'm fine. I fell in. I'll need another candle and please hurry, it's dark in here and I can hear things moving."

Fey, with more caution, wriggled in through the hole. The sand dropped away sharply in a steep bank and in the dim light Fey saw Rosalyn standing thigh deep in water at the bottom. "Cecilia, I'll need a rope." She wriggled back out. Cecilia returned and Fey tied the rope around one of the broken stones. She squirmed into the hole, letting the end of the rope drop down the bank. Fey slid down to where Rosalyn was standing and passed her a candle.

Fey lit their candles and holding them aloft they peered into the gloom. Columns, arranged in concentric circles, rose up out of the water to support stone lintels. The walls for the most part were constructed of stone blocks. In places the bedrock had been carved back, giving what must have been a natural cavern a circular shape. One section of the wall had collapsed bringing in sand from the outside and it was through this collapsed section that Rosalyn and Fey had entered the chamber.

Fey scooped up a palm-full of water and tasted it. "It's fresh. I'm going to kiss that bloody girl when we go back up."

Before climbing back out into the daylight the women followed the wall of the cistern around, finding at one point a set of stairs which led to the surface. A stone slab blocked egress and they continued back to their starting point. Rosalyn crawled back up. "Look out, Cecilia; Fey is going to kiss you."

"What?"

Fey emerged from the hole and grabbed Cecilia around the waist, bending her backwards and knocking the bonnet off her head in the process. Her long blonde hair fell loose. "Fey, no!" Cecilia squealed and struggled. Fey managed to land a kiss on her cheek as Rosalyn watched, laughing.

"That's for the water." Fey let the protesting Cecilia go. "I'll get the water bags, Ses, you rest your pretty head."

"You're a monster." Cecilia turned to Rosalyn and smiled. "Don't worry; I'm sure you'll be next."

"Next? I don't want to be next."

"I'm sure you don't. Why would you want to be embraced by that uncouth colonial? She's quite beneath us." Cecilia gave Rosalyn a wink and walked away.

17

The Meeting Place

Sitting back in the shade of the stones the group tried to decide their next move. "I think now that we have water we should head south."

"Sounds like a plan to me, Roz. Not a good one but the best we've got."

"I still don't know how I'd be able to keep up with you. I really can't walk in these," said Cecilia.

"I'm quite clueless as to why you didn't bring a set of walking boots with you."

"I had in mind to buy something more suitable in Sydney, but we did rush off a bit didn't we?"

"I could try to make you a pair," said Fey.

"Thank you for your kind offer but I think I'll stay here." Rosalyn and Fey looked at her as though she'd taken too much sun. "Well? I have an abundant supply of water and the food on the Lightning will sustain me. You go and find a tree trunk and some branches, fix the airship and we'll be off."

"Just like that, hmm?"

"Yes, just like that. You'll have the airship compass to find your way there and back."

"We'll travel faster without you, I give you that. Much as your company can be oppressive I don't like the idea of leaving you behind, Ses."

"Cecilia is right, she has to stay. We can carry enough water to go out for two days. If we don't find suitable trees we come back and then try in another direction. Cecilia, if we don't come back after the fifth day you'll have to suppose we've perished and come to your own decision."

"Wait, let's not be rash here. If we go and the blacks turn up we might come back to find Ses holding the wrong end of a spear."

Rosalyn thought about it. "She can keep the carbine. We'll take the pistol and the axe."

"I'll be able to manage here. We need to get the airship aloft and continue our search for Doctor Phatts and the Green Wave. It's all right, Fey, I'm sure I'll cope without you. I'll spend my time catching bugs."

"Yeah, I think you're more capable than you present." Fey gave her a knowing smile.

"Whatever do you mean?"

"You may act the London princess, yet you somehow manage to shape up solid when things go adrift."

"I'll take that as a compliment, although you present it as a suspicion."

"Will you two stop it? I don't know what it is with you but I wish I'd left you both in Sydney. Now, Cecilia, keep the carbine loaded and with you at all times, especially when you go down into the cistern. You don't know what unpleasant surprises you might find when you come out again. I'd hate for you to be a giant lizard's breakfast."

Cecilia, who had forgotten all about the giant lizard, clutched at her skirts. Her voice trembled as she said, "Very well, I'll take the carbine, although I've seen no sign of any big lizards around here. I'll hide in the cistern if one comes. It wouldn't be able to fit through that little hole." She took a deep breath and added more conviction to her voice. "Honestly, I'll be perfectly fine."

Fey stared at her and nodded, "Yep, you'll manage if danger fronts." In the situation little else could be done. They gathered what they needed, including the ship's compass from the wheel housing. Cecilia bade them wait, went to her chest in the boat and removed a petticoat, hiding the little bottle at the same time. She cut the fabric into large rectangles so her companions might cover their heads and faces against the sun in the manner of the Arabs.

The heat haze shimmered above the stones of the avenue. Rosalyn paused and turned to wave goodbye to Cecilia before hastening after Fey to follow wherever the avenue might lead them. Some of the stones were completely buried in the sand and others showed only their topmost parts. Rosalyn measured fifteen paces between them but after about a mile or so they couldn't be certain as to whether the avenue had stopped or had been swallowed up by the sand. They looked back periodically to see the stones of the great circle jutting up from the desert against the backdrop of the cloudless blue sky.

"Look at them, Roz. Nothing around for miles in any direction and I have to go and fly into them. Talk about bad bloody luck."

"It was hardly your fault, Fey. I directed you to fly low in the dark. Cecilia has to sleep sometime and we were both at the wheel."

"Yeah, you're right, Roz. It was your fault."

Rosalyn gave Fey a slap on the shoulder. "Beast."

Fey smiled. "It wasn't anyone's fault, Roz. Nature of the game."

"God's game. If we hadn't crashed into those stones we never would have found them and Cecilia would never have been injured."

"So what?"

"So if Cecilia hadn't been injured she wouldn't have been resting where she saw Doctor Phatts initials and date. Now we know we're still on his path."

"And two years behind him."

The women fell into silence as they trudged on, the only sound being that of their feet in the sand. The water bags seemed to be heavier and the sun hotter with every step. Most of the vegetation consisted of large tufts of dry grass. Occasionally a stunted tree or patch of scrub broke up the visual monotony. A large flock of emus appeared in the distance but with only the pistol no energy was wasted in trying to hunt one. A large, orange kangaroo jumped up from the grass clumps close by and thumped off into the desert. It happened so quickly they didn't have time to fire off a shot at it. By evening, physically worn out, they lay together in a hollow amongst the grass tufts. Sleep didn't come readily and together they stared at the bright stars of the southern sky.

"It's magical, isn't it?" said Fey.

"The universe works like clockwork. Our God created all of this and gave it to us to work out for ourselves."

"I hope I'm not about to get a sermon."

Rosalyn smiled. "No, I'm not going to give you a sermon. I'll let you look at the stars in peace."

"Anyway, if it works like clockwork how did that thing happen all that time ago?"

"The thing?"

"Yeah, that thing—when the planet started rotating the other way."

"Oh, you mean the Ante Vidoram?"

"I dunno. What's that in English?"

"I think you're referring to the Temporal Displacement Setback. The Church calls it the Ante Vidoram which means something like, 'seen before'. It had nothing to do with the planet running the other way."

"Yeah, tell me about that. I like to hear you talk and I've always had a notion to learn more about that thing."

"The Church taught us all about it. We have to know it as part of our Understandings. Some time back, in the early seventeenth century, time reset itself."

"How did it do that?"

"I don't know. No one knows how, but we do know for how long. It was set back by exactly two minutes and eleven seconds."

"And how do we know that?"

"Because a German clockmaker, setting his clocks at the time, said they all showed they had been set back for that exact amount of time."

"What makes this Anne Viddy thing so important if it was only for two minutes?"

"Ante Vidoram. I'll tell you why and I'll use the example of Joshua Quinn as an example. He is one of the more important figures to emerge from the Setback. Joshua Quinn was hanged. We don't know what for but we are told he was hanged. A minute after he was hanged the Setback occurred and he was back up on the scaffold about to be hanged again. He pleaded for his life, claiming that as he'd already been hanged the sentence had been carried out and he should be allowed to go free. The attending priest was inclined to agree and asked the crowd if they too had seen Joshua hanged dead. The crowd said they had, so the priest claimed it was God's will and Joshua walked free."

"So what?"

"This wasn't the only known case. There were two men fighting a duel in which one was killed. The Setback happened and the dead man was alive again, the shots yet to be fired. He conceded the other had made his point fairly, apologised to his opponent and they didn't fight the duel again. Another case was of a battle being fought and when the reset happened the soldiers recoiled in confusion. The commanders lost control and so they withdrew their armies from battle."

"I still don't see the point."

"The point is that if the Ante Vidoram had not occurred then Joshua Quinn would have been hanged, the man in the duel would have been killed and that battle would have had a different outcome. We know Joshua Quinn went on to become quite a wealthy businessman and raised a large family. There are so many people alive today who would not have existed if the Setback hadn't occurred."

"So it changed history then? Is that what you're saying?"

"Yes but we don't know exactly by how much. There is a field of science devoted to the study of the Temporal Displacement Setback called temporology. Some temporologists travel the world to find other peoples to learn what stories or tales they may have of the Setback. There are records of it in China and India."

"I don't get it. If everything was set back two minutes how come people at the time remembered the events that happened in the future." Fey pondered as she stared at the stars. "Or is it that they didn't occur? Because if they... This is making my head spin."

Rosalyn laughed. "It is hard to understand. Philosophical Temporology concerns itself with just that point. If Joshua was hanged then how could he walk free? That means he wasn't hanged, and yet he was. As for memories, the memories were not affected. Whatever caused the Setback didn't have any effect on the human mind. This is taken as proof of the existence of the Divine Creator."

"How so?"

"We think God created the universe but when humans were created we were given free will. When God caused the Setback it had no effect on our minds because they were our own and beyond God's reach. It's how our Deity created us."

"So how would this have had much of an effect on future history? So what if a few people lived who wouldn't have. Things couldn't change that much could they?"

"That is what temporologists study—how much change has occurred. They trace the lives and descendants of people who were affected by the Setback. They found that the Mysterious Captain Hivetree is a direct descendant of Joshua Quinn. If we hadn't had the Setback we wouldn't have airships." Rosalyn let that sink in before continuing. "The man who fought the duel, he went on to fight another duel and killed his opponent. That opponent was about to marry. Apparently the duel was fought over the woman.

The point is that if the man had lived he would have married and had children. A whole line of people no longer exist who would have."

"Yeah. I see what you're pointing at. This Setback, it started a chain of events."

"Yes, like throwing a stone in a pond, as the ripples travel outwards they grow bigger."

"But the Setback itself, how could it have happened if the universe is God's perfect creation like you preachers say?" Fey sat up, took out her pipe and lit it. Rosalyn coughed, waving away the smoke before continuing her explanation.

"It wasn't only the dawning of the age of Enlightenment that caused the schism between the churches. The Setback was seen by some as evidence of an imperfect universe, a flaw in the divine creation." Rosalyn coughed again. "Think of God as a clockmaker but the clock gains a little time over the centuries. When it was two minutes and eleven seconds ahead the clockmaker reset it."

Fey's pipe went out and she relit it. "That would mean there may have been other setbacks."

"Yes. We think there may have been others in the distant past. Julius Caesar writes of a peculiar event in his De Bello Britannica which temporologists believe refers to a Setback event."

Fey picked up a handful of sand and let it pour through her fingers. "And this Hivetree bloke, why is he so mysterious?"

"It's not that he's mysterious as such. It's a title. Anyone known to be descended from a line which exists only because of the Ante Vidoram is given the title, 'Mysterious'." Rosalyn paused. "Although, upon reflection, with the Mysterious Captain Hivetree it could be said he really is mysterious. No one knows his location. He once lived in a country house in Wiltshire. Around the time the first airship flew, he disappeared."

"So he's some kind of religious feller?"

"No. The title has nothing to do with religion, however there's a sect which venerates those descended from the setback, believing them to be God's chosen. Another sect believes the opposite, that they are children of the Devil."

Fey sighed and shook her head. "I'm glad you told me all this Roz, it's put me close to sleep." She lay down and closed her eyes. Rosalyn watched the stars until the night grew colder, and snuggled up against Fey for warmth.

Regular checking of the compass ensured they didn't veer off their course. Heads bowed with fatigue, they trudged onward. Small birds, frightened from the grasses by their passage, were the only break from the monotony of their journey. The sky was a perfect blue dome without a single cloud. Towards the end of the day the sight of the avenue stones protruding above the surface of the sand boosted their morale. Sitting exhausted on one such stone, sweat dripping from their dust-covered faces and sipping water, Rosalyn happened to glance up. Her eyes opened wide and she tugged at Fey's sleeve. "Fey."

Fey looked at Rosalyn and followed her gaze. In their fatigue they'd come to rest at the top of an escarpment that formed the bank of what must have once been a lake. The avenue narrowed here and continued across the dry floor of the lakebed. The stones still standing were much taller than the ones in the avenue. A jumble of other stones lay around them and across the avenue, many of them buried with only portions protruding from the dry lake floor. The avenue stretched across the lake drawing their eyes to the further side.

"Do you see that, Fey?"

"Yeah. Looks like buildings."

A shower of dust and stones accompanied the women's scramble down the escarpment. Finding the fallen stones on the lake floor an impediment to easy movement they walked off to one side. "Fey, I think this was a causeway or a bridge. These fallen stones here are lintels." Rosalyn stopped to stare at them. "But look, there can't be enough lintels here to make a complete bridge. They must have used timber which has since rotted away."

Fey looked around. "They must have used all of it. There's not a useful tree for bloody miles now."

"This must be thousands of years old, perhaps tens of thousands."

"It's fascinating and all but we have to find a mast for the Lightning."

"Yes, quite."

The bank was less pronounced on the furthest shore and climbing up it they came to the buildings they had seen from a distance. They found themselves standing in front of a ruined gateway to what had once been an ancient town. Many of the remains were mere outlines of stones, mounds of sand showing where buildings had once been. Columns of rock, some intact, and some broken, stood amongst the scattered, crumbling buildings. "This is most extraordinary."

"It's something isn't it? I still can't see any trees. Maybe we can find some water. There could be one of Ses's cisterns here somewhere."

They walked down what must have once been a main thoroughfare, noticing the circular floor plans of the buildings. The doorway of the first one they came to had a low stone lintel, forcing them to stoop under it to enter. Broken stones from the collapsed roof covered the floor, all of it carpeted by a layer of sand. Large stone slab walls, set on their edges, were decorated with relief carvings in the same style as those they'd seen in the lizard chamber days earlier. The mural played out across the walls in a haphazard way, without borders. Rosalyn leaned forward and blew onto one of the carvings, sending the dust into clouds. "I can't make out what these patterns are. They look like an incoherent arrangement of people and animals."

"I'd marvel with you but we have to keep going. I don't think there's anything here that can help us, Roz. Let's try the next one." They meandered on into the next building and found it was much the same. Fey examined a jumble of fallen stones and sand, tracing her finger along a line at the top of a large stone block. "Roz—this block isn't solid. This is a lid of some sort." Together they cleared the top of sand and debris and Fey, bracing herself against a wall, pushed the lid a short way across the stone. Expecting to see the bottom of the stone container they instead found themselves peering down into darkness. "Is that a cistern?" asked Fey.

Rosalyn dropped a rock in. It took longer than expected to reach the bottom and landed with a splash. "We need a light."

"I've only got my matches. Did you bring candles?"

"No. It wasn't dark when we left."

"It will be dark soon. Roz, we're not short of water, not yet. Let's leave it and make camp."

After clearing a space between the stones in the interior of the building they settled in to eat a meagre meal of dried meat and raisins. Rosalyn leaned back against the wall, writing in her journal, while Fey sat outside with her pipe waiting for the sun to set. For some time Fey stared out across the ruins, taking in the details. A peculiarity caught her eye. At the far side of the ruins there appeared to be a dead tree. She was sure it hadn't been there before. As she watched it the 'dead tree' sank to the ground. Fey tapped out her pipe against the stone and quietly walked back in to where Rosalyn sat writing. She took out the pistol and loaded it.

"What is it?" asked Rosalyn, alarmed.

"There's something out there. Something big. I think it's one of them lizards."

"Are we safe here?"

"I don't think so. Maybe. If it's a lizard it won't be hunting during the night. We'll bed down here. If we get into that crawl space there where those stones are forming a lean-to against the wall we'll be safe enough." The space, not quite cramped but cosy, forced them to lie huddled closely. Rosalyn lay her head on Fey's shoulder and draped an arm over her. Fey impulsively kissed Rosalyn's forehead. Rosalyn, exhausted from the day's walk, barely noticed and was soon asleep.

Rosalyn looked up from her bed on the sandy floor to see the early morning light shining through the doorway, illuminating the rear wall. Centred in that warm glow was the shadow of Fey, standing with pistol in hand. Rosalyn crawled out and Fey turned to the sound. "Good morning, Roz. Sleep well?"

"Yes." She stretched her arms, standing up on her toes. "I'm a bit sore and cramped."

"We should get moving. We've been two nights away now. What say we give it another half day and head back. Cecilia will be all dizzy with fear if we're late."

Rosalyn nodded. "I dare say she would be. She'll be fascinated when we tell her of these ruins. I think we should finish exploring them rather than head back immediately."

"I don't think we're going to find anything in the way of a mast but we might find something useful to us, and Roz, stay close."

The advice was driven home by the presence of the tracks of a giant lizard. They stopped and studied them in silence. Continuing on they came to the remains of a large building. The walls, much reduced, were still high in parts and like the other buildings had a circular floor plan. Around the base of the walls, and mostly covered by the debris of the fallen roof, were large hollow cylindrical stones. Some of these had lids while others the lids, and even the containers themselves, had been smashed by the falling roof.

The open containers were filled with sand, and thinking they might find something of more interest in one with a lid intact they opened one up. Rosalyn recoiled with fright. Inside were the bones of some long perished individual, the skull facing upwards on top of a tangle of bones. On the skull was a band of shining gold and set in the centre of it was a clear quartz crystal. As Fey reached in to pick it up Rosalyn yanked her hand back.

"What are you doing?"

"Getting rich. What are you doing?"

"Stopping you."

"Why are you stopping me from getting rich? I'll share it with you of course."

"It's not that. This is a grave and you're taking from it. It's grave robbery"

Fey withdrew her hand. "I didn't look at it like that. Looked to me like that were just a pile of bones in a stone." She looked around the rest of the building. "So this is a cemetery?"

"More of a crypt, I think."

"Yeah, that's what I meant. Do you see that crystal on the gold there?"

"Yes, it looks like a common quartz crystal."

"You don't think it's that Aqua Glass stuff."

"I wouldn't think so. It's not aqua."

"That's a bit disappointing. I thought we'd cracked it."

Rosalyn gave her a brief smile. "It's not going to be easy. We're in a bit of a pickle." They didn't waste time looking into the remainder of the stone coffins and continued their search of the ruins. Tracks of giant lizards criss-crossed the sand in the south end of the city and they swung their search up and around through the west side.

"Fey, over here." Fey wandered to where Rosalyn stood. In the sand, human footprints could clearly be seen; not of a barefoot black, but of someone wearing boots. Fey signalled with her finger to be quiet and they followed the footprints into a building, to a pile of rubble against a wall.

Fey raised the pistol. "Come out. We know you're in there."

"Don't shoot! Don't shoot!" A man emerged waving a dusty white handkerchief. He was unshaven, his clothes dustier than his hanky. Over his shoulder he carried a battered leather satchel.

"Doctor Phatts, I presume."

The man turned to Rosalyn. "Doctor Phatts? Oh no, I'm not Doctor Phatts, I'm Doctor Gilroy, Watson Gilroy."

"Really?" said Fey. "It's no great wonder I couldn't get a bloody doctor when I come down crook in Sydney. They're all out here roaming around the desert."

"I'm not that sort of doctor." The man looked at Fey's pistol. "Do you mind putting that away. You're making me terribly nervous." Fey lowered the pistol and the man turned his attention back to Rosalyn. "You must be the Reverend Missionary Rosalyn Flynn. I'm pleased to make your acquaintance."

"How do you know who I am?"

"We were looking for you. That is, they were. I wasn't really looking for you. I was looking for rocks."

"Doctor Gilroy, who was looking for me?"

"The Order, the Divine Order of Mechanics—the Mechanical Order. Surely you saw the red airship. You passed over us in daylight and again before that horrible dust storm. I thought you were them coming back for me."

"Why are they looking for me?"

"To kill you of course."

"What? Kill me? Why would they want to kill me? I know about the butterfly and the Aqua Glass but I'd hardly think that's a reason for my assassination."

"And the Mechanical Order knows you know and the Order does not want competition. It means to find the Aqua Glass and take everything for itself."

"What are you doing here if you're with them?"

The doctor mopped his brow with the handkerchief. "I was invited to come along on an expedition with them to the interior. They told me it was a scientific expedition. I only found out the true nature after we were aloft. I'm a geologist you see. I couldn't pass up such a chance. And then I found they were after this ridiculous Aqua Glass. Later still, when you flew overhead, is when I overheard them discussing plans for your demise."

"You still haven't explained what you're doing here. How is it you're not in their airship with them?"

"Yes, well. I didn't like the scoundrels. We felt quite unsafe with them. Then when the lizards attacked I was separated from them and departed the area in a hasty fashion. I found this place and have been hiding here for the last two nights." He paused. "I don't suppose you have anything to eat do you? I haven't eaten since yesterday morning."

"Back up a little, Doc. When the lizards attacked?" Fey asked.

"Yes. You've seen them haven't you? You must have seen them."

"We saw one to the east a few days back and we've seen their tracks here. Fey thinks she saw one last night at a distance. Tell us about the attack."

"Yes, of course. I see you have a pipe, could you spare me some tobacco? I'm in great need of a smoke. My nerves, you see, my hands tremble." Fey pulled out her tobacco and they sat on a stone, packing their pipes. "The lizards. We stopped you know, further on to the west. We passed over this place in the night. I think I was the only one to see it. Some of the stones reflected the starlight and I thought they looked most regular in their arrangement. I didn't mention it to the others of course, except to my good friend Geoffrey. He's my travelling companion and fellow scientist. I was thoroughly sick of their company, their aims and their methods. We stopped to the west of here to take on water at a spring of some sort. Sir Rothwell wanted to scout around and perhaps find some blacks."

"Who?" interrupted Fey, as she exhaled her smoke.

"Sir Rothwell—Sir Rothwell Blaze. You haven't heard of him? No?"

"The name doesn't sound familiar," said Rosalyn, waving away the pipe smoke.

"Not to worry. He's the man in charge of the Mechanic's expedition. We stopped for water and to gather intelligence. I'd wandered away from the main body of the party, scouring contentedly among the rocks and trees for samples, when my peace was disturbed by a great commotion and gunfire from the direction of the Eyrie—that's what they call their airship. Running back as quickly as I could—I must add that I don't run swiftly—I circled around the edge of the trees to come up at a distance to the rear—or is that aft? I came up behind the airship. The sight was most astonishing."

Watson stopped for a sip from his canteen and a good strong pull of his pipe. He waved his hand in front of him as he recalled the event. "There before me were these huge lizards attacking the boat. Monstrous things! I've never seen anything like it, and I might add that I hope I never see the like again. The airship itself was not firmly aground but had the keel at rest with the hooks down. We'd disembarked by rope ladder and the engine was still running. The lizards—I can barely reconcile the thought of those beasts as lizards—they're not at all what I have in mind when I think of lizards. They're like some ancient creature whose bones we find fossilised." His gaze was fixed on the ground and he panted heavily.

"So big lizards then? Go on will you, the suspense is fair gnawing at my guts."

"Yes, frightfully big lizards. The biggest was rearing up, clawing at the boat, ripping off boards and railings. The men were shouting and shooting and those aground were running to try to get back onto the boat." He stared into the distance as he recalled his disbelief. "I saw a man eaten. This reptile, it took him from the sand as he ran screaming to the boat. Just snatched him up, just like that! A couple of gulps and the man was gone. It was horrible, just horrible." Watson stopped to gather himself, drawing on his pipe, shaking his head from side to side before continuing.

"The shooting went on. I don't know how many men were lost. I think there were others. I heard Sir Rothwell yelling out to unhook and amidst the sounds of the shouting and yelling of orders, the gunshots and the crash of the swivel cannons, the smoke and the dust, I saw the Eyrie start to rise. They were taking off without me. Can't say I blame them really, the safest place was in the air. If they'd stayed on the ground the lizards would have ripped that airship to pieces. I certainly wasn't going to wait around for the dust to settle only to find myself alone with these hideous reptiles. I ran."

"Not very fast though," said Fey.

"No, not very fast, but I think quite a bit faster than I've run before. I headed straight back here to hide in the ruins. I've seen the lizards crawling about. Horrible things, horrible. I've spent two nights in this place now and I've had quite enough. Where is your airship? We must leave immediately."

"Bit of a hitch there, we won't be leaving for a while yet."

"Doctor Gilroy, you best have something to eat. We don't have much, there's some dried beef that might blunt the edge of your hunger."

Watson took the proffered food. "Thank you, Reverend. I'm most indebted to you."

"When you've rested we'll have some more questions for you. One thing has me most curious though, you've only got one water bottle and still have water, you've been away from your airship for two nights and the first thing you ask for is food and tobacco. Where are you getting your water from?"

"That's no secret. I assume you haven't been underground here yet?"

"No, Doctor Gilroy, but we're aware of a body of water beneath one of the buildings. It was too far down for us to reach and we have no light."

Watson looked at them. "Where is your airship? Surely you have it here?"

"We had a slight mishap."

"Yeah, Roz steered it into the ground." Fey caught Rosalyn glaring at her and added, "I helped."

"Do you mean to say that your airship is no longer airworthy?"

"That's what we're saying, Doc."

"Oh dear. We are in a bit of a pickle aren't we? I'll show you where to get to the water if you'll follow me, but we must be careful—the lizards."

Watson led the way to a smaller building, almost covered with sand. Grass and a few small bushes grew on it. The structure looked like it had collapsed but had in fact been constructed as a rough dome. A big slab of stone barred the way to the interior "I found this place by watching the flights of birds," explained Watson.

"Friend of Ses, are you?"

"Who?"

"Never mind. How do you open this thing?"

"It's quite clever, really. One simply pushes hard on this side here." Watson put his shoulder to the stone and the door pivoted in the middle. "Come in. I think this place is safe from lizards. I have a small lantern here and some candles."

Light filtered into the room through cracks between the stones. A large hole in the floor took up most of the space on the far side. Watson lit the lantern and gave them a candle each. "Watch your step here, it's quite steep." The hole was the top of a narrow set of stone stairs descended into the gloom below.

Watson proceeded down them, followed by Rosalyn and Fey. The stairs had been cut through the solid rock and descended for about fifty yards before opening onto a wide ledge. Around the ledge a body of water stretched into the blackness. "We're on an island," said Watson. "The stairs we came down are carved into an enormous natural rock pillar. I haven't explored any further than this. I'm not too keen on immersing myself in dark, cold water while trying to swim holding a lantern."

"Yeah, I can see your point, Doc. That would be difficult even for a brave, skilled, soul like myself. We might just fill up our water bags while we're here."

The cavern was cool and refreshing after the heat of the day. Rosalyn lay on the cold stone, watching as Watson helped Fey fill the bags. A splashing sound in the distance froze them in their movements. They peered into the darkness.

"I don't like the sound of that," said Watson. He put the stopper in a water bag. "Whatever made that splash was big."

"Can we start backing up the stairs? This place gives me the creeps." Fey, who had been crouching at the water's edge, got up and turned to go.

Rosalyn stood up so abruptly she almost knocked Fey into the water. "Let's go fast." Watson didn't stop to look at what Rosalyn might have seen. He rushed for the stairs. Fey turned back for a last glance. She could see, at the edge of the darkness, the huge head of what she took at first to be a giant lizard. The light caught the ripples further back, she saw it wasn't a single thing, but several, and snake-like. Wasting no time, she pushed Watson up the stairs in front of her. At the top they stumbled over Rosalyn as Watson scrambled to get the door open.

"It's coming—can you hurry it up in front?" Fey turned to face back down the stairs and fired the pistol. The crack as it went off echoed around the chamber and filled the air with the white smoke of the gunpowder. They tumbled out into the light. Watson lost no time in shutting the door. Fey reloaded as they moved back away from the door. Whatever it was hadn't followed them.

"Damned lizards!"

"Doc, that wasn't a lizard."

"What was it, Fey?" asked Rosalyn.

"Snakes—big, pale snakes."

"Big? How big?" Watson mopped his brow again.

"Lizard big, and behind them some other monster, like it was directing them."

"Astounding, most astounding."

"Yeah, bloody marvellous. We need to get out of here."

"Doctor Gilroy, you mentioned trees?"

"Yes I did. To the west. Do you have an interest in botany?"

"No, we have an interest in timber for our mast. It snapped in the crash. Do you remember seeing anything there that might have been suitable?"

Watson took a breath as he considered the question. "I think so, yes, I'm sure there must be something suitable. I've seen your ship and it's quite small—but the lizards, you know? The place is home to several of them. How would you get the timber? The noise of the axe will surely bring them."

"Lizards are daylight creatures. They like the sunlight. We'll have to get what we want at night but what'll we do about Ses? If we go for the timber we'll be a couple of days late back. She might do something stupid if we're late."

"Who is Ses?"

"Cecilia Spotswood. She's our companion who is waiting back at the airship," said Rosalyn.

"Cecilia Spotswood? Young Cecilia? I think I met her at a ball held by the Royal Society. Short, dark-haired girl?"

"Close, Doc. More on the medium to tall side with fair hair."

"Yes, of course. Studying ornithology I believe."

"If that's a fancy way of saying bug catcher then you're spot on."

"We really haven't got time for this. We're going to have to forget about Cecilia and hope she remains where she is. Doctor Gilroy, can you lead us back to the trees?"

"Of course, but I must warn you again of the lizards."

"Yeah, Doc, lizards, big ones. Got it. I can see they hold a special interest for you. Tell you what, we'll name them after you."

Watson mused, "Hmm, giant monitor lizards. I think Varanus Rex Gilroy has a lovely ring to it but a trifle vain perhaps. I'm sure Varanus Rex will do nicely."

"You can christen the lizards later; we need to get the timber for the mast and return to the airship."

18

HUNTED

Rosalyn scanned the landscape from the shelter of a low wall at the edge of the ruins. "I can't see any lizards. We should move now." With Watson leading they made their way back out into the desert. They didn't make it to the trees on the first day but stopped for the night and slept in the dunes, each taking it in turns to keep watch. It was midday the next day when they came to the top of a rise, giving them a view of the trees in the distance. It was a much larger patch of woodland than they'd expected to find. The rest of the day was spent watching for any signs of the reptiles. One was seen coming in from the more open country and disappearing from view into the patch of forest.

"Do we have a plan should one of those things appear while we're chopping wood?"

"I found running worked quite well for me, although I don't think the lizards saw me. If they had I'm sure they would have caught me as I can't run at all fast."

"So the plan is this—if one comes at us, me and Roz will run faster than you."

"Fey, we will not leave Doctor Gilroy to the lizards." Fey smiled and Watson looked much relieved. "The lizard we saw in the chamber was scared off by the noise of our guns but in that small, stone space the sound was deafening. Apparently the noise of gunfire didn't work when the lizards attacked the Mechanical Order's airship so we can't rely on shooting at them. Perhaps fire might work. I'm sure the blacks have found a way of protecting themselves from these beasts and I presume they use fire to drive them away."

"Have you seen any blacks around?"

"No. Come to think of it we've seen no sign of them, not even smoke from their fires."

"Do you suppose the lizards have eaten the blacks hereabouts?" asked Watson nervously.

"I think you might find there are other reasons for the absence of blacks from the area. In my studies in comparative religions we were taught that indigenous peoples have a superstitious dread of certain places, or even taboos such as Captain Cook described from his observations in Tonga."

"That would certainly explain why they're not making use of the ruins and the reservoir beneath it."

"I thought the giant snakes and their minder explained it better," said Fey.

"Regardless, we have to get this mast."

As the sun set, and with Watson's lantern lit, they walked with great dread to the tree line. Finding something suitable was going to prove much more difficult than they had imagined as the trees of the right girth lacked a good, straight length. With some searching they found one of a suitable size. Fey took the axe from her belt and gave it to Watson, who insisted on doing the chopping. Fey and Rosalyn gathered up dead wood and sticks that lay around and started a large fire. The two women sat back to back and stared into the gloom, their attention focussed on the dark spaces between the pale trunks of the trees. Frequent sounds in the darkness kept them in a state of heightened vigilance.

After strenuous effort on Doctor Gilroy's part, the log crashed down making a frightful noise and they crouched silently until the stillness settled back around them. Satisfied that their activity had not wakened any sleeping giants, Watson continued working on the trunk, chopping the side branches from it. With that finished, four thinner lengths of timber were collected for the struts. Rosalyn looked at her watch. "We made good time. Let's get ourselves out of here."

Doctor Gilroy put his jacket back on and gave the axe to Fey. With some effort they managed to get the lumber onto their shoulders. Although the three of them carrying it made the load easier they decided two would carry it in turns while the third walked ahead with the lantern and pistol. The sun started coming up as they were about half way back to the ruins and they stopped to rest and to assuage their growing hunger by eating the dried beef. The sun rose with a changing display of every hue, yellow through to red. As the light spread along the horizon, turning the black sky to blue, Rosalyn and Fey sat shoulder to shoulder, watching.

"I never tire of that sight. Day after day it appears, the endless stutter of creation."

"It's quite something isn't it, Roz. When we get out of here and back to where there're civilised folk maybe we can sit and watch the sun rise together without having to look over our shoulders."

"That's a lovely thought."

Watson brought them back from their appreciation of the glory of Eos by a sudden interjection. "I say, I don't mean to alarm you but I think we might be in a spot of bother." The women turned to see Watson pointing. "Back there, some distance away yet." A large lizard headed their way, the rays of the morning sun glinting on its scales as it moved. Every few paces the beast turned its head from one side to the other.

"Move," said Rosalyn. "We're going to have to travel as fast as we can but we're not leaving the log." Fey and Watson picked up the burden and started trotting through the grass, Rosalyn taking the rear. She turned often to see if the reptile persisted in its pursuit. Sometimes she saw it stand on its hind legs, balanced by its tail, just as Fey had seen the one do in the distance in the ruins.

"It's not gaining on us but I'm not sure that we're leaving it behind either. We have to keep going—there's no doubt the lizard is hunting us." Rosalyn urged them on.

The day warmed quickly and the combination of burning heat and exertion had them dripping with perspiration. Sometimes stumbling, the sand and dust adhered to their sweat-soaked clothes and skin. In spite of their load they kept a good pace and with relief they spied the ruins in the distance. They aimed for the north side of the city but were dismayed by what appeared to be fresh lizard tracks across their path.

The sweat dripped from them as they came staggering to the first building. It had a partial roof and solid walls and they dropped the log outside. The interior was barely defensible. Exhausted, the three of them flopped down behind the stones to recover from their forced march. "We'll have to leave the log for now," said Rosalyn, at last. "We need a better place to hide. When the sun sets we'll come back for the log and return to Cecilia." The other two nodded in assent. "I don't know how that thing is following us but I assume its tracking our footprints. If we can…"

"It's not our tracks it's following, it is our scent," interrupted Watson. "I don't know if you've seen its forked tongue but that tongue is used to scent the air." They recalled the big flickering tongue of the lizard as it entered the chamber.

"What can we do?" asked Rosalyn.

"I found in Sydney when being pursued that hiding works well," said Fey.

"Yes. We must hide," said Watson. "But where?"

"I've got it," said Fey. "Roz, you remember those big stone jars, the coffins. Maybe we can hide in them—pull the lids over us, lie doggo until it's dark and then get the bloody hell out of here." Rosalyn agreed and they picked their way through the ruins almost frantically to find the crypt that held the sarcophagi.

"This is most remarkable," said Watson, when the crypt was located. "There is so much here. I must inform Geoffrey, he adores antiquities."

"Doc, we don't have a lot of time. Find yourself a big stone jar and get inside it or you're going to find yourself inside something warm and wet and it won't be something pleasant."

"Fey, I hope you're not being uncouth."

"Sorry Roz, I forgot you're brought up on the social niceties. Find a jar and I'll help you get the lid on."

Rosalyn climbed into a large sarcophagus and Fey and Watson slid the lid over it, leaving only a small gap for air. Watson located a bigger jar and with Fey's assistance secured himself inside. Fey found that the nearest sarcophagus of a suitable size was the one which she and Rosalyn had examined earlier and with effort, managed to slide the lid far enough off to crawl inside it. She grunted and strained trying to get the lid over her, the bones of the original occupant crunching under her boots.

In her sarcophagus, Rosalyn too, could feel the bones splintering under her weight. The desecration of the dead caused her spiritual disquiet. She prayed for the souls and the forgiveness of the people whose remains she and her companions were disturbing. The only way to sit in the coffin was in a foetal position and she soon became severely cramped. Rosalyn wriggled ineffectually, trying to find a comfortable position. Her limbs ached and she imagined the others must be enduring the same discomfit. As the minutes turned to what felt like hours the position became torturous. In spite of the small breathing space, the air was stifling and the heat added to her misery. It felt like she was slowly cooking.

Her mind wandered. She wondered how poor Cecilia was doing, alone and no doubt sick with worry. Her thoughts turned to home, her parents, her sister, and to the seminary where she had had so many wonderful times. Those thoughts led her to the Dean and the Church Council. They knew they were sending her on a perilous Mission but had given her no warning and no word. "They used me," she said aloud at the realisation, and a tear mixed with sweat rolled down her cheek at the thought of how she had been betrayed by those she trusted. Mercifully at this point she passed out.

She woke to something grabbing her. She cried out and tried feebly to hit at whatever it was clutching at her. She heard voices, soft and soothing and so ceased her resistance. Fey and Doctor Gilroy dragged her out onto the sand and the fresh night air revived her. Fey was trickling water over her face so that it ran into her mouth. Rosalyn drank thirstily, her head aching as though she'd been hit with a brick, the pain rivalled only by the burning sensation in her cramped legs.

"That's the way, Roz, drink some more. Not too quick now— steady girl." Eventually Rosalyn's full awareness returned. It was dark, but the moon was almost full and its light gave the ruins a gentle, mystical glow. Watson was holding the lantern.

"The lizard?"

"It passed us by," said Watson. "The tracks show it went right by the entranceway here."

"The time, what time is it? The mast! We must get it back."

"Rest for a bit Roz. We thought we'd lost you. Stretch your legs, get some movement into them."

Rosalyn tried to move her legs and found that any stretching of them caused the pain to intensify. "That's the girl. Keep trying, we had to do the same thing. Wasn't much space in those coffins but more than inside a lizard. You'll get past the pain quick but you've got to push it a little." After some time and with help from her companions, Rosalyn staggered to her feet and limped around until full mobility returned to her. "Roz, we don't have a surplus of water and neither of us feel much like coming face to face with those snakes in the underground chamber."

"How much water do we have left?"

"There's about enough for a day if we're careful."

"We'll have to be extra careful and make it last two days. There's plenty at the other end. Standing here won't get us there either."

"That's the spirit."

Rosalyn looked at the moonlight reflecting in Fey's eyes. They were moist, and it looked to Rosalyn as if Fey had been crying. She chose to say nothing, instead leading her companions to where they'd left their timber.

The log retrieved, Rosalyn checked the compass to ensure they were headed north. Travelling as fast as practical while they had the relative coolness of the night, they covered a good distance. The ruins were far behind them by the next morning. As day came, a wind sprang up, gathering with it large amounts of dust and sand. This wind was nothing like the one they had flown into some nights ago and it subsided not long after it started.

During the mid morning, as they were resting amongst the clumps of grass, they saw a band of Aborigines far off in the distance. Not wanting to have any encounters they couldn't readily flee from, they lay low until the threat passed. The hot sun slowed them down under their log burden and by late afternoon they were struggling to keep going. Rosalyn called a halt and they rested and dozed until sunset, continuing on by the dull light of the moon.

As the dawn broke they staggered into the stone circle, collapsing in the shade of the stones. Cecilia was nowhere to be seen. "I'll go and have a squiz in the cistern, she must be in there to keep safe and out of the heat." Fey pulled herself to her feet. Rosalyn remained in the shade with Watson who was lying with his eyes shut and breathing heavily. Both he and Rosalyn were asleep when Fey returned. "She isn't here," she stated flatly.

Rosalyn stirred. "What?"

"Ses. She isn't here."

"She's gone?"

"I suppose that's what I meant when I said she isn't here. She may have gone out into the scrub for a bit to catch some bugs or have a bit of a squiz for us."

"Cecilia can't go out there alone. She can't survive."

"Yeah, maybe. I wouldn't dismiss her abilities. I'll climb up the stones, see if I can spy the wayward molly from up top." In spite of her fatigue, Fey clambered up and walked around the lintels, staring into the desert looking for any sign of movement. She put her hands to her mouth and shouted Cecilia's name but received no response. She climbed down and sat in the sand next to Rosalyn. "Sorry."

"It's hardly your fault. Where could she have gone to? We didn't pass her heading south to look for us, unless she was sleeping in amongst the grasses and we passed her in the night."

"I'll check to see if her things are still there." Fey walked over to the airship, looked in Cecilia's trunks and returned to Rosalyn. "All her clothes are there, even the ones she was wearing. There're some jars and such but her journal and notebooks are missing, and so is her net."

"Did she leave a note?"

"I didn't see one, but I did see something peculiar."

"What?"

"As I was ratting through her stuff I found a bit of her dress caught in the bottom of one of her trunks. The reason it was caught is that it was stuck in a false floor."

"A hidden compartment? That's not so unusual. What was in there?"

"Nothing. Whatever was in there she's got with her."

"It may have already been empty."

"I don't think so. If it was already empty then she wouldn't have had to lift it and her dress wouldn't have got caught."

"That is a trifle unusual. I wonder what it could have been that she was hiding in there."

"I knew we couldn't trust her."

"I'm sure you're wrong, Fey. We'll find Cecilia somewhere close by, engrossed in the six legged creatures of the desert."

"Yeah, maybe. I don't have your faith in her."

"She can't have vanished. She'll return soon."

Without further discussion they both walked around the circle looking for any sign of their companion. "Look at this, Fey." Fey came to where Rosalyn stood next to a pillar. As Fey approached, Rosalyn pointed at the ground. It was littered with fragments of broken glass. "What do you make of that?"

"Dunno. Maybe when we didn't return she came over all hysterical and went mad."

"Do you suppose she had laudanum in her luggage and took too much of it?"

"If it was laudanum she would've been more relaxed—unless she run out." Fey picked up one of the larger pieces of the broken bottle and sniffed it. "I can't smell anything."

"I find it perplexing. If she had wandered off looking for us I'm sure she would have left a note. Something terrible has happened to her."

"Let's not get too worked up about it yet. She may turn up. We're going to have to wait and right now I'm bloody exhausted. I'm going to make like Watson and have a snooze."

Rosalyn walked with Fey to the shade of the stone to reflect on her Mission. She hadn't achieved either of the Mission goals of finding Doctor Phatts or bringing Enlightenment to the heathens. The airship was a wreck and one of her companions missing. She took hold of the cross hanging around her neck and knelt and prayed. After half an hour of this she found her knees were getting sore. She asked herself again why the Church would have sent her on this Mission so unprepared and without telling her in advance. It all rested on this Aqua Glass, but even that didn't make much sense. The Mission the Church had sent her on was much more expensive than most due to the cost of the airship. The Mechanical Order expedition must have been even more costly. She resolved to ask Watson some questions when he awoke. Fatigue caught up with her and she fell asleep where she lay.

Rosalyn awoke to find Fey and Watson sitting cross-legged on the ground, smoking their pipes and boiling water on a coal brick. "Thought you might like a cuppa when you woke."

"Yes, good idea. Is there any sign of Cecilia?"

"No, I had a good look around again—couldn't even find any tracks."

Rosalyn became quiet for a while and then turned to Watson. "Tell us about this expedition you were on."

Watson took a pull on his pipe. "I'm from the Society—the Royal Scientific Society for the Exploration of the Antipodes."

"So was Ses. I thought she was the only one."

"Well, I was in the Society but circumstances insisted I part company with them. I was recruited by the Mechanical Order to take part in their expedition. I'm sure you know about the Mechanical Order—The Divine Order of Mechanics. They needed a geologist and me being a geologist, I jumped at the chance."

"How many men are there in the Order's expedition?"

"Let me see now," said Watson as he gazed at the canopy of the sky, "There were fourteen of us including myself. There were four crewmen including Sir Rothwell Blaze—the captain—and the rest of us were expedition members. We all had to take part in the running of the airship. That's how I came to see the ruins and no one else did. The wheel officer can't really see the ground below and it's the job of the forward watch to look for anything of particular interest. It was my turn on watch and no other soul was awake at that hour."

"What was the goal of your expedition?"

"It was a voyage of scientific discovery. That's what I'm told anyway. We had on board people from other fields of enquiry. The Order also had funded a botanist, a temporologist, a biologist and myself. The other six are private soldiers from the Mechanical Order. I suppose only five now after the lizard ate one of them." Watson took a sip of the tea that Fey handed him. "That's frightfully hot and it smells delicious. Thank you, Fey. The expedition—I became disillusioned with it, as did Geoffrey, my companion. I mean, we all know the blacks are savages destined for extinction, but the way he and his men would shoot them was something I didn't agree with at all. I told Sir Rothwell what I thought."

"Did he change his style?"

"No, Fey, he did not. He simply reiterated the philosophy of the Mechanical Order; that either you are part of the ordained order of things or you are not, and the savages were not and therefore had to be shot."

"That's their philosophy is it?"

"I believe this is my field," said Rosalyn. "When the Schism occurred and the Enlightenment Church engaged with the new rise of science and knowledge, the Mechanical Order broke away from our Church. The Enlightenment Church believes all things follow a natural order which is regulated by divine decree. Science has shown us there is order in the universe and that it is run in the manner of a huge automaton. The centre of our particular part of it is the Sun. We are part of the rest of the universe but also a separate part of it."

"You're giving another sermon aren't you?"

"No, Fey, but I think it's important that you should know what manner of a society you live in."

"I don't think your Church knows much at all about the society I live in."

"Be that as it may, I'm sure your society in Sydney has its own order. Everything does. Regardless of whether or not there is an underlying connection between societies there is order to them. The Church recognises the difference but sees that like the cogs in a machine each separate piece must mesh together."

"What does that mean for us mortals?"

"It means, Fey, that in a case such as the blacks we must bring Enlightenment to them so they may become part of the divine whole. They must find a place with the rest of humanity."

"And what's that got to do with the Mechanical Order?"

"The Mechanical Order believes society must be strictly ordered; that there can only be one authority, one society, and the best hierarchy for a well ordered society is a military one, well disciplined, well regulated. Their goal is to create a new world order in which everyone must have a place or perish. They have as a central tenet of their faith that the Ante Vidoram, and other Setbacks which may have occurred before it, are a result of a disordered world. If the world is ordered there will be no further need of divine intervention to set things right again by creating these Setbacks."

"This is why I like fishing on Sunday mornings."

"Why is that?"

"So I don't have to listen to sermons."

"You're not going to catch any fish out here."

"Thanks Doc, you're a real help."

"I'm not sure it's Sunday either."

"Doctor Gilroy, did Sir Rothwell make any mention of Doctor Phatts?"

"He did, and he was just as interested in where Doctor Phatts might have been as to his current whereabouts."

"Do you know why?"

"Yes, it became apparent after we left Sydney that he was seeking the Aqua Glass. Silly idea, really."

"Why do you say that, Doc?"

"The connection between the butterfly and the Aqua Glass is a tenuous link. The expedition is quite expensive as you can imagine—not that I or the other scientists mind of course, being the first in our fields to explore the wonders of the interior is a unique opportunity."

"So are you saying this Aqua Glass doesn't exist?"

"I suppose it might exist but finding it is going to be a case of luck more than planning. Even if it is found the idea of being able to use it to move a person from one place to another is quite preposterous. I mean... what would you do? Swallow it?"

"It does sound preposterous. I don't understand why the Mechanical Order would mount such an expensive expedition if it thought it was for nothing, nor would my Church have me looking for Doctor Phatts."

"That's the thing though isn't it Roz—why would your Church want you to find Doctor Phatts if he doesn't even know himself where the butterflies were? He was already lost when he found them."

"I assume they would like to interrogate him for any details he might possess which would lead them to the butterflies and thence to the Aqua Glass."

"I know one thing for sure, and that's we're not going to find anything by sitting here."

Shaded by a lintel, they set to work to trim a new mast from the log and managed to fashion something serviceable. The broken struts were replaced with the slender trunks they'd collected with the new mast. The work took them into the dark of night and continued into the morning. With difficulty they managed to remove the propeller, and Watson, using heat from a coal brick, the hammer from the tool box, a stone as an anvil, and with Fey's assistance, straightened the shaft. The bent propeller blades were similarly treated.

After a mixture of patience, swearing, prayer and perseverance, the *Lightning* was brought back into a serviceable state. Rosalyn stepped back and looked at their handiwork. She examined the entire craft with a critical eye, checking every detail. The shattered bow section was no longer tapered and graceful. Rope netting was now fixed around it to cover the gap caused by the crash. Satisfied, Rosalyn instructed Fey to fill the boiler and ignite the coal bricks to test the repairs.

Rosalyn took the *Lightning* off the ground and when clear of the stone circle, engaged the propulsion. A loud screeching noise emanated from the propeller shaft, the *Lightning* gave a shudder and moved forward. She circumnavigated the stones and returned to ground safely in the centre of the circle.

"She makes a bit of noise and doesn't handle quite as well as before We'll have to put some weight forward for balance but she's flyable."

"Splendid." Watson clapped his hands together with joy.

"We'll get her loaded, Roz. What's our plan?"

"We can't give up on Cecilia. I propose we fly from the circle in a spiral to see if we can find any sign of her. If we see any blacks I think we should try to make contact and learn what we can."

"Our food is running low. We'll have to find something soon and Ses has the carbine. I have an idea that might enlarge our larder."

The other two waited by the airship while Fey waited inside the tunnel to the cistern. After many hours had passed Rosalyn and Watson were awakened from where they dozed by the sound of a shot. Fey returned to them grinning, a dead wallaby slung over her shoulder. "Fresh meat." After skinning it they carved off pieces and cooked what they could on a coal brick. Their bellies stuffed, Fey walked away from them. "I just want a quiet moment, me and my pipe."

As Watson salted what remained of the wallaby, Rosalyn watched Fey wander. Fey puzzled her. Something about Fey's behaviour appealed to her, yet infuriated her too. Not only did she have no respect for authority, she had no respect for social conventions. It was that same lack of respect for everything Rosalyn held dear that she found so attractive. It dawned on her that Fey had a freedom she herself did not possess; a freedom from social conventions that were as tight as any corset.

Rosalyn gazed up at the stars and the waxing moon, recalling the image of Fey's naked candle-lit body when they'd stood in the water in the chamber of the lizard. She recalled also the words that were spoken as they looked at each other. Bothered by such thoughts she turned her mind to England and her parents.

Fey returned from where she'd been sitting on the other side of one of the big stone uprights. "I made you something, Roz. Here, you put this on your head to hold that white piece of Ses's petticoat. It'll stop it coming off your head when we're flying. I made myself one too—it's hide from that wallaby." Fey handed her a band of plaited fur strips. "It's a bit fresh but it'll dry out in no time in this heat." Rosalyn thanked her and put it over the petticoat fabric draped over her head. Fey did the same, causing Watson to remark that they looked like they'd stepped straight out of a bible illustration.

19

AIRSHIP PIRATES

Fey was up at first light collecting the waterbags and stray bits of equipment and stowing them onboard. Her companions awoke as she was completing the task. Rosalyn started the engine and Watson unhooked and clambered aboard. They first headed north until they were almost out of sight of the stone circle and then started circling it in an ever widening pattern. Hidden by the tufts of grass somewhere below, a pair of blue eyes observed their passing.

Their search was unrewarding. Fey watched from the port side and Watson, who had his own telescope, kept lookout from starboard. "There's nothing. It's just this dry grass and stunted trees spreading for miles. Not even so much as a kangaroo or emu."

"Nothing out my side either. Even if Ses was lying down there injured or dying of thirst we might not get a fix on her."

"I think if your friend is not dead the blacks might have her. Perhaps she went walking and they came upon her."

"What would they do to her?"

"I don't know and I wouldn't like to imagine."

As the day passed into night they dropped to a low altitude and threw out the hooks lest they pass Cecilia in the night. A lantern was lit to create a light for Cecilia so she might see it and make towards them. Rosalyn considered it was worth the risk of being discovered by the *Eyrie*.

Watson and Fey sat and smoked their pipes before settling in. Fey curled up with Rosalyn in the stern behind the engine while Watson made himself comfortable between the seats. Fey awoke to Rosalyn's finger on her lips. Rosalyn moved in close and Fey put an arm around her and kissed her. Startled, Rosalyn pushed Fey back and whispered, "I think there's someone climbing up the hook rope." Fey withdrew her arm and lay still. The boat was rocking from side to side but in a manner different from the motion when flying or sitting in a breeze.

Fey took out the pistol, cocked it, leaned over the side and whispered, "Ses, is that you?"

A dark shape was on the rope below her but she couldn't see the detail of it. On hearing Fey's voice the movement on the rope stopped and all was silent. "Damn you, I'll fire if you don't speak."

The shape started up the rope again. Fey fired. The loud crack of the pistol produced a grunt from the shape. The noise woke Watson and the three of them leaned over the side. A soft thump told them the target was back on the ground. The dark shape could barely be discerned as it moved swiftly away from the airship. Fey reloaded.

"Did you hit it?" asked Rosalyn.

"I'm bloody sure I did. The ball hit something, I heard it."

"It still moved."

"I'm positive I hit it, must have winged it in the arm or shoulder."

"What was it?" asked Watson.

"Someone trying to climb up the rope into the boat. Must have been one of the blacks."

"Pull the hooks," Rosalyn commanded. "We're going up." Watson and Fey obeyed as Rosalyn took the wheel. With some extra distance between themselves and the ground, Rosalyn held the position and turned to her companions. "We can't hook for the night without being in fear of the blacks. If we stay at rest we'll drift and lose our search pattern. I don't think we'll find Cecilia now but I do know that if she went in search of us she went south. We're going to return to the city of the lizards." Fey and Watson nodded their acknowledgement.

In the dim glow of the light from the firebox windows, Rosalyn's gaze met Fey's. Rosalyn turned her eyes immediately back to the instrument panel and when she dared glance up again saw that Fey was kneeling, leaning her arms on the skyrail, looking over the side into the darkness. Rosalyn studied her, wondering about the way Fey had kissed her when she had been motioning for Fey to be silent. Was it the action of someone half awake, or was there deliberate meaning behind it? Rosalyn felt her pulse start to race and when Fey turned to look at her, Rosalyn chose to study the compass heading.

The *Lightning* drifted in the night, but the breeze was almost nonexistent and they didn't move far from their original position. Rosalyn woke early, took them to a high altitude and commenced the search for the ruined town. It took no time at all to find it and Rosalyn descended to conduct a more intensive search. The view of the town from the air showed up the extent of it. No walls could be seen and most of the town consisted of a maze of sand-covered circular mounds of various sizes from which the surviving columns and ruins protruded. They spied a circular central plaza they hadn't seen when they were on the ground. There were no lizards visible although they did see signs of tracks, and holes which they presumed the lizards had dug.

A heavy thump on top of the balloon captured the attention of all three of them. They looked at each other but before anyone could speak a man dropped down beside them, hanging on the end of a rope and secured to it by a harness. Rosalyn screamed, Watson sat back stunned and Fey went straight for the pistol.

The man held a pistol of his own but the movement of the airship caused him to spin and he couldn't bring his weapon to bear. Fey aimed to fire a shot at him when a second man, armed with a carbine, appeared on the other side. Rosalyn gave the wheel a hard turn and pulled the vent lever, cutting off the blue ascension. The airship gave a shudder which, although small, threw the dangling men further off balance. This also had the effect of throwing Fey off balance and she landed heavily on top of Watson. The airship started its descent.

The man with the pistol tried to swing himself under the balloon and into the boat. The other yelled to Rosalyn to give over or he'd shoot. Rosalyn had no such intention and continued flying. Fey untangled herself from Watson, knelt on the floor of the boat and fired off a shot at the man with the carbine. The pistol spewed out its flame and smoke and the ball found its target. The man gasped and slumped in his harness. Fey reloaded as Watson, having recovered from his initial panic, took out the axe. The surviving man scrambled frantically to climb back up his rope and disappeared out of sight before Fey could bring the pistol to bear on him again.

Rosalyn, about to reactivate the injector to try to gain altitude, saw they were now already perilously close to the sand and the ruins. With little choice, Rosalyn grounded the vessel. "Hooks out!" Her companions scrambled to obey and they waited in silence, peering out from under the balloon. A shadow passed over them and they knew the *Eyrie* was above them.

Fey handed the pistol to Rosalyn and climbed out of the boat, taking her knife from its sheath as she did so. She cut the strap attaching the carbine to the dead assailant, taking also his waist belt containing shot and powder and threw it over her shoulder. Watson motioned that he thought someone remained on top of the balloon. Rosalyn nodded and said quietly, "The rest of them are going to be coming down soon, we can't hold them."

The *Eyrie* glided past them and came to rest in a position fifty yards forward of their bow. Hooks were cast out, thudding into the sand, and men descended on rope ladders. Having formed a line they moved towards the *Lightning*. Watson pointed out the *Eyrie*'s two swivel guns trained on them. Rosalyn whispered again. "If we run, the man on top of our balloon will shoot us in the back. We have to surrender."

"I think you're right, Roz. I don't see any other way out of this."

Rosalyn called out, "Don't shoot. We're coming out. We're unarmed." She laid the pistol down in the boat and Fey flung the carbine and belt out into a pile of fallen stones.

"Stay where you are," came the voice from above. The line of armed men closed the distance to within a few yards of the *Lightning*. One of the men, tall, with dark hair and a Roman nose, wore a red and black uniform, the rank insignia marking him as an officer of the Divine Order of Mechanics. He approached them and looked at Rosalyn. "Reverend Missionary Rosalyn Flynn, I presume."

"Yes, and I presume you're Rothwell Blaze."

"Sir Rothwell Blaze. Yes, I am he indeed. Doctor Gilroy, I see you're alive and well. We feared the lizards had eaten you but we returned to search anyway. It will be good to have you aboard again. As for you..." and he looked back to Rosalyn and Fey. "I don't know what to do with you. I'm sure I can come up with some ideas."

"You do realise, don't you, Sir Rothwell, that I am an Enlightenment Church Missionary on Church business, sanctioned by our Queen Herself, and what you are doing is nothing short of piracy."

"Tsk tsk. Such harsh words. Church business, you say? Why would your Church have business in this dry country?" Sir Rothwell gazed around the sandy ruins.

"I'm tasked to bring Enlightenment to the heathens, of course."

"I understand you were to set up a Mission on the frontier. This is hardly the frontier, my dear Reverend. We're well past that, and I can see no heathens about."

"We made a navigational error and were about to turn back."

Sir Rothwell didn't look particularly taken by her answer. He turned his attention to Fey. "And you're the companion? Odd. You look nothing like how I imagined. You're just like one of those wretched colonial types."

"I am one of those wretched colonial types, and quite happy with it, too."

Sir Rothwell studied her more closely. "Doctor Gilroy, is this girl a colonial or is she from mother England?"

Watson, glancing from Fey to Sir Rothwell, stammered out, "Y-y-yes, as far as I know she's a colonial, and quite a nice young woman."

"I have little interest in her personality. I want to know who she is, and she looks to me like she might be the woman calling herself Cecilia Spotswood, passing herself off as a young colonial man." He looked Fey up and down again. "You're clever with your disguise—cunning, even down to the colonial accent. You have Watson fooled but not me."

"Listen, you stiff-necked bastard, I'm not who you think I am. I'm Fey Grey, Sydney-sider. If you don't like it you can go bugger yourself."

Sir Rothwell studied her for a few more seconds and spoke to his men. "Take them back to the ship. You," he said, indicating the man who was climbing down from the top of the balloon. "Is your mate dead?" The man nodded. "I'm terribly sorry. I know you were good friends. Cut him down and we'll bury him here."

Rosalyn, Fey and Watson were escorted back to the *Eyrie* and taken onboard. A group of men who had been standing at the bow turned to look at them and one of their number rushed forward, his face aglow.

"Watson!"

Watson grinned and held his arms out. "Geoffrey!"

Geoffrey embraced him and stood back, still holding Watson's arms. "We thought you lost to those hideous reptiles."

"Almost, but I ran."

"Not very fast though." Fey's eyes narrowed as she looked at Geoffrey. "You're not one of these ratbags are you?" She indicated the Mechanical Order soldiers guarding them.

"No," said Watson. "Geoffrey is not with them." He turned to his friend. "Geoffrey, this is the Reverend Missionary Rosalyn Flynn and Miss Fey Grey."

Geoffrey lifted his hat. "Geoffrey Ovens at your service. It's a pleasure to meet you."

Their guard interrupted them and instructed Watson and Geoffrey to go to the bow of the vessel. Rosalyn and Fey were made to sit against the skyrail and wait. Rosalyn looked around the deck and noted the solid construction—the airship had been well made. Hatches set at intervals on the deck roused her curiosity. She asked the guard what they were for.

"They're our coffins."

"Coffins?"

"That's what we call them. They're sleeping bays. We crawl in and sleep, not much room but enough to stretch our legs out."

"How do you breathe?"

"Through a small hatch in the side near your head."

"I see," said Rosalyn. "And I suppose the cabin in the stern belongs to Sir Rothwell."

"You suppose correctly, Reverend."

A bucket of water and a tin cup were brought for them and they sat and waited. Rosalyn leaned over to Fey and whispered. "What is it with Cecilia? Sir Rothwell has this idea that you are her."

Fey shrugged. "I think the man is confused, but I'd like to know what it is with Cecilia myself."

The whispering provoked a rebuke from one of the guards. Fey responded to him in the currency tongue. "Piss off you ratbag. You know piracy is a hanging offence? Tell you what, if you give over your guns I'll put in a good word for you with the guv'. He's a close personal friend of mine. Hand them over quickly before your owner comes back."

The guard glared at her and spat out, "I ain't got no owner. I serve the Order and Sir Rothwell. You mind your tongue you dirty tramp—dressing in men's clothes. You got no decency."

Sir Rothwell came back on board and approached Fey. "Young

woman, I don't know who you are but I want to know who you work for. You can drop the act about being this currency lass, Fey, and you can forget about trying to claim you're Cecilia Spotswood. I want the truth now."

"The truth is you're an idiot."

Sir Rothwell did not respond to the insult and instead went and talked to Watson who was still standing at the front of the boat. After a brief discussion he returned and studied Fey carefully. "It seems you really are this Fey person."

"Glad you got that sorted out; I'd hate to be someone else."

"I do know however, that you had another woman on board your vessel and she is going by the name of Cecilia Spotswood. Where is she?"

"Sir Rothwell, we did have Cecilia on board but she has gone missing as I'm sure Doctor Gilroy has already told you. Do you mind telling me why you think Cecilia is not who she says she is?"

Sir Rothwell beckoned Geoffrey over. "Geoffrey, tell the Reverend here about Lord Spotswood's children." Geoffrey looked at the two dejected women sitting on the boat's deck.

"Lord Oswald Spotswood had only one son. He died a few years back in an unfortunate hunting accident when his horse threw him. Lord Oswald has been a recluse since then, allowing only a few of his closest friends into his company." Rosalyn and Fey looked at each other and back to Geoffrey.

"Are you sure?"

"Yes Reverend, I am most certain. I have been a friend of Lord Spotswood for many years. He was most upset at the death of his son. You see he was only a young man, little more than a boy, and his mother said he was too young to be riding on a hunt but Lord Spotswood insisted."

"Thank you, Geoffrey. You may return to your position now." Sir Rothwell turned back to his prisoners. "Do you understand now that this Cecilia is a fraud, an imposter?"

"Her dad must be a different Lord Spotswood, probably his

brother or second cousin. You should go home and check that."

"I think not," said Sir Rothwell. "Your companion is not who she claims to be."

Rosalyn sat, stunned. "But... But... that's incredible. If she is not Cecilia Spotswood who is she?"

"I had sincerely hoped you would be able to provide me with that intelligence, but I can see you're as ignorant on this matter as I am."

"Looks like you won't be needing us then. Sorry we couldn't help you. You have a nice day and all and we'll get back to the Lightning." Fey started to rise.

"Sit down. You're not going anywhere." Fey sat back down.

"Sir Rothwell, what you are doing is an act of piracy and to that you are adding kidnapping. You know you'll hang for this."

"I don't think the gallows will be seeing me, Reverend. I have a great many friends and in all the right places. You might find it's yourself facing charges of theft."

"Theft? Whatever do you mean?"

"The airship, the one you call the Lightning, it was the property of the Moreton Bay penal colony was it not?"

Rosalyn leapt to her feet, fists clenched. "That was you? You sent my airship to Moreton Bay?"

"Tsk tsk, Reverend. Save your fire and brimstone for your sermons. I had nothing to do with that at all."

"Then it was your man did it."

Lord Rothwell smiled and feigned the wounded innocent. "My man? My dear Reverend, I know nothing of which you speak. Don't be too concerned, I'm sure you'll find a decent solicitor and wriggle free of all charges."

"What do you intend to do with us?"

"Keep you for further interrogation. I also have another purpose for you." He turned to Fey. "I'm not sure I have any use for you, however, and I need to hang someone for the death of my guardsman." Fey glared at him.

"You can't hang Fey. She was defending the airship from your piracy."

"Your concern is so touching. She's only a convict. No one will even miss her."

"I'll miss her. And she is not a convict and you are not hanging her! We'll see about this when we arrive back in Sydney."

Sir Rothwell smiled at her. "I won't be hanging her just yet. Keep it in mind that your cooperation will be a cause of leniency on my part. In the meantime I have a task for you." He turned to one of the guards. "Fetch Doris."

The guard disappeared down a hatch. He reappeared shortly, grunting as with some load. He dragged an Aboriginal woman up through the trapdoor by her hair. Her hands were fastened behind her back and she struggled to retain her footing on the ladder. The guard pushed her to the deck between Sir Rothwell and his prisoners. "Reverend, I'd like you to meet Doris. Doris, meet the Reverend Missionary Rosalyn Flynn. She's come here to enlighten you."

Doris stayed where she had been pushed and gave no sound. Rosalyn studied her. She was wearing an old shirt and trousers given to her by a crewman. "Doris doesn't speak much. In fact Doris doesn't speak at all. It's possible she doesn't want to speak because we are men. You are not."

"You're an observant bugger, I'll give you that," said Fey.

Sir Rothwell turned to the guard. "Strike her." The guard struck Fey on the head with his musket butt. Fey's eyes flashed with anger. "You'll pay for that. Both of you."

"Yes, I'm sure. Now be a good little currency girl and keep your damned mouth shut." He turned to Rosalyn. "Reverend Flynn, I'm charging you with the task of enlightening Doris with the knowledge of the Queen's English, or..." Sir Rothwell looked at Fey and gestured as though hanging himself in a noose.

Rosalyn sat silently, weighing up the situation before she spoke. "You, Sir, are not a gentleman. Under the circumstances I accept. I do however expect fair treatment for myself and my companion."

"Agreed, as long your companion learns to hold her tongue."

Sir Rothwell had Fey's hands bound behind her back in the same manner as Doris and she was bundled below deck, her face red with anger. Seeing her safely away, Sir Rothwell turned back to Rosalyn. "Reverend, you'll have some freedom to move around the deck but you will be escorted at all times. If you try to act the heroine your friend will suffer. Am I understood?"

"Yes, you're understood."

"Good. You can start work after the burial. I'm assuming as a Reverend you will be so good as to say a few words for the unfortunate fellow whom your friend murdered."

Rosalyn gritted her teeth.

The dead man's friends buried him not far from where the *Lightning* sat at rest. Sand was heaped over the grave and his fellows built a cairn of rocks. Rosalyn kept her service brief and returned to the *Eyrie* to start the lessons with her unwilling pupil. She instructed the guard to untie Doris's hands, an instruction which caused the guard some consternation. Sir Rothwell intervened and compromised by having the rope tied around the woman's waist, the loose ends fastened to a tie point on the skyrail. This allowed Doris a much greater degree of movement.

Doris cowered whenever the guard approached so Rosalyn told him to stand further away. Doris trembled in fear and refused to look at Rosalyn. Rosalyn reached out and took Doris's hand in hers, gently stroking the back of it. "Hand," she said. Doris glanced at her and turned her eyes back to the deck. Rosalyn could see her task wasn't going to be an easy one. She persevered for some time but made no progress.

Sir Rothwell took a party, including the scientists, to explore the ruins. Rosalyn stood and watched as they went aground and walked away. She noticed one of Sir Rothwell's guardsmen kept close by Watson. Thus engaged, she felt someone pulling at her fingers. "Hand." Rosalyn looked at Doris and gave what she hoped was a reassuring smile. She sat down beside her pupil. By the time the explorers returned Doris had learned a dozen words.

For the most part Rosalyn was kept isolated from the scientists. This brought a measure of protest from both Watson and Geoffrey but their protests were ignored. As night fell, Sir Rothwell, unconvinced of the diurnal nature of lizards, had the ship rise to a holding position deemed safe from their reach. Doris was secured again below deck and Rosalyn was allowed to take food down to both her and Fey. The guard waited at the top of the hatchway. Rosalyn couldn't stand upright under the low ceiling. Stores took up most of the space, the bound captives leaned against sacks of flour. "Are you all right, Fey?" In the dull light of the confined space Rosalyn could see Fey's eyes, red and wet with tears.

"No. It's bloody cramped and hot in here, and they don't take me to answer nature's call as much as I'd like. That, and I feel like punching someone's snout. How is it going up there? Any news?"

"Nothing much. Sir Rothwell went out exploring the ruins today but I don't think they found much of interest to them. I've spent most of the time teaching Doris to speak English."

"We have to find a way to get out of here and back to the Lightning and we're going to have to do it at night."

"I don't know how we're going to manage it. We're at too high an altitude."

"Maybe if we climb down the hook ropes."

"I don't know if I could manage that either. We'd still have the guards to contend with."

"What can you manage?"

"I can manage to feed you if you'll give me a chance—now enough with being a bad-tempered sook and open your mouth." Fey settled back and let Rosalyn spoon feed her.

Fey leaned back. "I've seen him before."

"Who?"

"That Rothwell bloke. I saw him on the docks about a week or so before you arrived. He was met by another man. I knew he was military when I saw him."

"Who was the other man?"

"Dunno, but I think he might have been the bloke who was looking at you when you arrived."

"It's of small matter to us now. We have to find a way to escape this vessel and return to the Lightning."

Watson came over to Rosalyn as she sat on a pile of sacks on the deck, leaning over the skyrails, staring out into the ruins. "What are you thinking, Reverend?"

"How Fey and I might get off this boat."

"That will be difficult. They're watching you closely."

"Can we expect any help from the other scientists? What's their mood?"

"I've discovered the other two are members of the Mechanical Order. I suspect they're keeping me under observation, too. My good friend Geoffrey feels as I do but there is little we can achieve. We haven't the vigour of youth and are men of science, not action."

"I understand that, Watson, but sometimes we must pray for courage and God's guidance to get us through the more difficult times."

"Perhaps your God sees fit to answer your prayers. He's completely oblivious to mine."

"Do you think you might at least keep me informed of anything you learn that could be to my advantage?"

"Yes, of course, Reverend, I'll do that."

20

Close Encounters Of The Odd Kind

Hands reached out of the darkness of the night and grabbed Fey under her arms, roughly hoisting her up and dragging her onto the deck. She struggled against their grasp. A man's voice said, "Settle down girl or you'll get 'urt."

"What the bloody hell are you doing? I was having a nice sleep there."

"Sleepin' times over darlin'. You're being put to ground." Fey, lifted onto her feet, looked around. The faintest line of grey showed on the eastern horizon.

"Where's Roz—the Reverend?"

"She's at your airship waitin' for you. Don't give us any trouble now or you'll go to ground the fast way."

"Bullshit, you're not on the square."

"No, and we don't care. Now I'm goin' to put this 'ere rope around your neck and untie your 'ands so you can climb down the net."

"Pig's piss hole you are. You're not putting a rope around my neck. You bastards are going to hang me." Fey started kicking.

"No we ain't. Stop fussin' now, sweetheart. If you squirm too much my mate Rattrap here will put a ball into you."

Rattrap had a lean face and his sideburns almost joined at the chin. His gold tooth glistened and he grinned at her in a most disturbing way. Fey stopped resisting and descended the ladder, covered by Rattrap's pistol. On reaching the ground the other man led the way, dragging Fey with the rope, Rattrap following behind. "I don't think this is the way to the Lightning. We have to go up this way." Fey pointed. The lead man gave the rope a strong pull and Fey stumbled. "Steady on. You could've done me an injury." Fey's voice started to shake. Her captors didn't respond. Fey became increasingly worried. "Rosalyn isn't at the Lightning is she? What have you done with her?"

Rattrap kicked her and told her to get a move on. Fey responded by screaming out Rosalyn's name. That earned her a crack on the head from Rattrap's pistol butt. She stumbled again, her petticoat head-covering falling to the sand. Fey didn't know if it was perspiration or blood running down her face. "You bastards. You've done away with her, haven't you?"

"No, my lovely. Your Reverend is safe and snug aboard and heavily doped by Sir Rothwell. It's you that's being done away with, but we might have a bit of fun with you first. What do you say, Mince?"

"Yeah, wouldn't be no harm in pluggin' her before we plug her." Mince laughed at his own crude joke and reached with one hand to rip at her shirt. Without thinking, Fey head-butted the man's nose and ran. Mince recovered quickly and grasped the end of the rope; as it closed tight around Fey's neck a shot rang out. A lead ball whistled past her head and the rope around her neck fell loose—nothing held her back.

Another two shots sounded close by. A ball struck the ruined rock wall beside her, splintering the stone, the tiny fragments stinging her face. Her captors yelled, their loathsome tones flecked with fear and anger. Fey, didn't hear their words, didn't look back. Her feet pounded on the soft sand, her hands grasped at the rope as she raced for freedom. The sound of another shot reached her, distant now, and she felt a surging hope that she might make good her escape. The *Lightning* loomed up out of the morning gloom ahead. She knew she would have no way of getting it started and away before the men were upon her. The *Lightning* wasn't her goal and she hunted around in the sand between the stones where she had thrown the carbine and belt when they'd been taken prisoner.

Fey's fingers closed around the weapon. She breathed a sigh of relief. More frantic searching revealed the belt with its pouches of powder and ball. Knowing the first place a search party would look would be the *Lightning*, she put distance between herself and the airship. The sound of a single set of heavy footfalls came from behind her. The pursuer had gained on her while she'd searched for the weapon. Lungs aching and the muscles in her thighs burning she dropped down behind a low wall and made ready to fire at her pursuer.

The person who appeared around the corner wasn't at all who Fey was expecting. She moved her finger from the trigger. Dressed in black, with a black hat, the man carried a carbine. He ran bent over, in the same way Fey had run when she was being shot at. She stood up, levelling her carbine at him as he came running by. The sight of the woman standing up before him arrested his movement and he came to a stop at the point of Fey's carbine's muzzle. They both spoke at once with Fey saying, "Who the bloody hell are you?" and him saying, "Oh good, there you are." Another gunshot sent a lead ball flying past and cracking into the wall next to them.

"Lovely to meet you, chat later. I really must be off now. Come along if you wish to." The man ran off and Fey paused only a second before sprinting after him. She caught up and with a gasp managed to ask, "Where are we going?"

"I don't have the foggiest of ideas, but when they get their airship up in the air our goose will be well and ... there're two of us so perhaps that's geese. Still, no time to quibble over spilt grammar. We're being hunted and we need to hide."

"I've been making a habit of that."

"Hiding?"

"Being hunted. Hiding too."

"Now would be an excellent time to hide."

"I know somewhere if we can get to it."

"You do? Marvellous. Lead the way."

Fey wasn't entirely sure of the way and they followed a winding route to reach the place she had in mind. In the distance, the sound of the engine of the *Eyrie* could be heard. The sand-covered dome appeared before them and Fey brought them to the door. "This is it. We have to push this stone." They put their shoulders to it and the door swivelled on its hinge. Safely inside they sank to the floor gasping for breath, their backs against the door.

"What is this place?" asked the man. He looked at the top of the stairs in the soft light filtering through the cracks in the stonework.

"It's a cistern. We'll have to be careful—there's a snake or two."

"That shouldn't be a problem at all for a seasoned campaigner such as myself. I'll simply decapitate the creatures with my sword."

"You'll need a bigger sword."

"Are they big snakes?"

"Have you seen the big lizards?"

"My word yes. Extraordinary creatures. Huge. They remind me of—"

"The snakes are close to lizard size," Fey interrupted.

"I see. And they're downstairs, I presume."

"That's where we saw them."

"Who else knows about this place?"

"Roz and Watson. It was Watson who showed it to us. I don't know if that Rothwell cove knows about it. They've been poking around the ruins so they may well do."

"We must entertain the idea that they'll eventually come here looking for us."

"Yeah. I think we're done. I can't give up though, they were going to shoot me."

"I noticed that. It's fortunate for you I happened along. Is there any other way out of this cistern?"

"Dunno. The stairs lead down to a central island in a lake. The thing looks like it might be a natural cavern. There're the snakes too, we can't forget the snakes."

"No, let's not forget the snakes." They waited, still recovering from their hurried flight. "A cup of tea would be nice."

Fey looked at him. "I think we have other bloody things to worry about. Look, we can see out through these cracks here. One of us better keep watch so we know when those bastards are coming."

"Good idea, yes, keep watch. Time is important. I have a watch here I think. No, that's right, the blacks have it. Still, we know it's tea time."

Fey looked at him in an effort to appraise the man's sanity but saw nothing that could decide her opinion either way. She turned her head to a crack, looking out into the ruins. "You better tell me who you are. I like to know whose company I'm keeping."

"Why, of course. I'm Max... No, wait. I'm not Max, I'm Samuel, Samuel Bluetooth." He lowered his head and stared at the sandy floor. "That's not right either, Bluerose. I'm quite sure of it now. I'm Samuel Bluerose."

Fey gave him a queer look. "You're the bloke who came through Max's station aren't you?"

"Max? Hmmm. I'm not Max you know. I'm Samuel. The station. I do recall that Max has a station in his life. Yes, you're quite right. I did pass through Max's station. My goodness, it seems so long ago but it couldn't have been much more than a week or two. Time flies you know? It's a peculiar thing."

"So I've heard. You're a bit old to be waltzing around in the desert."

"Grey hairs are not a sign of a grey mind and although one must take into account the brain is grey matter we must put our minds over it."

"I can't smell rum on your breath so I'm guessing you've been out in the sun too long. You're the Guardian aren't you? The bloke from

Roz's church."

Samuel pondered. "Guardian, you say? I haven't heard of this Roz. You must be talking about the Missionary chap."

"She's not a chap. She's the Reverend Missionary Rosalyn Flynn, and right now she's on that big red airship in peril."

"I do know her now. Yes, I was looking for her. She has the airship doesn't she?"

"Yes and it's still there. We could get away in it but not in daylight. The Order would be on us in no time and I'm not leaving Roz."

"Quite right, we're not leaving her. We must effect a rescue at the earliest hour."

"That's going to have to wait a bit. Do you hear that?"

The sound of the *Eyrie*'s engine came to them from the distance and as they waited the sound became louder. Fey and Samuel looked at each other as they listened. The crash of a gun was instantly followed by the deafening crack of something hitting the stones with force. They flinched and cowered against the sides of the dome. "I say, that was rather a big calibre."

"Yeah, they have swivel guns."

A voice shouted to them as they huddled in their shelter, fingers curled around their carbines. "We know you're in there. Come out with your hands up and you won't be harmed."

"I don't believe the bastard—they were going to kill me. Why would they have changed their minds?"

"I'm inclined to agree with you; they're not quite the sporting sorts. I suggest we take the stairs. We have the powder and shot if those snakes of yours put in an appearance."

"We don't have any light. That's going to put a damper on our descent. Taking on giant snakes in the dark puts me a long way from where I'm comfortable. There's that other thing too."

"Other thing?"

"Something followed behind the snakes. I didn't get a good look at it but it was big."

"My dear girl, so are elephants and I bravely slew one or two of those frightful beasts. One of them was a monstrous bull elephant, as big as they get in India. As for light, I did come prepared for such eventualities as darkness. I may be a fool but not a complete fool, I'll have you know. A partial fool perhaps, but not a complete fool." Samuel reached inside his coat to a pouch on his belt, pulling from it a small brass box with a handle on the top. "Now, if this thing works... Let me see... I think I push this, yes, I turn this wheel and flick this little lever and..." A glass window at the front of the box lit up and shed some light in the dimness of the interior. "You see? Only part of me is foolish—the other part is complete genius. Shall we?"

"Yeah, let's get down there, those blokes will be coming in after us soon. You have the lantern, you lead."

"Certainly my dear girl, certainly. I'll shoulder this carbine, and yes a pistol will be much better one-handed. I really must mount the lantern on the carbine. That will work, yes, of course, I'll work on that."

They headed down the stairs as the men above them shouted at them to surrender. As they reached the bottom they heard the stone door above them scrape its way open. Fey stood behind Samuel as he shone the lantern around the chamber. The beam of light failed to reach the sides so they continued around the ledge without seeing any sign of a far bank on to which they might exit.

"We'll have to go in or give up."

"Give up? Dear me, no. I've been in much worse pickles than this. No surrender I say. Let me... here, you hold this." Samuel gave Fey the lantern and took off his back pack and coat. This revealed another peculiar arrangement of pistols and pouches attached to a harness which he also removed. Following that, he took off another belt which held two more pistols, a sword, a knife and sundry other pouches. He inched himself into the water and found it to be a depth of only a few feet.

"Ooh, that makes my balls retract."

"What?"

"I said, 'we're having a ball in fact'."

"Yeah right, can we get moving? This place creeps me out."

"Of course. Careful as you get in—the water is a trifle cold."

He put his pack back on, wrapped the remaining items in his coat, making a neat bundle, and placed it on his head. He took the lantern from Fey and she slid carefully into the water. The men above, having had to delay their pursuit while a lantern was procured, began descending the stairs.

"Be a dear and fire a shot up there will you?" Fey turned and fired the carbine at the opening. "That's the way. They'll be giving careful consideration before following us—more time for our escape."

Fey squinted as she looked into the darkness. She stood waist deep in the cold water, wondering how this escape might be made effective. Samuel waded on with Fey following him closely, turning occasionally to see if the light of the men's lantern showed them to be in pursuit. The sounds of leather boots on the stone stairs echoed through the cavern as their pursuers found the courage to again attempt to follow them.

A shout was followed by a shot and the lead ball splashed into the water next to Fey. "Hurry it up in front, we need to get out of musket range."

"I can assure you, I'm wading as fast as I can."

Another shout pierced the darkness followed by a scream. More shouting echoed through the cavern. Fey looked back and saw the muzzle flashes of muskets. They weren't aimed at her or Samuel. The shouting continued amid the sound of churning water. More shots sounded and then silence and darkness.

"I think the snakes got them."

"Let's not count on it. They may be back. And you might think that if the snakes didn't get them then those wretched serpents will come for us." Samuel held up the lamp. "Ah look! There, you see? A bank on which we might climb out of this water. I feel my feet are growing quite numb with the cold."

The bank was a mixture of bedrock, sand and gravel and they

waded out onto it. A quick play of the lantern light revealed a large opening in the cavern wall. After Fey reloaded her carbine Samuel gave her the lantern, broke open his bundle and reequipped himself. "This is the way." Samuel's tone was strong and confident.

"'How do you know that? Have you been here before?"

"Not at all. It has to be this way. The other way has men with guns and oversize serpents."

"I see your angle clearly. This way it is."

The opening, formed by nature, showed additional shaping by human hand, making its navigation easier. They hurried along its winding length, unsure of where it was taking them. It opened at last into another large chamber. This one was filled with piles of rocks of all sizes with a pool of water in the centre. On the walls were strange depictions of animals and people, painted in a variety of ochres.

"Marvellous, absolutely marvellous. These things must be thousands of years old."

Fey looked at him and back up at the paintings, illuminated by the glow of Samuel's lantern. "I could paint better than that."

"That's hardly the point. These are the manifestations of a great spirituality and that is something which cannot be contrived. Marvellous, really extraordinary. If only I had some way to record it or someone to decipher it."

"I can tell you what it's about. See that one? That one is a kangaroo, and that one there is a man with a spear—you can tell he's a man by his long fellow. And that there, I think that's a giant wombat by the looks."

"Miss... you know I don't think you shared your name with me."

"Fey Grey."

"Short and sweet, like the last time I saw Bridget. Fey Grey. I like that. Miss Grey I can see what the figures are meant to represent but I do think there is some great undertone which quite escapes us." Samuel paused and studied the paintings more closely. "It does resemble a giant wombat. How odd."

"Bloody astounding as they are, if we loiter about here much longer the bloody snakes or those men will come down that passage looking for us. And I don't like the way these walls are starting to close in on me."

"Quite right. It would have been nice to stop for a spot of tea in amongst these rocks in this lovely chamber." Samuel shone the lantern around the cave. "Look at this here, Miss Grey, it's a stone box."

"Has it got bones in it?"

"I don't know; it has a lid on it and it looks heavy. Give me a hand if you could."

The box wasn't overly large, about two feet long and crudely carved from a single piece of stone. The lid, six inches thick, made a loud scraping noise as they pushed it from the container. Samuel shone the light into it.

"What's in there? Can you see anything?" asked Fey.

"Yes, wonderful things."

Fey leaned over the box and looked in. "Yeah, I can see gold and diamonds, and no bones."

"You wanted bones?"

"No. If there are bones I'm not allowed to have the gold. Roz says."

"There's more than gold here."

Fey picked up some of the nuggets, none of which were bigger than her thumb. "There is?"

"Yes, stone tools, see?" Samuel showed her a dark grey stone. "The edge has been ground down. There are several of them here."

"Yeah, rocks, and a bunch of painted sticks and other bits of wood, too." Fey raked her hand around in the box, "Aren't these diamonds?"

"Crystals." Samuel reached into the box, picked out a piece and held it to the lantern light. "Clear quartz crystal. I've heard it has special qualities for the black witch doctors."

Fey looked closely at one of the pieces. "Is it worth anything?"

"No, but the gold is. Gold is always worth something."

"Whoever put it here thought sticks and rocks were worth as much."

"Different people, Miss Grey, different values."

Samuel continued playing the light around the chamber. While thus engaged, Fey stuffed a good handful of gold specimens into her tobacco pouch, adding others into the pouches on her thigh belt. "Is there another way out?"

"Come, we'll search along the edges." He led the way past the pool, between the rocks, to the other side of the chamber, continuing on until they reached their starting point. "That's disappointing. Let's try again shall we? There must be some crevice or cranny we've missed among all these rocks and shadows." They continued their search, being much more careful this time, exploring every hidden nook. Fey drew Samuel's attention to a particular flat rock on the floor of the cave.

"Here. This one has carvings on it."

"My word, so it does. Look here, too. These grooves on the stone and the wear marks— the thing moves. We must try to slide it."

They pushed on the slab in the direction of the grooves. Although the grooves ran on a slight uphill incline it didn't take much effort to move the slab. It had to be held in place to prevent it sliding back again. Samuel was peering down the revealed hole when they heard a strange sound from the other side of the chamber. It was a low, soft, scraping sound accompanied by the clattering of small rocks disturbed from their resting places.

"Get in, Miss Grey. There's a ledge there." Fey dropped into the hole and Samuel, ridding himself of his backpack with impressive speed, followed her. As he reached up to pull his pack in, the slab slid back into place. The pack was stuck and to free it Samuel pushed at the slab. The strange, sucking, slithering noises were growing louder.

"It's a bit more difficult from this side—I can't do it one-handed.

Hold the lantern."

Fey took the lantern and in return gave some helpful advice. "Leave the bloody thing! Those are the snakes coming."

"Yes, thank you, Miss Grey, I'm well aware, but everything I need is in this pack."

"Then get a bloody move on or you'll be wearing a snakeskin suit."

Samuel continued to struggle in the narrow space as Fey directed the light at the problem. A large shape appeared in the beam of light on the other side of the hole. The head of the creature consisted of a single double-lidded eye. As it moved about they could see short spikes covering the upper side of it. The underside was pink with rows of small, tube-like appendages. It reared back and another creature, identical to the first, started nudging at the slab. The slab moved back and the pack, now freed, was released. Samuel, who had all his weight pulling on the pack, fell back against Fey leaving them balanced awkwardly on the ledge.

A creature wedged its head into the hole pushing the slab further open. Another creature tried to push in beside it and beyond that they could make out a third. "Shoot the damned thing, Miss Grey, shoot it." The creature slowly made its way towards them, the body swaying as it approached.

Fey held the carbine one-handed and without aiming, squeezed the trigger. The muzzle flashed and gunsmoke filled the confined space. Fey turned, trying to reach an ammunition pouch, slipped, and fell to the floor some ten feet below. The carbine caught the strap of Samuel's pack and it came with her. Samuel, not wanting to lose his precious cargo, rolled off the ledge and landed on top of Fey. Above them they heard the sound of the slab slamming back into place.

The lantern light showed through the haze of the gun smoke. They stared up at the slab. Silence. Confident of their safety, they got to their feet, dusted themselves off and looked around. A narrow stone corridor led off in two directions.

"Are you injured, Sam?"

"No. I think all my bits are where they should be. One might say between the fear and the cold I may be taken for a eunuch but it's nothing I won't recover from with a hot bath and a cup of tea. What about yourself, Miss Grey, are you sound?"

"I'll have a few bruises I think, otherwise good. Which way?"

"Why, this way of course." Samuel adjusted his backpack and set off.

"Why that way?" asked Fey, staring after him.

"Because this is the way we're going. You do ask some frightfully silly questions."

21

CECILIA SPOTSWOOD

Cecilia watched until her companions were out of sight and lay back against a stone, the carbine in her lap. She took her watch from her purse and glanced at the time. After an hour she stood up, walked over to the *Lightning* and opened her one of her trunks. The bottle lay where she had concealed it and with her small folding apple-knife she prised the top off. The paper had unrolled making it difficult to retrieve, so she threw the bottle against one of the stones. She walked over to where the note lay, picked it up and read:

'Dear Friend,

I'm lost. I can only assume my message balloon failed to return to Sydney. The companions who didn't desert me are dead to hostile blacks or from want of water. Friendly blacks saved me. I'll remain living with them until I'm rescued, for I do believe that others will follow and I will be discovered.

These large stones are an enigma to me as I'm sure they are to you. I cannot speak the language of the blacks who have nurtured me, but am hopeful of learning more and they may be able to shed light on the origins of this place. The blacks fear to come here and are waiting for me at a distance. I know such a structure as this will attract the attention of other explorers and in examining the rocks, will find my mark and so too, this message.

The people I am with are to the North-East of this point. Of distance I have no notion. Do try to find me, and be generous with these people. I have been with them for a month and they have been so kind to me in their own primitive way.

Yours in hope,
Doctor Norman Phatts
1836'

Cecilia read the letter twice and found no mention of the Green Wave but she didn't really expect there to be. To Dr Phatts it was an unusual butterfly, one of many unusual things he had seen, and the knowledge of its significance was yet to unfold. What she had learned was the general whereabouts of Dr Phatts and the chance he may still be living. She returned to the *Lightning*.

The bottom of her clothing trunk had a false floor, accessed by working a cunningly disguised latch. She opened the compartment. Everything was as she had placed it. After removing her corset and divesting herself of the rest of her attire, she stood naked, her clothing crumpled around her feet. She looked around the stones and beyond them, seeing only the still, empty landscape. Her body was pale, almost white and she could feel the sun burning her.

She reached into her trunk and proceeded to dress herself in the clothes concealed there; clothes less cumbersome and impractical than the garments of gentle ladies. The hot, layered skirts she replaced with leggings akin to trousers. A plain, long-sleeved blouse covered her top and it tucked into a short skirt. Over the blouse she put on a sturdy, brown leather corset, which, after years of practice, she expertly laced herself into.

To fit the boots into the trunk she had squashed them as flat as she could and now she sat on the skyrail, pulling them on, ensuring the laces and buckles were tight. On her wrists she wore leather bracers, a compass artfully riveted into one of them and a timepiece in the other. She buckled on a wide belt containing pistols and a dagger. Another belt was worn diagonally across her chest and this contained pouches of shot and gunpowder.

Lastly she took out a satchel which she wore from her shoulder so it lay diagonally the other way to her ammunition belt. The satchel contained goggles and two soft, leather, water bottles. She took out the water bottles and put in her journal and note books. The hat she had packed was of a light cylindrical type with a wide brim. It had been collapsed for packing and she pushed it back into shape. She tore a length from her ruined petticoat and wrapped it around her face to protect her skin from the sun. Carelessly throwing her other clothes back into the trunk, she slithered into the cistern and filled the water bottles.

That done she climbed up the broken stones, jumping from one to another with goat-like confidence, and from the rocks clambered onto a lintel of the stone circle. Using her goggles she looked in the direction Rosalyn and Fey had taken. The scene was magnified as though looking through a telescope. Nothing was out there but grasses, scrub, rocks and heat haze. She gave the east and west a quick perusal before turning her attention to the northeast. At a great distance was a single plume of smoke. She climbed down, collected the carbine and her insect net and set off in search of the source of the smoke.

Travelling by foot across the desolate terrain was so much harder than it had looked from the air and Cecilia was not accustomed to long walks. The task was made more difficult by her attempts to cover her tracks. She was sure Rosalyn would not even think to do so but Fey was cunning enough to try to follow her. From the top of another grass-covered dune she stared off into the distance. The plume of smoke she had seen earlier was gone now but she still had the bearing.

Several times she came across large species of lizards; not the giant size that entered the grotto but large enough to give her the chills. The lizards in England she'd thought of as large were mere specks beside some of the specimens crawling through the grass around her. She gave them a wide berth and did her best not to look at them. Only one snake crossed her path; a small one focussed entirely on making its escape. No time could be spared to look for insects but she was sure there were enough for at least two leather-bound, illustrated volumes.

After hours of nonstop travelling and seeing nothing more interesting than a small flock of emus, Cecilia stopped by a clump of stunted trees. The important thing now was to make contact with the blacks. She remembered Daddy saying once that it didn't matter where in the world you were, when entering into the space of another, one should always announce one's arrival loudly lest one be taken for an intruder or a snoop.

One of the trees had died and fallen some time ago, its form silvered and broken. She gathered up the loose pieces and made a stack of the wood. Into its base she stuffed a mass of dried grass and using a lens from her sunglass to focus the sun's rays she soon had the pile ablaze. The fire didn't produce as much smoke as she wanted so she added some green leaves torn from one of the dead tree's living relatives. She sat down to wait.

Cecilia fell asleep watching the stars appearing as the sky darkened. She awoke early and sat backed up against a large clump of grass, hugging her knees, the rising sun warming her. A feeling came over her of being watched. She took a pistol from her belt, primed it, rose to her feet and turned around.

The man standing before her had grey hair and beard and his shoulders, torso and thighs were covered with raised scars. By their arrangement they must have been deliberately created. Cecilia saw behind him two more men, younger, their bodies lithe and muscular. She kept her weapon lowered and the Aborigines made no move to use their own. They stood for a time in silence, staring at each other. The older man turned to one of the younger men and said something, an instruction, and the young man turned and trotted off. The greybeard said something to Cecilia and made indications to her to follow him.

For half a day they walked through broken country and came at last to a waterhole where other Aborigines had gathered, including women and children. Some of them backed away, most stood their ground. A man several shades paler than the others walked directly to Cecilia. "Who are you?" asked the pale man in perfect English.

"I'm Miss Cecilia Spotswood. And I presume that in spite of your lack of attire you are the Englishman, Doctor Norman Phatts."

"Yes, I am," said Doctor Phatts, covering his groin with his shield. "I assume you're from a party that has come to rescue me."

"Yes, I suppose I am."

Dr Phatts studied her before replying. "Why would they send a woman? Did they recover my balloon? How long has it been? Three years?"

"Your balloon arrived in England recently."

"England? It was supposed to go to Sydney."

"It was still on the manufacturer's settings. You had to reset the device and put in your own bearings for the Sydney beacon."

Norman stared at the sand. "Carson did the settings. I should have checked them. Poor Carson."

"And I wasn't exactly sent. I insisted on coming."

"Insisted? Why in God's name would a young Englishwoman want to come out into the Australian desert?"

"I'm an entomologist, see?" said Cecilia. She waved her butterfly net.

Doctor Phatts followed the movement of the net and returned his gaze to Cecilia. "Hmm, I do see, but it doesn't quite explain your presence this far out. Are you lost?"

"No. I'm looking for a butterfly—the Green Wave."

"You can't be serious. You've wandered out alone into this dry, wild country to catch butterflies?"

"Not exactly. I was part of a party but our airship had an accident. They wandered off for help leaving me with the airship and they never returned. While I was waiting for them I found your message."

"What message?"

"The one in the bottle at the stone circle."

"I don't remember it." Norman stared at the ground again and rubbed his chin. "And you've been wandering in the desert hoping to find me." Doctor Phatts gave her a concerned look. "How long have you been wandering? Have you been drinking enough water?"

"Not long, and yes, although if it's all right I'll need to fill my water bottles." She paused. "I was hoping to find you for my own reasons."

"Own reasons? Do we know each other? You look familiar."

"We've never met. And yes, own reasons. You described a butterfly that we call the Green Wave. I want to find it. You see, it's hard for a woman to make a place for herself in the sciences and if I bring back a specimen then, with it and other new species, I'll make quite the name for myself."

"So you came looking for me in the hope that somehow in the middle of this vast continent you'd manage it? You are quite mad young lady."

"I wasn't alone, but I did manage it. See, here you are and here I am standing next to you." Cecilia smiled up at him.

"Yes, you're here but how did you know I found the green butterfly? Wait—it was mentioned in the notes in the message balloon wasn't it?"

"Yes, it was. So where is it? Does it even exist?"

"Miss Spotsdick..."

"Spotswood, Cecilia Spotswood."

"Miss Spotswood, I have no idea where I saw the green butterfly. I barely remember it. I was lost at the time."

"Well that rather spoils it. Can you give me a clue?"

A man ran into the camp, talking loudly. He took the attention of everyone, including Doctor Phatts, leaving Cecilia standing by herself. Angry faces turned towards her and she could see from his manner and gestures that Doctor Phatts was arguing vehemently on her behalf. After much heated talk, Doctor Phatts turned to Cecilia and explained, "There's been trouble with some other pale-skinned people. I can only assume they are your companions. I really must go, and so must you. I've arranged for three of the older women to travel with you to where my people first found me. After that I'm afraid you're on your own."

"Your people? But..." Cecilia tried to ask questions but Doctor Phatts had already turned his back, following the other men into the dry scrubland.

22

SIR ROTHWELL'S CORROBOREE

Rosalyn woke to the rocking of the boat as the airship ascended. Doris was sitting beside her, her wrists still bound; a guard sat next to them smoking his pipe. Rosalyn sat up. "What's happening?"

"We're going up. 'ere, 'ave a cuppa. I've kept it on the 'eat for you. You'll feel better."

Rosalyn took the proffered cup of tea. The ship was hazy and dreamlike and she entertained the idea that she might still be asleep. The men on deck were agitated and one of them was having a wound dressed. "Was there a storm, or were we attacked by a lizard?"

"No storms, Reverend, and no lizards. Your friend 'as done a runner."

"Whatever do you mean?"

Sir Rothwell appeared from behind her. "He means your friend ran off. She left you."

"Why would she do that? She said nothing to me."

"She's of the convict class. What do you expect? You were sound asleep and you have your task with Doris. I thought I would make your friend useful and had some men take her to your airship to see if it was in good repair. Unfortunately she snatched a gun from one of my men and shot him. He's lucky he wasn't killed but he took the ball in the arm."

"Fey wouldn't do that—she wouldn't leave me without a word." Rosalyn stopped to consider the idea and the ugly thought entered her head that perhaps Fey would. "Where is she now?"

"We're going to find out. We'll see if we can spot her from the air. If not, I'm afraid we'll have to leave without her. You keep yourself busy teaching English to the savage." Sir Rothwell left them to join the watch at the prow.

Rosalyn sat stunned and stared into her tea. Doris wriggled up closer to her, drawing Rosalyn's attention. Doris looked down at the mug in Rosalyn's hand and said, "Tea." Turning to the guard Rosalyn asked if Doris' hands might be untied that she could have a cup of tea. The guard grunted and secured Doris's waist rope and untied her hands. He thrust a cup of tea into her hands with such bad grace that the hot liquid sloshed over the sides. The man withdrew and engaged himself in the serious business of cleaning his pipe.

Doris looked at Rosalyn again. "Tea."

"Yes, Doris, tea. Drink it."

"Tea, sleep."

"No, sleep is when you close your eyes to rest at night. You know sleep. I've taught you that word."

Doris indicated Sir Rothwell at the other end of the boat, leaning over the bow trying to spy Fey. "Tea, man, sleep, Roz." She made a move to indicate putting something into the tea and Rosalyn understood. Her eyes flashed with anger and she made to get up. Doris pushed her back and put one hand over her mouth and kept her other hand on Rosalyn's chest, steadying her. She glanced at the guard who looked up from his labours.

"Trouble there, Reverend?" asked the guard.

Rosalyn pushed Doris's hand from her mouth. "No, no trouble at all. Teaching Doris the words for mouth and body. It gets a little frustrating sometimes." The guard nodded and went back to his pipe. Rosalyn mused to herself, "Why would he drug me? He didn't want me awake." Her eyes opened wide and she made a quick appraisal of her physical self. Her clothing was in place and she felt no sensations in her body that shouldn't have been there. "It had to do with Fey, but if Sir Rothwell didn't want me awake he meant her violence and he didn't want me hearing." She turned to Doris. "Fey?" If Doris did know more she was unable to communicate it. She merely repeated Fey's name and said something in her own language.

A commotion from the crew at the bow drew Rosalyn's attention. She made to rise but the guard motioned her down with a wave of his pistol. One of the more deep-voiced men was calling on Fey to come out of somewhere. This was followed by silence and Sir Rothwell, now next to the swivel gun, instructed the men to fire. The loud crack of the gun was followed by the distant sound of the ball hitting rock. More shouting at Fey to come out failed to induce her to surrender. Sir Rothwell ordered men to be lowered and four of them went over the side in harnesses.

Rosalyn waited, silently biting her lip. Doris huddled up next to her, holding Rosalyn's arm. When they heard the distant sound of shooting and shouting they clutched each other. More time elapsed and the crew on deck moved to lower a scaling net. The men on the ground clambered up it, over the skyrail and onto the deck in a state of panic; black powder stains on their cheeks and breathless from running.

"What happened?" asked Sir Rothwell.

"We saw them. There's a bloody big cave down there filled with water. We saw them and fired and then those Hell-things came." The man supported himself with his musket, panting for breath.

"What Hell-things? Talk sense. What are you blathering about?"

"It weren't lots of them—it were only one," said another man.

"It were giant snakes, sir, all pale and thicker than a man's thigh, thick as a mast, as big as those lizards, sir, bigger. And there was more behind them."

"They were all part of the same creature," said his mate.

"There was lots of 'em, giant snake things, I saw 'em."

"You, you say it was only one creature. What did you see?"

"I saw what he saw first, like, dozens of giant snakes, only it wasn't. Something else moved behind them, in the centre, a big pale round thing, and these things, they weren't snakes, they was joined to it."

"Like a squid, or an octopus?"

"Not like any squid I've ever seen, sir. It was big and it could move fast."

"Not as fast as you, I see."

"No, sir, I could outrun any man in England with that thing behind me. I was scared, sir, I couldn't 'elp it and I'm not ashamed to say it. It was worse than them lizards."

Sir Rothwell studied the man and looked at his companions, red-faced and sweating from their rapid flight. Even if he hadn't seen the giant lizards, the look of the men alone would have convinced him they had seen something terrible.

"We fired everything we had, sir, and we ran. I'm sorry to say, sir, but we ran. We come back up those stairs like a shot from a cannon, sir. We ran."

"Yes, yes. I see. Get yourself some water and then you and your fellows have a pipe and a shot of rum. Damn it, have two shots. You'll feel much better after you've got your breath back." Sir Rothwell turned around to see Rosalyn glaring at him. He walked over to her.

"I'm terribly sorry, Reverend. We did ask your friend to surrender herself. She's dangerous you know and she caused a spot of bother. Tell me now—this Cecilia—she's here isn't she?"

"I don't know what you mean."

"Your friend Fey, she's with someone. I think you know more than you're letting on."

"I can assure you I have no idea. All I know is that Cecilia Spotswood is an entomologist who was accompanying me to the frontier to study beetles."

"What do you know of Doctor Phatts?"

"Doctor Phatts? Hmm, I believe he was an explorer who went

missing."

"You have no other knowledge of him?"

"Why should I? I'm a Missionary tasked with bringing Enlightenment to the heathens."

"But you're more than that, Reverend Flynn. I've read your Orders and they state that you're to find and return with Doctor Phatts—if he's still alive."

"Oh, that Doctor Phatts. Yes, apparently I'm to find him but I know nothing other than what you've read in my Orders, and those are Church documents. You had no right to read them."

"Reverend Flynn, can you see why I'm suspicious of you? You were in the company of the impostor, Cecilia Spotswood, you have as another companion a dangerous convict who has killed one of my men and wounded another. That same colonial is now roaming around, armed and dangerous, in the company of a person unknown who is more than likely Miss Spotswood. You know more than you're telling me."

"I can assure you I know nothing else. I'll swear it on my Bible if it will help convince you." Rosalyn could see Sir Rothwell trying to control his growing anger. "You, Sir Rothwell, might tell me why you drugged my tea the night before you had Fey taken out to be shot. You are the one keeping secrets, not I."

"Who told you such nonsense?"

"Don't think me stupid, Sir Rothwell. I know the Order's attitudes to women but you are making a terrible underestimation of my cognitive abilities."

Sir Rothwell glared at her. "Go back to your English lessons with Doris." His tone was so icy and imperious that for the moment Rosalyn let drop her opposition. She turned her back on him and sat with the terrified Doris. Her motivation in instructing Doris was no longer fear of Sir Rothwell but in enlisting her as an ally in whatever might lie ahead. If she was to bring Enlightenment to the heathens or to find Doctor Phatts then Doris might provide the doorway to success.

The airship started moving again, the nose turning around and the engine operating at a low speed. They came to a gliding halt and Rosalyn stood up to see what was happening. A man was being lowered overboard. She saw they were adjacent to the *Lightning* so she approached Sir Rothwell to enquire as to the activity. "Quite simple, Reverend. We're leaving here and taking that airship with us. I'm putting a man aboard. We can't take the chance that your friends are still lurking about, although I daresay they're being digested by a subterranean denizen of the Antipodes even as we speak." Sir Rothwell smiled at her discomfit.

Rosalyn said nothing to Sir Rothwell's remark. "Who is the man being lowered? I haven't seen him before."

Sir Rothwell turned, looked briefly as the man disappeared over the side and turned back to Rosalyn. "You should hone your observation skills, Reverend Flynn. The man has been with me the entire voyage. Now back to your duties. If your pet savage doesn't learn English quickly I'll have no use for her—or for you if it comes to it."

Seething with anger and clenching her teeth, Rosalyn returned to Doris. She breathed deeply while Doris held her hand. Watson came to her with a couple of mugs of tea and spoke in low tones. "I don't have any news, I'm afraid."

"Do you know who the man is they have lowered? He's going to take the Lightning."

Watson sat down beside Rosalyn. "I didn't pay him much attention but he looked unfamiliar to me. He came aboard immediately after Rothwell's men returned from the cavern. I assumed he was one of the crew but dressed for fighting."

"I wish I knew what was happening down there."

"I think you know Sir Rothwell was planning to have Miss Grey shot. I was most distressed when I heard that, and relieved to learn she'd made good her escape with your other companion, Miss Spotswood."

"I really don't know that it was she who assisted Fey. Cecilia is incapable when it comes to activity of such excitement."

"I'm sure they're both still alive but your Miss Spotswood isn't who she says she is, and if she's not Miss Spotswood, who is she?"

"I really don't know. I think perhaps Sir Rothwell is mistaken. The false bottom in Cecilia's travel trunk need mean nothing at all except a traveller's caution. It's not uncommon."

"She wasn't here with the Society."

"What do you mean?"

"I've asked the other scientists, and heard them and Sir Rothwell talking. The expedition of the Royal Scientific Society for the Exploration of the Antipodes never left England."

"Nonsense. Cecilia was on the expedition and she planned to meet her Society companions in Sydney."

"Nevertheless, the man they'd selected to lead the expedition had an unfortunate accident and then the expedition stores warehouse caught fire and burned. If they were putting together another expedition no one has heard of it."

Rosalyn rested her head in her hands. "None of this makes sense." She sighed deeply. "All I wanted to do was fly my airship and Enlighten the heathens. It was supposed to be simple." She turned to Watson. "How well do you know Mister Ovens?"

"I know Geoffrey intimately. We have been the best of friends for many years. Like me, he's a scientist but he's not of the Mechanical Order—we've both embraced the Church of the Sun Cog. That is, I mean to say, the Enlightenment Church."

They sipped their tea, Rosalyn sharing hers with the melancholy Doris. "There are ten of them if you count the other two scientists, and there are four of us. Do you think we could take the ship?"

"Good heavens no. Geoffrey and I could never undertake such a task. It would be tantamount to piracy. We'd all be hanged."

"Piracy? That dreadful man attacked our airship. He is the pirate."

"He has a sound defence, Reverend Flynn. He claims you stole the Lightning from the government and he was merely reclaiming it. It doesn't matter that you are innocent of the charge. Sir Rothwell won't be convicted of anything and that will leave you to face piracy charges." Watson paused and sipped his tea. "There is no way we could seize the vessel even if we were fighting men and had the will. Sir Rothwell has too many men; it's too tough a proposition. I'm afraid it is out of the question, Reverend."

"It need not be. What of the sleeping draught Sir Rothwell put in my tea?"

"The what? I know of no such thing."

Rosalyn explained what she had learned from Doris and her own assessment of what had transpired. "Perhaps if we find the draught we can drug them."

"Still out of the question. There is no way we could drug the entire crew. How are we going to do it? You can certainly pilot the vessel but the rest of us? Then there is the securing of the captives. How do you propose we look after them all? We can't just abandon them in the desert. We'd still be facing piracy charges on top of that."

"I have another idea, Doctor Gilroy. What if we drug the night crew? I can then fly the ship low enough for us to make good our escape." Rosalyn looked at him expectantly.

"Dropping off into the middle of the desert in the dead of the night? Reverend, that would be a certain death sentence."

"No, we will have Doris here. She can help us to find food and water, and we'll take some with us from here anyway. The question is, can we gain possession of the concoction and induce the night watch to drink it?"

"Getting the watch to drink it would be the easy part. Getting hold of whatever it was that Sir Rothwell used would be a harder task. No doubt he keeps it in his cabin and only he and his first mate are allowed in there. You've seen how crowded it gets on deck here at times—there's always someone watching."

They continued sipping their tea as they thought about the problem. "I've got it," said Watson at last. "This airship doesn't have a large cargo carrying capacity and they have to stop frequently for water and to hunt. Sir Rothwell always goes ashore with the hunting party. Everyone likes a chance to stretch their legs. When they go to ground will be the best chance to find the sleeping potion that Sir Rothwell used on you. The only problem is that there are always one or two men left on deck to keep watch. We'd need to distract them."

Rosalyn smiled. "I have an idea."

Shortly after this point Geoffrey became terribly ill, complaining of the heat and of stomach cramps. The sickness lingered.

A couple of days later Rosalyn approached Sir Rothwell. "I'm sure it will work, Sir Rothwell. Please indulge me in my endeavour and when you have what you want, release me. I'll take Doris and bring Enlightenment to her people. You and I will both obtain our goals."

Sir Rothwell leaned on the skyrail as his crew made ready to go to ground. "Very well. I'll assemble all the available hands. You have a drawing of this, you say?"

"Doctor Gilroy has. My own artistic abilities are somewhat lacking."

Rosalyn, Watson and Doris went to ground with the rest of the crew, bar the ailing Geoffrey and the wounded man who remained below deck. On the ground, they assembled with their backs to the *Eyrie*, Rosalyn arranging the men in two rows. "You too, Sir Rothwell, we need to make this as effective as we can. Have your men hold the clumps of grass. Yes, like that, one in each hand. I'll stand in front and you follow my actions." Watson stood facing Rosalyn, his journal open to the page displaying his illustration of a green butterfly. Doris stood next to Rosalyn.

Rosalyn called out in a loud voice, "Is everyone ready?"

"Can we just bloody well get on with it. I'm already having second thoughts, Reverend."

"This will work, trust me, Sir Rothwell. If Doris knows where it is she'll show us. I'm sure of it. Now, here we go."

Rosalyn brought her hands together over her head, each hand holding a clump of grass. The assembled men followed suit. Rosalyn spread her arms out and brought them back together and the men did the same although with a great deal of amusement. She leaned over to one side and then the other as Watson constantly brought Doris's gaze back to the picture of the butterfly. Quietly Geoffrey rose from where he lay and crept into Sir Rothwell's cabin.

Doris appeared bewildered by the activity taking place until Rosalyn asked loudly, "Where?" Doris looked at her and Rosalyn became worried that the small amount of coaching wouldn't pay dividends. Rosalyn repeated the word and Doris made a show of looking around and pointed off into the south. "You see, Sir Rothwell. Results."

"Look, there's Geoffrey up." Watson closed the book and turned to Rosalyn. "You've done marvellous work."

"Can we stop doing this silly dance now, Reverend?" Sir Rothwell and his men were still standing with their arms outstretched holding their grass clumps, the men now in a fit of uncontrollable giggles.

"Yes, of course, Sir Rothwell. We have achieved our purpose. If you don't mind I'd like a cup of tea, and for Doris, too." Sir Rothwell made some kind of aristocratic grunting noise which Rosalyn interpreted as assent. Taking Doris and followed by their guard, they climbed back aboard the boat. "Geoffrey, how are you feeling?"

"Much better thank you. It was good to get on my feet and witness your wonderful dance."

"All is well?"

Geoffrey smiled. "Yes it is."

The crew killed a kangaroo and everyone ate well that evening. Sir Rothwell instructed the helmsman to head south and the great airship turned, its red balloon glowing in the light of the setting sun. Early in the morning hours Geoffrey came on deck. After relieving himself over the side he casually asked the wheelman and the watch if they'd like a cup of tea. They both accepted and Geoffrey set the pot on the boiler to heat the water. After serving the crewmen their tea he sat drinking his own. He stared out into the night sky, occasionally glancing at the two crewmen. He could see the bow watch starting to drift off and took the chance to go to the helmsman.

"I say, do you mind if I have a steer? It doesn't look frightfully difficult."

"I don't mind. You have a go if you want. You keep that heading there." He pointed to the compass. "I'll sit here and watch. If you have any trouble you give me a nudge, all right?"

"Absolutely. You can count on me. This is astounding. Me, a pilot. Thank you, good man, thank you." The man sat down behind him as Geoffrey took the wheel and with the warm breeze, the motion of the boat and the effects of the drug it wasn't long before he heard the sound of snoring behind him. He walked over to where Rosalyn lay in the cargo hold with Doris and gave a light rap to signal them. Rosalyn climbed out, gave Doris a hand up and took the wheel. Geoffrey fetched Watson from his sleeping bay. Watson handed them each a bag of provisions and a water bottle, surreptitiously collected over the preceding days.

"This next bit will be tricky. We'll have to harness up and drop over the side. Watson you go first, Doris can go next. Geoffrey you'll have to help her over the side. I'll bring the airship down to a low altitude before you go over. When you're all safely to ground I'll set the Eyrie on a fixed course to the southwest on an increasing altitude. We'll have to find each other in the dark as best we can."

Watson and Geoffrey helped Doris into her harness and when Rosalyn had the airship at the right height he dropped over the side. Doris, aware of the need for silence, still tried to reach out to Rosalyn as Geoffrey led her to the skyrail. He had her sit on the side but she took the harness off and dropped it, choosing instead to climb down the rope. Geoffrey dropped after her, the rope through the pulley making a soft whirring noise as he lowered himself down. The boat rocked slightly as the weight of each person left the airship.

Satisfied her comrades had reached the ground safely, Rosalyn turned the ship, setting the injector to send the *Eyrie* up and away from them. Having a last minute thought, she took the carbine and belt from the bow watch before putting her harness on. The airship was already rising when Rosalyn climbed over the side. She stared down into the gloom as she reached the end of her rope. The ground was already some twenty feet below and the airship was still rising. With a quick prayer she released the clip and dropped the remaining distance, landing with a thud in the sand. Stunned, she lay staring into the sky and the dark shape of the disappearing airship. Her eyelids closed over.

Someone called her name, voices came to her in the darkness— whispering, urgent voices. Rosalyn murmured, hands touched her, gripping her arms, pulling her up. Something was placed to her lips; water ran into her mouth and down her chin. She coughed. "Welcome to Earth, Reverend." Watson helped her to her feet. "We need to plot a course."

Rosalyn brushed herself off. "A course? What sort of course? Yes, of course. No, we don't need to set a course. We'll follow Doris." Doris pressed close to her and Rosalyn looked into her starlit eyes. "Doris, you go, we follow. " This was outside the means of Doris's limited vocabulary so Rosalyn pushed her, trying to get her to move. "Fey. We need to find Fey." Doris clutched at her and Rosalyn tried again. Eventually she conveyed to Doris that she would be coming with her and Doris started walking. Rosalyn and the two men followed behind in single file.

23

STRIDERS

Baker pushed his horses hard but they couldn't keep up to the task. It had been over a day since the last positive reading indicated the presence of an airship. It had been somewhere ahead of him, heading west. He needed to travel faster. He unpacked and unsaddled his horses.

One of the large leather cases carried an expensive piece of equipment. To use it he would have to abandon his horses and some of his stores. The decision was a simple one and he knew it would come to this. It was only a matter of when. He put what he could into his backpack, his bedroll folded over the top. He slung his carbine over his shoulder and strapped the atmotic indicator to the top of his bedroll.

The items in his case were constructed of brass, iron, and leather. Some assembly was required and when he had put them together he had a pair of large, stilt-like, automated boots. They extended the length of his legs with shafts projecting upwards to take the weight of his pack. The device, when assembled, formed a single piece and it was wound by a handle at the front. It had taken Baker weeks of practice to master the device, testing his ability in the Scottish Highlands. The amount of food and water he could carry was much less than he was able to take on his horses so he would have to be opportunistic in hunting game and refilling his water bottles.

Baker thought of shooting the horses lest they fall to the cruelty of thirst or the blacks but decided their carcasses would attract birds and draw attention to his presence. With the rig firmly strapped on and every buckle and piece of equipment checked, he wound the handle. Checking his compass bearing one last time he chose a spot in the distance and pulled the release handle. The legs started moving immediately.

The speed, on the lowest of three settings, put him at a fast stride. After a couple of hundred yards he increased it to the second setting: 'canter'. Comfortable that the legs were working as they should, he turned them up to the high setting: 'gallop' and he lowered his goggles over his eyes. Baker didn't take much enjoyment from life but he exhilarated in this fast running. It was almost as if he were a passenger on the legs. The ground needed watching but he'd trained so hard on the legs that they were now something of an extension of his body.

He looked over his shoulder, half expecting to see the Guardian coming after him. Word had reached the order that the Sun Cogs had also been interested in purchasing horse heels for their Guardians but it wasn't confirmed. If the man who had shot at him had such a device he could stay in pursuit. He considered the possibility that the man had already passed him and was further west. Regardless, he kept a good eye on the landscape, checking details with the 'telescope' function of his goggles.

With great delight he ran down a kangaroo whose misfortune it was to cross his path. While it cooked he set up his atmotic indicator. The machine gave him a positive reading. Evening was a few hours off and he didn't want to let the airship get away. If it was Sir Rothwell he needed to make contact. If it wasn't, he needed to find out who crewed it, and if necessary put them out of commission. He checked his weapons and packed away the indicator. Eager to be on the move, a half-cooked chunk of kangaroo meat made do for his meal. He gave the legs another wind and set off, eating as he ran.

As the light began to fade he stopped to set up the indicator and took a reading. The airship was to the south. He looked through his goggles and in the late evening could make out a light in the distance. He kept the atmotic indicator out, slung it over his shoulder and ran towards the airship, stopping once to take another reading. The airship hadn't moved. He checked again with his goggles and could see more clearly. It was still difficult to make out the airship itself. With the ship stationary and in visual range he no longer needed the indicator and packed it away.

Moving slowly now, he approached to within five hundred yards of the ship. His blue eyes sparkled with the thrill of the hunt. The airship was not the *Eyrie* and too small to be the *Bennelong*. It had to belong to the Missionary. A stunted bush served as a place to stow his gear. He took off his pack and his horse heels, leaving on the leather harness. He checked his weapons and moved forward.

It was night but the countless stars illuminated the landscape. Baker kept to the deeper shadows until he was below the airship. As he suspected, the airship was hooked. The sun had not long set and whoever was on board was still awake; he could hear their voices. At least one of them was male and he could discern one, perhaps two women. He counted on there being three people.

Baker sat down next to the hook to wait. He checked his watch. He'd give them three hours before climbing the hook rope. Every movement would rock the boat and might wake the crew so he would need to be slow and careful. When he reached the skyrail he'd have to draw two pistols, shoot quickly and then draw his other two pistols to take care of anyone else who might be there. He was confident he could kill all on board before they could react.

Gently he took the rope in hand without letting it immediately take all his weight. He increased his weight gradually and gripped with his other hand until at last all his weight was on the rope. After spending ten minutes climbing twenty feet, came the sound of a pistol being cocked followed by a voice. "Ses, is that you?" He froze and looked up. He had no more than ten feet left to climb. The voice called out again. "Damn you, I'll fire if you don't speak."

He continued up the rope, trying to rock the boat. The figure above shot at him, the ball thudding into the leather harness and tearing his shoulder. It was too close for comfort and he'd lost the element of surprise. He let go of the rope and dropped to the sand, landing with a thump. The darkness concealed his rapid departure.

The old spear wound in his thigh ached by the time he reached his pack and blood ran down his back from the gunshot wound. He didn't have much time to waste. If they searched for him in the morning they could easily spot him from the air. He strapped his horse heels on, donned his pack, wound up the legs and ran. If observers on the airship had seen him running away they would know he went north. After a few hundred yards he ran east for the same distance before turning south again, giving the airship a wide berth.

With the presence of the Missionary confirmed, it became more imperative that he find Sir Rothwell. His indicator would pick up the closest airship so he took a reading. It pointed north. Without any way of knowing where Sir Rothwell was he could only keep moving away from the Missionary's airship. If he got a reading from any other direction then it must be the *Eyrie*.

He travelled through the darkness on the slowest walking setting. A flickering light in the distance indicated a campfire; most likely blacks. Baker, too exhausted now for an encounter, folded back the lever to shut down his legs. Without unpacking he lay on the sand and drank some of his precious water. Even that was getting low—he'd have to find more soon.

At first light he wound his legs and checked his weapons. An indicator reading showed an airship to the south. That would have to be Sir Rothwell. The campfire he'd seen the night before lay between him and the airship. He had no fear of blacks, at least not when he was prepared for an encounter. He inhaled the crisp morning air and started out. As he drew closer to the spot where he'd seen the campfire he could make out a figure and it wasn't a black. It was the Guardian.

Baker was surprised the man had made it this far; he saw no sign of horses. He appeared to be engaged in some task—unsuccessfully apparently as Baker could hear him cursing. Baker decided to rush the man and set his horse heels to 'gallop'. He drew two pistols. The man looked around, saw Baker running at him, picked up a carbine and fired. The ball hit one of the mechanical legs, instantly slowing it. The other leg, still moving at the fastest pace, caused Baker to start running in a circle. Baker fired a shot off in the direction of the Guardian and shut off the legs, falling prone as he did so.

A gunshot and a splash of sand within inches of his face gave him cause to keep his head down. He wriggled behind a dune and un-strapped his legs and pack. Crawling through the tussocks of grass, he circled around to the Guardian's campsite. The man had gone. Staying low, Baker searched the area, finding the man's tracks in the sand. He'd headed south. Satisfied the Guardian had left, Baker examined the items he'd left behind.

As he had suspected the Guardian had also been in possession of a set of horse heels. One of the legs was badly bent and it appeared the Guardian had been trying to straighten it on the fire using a rock as a hammer. Baker collected his own horse heels and pack and returned to the camp site. If the Guardian had horse heels he may also have an atmotic detector, which would mean he also knew of the airship to the south.

With a damaged horse heel, Baker would have to pursue on his own feet. He examined the damaged leg and the ones left behind by the Guardian. With some work he'd be able to get his own horse heels fully operational. It took him longer than he estimated and it was nearly two hours before he was ready to start out again. He took a final reading—the airship was still to the south of him. He felt sure it was Sir Rothwell's ship and if so the Guardian would cause some mischief. With his heels set to 'gallop' he ran off in pursuit of the Guardian, hoping to reach him before the man got as far as the airship.

Coming to the top of a rise he could see on the far side of a dry lake bed what appeared to be a ruined city. To his relief he could also see above it the red balloon of the *Eyrie* coming in to ground. He put his lens on for a closer look. A second airship could be seen on the ground in the ruins, a smaller one. He could make out a figure standing on top of it. On the far side of the lake bed the Guardian climbed up the bank and disappeared into a jumble of stones.

It was time to report in to Sir Rothwell.

24

THE PASSAGE OF TIME

The tunnel, although barely wide enough for two people to squeeze past each other, was so high that one could barely touch the ceiling with an outstretched hand. Samuel led the way, the sound of every footstep echoing along the rock floor. They came to a small chamber containing a pool of fresh water, fed by a seepage on the wall above it. Hand prints covered the walls on one side and a picture of a snake portrayed in red and yellow ochres with dots and hatched lines of white pipeclay sprawled across the other. "I'm given to wonder what manner of mind produced this. Fascinating stuff, unworldly."

"Yeah, dreamlike and all." Fey knelt and drank as much of the water as she could manage. "Where do you think this passage leads?"

"To Hell. We're in the underworld. You know, young lady, it quite reminds of the time I was led into a cave by a talking bat in the jungles of the Yucatan."

"You've been drinking, haven't you, you old bastard."

"Bastard perhaps, but drinking I have not. Not such a bad idea though. Never mind, shall we keep moving? Never miss an opportunity to pass water as the Duke said, and here we are passing water.

Go ahead, I need to pass some of my own."

"Yeah, and I'm getting a bit of a queasy feeling, like these rocks are going to start pushing in from either side, and the air in here isn't so fresh."

"Squeezed by the rocks, disagreeable air, yes, well, on you go. I'll catch up."

When their legs grew tired from walking they sat facing each other and Samuel shared his meagre rations and water with Fey. He took out his watch. "Good heavens, we've been walking for twelve hours. Did you know that? Where does time go?"

"I think it travelled along this passage with us, Sam."

"Ha ha! Clever. It travelled with us. Therefore no time has passed at all. You're quite right of course; here we are right in this moment and no other. Funny thing, time. No don't eat that, that is my special... don't eat it. You won't like it and I need it to freshen things up."

"Freshen things up?"

"Yes, from time to time. Don't you worry your shaven, Antipodean head about it. Special medical concoction I use made from different herbs and fungi. Quite escapes me where I found them all but you wouldn't like it. Bitter it is. Here, let me take it from you, I'll put that back in my pack this instant."

Fey gave him a queer look and chewed on salted pork instead. "You're a weird one, Sam, but you're not a bad sort of a cove."

"Very nice of you to say—a drunken old bastard, but not a bad cove, hmm? Is that your assessment, Miss Grey?"

"Yeah, forget the drunken bastard bit, you can hang onto the 'not a bad old cove'. Putting to one side the measure of your personal worth, we'll have to find more water soon and I'm of a mind to go back."

"Back? Oh no, not one step backwards. We'll show the scoundrels. Do you think we should sleep? Perhaps a good kip would do us entire worlds of good."

"You've got a smart idea there. I'm as knocked up as a racehorse and could do with a rest."

The narrow passage gave them no room to sleep side by side and they lay stretched out head to head. Fey tossed and turned, trying to ease her mind into rest but thoughts of Rosalyn kept coming to her. She told herself Rosalyn would be safe aboard the *Eyrie*; that Sir Rothwell wouldn't harm her as she was a Reverend. "I'd feel happier if she was lying beside me though."

"Lie beside you? Not much room in this passage."

"No Sam, I was... I suppose I was dreaming."

"Go back to them."

Fey drifted off to sleep, but the dreams she had were of strange creatures of vivid ochre hues and the creatures were mixing and mingling with her, dancing around until she too was dancing with them.

Fey woke abruptly, sitting bolt upright. "What was that?"

"Hullo dear. A touch of smelling salts. Does wonders don't you think? Bright, alert, ready to go."

"You could have just given me a shake."

"Not quite the same thing though, is it?"

"And who in the name of the great, bearded creator carries smelling salts out into the desert?"

Samuel paused, furrowed his brow, looked at the ceiling, stroked his sideburns and answered. "Why, that would be me of course. One never knows when one might encounter a fainted woman. We best keep going, water is low."

They continued on, stopping every few hours for a rest, and just as the last of their water ran out they came to the end of the passage.

"It's a bloody dead end—they never finished it."

"I don't believe that is the case, Miss Grey. Do you really think whoever went to this much labour would bring the passage to a sudden stop? Now, young lady, do you remember back in the ruins—the stone door to the cistern?"

Fey remembered it at once and put her shoulder to the stone. "I'll need a hand here, Sam. If it's going to move its going to take more than me to make it so." Samuel lent his own aged strength to the task and with much grunting and sweating the stone started to give. It moved a few inches and swung suddenly so they both toppled forward landing with a splash.

"Wonderful, Miss Grey, we've found water."

"And light, Sam, we've got light." Fey knelt up and looked about. "I know this place."

"You're quite well-travelled, Miss Grey."

"This is the cistern. This is the place where the Lightning crashed."

"In here?" Samuel looked incredulous.

"No, not in here. See where that light is coming from, past the pillars? That's how we get out. Up above is the stone circle."

"Wonderful. Let's quench our thirst, fill the bottle and we'll go and have a look shall we? Two days in that dank passage was a trifle too much for me."

The daylight blinded them and they sat outside the hole in the sunlight, shading their eyes with their hands until they could see again. Fey searched around the pile of stones with Samuel in tow. "Are you looking for something, Miss Grey?"

"Yes, and here it is. It's a note we left Ses telling her we found the city to the south. See here? We wrote that it's two days walk so she could come looking for us. I don't think she... Wait, here's another note. That's not one me and Roz left."

Samuel and Fey read the note together. "Centre yourself and go deep inside."

"That doesn't make even a ha'penny of sense, does it?" asked Fey.

"It's terribly nonsensical. Could it mean the cistern?"

"I don't know. I'm not even sure that's Ses's handwriting and from any angle, she knows we already know about the cistern."

Samuel, sticking a monocle to his eye, took the note from Fey and studied it in great detail. "I do believe the hand writing looks much like mine."

"Yours?"

"Of course it's mine. Centre yourself." Samuel walked out to the centre of the stone circle. "You see? And now I go deep inside." Samuel started to dig while Fey watched, bemused. She was surprised when Samuel pulled out a leather case, and from it a strange brass object that looked like a peculiar telescope. He shook the sand off it and showed it to Fey. "You see? Makes sense doesn't it?"

Fey thought nothing about the man made sense, but kept the thought to herself. "Could you explain? I find I'm a bit simple minded when it comes to your affairs."

"I left a note. I remember. I read yours so I wrote one of my own and buried this here. I thought I would catch you in the ruins, you see, so I didn't have any need of this anymore."

"Why did you leave a note?"

Samuel looked flustered. "Ah, that. So I wouldn't forget of course. Why do you leave notes?"

"We left that one so Ses could find us."

"Yes, quite, and I found this, thanks to my note."

"It's fancy looking."

"Really? Is the sun too much for you? It's a plain and ordinary note."

"Not that—your telescope. I've never seen anything like it before. What's it do?"

"This, my dear, is a hand-crafted atmotic vessel directional indicator." Fey gave him a blank look which Samuel picked up on immediately. "I see by your empty expression you're in dire need of further explanation. Blue ascension is what is injected into the steam and gives airships their lift."

"Yeah, I know about blue ascension."

"Well this, my dear girl, indicates the whereabouts of blue ascension." Fey gave him another blank look. "It really is straightforward. Here, we unfold these legs, they're tripod legs and work like telescopes, only they're legs so you can't see through them." He glanced up and saw Fey watching, fascinated. "We level it, like so... and..." He flipped a little hatch on top, revealing a strange dial. "Now we simply..." And here he unfolded another attachment which turned out to be a handle. "Wind this for me." Fey wordlessly obeyed. "Stand back so we don't impede its movement. I'll deftly release this lever here and... there we are."

The main body of the device slowly turned on the tripod. Fey noticed Samuel smiling with satisfaction as he watched it turn. The machine gave a sudden loud beep and emitted a cloud of blue smoke. "Has it broken?"

"No, my dear girl. It has found an airship."

Fey looked at him in disbelief. "An airship?"

"My word these stones echo don't they? Look here." Fey looked over at the dial Samuel was now pointing to. "You see here, the fuzzy blue spot, that's an airship, or if not an airship then a quantity of blue ascension. As we know there are two airships in the region I think we can safely assume the dial is showing us an airship... and... look here." He flipped another panel on the device to reveal a compass. "You see, the airship is somewhere to the southwest."

"Can we tell what airship it is?"

"I'm afraid not. My atmotic indicator only shows the closest source of blue ascension. Mind you, I haven't fully tested it. What we do know is that even if there is an airship at the ruins, there's a closer one to the southwest. If the closer airship was at the ruins then the indicator would be indicating the south, not the southwest."

"What if both those airships are no longer at the ruins?"

"In that case we know that the closer airship is somewhere to the southwest at an unknown distance."

Fey let that sink in. "And why did the thing start smoking?"

"Did you like that? It's something I added for the dramatic effect."

"Speaking of smoking, I need a pull of my steamer." Fey extracted her pipe from its box and hunted around in the pouch for a pinch of tobacco. She sat down next to the device. "Do you want some tobacco? I have a bit left here."

"No thank you Miss Grey, perhaps later."

"So how does this thing work?"

"You put the tobacco in the big hole, set fire to it and inhale through the small hole."

"The indicator. I know how to smoke a bloody steamer."

"My dear girl, I can't explain everything to you. You really must learn things for yourself."

"I try."

Samuel appraised her. "Yes, I suppose you do."

"So are we heading southwest? We only have one water bottle."

"I'm not sure leaving here right now would be the wisest course. The airship is perhaps still moving. If we wait here a night we can see if the airship has changed position. If it comes to rest we might consider heading to it. But really, I don't see what your concern with the airship is."

"It's Roz I'm concerned about. The airship can crash in a sea of sparks for all I care."

Samuel studied her again. "You have quite the passion for Missionary Flynn. I didn't take you to be a Sun Cog girl."

"I'm not." Fey's tone sounded much to Samuel as a full stop in a sentence and he asked no further questions. Fey sat scowling to herself as she puffed on her pipe, every thought returning to Rosalyn. When she spoke it was to ask of Samuel, "You're a Guardian yet you don't have any great urgency to rescue Roz?"

"Roz? I see, yes, Reverend Missionary Flynn. Brave woman she is, coming all the way out here to... Now what was she doing out here?"

"She was going to teach the blacks how to pray."

"Hmm, a noble cause I suppose—rather like a knight might tilt at windmills. It's a long way to come to do that. She might have stopped at Bathurst."

"We have to find a bloke by the name of Phatts who got lost out here a few years back. Didn't I tell you this already?"

Samuel, who had been fiddling with the device, stood back and stared at the deep blue of the sky. "Phatts. Doctor Phatts. Unfortunate that, him getting lost and all. I suppose he's lying dead and desiccated in the desert. Yes, dead and desiccated. It's a hard country; I don't know how the blacks do it."

"He was alive two years ago. He left his initials on the rock over there."

"Really? You must show me."

Fey led him to the inscription on the stone and Samuel pulled out his monocle and scrutinised it. "Yes, I see, N.P. 1836. That would be him." He stood up straight and looked at Fey. "And your friend Cecilia saw this?"

"Yes, she was the one who found it."

Once again Samuel pondered the sky. "It's a magnificent blue. Shame I don't have my cyanometer. Lovely really. Blue sky—and look at the soft red sand and these wonderful grey stones."

"Whatever tickles your throat, Sam. I think we need more of a plan than waiting for an airship to stop somewhere in some direction. Even if we walked there, it would be gone again by the time we got to it. That's if we don't die of thirst and hunger."

"It would be a hard task. Do you have any idea where this Cecilia went?"

"Not the slightest. She weren't here when we returned from the ruins, not so much as a note. She'd left all her clothes, even her shoes, but she's taken her journals and bug net. We thought the blacks might have took her."

"That would be something. I suppose we could do the same."

Fey gave him a peculiar look. "Let the blacks take us?"

"Yes, certainly. Any port in a storm as they say on the sea. If we stay here we're sure to perish of starvation over time. If we move we'll suffer thirst. If the blacks don't kill us they might feed us and show us water."

"I think they're as likely to kill us as to take us in like long lost relatives."

"They did spear my horses mind you. That was an awful close thing. Different lot back there I suppose. They were unfriendly, hostile I would say. Perhaps the ones around here have a different nature, I mean, you have a think about it—Norman left the inscription in 1836."

"So what?"

"So he'd been out here for a long time. How could he have survived without assistance? We know from the message he sent that his companions had deserted him or were killed."

"He had help from the blacks, did he? Is that what you're saying?"

"My word you're a sharp lass. Yes that's what I'm saying."

"If he had help then he might still be alive and that means Ses might be too."

"Of course. Yes. Bravo! I do believe you've got it."

Fey sat and leaned against the stone, using a small splinter of wood from the *Lightning's* bow to clean her pipe. "And how does that help us find Roz?"

"Who? I see, yes, her. The Reverend Flynn. I suppose we must find her. Can't leave her in the hands of that wretched blackguard, Sir Rothwell. She'll have to wait though, more important things, yes much more important."

"You can't be bloody serious. Roz is out there in the desert somewhere with that rotten bastard and you, a Guardian, say there're more important things?"

Samuel looked at her, "More important, yes. I suppose. Staying alive is of vital importance, wouldn't you agree? And this Rosalyn, this dear friend of yours, she's safe on an airship, plenty of food and water, protection. She's not in any immediate danger is she?"

"All right, I was thinking the same thing myself earlier. But I'll feel much happier when I see her smiling phiz and we're safe on the Lightning again."

25

THE WATERHOLE

Light from the moon and stars glinted off the rocks and grass, giving the landscape a spectral appearance. Doris darted with ease from one rock to another over the broken ground. Rosalyn frequently called on her to stop so Geoffrey might catch up. Every time they stopped, Watson and Geoffrey would lie on the sand together looking awestruck at the stars. Rosalyn too, would find herself staring up at them and wonder if somewhere Fey might also be doing the same, or if she was still stuck in the cavern—or even dead. At such thoughts her gaze would drop from the stars to the rocks and sand beneath them, her head resting on her bent knees, absentmindedly pouring sand from one hand to the other.

She saw Doris staring at the stars and wondered if she was thinking of her family. However, Doris observed the stars for reasons more practical than spiritual. Inevitably, Doris would rouse them again, tugging at Rosalyn's hand, repeating the words, "Roz, where." They followed her with no notion as to what direction they were travelling or how far they'd come or how far they had left to go. The only certainty at all was the conviction that Doris had in mind a fixed destination.

After daybreak the three Europeans kept an eye on the sky, watching for the red balloon of the Mechanical Order's airship, but they saw nothing of it. Geoffrey, tired as he was, examined every new shrub or bush and stripped foliage from it to sandwich in the pages of his notebooks. Watson, already lagging, stopped frequently to pick up any interesting stone or pebble and wonder at its origins. Rosalyn plodded along behind Doris, who by her gestures and the imperative tone of her voice, was urging them all to walk faster. By midday Geoffrey sat down and refused to walk any further.

"You must go on, Geoffrey. We really can't afford to stop here."

"I can't. I need to rest. It's all right for that damned savage; she's born to this place. I must rest my feet."

Rosalyn looked at him in despair and tried in her best pantomime to ask Doris how much further. Doris tried in her own way to explain her course of action but the communication gap between the two of them, in spite of the best intentions, was still too vast for comprehension.

"I've noticed she's become more excited over the last few hours," said Watson.

"I think we may be drawing close to wherever she's taking us. Please Geoffrey, find your strength."

Geoffrey, red-faced from his exertions and with great reluctance, clambered back to his feet and without a word passing his sunburned lips, waved them on. Watson kept beside him, taking his arm here and there, gently urging him forward. Some hours later they came to a line of granite boulders. Thick vegetation and stunted trees with their sun-hardened leaves rose from among the stones. Doris pointed to the bottom of a small cliff and said, "Where—water." Sighing with relief, the three Europeans flopped down in the shade of the boulders next to the precious water hole. Colourful finches darted from tree to rock and the travellers sat in silence, one by one falling asleep. Doris watched them and satisfied they were all deep in their dreams, she crept away.

In the late afternoon Watson woke and at first was unconcerned by Doris's absence. After a time, with Doris nowhere to be seen, he woke Rosalyn. She searched between the rocks and trees, calling Doris's name. No answer came. By the last of the daylight Doris had still not returned.

"I think your black girl has left us, Reverend."

"I don't think so, Watson. I'm sure she'll be back."

"Why? She's out here, she's free. I think the dusky wretch has abandoned us and rejoined her people."

Rosalyn considered his words and her heart sank. She realised Watson was in all probability quite right. She sat, her back to a boulder, resting her cheek on her hand. The success of her Mission was now an impossible thing. She'd lost her airship, her friends and her hope. She looked at the two men with her and wondered if they would even be able to get out of the desert alive.

"A penny for your thoughts, Reverend?" asked Watson.

Rosalyn gave him a smile. It disappeared as quickly as it had come. "I was thinking, Doctor Gilroy, that we are quite marooned. If we leave this waterhole we are done. If we don't leave we are still destined for extinction, although perhaps a little slower."

"Let's not give up hope so quickly, Reverend. Let's sleep again tonight and in the morning we'll have a thorough search of our locale. We'll see if we can find something that might ease us out of our predicament."

Rosalyn nodded. "Yes. I'm tired and my head is muddled. This whole Mission has taken a dreadful turn. Nothing is like I thought it would be. I'm beginning to think I should never have left England." A single tear rolled down Rosalyn's cheek. "We'll talk again in the morning." She rolled onto the soft sand, vaguely aware of Watson covering her with his jacket.

Waking early she pulled herself into a sitting position, leaning against a rock. She rubbed the sleep from her eyes and looked up. When Watson awoke, Rosalyn spoke to him quietly. "Don't move suddenly, Doctor Gilroy. Have a look around you."

Circled at the distance of a spear throw, a number of Aboriginal men stood watching them. They ranged in age from young men to greybeards, their sinewy bodies decorated with scars on their chests and shoulders, and rough patterns in white ochre. They carried spears and shields and throwing sticks.

Watson leaned over and woke Geoffrey. Rosalyn slowly rose to her feet. She ventured a nervous "Hullo" as greeting. This was met by a complete lack of response from the encircling warriors. Rosalyn moved forward a few steps and the men still did not move from their positions. The grey-bearded man closest to Rosalyn turned his head and spoke. The grass behind him moved and Doris emerged into view.

She walked straight to Rosalyn, turned and faced the greybeard. He spoke out in a loud voice to those around him. The warriors laughed and they all started talking at once. Other women, some with children, appeared behind the warriors. Greybeard approached and Watson and Geoffrey stood up as he neared them.

"They're friendly, Reverend. We might be saved."

Rosalyn smiled at Doris. "You didn't desert us. You came back. Bless you, you came back."

There followed a close examination of the men's clothing by the warriors and Rosalyn found herself drawn away by the women. They too, took delight in pulling at her garments and her bag, examining everything and commenting to one another at each new discovery. Hands pawed at her skin and Rosalyn, remembering her first experience with the women at the gorge, stood smiling, letting them assuage their curiosity. Watson and Geoffrey also let the men explore their clothing and skin. They felt emboldened enough to return the examination, tracing their fingers along the scars on shoulders and chests, studying the decorated shields, the spear-throwers and spears.

After this initial meeting the group indicated to Rosalyn and the two men that they should accompany them. They formed into a file with Rosalyn again following directly behind Doris and they set off through the scrub.

As the day progressed they came upon the tracks of an animal whose life would soon be cut short. Two of the men detached themselves from the party to pursue the prey. The others carried on and topping a slight rise in the ground, found themselves looking out onto a narrow valley which cut across their path. The group paused only briefly before descending into it.

Majestic, ghost gums grew in stands or in isolation along the floor of the valley, contrasting with the oranges and reds of the rocks. Sulphur-crested cockatoos rose like spirits as they screeched up from the treetops. The path took them around large slabs of stone, fallen from outcrops on the valley walls. Reaching the valley floor and arriving at a large clearing, they stopped. Patches of black ash in the white sand showed where fires had burned. Some still smouldered.

The group split up and Rosalyn, Watson and Geoffrey were taken to one of the campfires by Doris. Other Aborigines gathered around, and children, some shy and some bold, approached to study the strange new-comers. The Aborigines shared their food and the trio of Europeans offered what little they had of their own. Geoffrey had a tin of peaches he'd carried all the way from the *Eyrie* and he opened it and shared them out. The juicy slices were met with favour by the recipients. With the tin empty, Watson took it and filled it with water, setting it on the fire. He made tea, adding a quantity of sugar. The old people tasted it first, the can passed mouth to mouth until empty.

"I think that was a splendid ice-breaker, Geoffrey. Well done," said Watson. Geoffrey sat back watching the fire.

"We'll be safe here for a time. I pray Fey and Cecilia are safe, too. I don't know what's happened to them. They must still be at the ruins, if they're alive at all."

"Reverend, do you think you can communicate the idea of the ruins to Doris? She has been there, she knows Miss Grey."

"I thought she was leading us there but she brought us here. I'm no wiser to her purpose than you are. I'll try again in the morning."

The sand of the creek banks provided their bed for the night, Rosalyn curling up with Doris and another woman. Rosalyn touched

Doris's arm and asked, "Fey?"

Doris looked at her and her reply caused Rosalyn only frustration and despair. "Fey, where."

Rosalyn, curled up against the morning chill, didn't want to move from her hollow in the sand. Smoke from the smouldering camp fires wafted over her. The grey-green leaves of the eucalypts swayed in the breeze and birds flew in and out of the branches calling to each other. On the floor of the gorge, the people were rising from their slumbers. The sounds of their voices did nothing to disturb the tranquillity Rosalyn was experiencing but instead enhanced it.

The gathering broke up with the men setting out in small groups. Three old greybeards came to Watson and Geoffrey, urging them to follow. With consternation the two men went with them. The women divided into two groups and Doris took Rosalyn in hers.

The day would have been an exciting one for Rosalyn if Fey hadn't been so thoroughly on her mind. This was the opportunity she had needed to bond with the blacks to teach them God's Enlightenment but it was soured by the loss of her friends. She had no idea where Cecilia might be and doubted she would see her again. Doris kept close to her, teaching her how to gather the grass seeds. Many times Rosalyn caught Doris looking at her. After hours of this toil Rosalyn sat back and with elbows on knees, leaned on her hands and quietly wept. Doris came to her, put her arms around her, and spoke. "Fey."

Rosalyn nodded. "Fey." And with Fey's name uttered, the weeping became loud sobbing.

The other women, hearing her sobs, came to her and gathered around in a cluster, hugging and holding Rosalyn and each other. This display of compassion and empathy only encouraged the tears and her crying intensified. Some of the women huddling with her began to cry, too. Only after her tears had ceased and her trembling body became still did the women disperse, leaving her alone again with Doris.

Strands of hair fell in front of Rosalyn's wet, red eyes. Her face was grubby from the toil. She wiped the tears from her face and gave Doris a smile. "Thank you."

Doris gave Rosalyn a smile in return, stroked her arm, and returned to collecting grass seeds.

To Rosalyn, the women appeared to be wandering aimlessly. Only the discovery of the tracks of animals interrupted the quiet work of collecting seeds. On the occasion of finding tracks, the women would take their big digging sticks and follow the creature to its hiding place. Sometimes this would entail routing the poor animal out by digging deep into its hole. At other times the animal would be caught as it tried to creep or slither through the grass. Snakes, lizards and small kangaroo-like animals were rounded up and went into the string bags the women carried.

Towards the end of the day they returned to the previous night's camp ground. Some of the men, their hunting forays successful, were sitting by a fire and as each group came in they greeted them and chatted. Rosalyn was left in no doubt that nearly all such communications had been in regard to the successes and failures of food gathering. Watson, Geoffrey and the greybeards were the last to come in and they were in good spirits.

None of them rushed to press matters forward, being grateful instead to have this temporary sanctuary from the rigours of the dry, scrubby desert country.

The next day was passed in much the same manner, with Rosalyn accompanying the women and Watson and Geoffrey going out with the greybeards. Rosalyn became concerned on the following day when Doris disappeared with the other women, leaving her behind at the campsite. An old woman stayed with her but without a common tongue all the two could do was smile at each other every time their eyes happened to meet. For the most part the old woman stared away down the gorge. She abruptly stood, turned and uttered something to Rosalyn. Rosalyn looked at her, bemused. The old woman came to her, took her by the arm and led her along the gorge. The woman, surprisingly agile, picked her way through the labyrinth of stones and bushes. Rosalyn followed as best she could.

A large pool of water lay in a bend in the gorge floor and the old woman insisted Rosalyn sit on one of the stones by the water's edge. Rosalyn watched as the naked, scarred elder knelt and drank directly from the water before joining Rosalyn on the stone. The woman once again took up her vigil.

She didn't have long to wait. A family of Aborigines appeared around the bend. Two women, one carrying a small child, followed a man. It was the man who interested Rosalyn. He carried two spears, a spear-thrower, a shield and over his shoulder was a bag. The man's skin was scarred in the manner of the other Aboriginal men she had seen, but his skin was paler. When he caught sight of Rosalyn, he stopped, but the women, seeing the elder with Rosalyn, walked to her. The man followed cautiously behind them.

"Reverend Flynn, I presume?"

Rosalyn, taken aback by his use of her name, quickly recovered herself and looked into the man's grey eyes. "Yes. I am. And you must be Doctor Norman Phatts."

"I am, but I'm not so sure about the must. You're a long way from home, Reverend."

"So are you, Doctor Phatts."

"I wouldn't be so sure about that, Reverend Flynn."

Rosalyn looked at him curiously, doing her best to ignore Doctor Phatts lack of attire. "Please, Doctor Phatts, let's not stand on ceremony. You can call me Rosalyn."

"Everything stands on ceremony, you must understand that. But yes, and please, call me Norman."

Rosalyn nodded. "Norman, I've been given a Mission by the Enlightenment Church to find you and bring you home."

Norman looked at her in silence and he gave her a curious little smile. After a pause he said, "Rosalyn, I am home." On seeing Rosalyn's look of consternation he turned to the women who were accompanying him and added, "Allow me to introduce my wife, Ripples in Water, and her sister Half Moon. This little one who Ripples in Water carries is my daughter, Red Sand Blowing and this elder here who you are with is my adoptive mother, Squirrel Glider." Norman turned to Squirrel Glider and spoke at length while Rosalyn stood, still stunned at the unexpected arrival, appearance and relations of Doctor Phatts. He turned back to her. "You see, Rosalyn. I'm quite at home. Come now, we'll go back to the camp." He spoke to the women and they formed up behind him in file and walked back up the gorge.

The two hunters who had left the party days earlier, when they were travelling to the valley, had come into the camp with the results of their hunt: a red kangaroo. It lay beside a cooking fire, flies buzzing around the dried blood from the spear wound. Norman sat cross-legged on the ground, conversing with the hunters at length—it appeared they were telling him the story of the hunt. Rosalyn watched them as she sat with Squirrel Glider.

The other men returned and Rosalyn rose to greet them. They didn't notice the presence of Norman. "Watson, Geoffrey, I'd like you to meet someone." Norman stood. The two men looked at him, taking some seconds to register that an Englishman stood in front of them. "Please make the acquaintance of Doctor Norman Phatts."

"My word, Doctor Phatts! You're alive! Gilroy is the name, Doctor Watson Gilroy, geologist."

"Yes, alive. Here I am. And you?" he said turning to Geoffrey.

"Mister Geoffrey Ovens, botanist. We really thought you must be dead and yet here you are with these savages."

Norman gave him a peculiar look. "Savages? These 'savages' saved my life you know. Come, I expect you'll want to hear all about it. Sit over here."

They listened enthralled to Norman's story, from the beginning right up to their meeting in the valley. "Norman, you didn't mention the big stone circle."

"No, that's a taboo subject with my people."

"You carved your name and date on one of the stones two years ago."

"Was it that recent? It feels like forever. I was already in the company of my people when I visited the place, although if my memory still serves me it was before I was initiated. I'm sure I hadn't been with them terribly long at all. I saw the stones from a distance and when I indicated my desire to go to them they tried to dissuade me. I've learned since they believe there are malevolent spirits there, you see?"

Rosalyn placed a hand on his arm. "Norman, are you going to return with us to Sydney and to England?"

"What on earth for?"

"Don't you miss civilisation?"

"Not at all. I did at first. I pined terribly for the grey, stone houses and their slate roofs, the smoke of those towering industrial chimneys and the whirring of the machines. One gets used to living without things you know. Look around. I have everything I own and love right here: my spears, my axe, my shield, my people."

Rosalyn changed the subject. "Norman, there are two other women travelling together—Fey and Cecilia. Have you seen or heard of any other white women?"

"Yes, I have. I was going to mention it. I met only one woman and that was Miss Cecilia Spotsdick."

"Spotswood. It's Cecilia Spotswood. When? When was this?"

"It was perhaps a week ago. I no longer keep a calendar."

"Did she say anything about her companion?"

"No, she said she'd crashed her airship in the sands while engaged on a scientific expedition and her two companions left for help and failed to return."

Rosalyn sat back. "I don't understand. Cecilia helped Fey escape so she must have gone to the city after meeting you."

"I really don't know. I didn't spend a great deal of time with her. I was called away on business. There had been some killings by pale people and my companions weren't too happy about having her with us. She was intent on finding a strange green butterfly I'd described in the notes I sent back in the message balloon. She told me the message had taken three years to reach England. Remarkable. It was my fault. I should have checked it was set to the Sydney beacon."

"Cecilia wasn't intent on finding Fey and myself?"

"No. She did express some concern but her focus was on the butterfly. She asked me where she might find it. I think the poor girl was quite addled. She said she was a naturalist—an entomologist—and how she wished to make a name for herself. She explained to me how hard it is for women to be taken seriously in science and this find would open doors for her. Quite fixated she was. As for the butterfly, I have no idea where it is—I was lost when I came across it. And still wandering lost and in a distressed state when these people found me."

"Did Cecilia wander off on her own?"

"Good heavens no. I wouldn't let her do that. I did send her with some women to where the blacks first found me and I asked them to help her find the butterfly, or failing that, to take her further east and pass her on to the next group. I hope she finds her way home but she was adamant that she absolutely had to find the butterfly."

"And you don't have even the faintest idea of where the Green Wave might be found?"

"Not at all. What is this interest that everyone has in this butterfly anyway?"

Rosalyn looked at Watson and Geoffrey and then back at Norman. "Have you heard of the Mysterious Captain Hivetree?"

Norman inhaled deeply and he replied in a cautious tone. "Yes, I have. He's the inventor of blue ascension and father of the airship."

"You've no doubt heard the stories told about him. One said he had found the blue fungus on another planet."

"My dear Reverend, there are so many stories about him. They are all contradictory, and he is the source of almost all of them. The idea he found the fungus on another planet is quite preposterous."

"Norman, sometime after you left on your explorations a story appeared in the press about the tales of Captain Hivetree. He claimed he accessed another world using a machine he created, powered by a strange substance he called Aqua Glass."

"You do know that Igneous used to dabble in strange drugs with the natives during his explorations in the Americas don't you? The man is obviously insanely deranged from all the substances he ingested." Norman picked up a stick and idly played with it, drawing lines in the sand.

"Igneous?"

"Yes, Captain Igneous Hivetree."

"He might be deranged but he described a green butterfly which fits exactly with your description of the butterfly you found. It's attracted to a flower which grows only in certain areas—the same areas where the Aqua Glass is found."

Norman stared into the fire. "I see. So the Society has sent an expedition to find this butterfly based on my missive."

"Yes."

"Not only the society," said Watson "The Mechanics have also sent an expedition looking for you or the Green Wave."

"The Mechanics?"

"The Divine Order of Mechanics. They're an offshoot of the Enlightenment Church. They see themselves as some kind of religious order like the old Knights Templar, with a mission to set the world right according to their view of it."

"Ah! Those Mechanics. Yes, I know of them. They were a small sect when I left Britain."

"Their popularity increased considerably after the release of their manifesto. That must have come out about the time you left."

"What manifesto?"

"Their plan for a future society. It appealed to a great many people, and not just in Britain," said Watson

"And they're looking for the flower, too," said Geoffrey.

"What flower is that?"

"The one Captain Hivetree called the Shellbean Flower. It looks like a bivalve shell. I don't suppose you recall seeing any do you?"

Norman looked down at his cracked, bare feet and shook his head. "Do you know if Captain Hivetree knows of the report I sent back?"

"I really don't know," said Watson. "It's more than possible. The papers you sent back excited much curiosity and were serialised in three parts in The Times. I daresay he read it but as no one knows where he is, how would we know?"

Norman frowned. "I don't suppose you would. And this information I sent back caused both the Royal Society and the Mechanics to mount airship expeditions to find it?"

"Not just them—The Enlightenment Church, too. The Lightning, my airship, is Church property. Cecilia was only on it by chance. The Royal Society didn't send an airship."

"So Watson and Geoffrey, if the Reverend Flynn and Miss Spotswood were with this other girl—the colonial—how did you get here? I thought you must be Society men."

The two men looked at each other sheepishly. "We were sort of excluded from the Society—something of a scandal you see. I won't bother you with the sordid details but we're quite innocent of course. We did nothing wrong. It made it hard for us and we were excluded from our social circles completely. Our respective fortunes declined. When the Mechanics approached us and offered us positions on their expedition we didn't hesitate to accept their generous offer."

"So why did you leave them?"

"They are scoundrels," said Geoffrey, clenching his fist. "Murderers."

"Murderers?"

"Yes. You see, sometimes during the course of the flight Sir Rothwell would order the shooting of blacks who we came upon. He didn't hide his reasons. He wanted to eradicate them as being unworthy of taking part in the great machinery of life. Not only that, he wanted to enrage them so any other Europeans who might come looking for the Green Wave would find the blacks in arms against them."

Norman winced, his fingers tightening on the stick he'd been playing with. It snapped. He muttered something in his adopted tongue before looking up again. "So he's the one responsible for the killings—the damned bastard. Sir Rothwell you say?"

"Yes," said Watson. "He heads the expedition of the Divine Order of Mechanics. It's well financed with the latest in airships. Their ship, the Eyrie, was built in Sydney in secret. The Mechanical Order has a shipyard and they were building wet ships for the coastal trade. However one of the ships being built was in reality an airship. We departed at night in secrecy. The Eyrie took with it four scientists. Two of them, we discovered, were members of the Order and the other two were Geoffrey and myself."

"We didn't know the true purpose of the expedition when we were recruited," said Geoffrey. "We only found out after we were well underway and beyond the frontier."

"We didn't know just how ruthless they were," added Watson. "When we did we were all ready trapped. The idea came to us that Sir Rothwell may have had us killed after the Green Wave or the Shellbean Flower were found. We're not exactly considered part of his new world order. Mind you, we're not exactly considered part of the old world order either."

Rosalyn asked Norman, "Haven't you heard more of these events from Doris?"

"Who is Doris?"

Rosalyn looked around and saw that the women had not yet returned so could not point Doris out to him. "She's a black woman I met on the Order's airship."

"Yes," said Watson. "She was kidnapped from her group by Sir Rothwell's men. He had in mind giving her instruction in English so she might assist in locating the Green Wave."

"Or the Shellbean flower," added Geoffrey.

"They weren't making any progress so when I was captured by Sir Rothwell he tasked me to take over the language teaching. He thought perhaps a woman might have more success with her."

"And did you?"

"Yes. I taught Doris a few words before we managed to escape. We put ourselves in the hands of Doris and she led us here."

The women entered camp at that moment, Doris among them. Rosalyn pointed her out to Norman who walked over to her. They had a lengthy discussion. He returned shortly and bade Rosalyn, Watson and Geoffrey to follow him. He took them only a short distance and had them sit down at the edge of a large circular area. The space had been cleared of sticks and stones. Norman sat down beside Rosalyn.

"What's happening?"

"They want to formally welcome you. They're putting on a dance, a corroboree they've been working on today." Most of the other Aboriginal people sat down around them at the edge of the clearing. Over the other side of it, dark shapes could be seen and the rustling of vegetation heard. Nearby, some of the seated men and women started banging sticks together and chanting. A line of dancers entered the arena in single file, making strange exaggerated shuffling movements with their feet. Their bodies were covered with designs of white ochre. Arm and headbands were adorned with fresh sprays of green leaves and in each hand they carried tufts of grass. The performers danced around the perimeter of the circle. Having completed a circuit they came in and formed two lines facing Rosalyn, Watson and Geoffrey, holding their grass clumps directly above their heads.

Another figure entered the scene carrying a sheet of bark. He stood in front of the dancers and held up the bark on which they could see an abstract painting in yellow ochre. The dancers and the 'painter' stamped their feet in time to the clapping of the sticks. Rosalyn was surprised when Doris entered the circle also carrying grass clumps. Standing facing the dancers she started moving her arms apart and then together, swaying from side to side. The dancers followed her movements.

Rosalyn nudged Watson and whispered. "Do you recognise that?"

"The painting?"

"No, the dance."

"Yes, I see. My word, they're doing the Green Wave dance that we performed to distract the crew of the Eyrie."

The dance was carried out with some imaginative embellishments. The three newcomers clapped their appreciation at the end of it and Doris joined Rosalyn. Norman introduced Doris as Deep Moving Water and sat with them acting as translator. He explained that Deep Moving Water was from another group, and had married into Norman's kin-group.

"Norman, I've been curious, can you ask Deep Moving Water if she knows who built the circle and the city of stone?"

"I can answer that question for you. It's one I was curious about myself. Their ancestors did."

Watson looked at him incredulously. "Nonsense. They're savages. They couldn't possibly have built such a thing. And if they did why did they abandon it?"

"I once thought the same thing and asked the same questions. The story is soon told. The people's ancestors stopped following the Law and started making food out of the ground. I suppose the story is referring to farming. Two spirit men came, called the Lightning Brothers and they had the ancestors make the big stones. The ancestors went to live in the big stones with the Lightning Brothers but some of the people got greedy and forgot the Law. By and by the Lightning Brothers quarrelled over this and had a big fight. One of the brothers chopped the head off the other with his axe. The Elders, who had stayed away from the stones, told the people that the big stones were bad and it wasn't the Law. They started an into-the-desert movement and the people left the big stones to the dead.

It is now a taboo to go there."

"Do you believe that?"

"Yes, Reverend, I do—at least I have no reason to disbelieve it. The stones must be thousands of years old and so the stories themselves may contain something of the truth of the matter."

Rosalyn left them and laid down in her sleeping place, wondering if Fey still wandered in the big stones or if she was now in the camp of the dead. She fell asleep and woke in the night dreaming of Fey stuffed into one of the stone sarcophagi. Deep Moving Water was lying behind her and put her arm around Rosalyn when she stirred. Impulsively Rosalyn kissed it and drifted back off to sleep.

"Where is Norman?" asked Rosalyn of Watson and Geoffrey.

"Over there, see? Among that group of fellows. They're jabbering away about something. Look—they have their spears and are thoroughly agitated."

Geoffrey moved closer to Watson. "Oh dear, I hope we're safe. Do you think we're safe?"

Rosalyn stood staring at them and looked around at the rest of the unsmiling faces in the camp. "I don't know. I think we're safe. No one is looking at us with devil eyes so I'm sure whatever it is, it's not about us."

Norman came back to them, his weapons in hand. "There's been a bit of bother and your presence here is causing some concern."

"What sort of concern?"

"They know about the killings of the people of Deep Moving Water and of other killings by the Mechanical Order. I explained to them that white people also have different kin groups or tribes and that your group is a friendly one but there is another—an enemy tribe. Deep Moving Water also gave an account which supported that."

"So what is the concern?" asked Rosalyn.

"My people think that having you here will bring your enemy tribe looking for you. They're scared and they think they'll be punished if you're here and it would be best for you to leave now."

"Leave?"

"Yes, Reverend. I've agreed to take you away."

"Where are you going to take us?"

"I think back to the circle of the big stones—it's not too far from here. That is, if you're accustomed to long walks through dry country. Someone will find you eventually and I'll personally see to it that none of you starve."

Rosalyn looked at her companions and then at the watching faces of the natives. She turned back to Norman. "If Sir Rothwell finds us I am certain he is going to kill us. He could well appear at the circle and if he does there is nowhere for us to hide, nowhere to run."

"I understand that, Reverend and I argued for you to remain here. Their response was predictable—if your enemies are going to kill you then they're going to kill the people you're with."

"I see."

"What I've arranged with my people is that they'll go and tell other groups to look out for the big red airship and warn you if it is in the area. They'll stay until your home people realise you are missing and send a party out looking for you."

"When do we go?"

"Now."

"So soon? I could see myself becoming accustomed to this place and these people. This would have been an excellent place to set up my Mission and teach the Enlightenment."

"Have a good look around you, Reverend Flynn, and see if you can see what I have seen."

Rosalyn looked and she saw women sitting in small groups chatting as they worked on various tasks. Children were running about squealing, playing and exploring. She saw the men standing watching them and waiting patiently. She saw people who were closely bonded to each other. Her attention was caught by a flock of white cockatoos flying past the orange cliffs and her gaze dropped to the footprints of the people in the dry sandy bed of the river and she understood.

"May I say farewell to Deep Moving Water?"

Rosalyn hugged Deep Moving Water closely and kissed her cheek. She turned and followed Watson and Geoffrey. Other men came with them and they walked up out of the gorge with its friendly wisps of smoke rising from the campfires on the dry river bed.

26

THE GREEN WAVE

The warriors took a slow and meandering route to the stone circle, interrupting the walk to hunt anything catching their attention. Signs of animals invisible to Rosalyn and her comrades stood out like beacons to the hunters. Norman explained life with the Aborigines as best he could but struggled sometimes to impart the correct meaning. When evening came camp would be made wherever they happened to be, a fire would be lit, food would be cooked and they'd sleep under the stars.

Late one morning the warriors stopped them below a rocky outcrop and bade them stay, sheltered from the harsh sun by the overhang of the rock. Norman went with the warriors and they didn't return until early afternoon. While she waited, Rosalyn amused herself by waving away the flies or trying to spot wildlife out in the spreading landscape. Watson and Geoffrey waited in silence, lost in their thoughts. The return of Norman and his companions roused them from their idle musings.

"There are two people at Big Stone Circle, but no sign of an airship of any kind," said Norman.

"What did they look like?"

"We didn't get close enough to see their features. I thought we looked at two men. My companions insist the smaller one is a woman."

"Fey. Could it be Fey?"

"I don't know," said Norman. "I've never met the woman."

"Reverend, if that is Fey and this is Norman, then who is the man with her?" asked Watson.

Rosalyn looked at Norman. "Don't look to me for answers. I have not the faintest idea. The desert is full of your people these days."

"They're yours too," Rosalyn reminded him. Norman made no reply.

"We had best be careful," said Watson. "This might be a trap."

"I saw no sign of anyone else."

"They could be hiding in the cistern," said Rosalyn.

"I really don't think they'd waste so much time setting a trap for us. I mean, think about it. They don't know if we're alive or which way we went. Sir Rothwell wouldn't bother—he has other things on his mind," said Watson.

"We'll go straight in. I'll lead the way." Rosalyn clambered to her feet.

"I'll come up behind. I might scare them with my appearance. My friends will wait here for me." Norman turned and spoke to his comrades who were quite at ease with him leaving them for a time.

Picking their way through the clumps of grass they came up to the stone circle. As Rosalyn entered the ring of stones she recognised one of the figures.

"Fey!" Fey turned around in surprise at hearing her name called, and on seeing Rosalyn she grinned, leaping up from where she'd been sitting in the shade of a stone. Rosalyn ran to her and wrapped her arms around her neck, hugging her tightly and kissing her cheek. "I am so glad to see you."

"Yeah, it shows, and I'm pretty bloody happy to have you in view, too. You got any food? The local wildlife is either inside us already, or have twigged that none of their relatives come back from the water and are keeping clear of us. My palate is needing a change from roast grasshoppers."

Rosalyn stepped back, her hands still resting on Fey's shoulders and whispered, "Who is the we?"

"Your Guardian."

A figure emerged from the deep shade of the stones and approached them. "Good afternoon. My, another young lady in the desert. How do you do? I'm Frederick. No wait, that's not right. Samuel, yes Samuel Bluethorn."

Fey turned and muttered to him. "That's Bluerose."

"Yes, of course, how silly of me, Bluerose, Samuel Bluerose. And you must be Missionary Flynn."

"I am. I'm Reverend Missionary Rosalyn Flynn."

"Glad to see you alive and well. Pleased to make your acquaintance. And who are these people?"

Rosalyn looked around as the rest of her party came up to them. "This is Doctor Watson Gilroy and Mister Geoffrey Ovens, and the man with the spears is Doctor Norman Phatts."

Samuel gave Norman a close scrutiny and Norman started to speak. "Igneous... "

Samuel interrupted him. "Samuel Bluerose. Call me Samuel."

Norman looked at him and nodded. "Yes, Samuel. Good. We weren't expecting to see anyone here. What are you doing here... Samuel?"

"Waiting."

"You travelled into the interior to wait?"

Samuel looked around him. "It appears to be as good a place to wait as any."

"Norman, what did you say?" Rosalyn gave Doctor Phatts an inquisitive look.

"Say? I asked him if he came here to wait."

"I thought you said 'Igneous'."

"He did, I heard him too. So what?" said Fey.

Rosalyn turned from Norman to Samuel. "Captain Hivetree?"

"Who? Never heard of the fellow, never heard of him at all." Samuel stroked his sideburns, looking from one to the other of the surrounding faces.

Geoffrey coughed loudly. "I say, we have more company. " He pointed into the desert and as they looked they heard the sound of an engine. An airship was approaching, flying close to ground level.

"That looks like the Lightning," said Rosalyn.

"It does," said Fey.

"The Mechanical Order took it. Rothwell's men will be on it."

"We need to hide." Geoffrey clutched at the worried looking Watson's arm.

"Too late for that," said Samuel. "We have weapons; form a line. It will be just like Waterloo all over again."

"I hardly think it's the same thing at all, Igneous. It's only a small airship, not the French cavalry."

Rosalyn, Fey and Samuel primed their weapons and Norman fitted a spear to his spear-thrower as the *Lightning* came close, its propeller shaft whining in its housing and kicking up dust. It grounded outside the circle. A hook was thrown out and a figure climbed over the side and walked towards them.

"Cecilia?" Rosalyn lowered her weapon and watched the woman approach.

Cecilia said nothing but as she drew near her eyes fixed on one person in particular.

"Daddy!" She ran up to Samuel and threw her arms around him. Everyone else stood back, stunned into silence at the unexpected reunion.

"Edain! Wonderful. I trust you're in as good a condition as you are spirits. I have this peculiar idea I'd told you to stay in Sydney."

"Yes, Daddy, I know, but I didn't and everything has gone splendidly well."

"Did you find any?"

"No, Daddy, but look." While the rest of the party stared, Cecilia took from her satchel a large, leather-bound notebook. She opened it up and there, squashed between the pages in a haphazard fashion, was a green butterfly. Underneath in fine copperplate was written the words, 'the Green Wave'.

Everyone started asking questions all at once so Geoffrey suggested they make a pot of tea. After calming themselves down they waited patiently in the shade until they were all equipped with a hot brew. Rosalyn spoke first. "I think I deserve some sort of explanation, Cecilia."

"Yes, you do. My name is Edain. I was helping Daddy look for the Green Wave, and if it existed nothing was going to stop me from finding it."

"That's hardly an explanation."

"What do you want, a novel?"

"No, I want to know why you never told us you were Captain Hivetree's daughter."

Edain looked at her father who answered for her. "That would be on my account. I told her not to tell anyone."

"But why?"

"Attention. There would be far too much of it. People would accost Edain with questions, And those horrible cults. Do you know we 'Mysterious' people are hounded, followed by people who revere us or hate us. I didn't want my precious child to attract undue attention. It would also bring more focus on me, and I do enjoy being unfocussed."

"I'm not sure why it needed to be such a secret," said Rosalyn.

"I didn't know you had a daughter," said Norman, "although I did notice a certain familiarity when I met her earlier."

"Yes, well, I do, see? And isn't she a remarkable young woman? She was at school in France when you and I travelled together, Norman."

"How do you both know each other?" asked Watson.

"We fought together at Waterloo," said Igneous, and added, "Or rather, fought alongside each other. We didn't fight each other, although we've had our spats."

"A long time has passed since Waterloo. We became good friends after that engagement."

"Yes, quite good friends. And after we thrashed old Boney we were in France together for the occupation. That's when I met Edain's mother."

"That woman you were seeing? Bridget?"

The others listened to the exchange in silence. "Yes, terrible thing. She died in childbirth."

"I knew nothing of it."

"I kept it quiet, hushed up, yes. We were young officers and ambitious—it wouldn't have done for the scandal to get out. I arranged for the baby to be sent to England to be cared for."

"You both went on the expedition to South America," Geoffrey said. "I remember reading about it."

"That's not quite right. It was to Central America we travelled," said Norman.

"Why were you hiding from us your friendship with Captain Hivetree?" asked Rosalyn.

"Out of respect for my old comrade. I know he likes to preserve his seclusion, even to the point of being a recluse. I had no wish to talk of him and it was unnecessary to do so. If his location was made known it may have put him in danger."

"But... So you're a friend of Captain Hivetree?"

"Yes, haven't you been listening?"

"How could knowing him put him in danger?"

"I'm right here you know," said Igneous. "As my old friend Norman has said, he did not want to be questioned too closely lest he divulge details I would prefer not be made known."

"Why not?"

"Apart from those wretched religious zealots, there are people who want what I've found, what I've made. Amazing things, yes."

"How did you come to be a Church Guardian?"

Igneous looked at her. "I'm not, my dear Reverend, I'm not. I've never said I was. Mind you I never denied it either. It's best I remain anonymous, it suits me. The last thing I want is people pestering me about this and that—and then there are those infernal Mechanical Order fellows."

"What about them?"

"The Divine Order of Mechanics? They are overly inquisitive concerning my activities. I'm quite safe from them of course. There have been a few close encounters but I've played my cards close to my chest. I dropped some of them—not sure at all I'm playing with a full deck but I get by."

"Why would you come out here and put yourself so close to them and so at risk?" asked Geoffrey.

"I couldn't in clear conscience send Edain out here by herself, could I? I needed someone I could trust in Sydney, to spy out what she could. We had more chance of finding, or perhaps disproving, the existence of the Green Wave and the Shellbean flower—and of learning if anyone else did."

"Oh yes, Daddy, I found the flower too." Edain opened her book and presented the squashed flower.

Geoffrey leaned in and had a close look. "Remarkable. I've never seen anyone press a flower like that."

Igneous asked, "Was there nothing else?"

"No Daddy. I didn't see any Aqua Glass and I had no pick-axes to dig into any rocks."

"Captain Hivetree," asked Rosalyn, "you've been here before, haven't you?"

"No. I swear by the great bearded cloud deity, no I haven't."

"I still don't understand," said Rosalyn.

"My dear, if you have heard of the Green Wave and the Shellbean flower you must certainly have heard of Aqua Glass."

"Yes, the blue-green, crystal-like substance you found somewhere."

"Where did you find it?" asked Watson.

"Far away from here."

"Does it do what you said it does?"

"My word. That and more. It is powerful and potentially useful."

"Why did you come here?"

"To see if there is more of course. I have to know."

"I don't understand," said Rosalyn. "Why is it so important that you come here?"

Igneous and Edain looked at each other and Igneous continued. "That is soon told." Igneous stared into the cup of tea he'd been holding. "Some time ago, I'm not sure how long, but some years back, a plan for a machine I was working on went missing."

"The one for moving between two locations?" asked Fey.

Igneous shook his head. "That machine is dangerously unworkable. No. A different machine. The loss of the plans caused me no great pain as the machine needed Aqua Glass for it to function. I did mention that particular point in the plans, and I know Aqua Glass can't be found on this planet."

"This planet?"

"Yes, my dear, this planet. There are other planets of course."

"Are you saying you went to another planet?" asked Watson.

"I found the Aqua Glass on another planet. Fogbound I call it, but the fog could have been in my head."

"Another planet? That's not possible," said Rosalyn.

"Neither is flying, my dear Reverend Flynn. At least that's what they said before I built the first practical airship."

"Did the blue ascension also come from another planet?"

"Yes my dear, the same one. Made me quite a wealthy man too, richer than I could possibly have imagined. Moving on, Norman's accounts of his travels here arrived back in England and I read his description of the Green Wave. I had to come to see if it was true or not. If the Aqua Glass doesn't exist here then all is well. If it does and it falls into the wrong hands—the hands that have the plans of that device—then terrible things could happen. I had no idea it might be found here on Earth and I never would have described the green butterfly I saw if I thought it could lead to finding it here."

The group fell silent, absorbing the revelations. After musing for several minutes, Rosalyn turned to Edain. "How came you by the Lightning?"

"It was purely providence that I chanced across it. Two days ago I saw the Lightning. The ship was in a search pattern, circling, you see. I thought it might be you and Fey searching for me. By then I'd found what I had come for and was more than ready to return to Sydney. The Lightning was a long way off. My black companions— the guides Doctor Phatts sent with me—helped me get closer to it. Eventually the Lightning grounded and I saw it wasn't you at all—that's when I decided to take it."

"Take it?"

"Yes, a man flew it—one of the Mechanical Order. You know they have their own counterpart to the Guardians? They're spies and assassins. The silly fellow was flying the Order's flag. I prayed you hadn't been killed but as the poor man died before I could ask him, I had no way of knowing your fate. I returned here to start searching for you."

"He died? What of?"

Edain tapped one of her pistols and smirked, "Lead poisoning."

Rosalyn sighed. "How did you find the circle again?"

"I keep detailed maps. It wasn't too hard."

"Cecilia," asked Rosalyn, "did you see the Eyrie?"

"Yes I did. It was the same time I saw the Lightning but the Eyrie was far to the south."

"My dear, which direction was the Eyrie headed?"

"It was heading east, Daddy."

Igneous stared off into the sky. "East you say?"

"Yes, Daddy."

Geoffrey coughed again. "Speaking of the Eyrie..." He indicated the brass tube on its tripod. "Captain Hivetree, what is this thing? Is it some kind of telescope?"

"No, Geoffrey, it's not. It's an atmotic vessel directional indicator.

Miss Grey can tell you all about it."

"I only ask because I noticed Sir Rothwell has a similar looking thing in his cabin only bigger and with an odd cable attached."

Igneous spat out his tea. "He what?"

"I didn't mean to upset you but Sir Rothwell has a similar device that he keeps in a long wooden box. I presumed it to be a navigational instrument."

"Good heavens, no. If it's what I think it is... Damn it."

"There's one of those atmotic indicators on the Lightning, too," said Edain. "That Mechanic fellow had it."

Igneous stared into his empty cup. "They must have got the plans. I don't know how they found me or obtained them. Could someone please make some more tea?" Geoffrey rose from his rock to fill the kettle.

"Plans for what?" asked Fey.

"For that device, the one that can cause great destruction if misused."

"Igneous, I have a small confession to make," said Norman.

"Yes Norman, what is it?"

"I... I took the plans of the thing you said was a weapon. I sold them to the Mechanical Order. I knew they'd be interested buyers."

Igneous's face turned white, changing to a bright red hue before resuming its usual shade and he asked flatly, "You stole my plans and sold them? Why?"

"It's like this: after our Central American expedition I was totally skint. Cost me everything to go on that journey and when we returned home I found myself struggling. I thought your plans were simply the work of an over-imaginative, drug-crazed madman and were quite harmless so I stole them and sold them to finance this expedition."

Igneous stared at the sand. "The machine made from those plans would be quite harmless as long as it doesn't have the Aqua Glass. It's useless without it."

Fey, who had been quietly listening, gave a loud cough. "I have some bad news—I think he got some."

"Why do you think that, Fey?" asked Rosalyn.

"Do you remember the gold headband we found in the stone jar with the bones?"

"Yes."

"Do you remember when you and Watson and I were hiding from the lizard?"

"Yes."

"Well, I took it. I wrapped it up in roo hide and was wearing it on my head with the head scarf thing that Ses made us. When I was taken off the Eyrie and made my escape I lost it. Sir Rothwell might have found it, or one of his crew."

"You found gold?" asked Watson.

"Yeah, I found gold and it had a crystal mounted in the centre."

"But, Fey, that was clear quartz. It had no colour to it."

"It didn't when we first saw it, but when I pulled it out again the night we were hiding from the lizard, the thing had a blue glow to it."

"That's it. The planet of Fogbound always has an eerie blue glow and a full moon, two of them."

"How odd," said Watson.

"Maybe it's like the stars," said Fey. "You can't see them when the sun is out."

The discussion came to a halt while more tea was made. Edain turned to her father. "Daddy, do you think the Mechanical Order has Aqua Glass?"

"Yes dear, they're heading east so we must assume they're returning to Sydney. They wouldn't do so if they were empty-handed. What I don't understand is why Sir Rothwell had the device with him. He couldn't have known he would find the Aqua Glass."

Fey fished out her tobacco and shared it around. "He wouldn't have to. He had it with him just on spec. What does this device he has do?"

"It's a mineral particle displacer, I think."

"Yeah, not what it is. I asked what does it do?"

"It displaces minerals. That is, it shoots out a beam of pale blue light, delightfully pretty I would imagine—I never built one—this is all theory. The blue light causes a momentary failure of certain mineral particles to adhere to each other."

"And then what happens?"

"Whatever it strikes falls apart."

"That can't be too devastating," said Rosalyn.

"Oh my word it can. I would expect all your bones would fall apart inside your body. Any iron nails, gun barrels, wagon rims, they'll all turn to powder if hit by this thing. I do stress this is in theory. I worked it all out but I have no idea what effect it will have or on what minerals."

"What's the range of this thing?" asked Fey.

"I estimate at least half a mile. I repeat, I never built one—I could see little point. When I understood some of the properties of the Aqua Glass I started designing things and thought perhaps such a tool might be useful in mining. I decided it was far too dangerous and even destroyed the only piece of Aqua Glass I had so that I might never be tempted to return to Fogbound and collect more."

"What is the Aqua Glass?" asked Watson.

"The most interesting substance." Igneous's eyes lit up and he stared skyward. "I couldn't classify it. The stuff defies analysis. It looks like mineral, but vegetable too—perhaps even animal. And I think it can grow."

"Peculiar," said Watson.

"Astounding, I would say," said Geoffrey.

"I have it figured," said Fey.

"You have?" asked Igneous.

"Yeah. I can tell you why they're heading to Sydney." Fey took a pull of her pipe. "They're going to take it for themselves."

"What do you mean?" asked Rosalyn.

"I mean they're going to take over the colony. A coup, like the

Rum Corps did to Governor Bligh in the old days."

"Could they do that?"

"If they've got enough people in the right places."

"It's quite possible," said Watson. "They have people everywhere. If they're in uniform you know them, but there are so many in different professions you just don't know who is in it and who isn't."

"Why would they want to take over Sydney?" asked Rosalyn.

"If they've found Aqua Glass it's reason enough. Where there's one piece there's more. When it becomes known that Aqua Glass is found in the colony, Sydney will become of vital importance," said Igneous.

"And the gold," said Fey. "Learning there's gold here will spark a rush. The colony will become rich. Sailors will be jumping ship to get a piece of the shiny."

"The Mechanical Order would also have its own region. It would become a power to be reckoned with," said Geoffrey

"Especially with having the only access to Aqua Glass. The Eyrie has the machine aboard so it can easily cover Sydney from the air, out of range of troops on the ground. It could force a surrender on its own," said Igneous.

"Political power will be won from the boats of the airships," mused Rosalyn.

"What's that you say?"

"Something a young officer told me on my airship training course. So what do we do?"

"Don't know about you lot but I think we better head back to Sydney," said Fey.

"Yes, of course, Fey, Sydney. Tiny little place it is. Can't go rushing in there. Not with the weapon they have, no, not like that."

"How are we all going to get there anyway? We can't fit the seven of us in the Lightning," Fey tapped the ashes from her pipe.

"Six," said Norman. "I'm not coming."

"I suppose we could stay here, Geoffrey and I, I mean. I've had little chance to study the geology and I know Geoffrey is aching to study the flora in more detail. If Norman could help us out with food from time to time, we could survive here until you come to retrieve us."

"I can see to it that you don't starve," said Norman.

"Can we fit four on your airship, Reverend?"

"Yes, Captain Hivetree, I think we can manage it. We'll have to keep our extra weight to a minimum."

"What do we do when we get there?" asked Edain.

"I'm sure we'll think of something," said Rosalyn.

"Miss Grey," said Igneous. "Do you remember that gallery, the one where those snake things chased us and we went down the trapdoor?"

"Yes, what about it?"

"There were crystals in there."

"Clear ones, yes."

"Clear by the light of my lantern,5 yes, but in the moonlight, perhaps not, like the one you say you found. We must get there and find this crystal and bring it up by moonlight. We need to know if it's Aqua Glass."

"I had a quick thought it might be the same as the piece I found in with the bones, but it was the gold that had me fixated. Anyway you're forgetting something, Iggy."

"What's that?"

"Those monsters are in there."

"What use are the Aqua Glass crystals by themselves anyway?" asked Rosalyn.

"I don't suppose they are any use at all," said Igneous.

"So why is it you want them?"

"I think I might be able to create something to help us. First we must get the crystal and see if it's Aqua Glass."

"What if it isn't?"

"Then the colony of Sydney will have new and unpleasant rulers."

"So we're going to fly back to the ruins?"

"I don't think that's a good idea. It's when we go through the cavern in the water we'll be at our most vulnerable. If we go along the tunnel we can come right up under the crystal."

"Back into the monster hole." Fey cleaned out her pipe. "It's two days walk through that narrow tunnel, and two days back. I don't fancy that. How about we fly down? We could get it all done in a day or so?"

"Miss Grey, that means walking twice through deep water with those snake things lurking."

"I'd go half an hour in the pond over four days in that narrow passage."

"You could stay here," suggested Cecilia.

"No, I'm not staying, I'm coming."

"We all have to face our demons sometime, Miss Grey," said Igneous.

"Glad you agree, we're flying down."

"That wasn't..." Igneous looked at Fey, "All right, let's fly down and get this business done."

"Norman, do you mind waiting here with Doctor Watson and Mister Ovens?" asked Rosalyn.

"Not at all," said Norman.

"Yes, yes stay here. I'll leave my atmotic indicator with you, keep it safe, I'll need that. We'll be back in a day or two if we're not devoured. Let's go at once."

"Hate to break it to you, Iggy, but while we've been exercising our chins the night got here."

"We're leaving in the morning." Rosalyn turned to Watson and Geoffrey. "I'm not sure how long it will take us exactly but we should be back tomorrow."

27

A SMALL SETBACK

Stars could still be seen in the morning sky as the circle of stones disappeared behind them. The four of them remained silent as the *Lightning* flew on through the dawn. Edain stayed in the bow, scouring the landscape for her first view of the ruins.

"It's substantial, but not a big city."

"Yeah, not as big as Sydney."

"Sydney isn't a city, it's a town," said Rosalyn.

"We should go down there," said Igneous.

"We should have a cup of tea first."

"Marvellous idea, Rosalyn. It'll give me time to make a quick map of the ruins." Edain took out a note book and started work while Rosalyn prepared the tea. Fey checked the weapons.

"We've a few extra guns here. Look at these ones." Fey held up a pair of handsome pistols made entirely from brass and iron.

Edain looked at her. "Those are mine. I took them from the man I killed. He was well-armed."

"You'll have to tell me about that sometime, Eddy."

"Call me Eddy again and you'll be the next one I kill."

Fey grinned. "Then for my own safety I'll be sticking with 'Edain'."

"We should take all the weapons," said Igneous. "There're quite a few of those monsters we'll have to deal with in the darkness."

Rosalyn manoeuvred the *Lightning* to an open patch of ground close to the cavern entrance. "We'll need to be quiet," said Fey.

"Are the things drawn by sound?" asked Edain.

"Light too, perhaps, light and sound, vibration, ripples in the water," said Igneous.

"We'll have to have light," said Rosalyn. "If we move like snails and just as quietly we may pass unnoticed."

"Iggy, do you remember which way it was from the ledge at the bottom of the stairs?"

"The way?"

"Yes. When we walked off from the ledge, which way did we go?"

"Don't you worry about that. I took a compass reading."

"You did?"

"Yes, I have a compass on this leather bracer on my wrist. Look. Comes in quite handy."

"How will you see it in the dark?" Fey peered at the compass face.

"The needle glows in the dark."

"Enough. Let's get this done with," said Rosalyn.

Fey opened the stone door and once inside, they stopped, listening for any sound that might be coming from the stairway. "Remember, no lights, no sound," whispered Igneous. "Follow me, keep a hand on my shoulder, single file."

They crept down the stairs and at the bottom they rested, their eyes adjusting to what little light made its way from the stone room above. Hearing no sounds apart from their own breathing, Igneous slid off the rock into the lake. He took Rosalyn's hand and guided her in. She stifled a gasp at the coldness of the water. Edain and Fey followed.

Over the years sand had made its way into the cavern, settling on the lake bed creating an even floor. Igneous kept a slow pace, stopping frequently to check his compass. At such halts every pair of ears listened for sounds. The chamber was silent and apart from the faint glow at the stairway, perfectly black. After painfully inching their way forward Igneous hit the wall with a soft thud. He fumbled around, produced his lantern and found the beach where he and Fey had exited the water days previously. He turned the lantern off and they made for the beach; relieved to be out of the water.

After a small amount of searching in the dark, feeling their way over the walls, they located the cave leading to the chamber of the stone box. Once safely inside, Igneous lit his lantern again. The women produced candles from their pouches and they gazed around the cave.

"This art is fascinating," whispered Edain.

"Yeah, it's spiritual. Iggy said so."

Rosalyn looked at it. "It's intriguing, yes. Let's not waste any time. We need to find what we're looking for and hurry out of here."

"If I remember proper, it's over there," said Fey. She climbed over the jumble of rocks, moving her candle around in front of her. "Here." Together they examined the contents.

"Do you think it's Aqua Glass, Daddy?"

"It's possible. If Miss Grey found a piece in the ruins it must have come from somewhere. This box could be the somewhere it came from." Igneous added, "How bizarre. I could have sworn we found gold in here, too."

"Gold?" asked Edain.

"I guess the monster took it," said Fey as she rummaged around the sticks and stones in the box.

"That sounds likely," said Edain drily. She reached into the box and took out several pieces of crystal. "This does look like ordinary quartz crystal, doesn't it, Daddy?"

"It does, but I'm having a notion the Aqua Glass goes dormant when away from the light for long periods. We won't know until we take it up into the moonlight, and I don't know if you've followed the calendar but tonight is a full moon."

"From what you've said the full moon will be the best time for looking at the Aqua Glass," said Rosalyn as she continued staring about the chamber.

"Yes, most certainly, Reverend Flynn. Moonlight is good, more moonlight must be better."

"Getting it up into the moonlight means wading waist deep in the darkness trying to find the stairs again while being hunted by monsters."

"Details, Miss Grey, details."

"I'd hate to be eaten by one of those details," said Fey, as she rummaged around in the box making a show of looking at the painted sticks and the ground stones.

"I'll go first again, Miss Grey. You can bring up the rear."

"No she won't." Rosalyn voice carried an edge of steel. Her companions stared at her. "Captain Hivetree, we need you to build the machine to stop the Mechanical Order. I have to fly the airship. Fey will go first. Captain Hivetree, you second. Cecilia can bring up the rear."

"It's Edain."

"Edain, Cecilia. I don't care. We have work to do. Fey, take the lead."

Fey didn't argue. She led the way back through the chamber to the underground lake. She stepped down into the dark water, her carbine raised to her shoulder in readiness. Igneous followed directly behind her with the lantern. The cold water made pleasant rippling noises as they waded slowly through it. Fey stopped.

"Do you hear something?" Rosalyn whispered.

"No."

"Why did you stop?"

"To listen."

"Keep moving."

After wading on a dozen steps further Fey stopped again. "Did you hear that?"

"No. What was it?"

"I thought I heard a splash."

"How close?"

"In the distance."

"Keep moving, keep moving," Igneous urged them.

A few minutes later a splash sounded close by to their right. The party froze and Igneous swung his lantern around. Rosalyn raised her candle higher. Ripples came towards them.

"Whatever that was, it was big," said Rosalyn.

The water erupted in a spray of reflected light, like a shattering chandelier. Large, snake-like creatures rose up and crashed down hard, splashing into the water between Fey and Igneous, drenching them as they dodged aside. The water calmed and the party stood still, waiting for the creatures to move again. "Where did they go?" asked Rosalyn.

"Dunno. Should I go look for them?"

"I have a notion those were tentacles, not snakes," said Igneous, scanning the water with his lantern.

A large ripple formed in the water, the water swirled and something swept Fey off her feet. She disappeared below the surface. Further back a fleshy, bulbous part of the creature projected above the water. Igneous aimed at it and squeezed the trigger of his weapon but it misfired. The water churned and the tentacles broke the surface again. Rosalyn reached for Igneous's belt, pulled out his sword and moved towards the monster.

Another of the creature's tentacles broke the surface, swiping at Rosalyn. She ducked, swung, and severed the limb. The water still churned and the creature began moving away. Fey still hadn't resurfaced. Rosalyn thrashed after it and felt a spiky limb of the creature brushing against her legs. Ignoring the spines she plunged the sword into it, cutting and hacking. Nearby Fey burst to the surface, gasping for breath in the swirling water, only to be knocked off her feet again by another tentacle.

Rosalyn fell back as the creature raised itself out of the water on several of its limbs. Fey took one look at it, turned, and made her way towards Igneous. He struggled to reload his pistol while holding the lantern. Edain dropped her candle and fired her own pistols at the central mass of the monster. It spun rapidly, bending its limbs, sending up large waves and sprays of water that blinded the party.

Igneous, who was now holding the only light, held it up high. The swirling waters became still. "It's gone."

"I don't think so," Fey said quietly.

"It's not moving. Did we kill it?" asked Rosalyn.

"Over there, in the distance," said Cecilia.

"What?" asked Igneous.

"The light reflected off the water as it moved. The creature has retreated."

"What was that thing?" asked Rosalyn.

"It was a cephalopod," said Cecilia.

"A what?"

"A squid."

"What would a squid be doing in here?" Rosalyn stared off into the darkness.

"Young lady, you should stick to your insects; it wasn't a cephalopod. It brought to mind a gargantuan form of asteroidea." Captain Hivetree passed his light to Fey and looked to his pistol. "Damnation. The powder is wet."

"What's asteroidea when it's home, Iggy?"

"A starfish. It looked like a starfish."

"We were attacked by a starfish?"

"Yes. Quite remarkable."

"Bloody oath it's remarkable. It's eating well if it got to that size. Nothing like the wee creatures I've seen in Sydney cove."

"It's remarkable because this is fresh water."

"I would have thought the size. Write a paper about it. We need to get out of here."

"Is everyone unharmed?" asked Rosalyn. "Fey? Are you hurt?"

"I'm fine now I have my breath back. Might have a few scratches and bruises." She raised her hand to find she still had her pistol clenched tightly in it. She tucked it into her belt. "What about you Roz? Did you suffer any damage?"

"I think I might have some cuts to my legs from that... that starfish's thorns. It's nothing serious. Let's move and quickly."

Igneous, with the lantern, now led the way. The others formed up behind him and with no attempt at stealth, rushed on to where the faint light in the distance showed the location of the stairs. They reached them without further incident and clambering to the top, pushed the door open, and ran back to the relative safety of the *Lightning*. Rosalyn insisted everyone clean their weapons before resting. The gunpowder was laid out to dry on a rock in the sun. None of them talked much and with the weapons cleaned and loaded they sat in the boat drinking tea, eating raisins and watching for giant lizards.

When evening came, Igneous turned to Edain, "Take out the crystals and set them up here on this slab, arrange them in a circle."

The four of them waited for moonrise, watching in expectation as the glowing orb climbed higher into the sky.

"Nothing is happening, Daddy. They're ordinary quartz crystals."

"Patience, Edain, patience. Look, do you see that?" Igneous closed the shutter of the lantern. The crystals started to glow a pale green and the party became entranced. The colour started changing. The light from inside them grew ever more intense until they were glowing a brilliant aqua colour.

"Aqua Glass! Wonderful."

"Daddy, look now."

The light from each piece of Aqua Glass spread to its neighbours, creating a pattern of lines of aqua-coloured light on the stone like the spokes of a wagon wheel. The spokes widened until the interior of the circle was a sheet of colour.

"It's stunning," sighed Rosalyn. Fey said nothing and slipped her arm around Rosalyn's waist. Rosalyn quietly put her hand over Fey's and held it.

"Daddy, what's it doing now?"

The light grew ever brighter and began pulsating within the stones. A mist developed around the crystals and the light formed itself into a dome, spreading outwards. Fey put her arm around Rosalyn's waist and Rosalyn put her hand over Fey's. She frowned as she stared at the intensifying colour.

"Daddy, this isn't right."

Igneous leaned forward, sweeping his arm across the slab, knocking the pieces of Aqua Glass like a temperamental chess player. The four of them stared in silence at the scattered stones, still glowing but no longer united in purpose.

"What just happened?" asked Fey.

"That happened twice didn't it, Daddy?"

Igneous opened the lantern shutter. His face was pale. "Yes my dear, it happened twice."

"That was an Ante Vidoram wasn't it?" asked Rosalyn in a hushed tone.

"A Setback?"

"Yes, Fey, a Temporal Setback."

Igneous picked up the pieces of Aqua Glass, putting them carefully into his satchel. "This is so dangerous. It's what I was scared of. It proves it, Edain, it proves I was right."

"It looked like they were smoking," said Fey. Her shaking hand reached for her pipe.

"That's the fog."

"What fog?"

"The fog, Miss Grey—the mist. It was in the fog that I arrived at Fogbound."

"You'd best explain, Captain Hivetree. I want to know what we're dealing with," said Rosalyn.

"The machine I made, it only used a single piece of Aqua Glass.

When I activated it a thick blue fog surrounded me. I found myself in another place and I presume it was on another planet. I wasn't there long when suddenly I was back in the room with the machine."

"You're leaving a bit out aren't you, Iggy?"

"Yes, how did you get the Aqua Glass in the first place?" asked Rosalyn.

"Ah, well, you see, that is, I had help."

"What kind of help?"

"That is soon told. I'd prefer not to have told you for I fear you'd think it deluded ramblings, and perhaps it is. It was bizarre." Igneous packed and lit his pipe. "It was shortly after returning from the Americas. Sitting in my study I smelled a pleasant odour so I knew it wasn't me. I looked up to see a thin, pale, blue mist forming in the centre of the room. The mist took a human form, tall I suppose, nearly six feet—and white. Not white like us but white like snow. A soft, white down covered it, something like the fur of a mouse."

Igneous leaned towards Fey for a light for his pipe. He inhaled deeply, turned his head from his audience and exhaled a long stream of smoke. He continued. "Its eyes were large and what would be white in our own eyes was a pale blue—the Iris was white. I stood slowly as this creature looked at me. In truth I thought it some apparition come to haunt me, or an hallucination. It spoke; its voice a series of purrs and clucking, like a cross between a cat, a pigeon and a whispering hen—if you can imagine a hen whispering."

"Was it dangerous?" asked Rosalyn.

"No. At first I trembled with fear but I saw it didn't mean to harm me. I could see immediately it possessed some intelligence; it wore clothing and carried satchels on its person. We tried to convey meaning to each other and settled on drawing each other pictures to communicate our ideas. Thus engaged, we spent a good amount of time together until the creature grew agitated, constantly looking about as though waiting for something. It calmed down but remained anxious.

"After many hours had elapsed, it expressed an interest in viewing the rest of my home. It stopped in each room studying every item, making notes in its notebook. I continued to explain things using drawings. A watercolour on my wall depicting Stonehenge caused it much excitement. When we arrived in the basement workroom it displayed what I assumed to be enthusiasm and happiness. It spent hours looking at each and every item I had there.

"I left it to browse and brought some food, thinking it might be hungry. By now I most certainly was; the visitor thought my rumbling tummy was speaking to it. It eschewed the cold meats and spat out the apple but feasted hungrily on pears, grapes and apricots. It had started creating something out of the bits and pieces in my workshop and enlisted me in its endeavours. I had no idea what manner of device we were building. On occasion I had to leave the creature to fetch parts it wanted."

"What was it making?" asked Rosalyn.

"I'm about to tell you. Next to my work room is an empty vault—you know the one, Edain. It assembled the machine in the vault and dug a hole in the floor to put the pipe through to the steam engine in the work room. The machine itself was an ugly looking contraption of copper and brass. Satisfied with our work, it took me back to the picture of Stonehenge and made it known to me that it wanted to see it."

"You took it out in public?"

"Not exactly, Reverend Flynn. I waited until late at night, wrapped it in a cloak and we drove by buggy to the henge. I remember it clearly. It was misty and I waited in the buggy as the creature walked the distance to the stones. Voices in the mist interrupted its walk around the circle. It returned to the cart and we left. It cooed to itself under the blanket all the way home.

"When we arrived home, the creature took a crystal from a pouch. It was the Aqua Glass of course but I didn't know that at the time. It placed it in the centre of the machine and instructed me by gestures that I was to start the engine in the work room.

"I stoked the furnace and pulled the lever and the mechanism started to turn. The creature put a hammer in my hands and I do believe it wanted me to smash the machine. It pushed me out of the room and shut the door. I put my ear to the door but could hear nothing above the sound of the engine. I waited for five or ten minutes and opened the door. The vault was filled with blue fog and I stood there in my leather apron and work goggles with my hammer, calling out 'hullo'. The creature didn't answer.

"I waited and the fog cleared. I was no longer in the vault. I stood under a strange sky, on a hill. The ground was spongy, covered with rocks and flowers. Being the curious sort of person I am I examined them closely and picked one—the one I called the Shellbean Flower. Around about were myriads of these butterflies—the ones Norman named the Green Wave. The rocks themselves contained the fossils of numerous seashells. Here I saw the Aqua Glass, glowing as if enchanted. I couldn't help but break a piece off with my hammer.

"I have no idea what time of day it was as the place was strangely lit, like twilight. It had a queer intensity. Two moons were in the sky. I walked a short distance over a rise and came to a curious-looking, dome-shaped building. I walked cautiously to it—the door was open and inside stood the creature. Several more of them lay dead on the floor, or at least I assumed they were dead, unless they decompose in their sleep. In the middle of the room I could see another machine, much like the one in the vault but more refined. The creature, on seeing me, displayed surprise and dismay and became greatly distressed.

"It soon recovered and tried its best to explain some important point to me but it was no use, I couldn't understand it. Taking me outside and away from the building it pointed out a city in the distance. Things were flying over it—airships. It took me back inside, gave me some sheets of rolled up parchment and a firkin filled with something. It made me wait. In about an hour the creature disappeared right in front of my eyes—it simply vanished. Shortly afterwards things became strange as though seeing everything from underwater by moonlight. That passed and all I could see was dark blue and I was back home in the vault with the creature.

"The pantomime started again and the creature withdrew the Aqua Glass from the machine, took my hammer and smashed it—the Aqua Glass—not the machine. It then put another piece in the machine and bade me leave the room. I did and this time I waited longer. On opening the door I could still see the fog but fearing I would once again be taken away by it, I did not enter but waited for it to clear. As soon as it had, I rushed in and took the Aqua Glass from the machine and smashed it. I tell you I waited for hours for the creature to reappear but it didn't."

"And the firkin, what was in it?"

"Blue mould. The rolls of parchment were plans for an airship, engine and all. It had given me a gift."

"Nice story, Iggy, needs more goblins." Fey relit her pipe.

"So you're saying you didn't actually invent the airship?" asked Rosalyn.

"Not exactly but I had to modify the designs so the thing would work here."

"Iggy, you didn't really go to another planet, did you?"

"I have related to you my memory of what I experienced."

Rosalyn sat back on a stone, a finger to her lips. "The creature was seen."

"Pardon?"

"At Stonehenge. Someone saw the creature and took it for a spectre. I was told about it by my flying instructor. If someone saw it then it lends some substance to your story."

"Could have been a different ghost," said Fey.

"All in the past now," said Igneous.

"What now, Daddy?"

"We take this back to the stone circle and I work on something to stop the Mechanical Order from taking over Sydney."

"I'm in full agreement with you there, Iggy."

Rosalyn spoke. "We'll leave now."

"That's what I like, Roz, a woman of decision and action."

The hooks withdrawn, Rosalyn took the *Lightning* aloft. The ruins below them took on a spectral and unsettling appearance in the moonlight. Fey stood next to Rosalyn at the wheel. Rosalyn looked at her and lowered her eyes. Fey kissed her—softly—her lips lingering, until Rosalyn pulled away. Fey sighed and sat in the front of the boat to pack her pipe.

Watson and Geoffrey, pleased to see their companions safely return, were apprised of the events at the ruins.

"Did you notice any extraordinary twist of time?" asked Rosalyn.

"No, nothing, but then we would have been asleep at the time you said this happened."

"You good people can rest for a while. I need some time to tinker on this machine."

"I'll give you a hand, Iggy."

"Thank you, Miss Grey. We'll use that slab there as the work bench. We need to take apart the atmotic detector. I need a lens. That's going to be a problem."

"No worries, Iggy, we have an old telescope here somewhere. One of the lenses was smashed but the other is still good."

"Excellent, find it and bring it here."

The others left Fey and Igneous to build the machine. Rosalyn went with Edain to fetch water from the cistern. The light from the entrance hole gave the space a mystical quality with the pillars reflected in the cool water. Edain broke the silence as she knelt to fill a water bottle. "She's different, isn't she?"

"Fey?"

"Yes, Fey."

"I suppose she is."

"Attractive too."

"In her own peculiar way."

"You're in love with her aren't you?"

Rosalyn looked down at her reflection in the water. Scooping the water in her hand she watched the play of light as it ran back into the pool, distorting her reflection. "You saw her kiss me didn't you?"

Edain laughed. "You hardly made a secret of it."

Rosalyn blushed. "I didn't kiss her back, and anyway, a kiss doesn't mean love, not that love anyway."

Edain smiled. "That kiss did. You liked it. Are you ashamed to admit it?"

Rosalyn turned her face away. "It's not proper. I don't love her. I don't understand it."

Edain took Rosalyn's hand in hers. "Rosalyn, I don't know you well but I do know you're in love. She loves you, too."

Their eyes met briefly and Rosalyn stared back into the water. "The Church wouldn't approve. It doesn't allow these types of... of friendships. And Fey, she's a colonial. I could never take her home, never."

"Are you crying?"

Rosalyn nodded and whispered between the tears, "I want her so much it hurts." Edain wrapped her arms around her, holding her closely, stroking her hair and calming her until the crying stopped. A shadow blocked the light. Edain looked up and saw Fey.

"I was after the water, but it looks like I'm interrupting. I'll come back later."

Edain called after her as Rosalyn looked around, startled by Fey's voice, but Fey had gone.

"I'll talk to her," said Edain. She turned to leave. Rosalyn took her arm and pulled her back.

"No, leave her. I have to let it go."

Edain shook her head. "I hope you come to your senses. Those feelings, the ones that make you think your chest is going to explode with the intensity of passion, they don't come around often. Don't waste the moment for a Church."

"I don't know what life you've led, Cecilia or Edain or whoever you are, but I was brought up well and I took vows. I made a commitment and I intend keeping it." Rosalyn scowled and with arms folded turned her back on Edain.

Edain sighed and finished filling the water bottles.

Rosalyn avoided Fey whenever she could and Fey was in a dark mood. "Is something wrong?" asked Igneous, as they tinkered on the machine.

"No," snapped Fey.

Igneous glanced up at her. "Then a rather odd species of well-being."

"I told you, nothing is wrong." Fey walked away, climbing to the top of the stones to sit and smoke. She saw Edain and spat, her face a study of anger and despair. A tear rolled down her cheek. She turned her gaze from the floor of the circle to the deep desert. She didn't see Edain talking to her father and her father looking up at her and smiling. Several smoked pipes later, Fey climbed down to continue helping Igneous at his work.

With head bowed as he screwed a piece of his watch into the machine Igneous spoke. "She loves you."

"Who?"

"Reverend Flynn of course."

"I don't know what you're talking about."

"Yes you do. My dear girl, I don't care. Denying it is useless—you can scarcely take your eyes off her."

Fey stared at him. "What do you mean you don't care? You're English and a gentleman."

"My dear girl, I'm no ordinary gentleman. I've seen many things. If we were in England I would be advising you to keep your head down, but we're not in England we're in the Antipodes—plenty of new opportunities here. There are worse things than being in love."

Fey worked on for a few minutes in silence before continuing. "But Ses, your daughter, I saw—"

"Tsh! You don't know what you saw. The poor girl was crying and Edain was holding her."

"How do you know that?"

"Because while you were up there puffing away on your pipe, contemplating the injustice of the universe and how you're sick of it all anyway, Edain came to me and explained."

"She told you that?"

"Yes, Miss Grey. She told me that."

Fey stood up straight and looked around for Rosalyn before turning her attention back to Igneous, whispering, "What should I do?"

"Miss Grey, I'm single and I'm old and I'm a man—I'm not really the person you should be coming to for this sort of advice. Talk to Edain, she's much more attuned to these sorts of affairs than I am. God only knows what she got up to in that French boarding school." Fey didn't move. "Go on, I meant now. You're not much use to me brooding and scowling and carrying on. We're almost finished here. Scat!"

Fey walked away to where Edain sat with Watson and Geoffrey. With a look, Fey beckoned to Edain who rose and followed her to the edge of the circle. In a low voice Fey asked Edain, "Are you in love with Rosalyn?"

Edain smiled, "No, Fey, I'm not, but you are. And she's in love with you."

"Then why did she not come after me? And why is she avoiding me? She won't even look at me anymore."

"She's scared, Fey."

"Scared of what?"

"Of loving you. She's concerned about the views of her Church and society."

"I don't give a koala's arse what other people think."

"She does. She's an English girl from a good family and has taken vows with her Church."

"She doesn't think I'm fit to be seen with?"

Edain looked at Fey with a touch of despair. "I don't think that's it. She's from England and you're from Sydney. She'll return to England, too."

"Then I'll go with her."

"I'm not sure that England is ready for you, Fey, and I don't think you'd like it."

"You're probably right there. From what I've heard it's cold and stuffy and has more old ruins than a geriatric's gin house. So what do I do? I've never had a feeling like this before."

"Don't give up. She may be aloof to you but inside she's screaming for you to hold her."

"How do you know about this? Did you love a girl at that school in France?"

Edain smiled. "I did have a brief thing going with the drama teacher but I didn't love her. It was the gardener there who I fell in love with. He was a beautiful man with a bewitching smile."

"What happened?"

"We were caught together in the greenhouse and it created something of a scandal. I threatened to expose the drama teacher—I wouldn't have of course but they weren't to know that. Daddy made a large donation to the school, the gardener kept his job but we stayed distant from each other afterwards."

"Do you still love him?"

Edain sighed. "I suppose not. It was some years back and he's a treasured memory now." She stared deep into Fey's eyes. "Don't let Rosalyn become a memory."

Fey impulsively leaned in and kissed her cheek. "Thanks, Edain. You're a bloody treasure."

From the broken stones, Rosalyn sat staring into the desert. She didn't turn to look as Fey took her place next to her. Fey quietly took Rosalyn's hand in hers and they watched the changing colours of the sand as the sun set. They were interrupted by Geoffrey bringing them a cup of tea each.

"I thought you might like something."

"Thanks, Geoff. How's Iggy coming along with the weapon?"

"He says he's finished what he can but he's missing a part."

Fey let go of Rosalyn's hand and they went to see Igneous who was standing with Edain. "What's the problem, Iggy?"

"I have many but most immediately I need steam power to give this device range beyond a few yards."

"Can't we feed it off the Lightning?"

"Yes, that's the idea. The one the Order has will no doubt have a connecting tube of sorts. That's what this is missing."

"What sort of range does it have now?"

"Close range, like when we gave it to Boney's Old Guard at Waterloo. We can charge this weapon with a tube from the telescope and then it has to be detached to fire it. I don't know how effective it will be. It can fire repeatedly but each successive burst will be less destructive until recharging is necessary."

"I can find you something when we get to Sydney."

"Fey, by the time we get to Sydney it will well be in the hands of the Order, won't it?" said Rosalyn.

"We can hook outside town—in the mountains or forests. I'll walk in and find the things we want and then we'll give Rothwell a surprise."

The boat of the *Lightning* provided the headboard of their sandy bed that night. The morning sun illuminated the row of sleeping figures; all except Watson who had risen to answer a call of nature. He woke them by nudging Geoffrey who passed the nudge along the line of sleepers until it reached Captain Hivetree at the other end. A Varanus Rex, still in the distance, kicked up sand with its tail. For several seconds they watched the lizard. It reared back on its hind legs, flicking its tongue in the air. Without a word they reached for their weapons and primed them.

With their backs to the fallen stones they formed a line across the path of the approaching lizard. The reptile drew closer, picking up speed and charging towards them. Dust flew up as its huge claws and tail struck the sand. Geoffrey fired his pistol, dropped it, turned and clambered up into the rocks. Watson fired and took off after Geoffrey. The thing was almost upon them. Rosalyn, Fey and Edain raised their weapons but before they could fire a burst of blue, sparkling light flashed and crackled from behind them. The blue light struck the lizard and its grey, scaly face contorted. At the last moment it tried to turn and it stumbled, crashing to the ground, knocking the women off their feet in a spray of sand.

The lizard scrambled to get upright. In the choking dust Rosalyn grabbed Fey by the arm and dragged her away. Edain ran past them screaming as another burst of blue light pierced the dust and struck the lizard in the back. It fell to the ground again, the tail thrashing about and its front legs clawing at the soft earth. The women looked over to the *Lightning*. On the deck stood Captain Hivetree behind his machine.

"It works awfully well. Reminds me of the time I blew the brains out of that spider monkey I found stealing fruit from my tent. I'm sure it would have looked quite surprised if it had had a face left."

Watson and Geoffrey, having run out of steam before they reached the far side of the circle, found the courage to return and climbed onto the fallen rocks. From their vantage point they stood and looked at the prostrate creature.

"My word," said Geoffrey.

"Its head," said Watson.

They stared at the once proud head of the monster lizard. The bones of its skull had turned to powder and the head had collapsed. One large eye, still full of life, stared up at them through the bag of scaly skin. It's long forked tongue hung limply from the gaping hole that had once been full of deadly teeth. The pelvis of the lizard had also disintegrated, immobilising its rear limbs.

"Poor creature," said Rosalyn.

"It could have been poor us." Fey walked over to the lizard and shot it in the back of the head. At close range and with no bone to protect it, the ball penetrated into the brain of the beast and the spark of life faded from its eye.

Watson and Geoffrey, their courage fully restored by the death of the creature, came forward and examined it closely. "We won't be recovering its bones for the museum," said Watson.

"No, but perhaps we could recover its skin."

"We've got more company." Fey nodded out to the desert.

"It's all right, you're safe. It's Norman returning to us." Norman walked casually towards them. His two companions watched from the distance.

"I see you got it. We were hunting that."

"Hunting it? With spears?" Watson looked astonished.

"Yes, we have a technique. My friends think the lizard belongs to them."

"They can have it."

"We'll share it with you. You might want to cut it into strips and salt it. There's plenty of good eating there."

Igneous walked over to Norman. "The machine works. The one you stole the designs for."

"Yes, so I saw, and I see it does what you said it would do. I don't suppose you can stop the Order and take the weapon back out of their hands?"

"Take it back? No. They'll have many copies of those plans. I have no doubt that if they've made one and risked bringing it here they'll have built others as well, waiting for the Aqua Glass to bring the machines to life. Those damned fellows had more faith in my invention than you did."

Norman stared at the lizard and turned back to Igneous. "I'm so sorry, old friend. I didn't have any idea your weapon would work. I thought it was another of your strange fantasies. I stole the plans but I want you to know that it wasn't me who stole the blue mould. I had nothing to do with that."

"Good heavens, no." Igneous paused and studied his fingernails. "That was me."

Everyone turned towards Captain Hivetree.

"You? You stole your own fungus?" Watson asked.

"Not exactly. It's mould, not fungus, and I reported it stolen and secretly sold it to various people and nations."

"Why did you do that?"

"I had to really. I wanted to fly and I can't hide an airship, not for long, so I had to make it known that I had one. Our government sent some people to see me and told me they were to take the mould and that I was to hand over my airship. The hide of the scoundrels! I told them most of the mould had been stolen. You see they were going to keep the secrets of it for Britain alone."

"What was wrong with that?" asked Geoffrey.

"They wouldn't have let me keep my airship—and of course I wanted this discovery to benefit all of mankind. You see..." Edain coughed and caught her father's eye. "That is, I wanted all of humankind to benefit. The joys and advantages of flying shouldn't belong to any one nation—things would be unbalanced."

"Igneous, if the government finds out you gave this advantage to other nations you could be hanged for treason."

"No one here is going to tell them, are they? I did make an agreement with the government in exchange for them not stealing my airship. I helped them with the technical details for their own airships. Britain did get an advantage, you see, and besides, I didn't give the mould to any nation we were currently at war with." Here Igneous scratched his head and studied a small blue beetle as it crawled across the stone. "Although I was a bit concerned about selling it to the French."

Rosalyn spoke up. "What of the Aqua Glass? You speak of balance. If the Mechanical Order has Aqua Glass then we must see that other nations do, too."

"Yes exactly. That is my point. Now we know the Aqua Glass exists on this planet we must see that every civilised nation has some and hope it is used for peaceful purposes or to counter the likes of the Divine Order of Mechanics. The world will know soon enough of its existence here and they'll all be after it."

Norman spoke again. "Igneous, I feel quite terrible that I've been the agent for the Order gaining such power. If they're as bad as I'm told and they seize Sydney they'll work on killing every black they see. You have to stop them."

"That's exactly what we're going to do. I'm not sure exactly how. The details are still foggy."

Rosalyn added, "We're leaving for Sydney this morning. I'd best get this engine going and the steam up. We'll have to throw out anything we don't need and carry as much in the way of water and provisions as we can."

With the *Lightning* prepared, Norman made his goodbyes. "So sorry to disappoint you on your Church Mission, Reverend Flynn but I really have no wish to return. Good luck to you all." He stood with Watson and Geoffrey as Fey and Edain unhooked. Rosalyn pulled the lever, the propeller shaft whined and the blades started to turn. The airship rose into the sky and Rosalyn turned its nose to the east.

28

THE ASSASSIN

Edain's ability at map making had improved considerably in the time since they had departed Max's station. The maps she had produced in her notebook were not all contiguous due to the time spent flying at night and the dust storm which had interrupted her cartographic endeavours, but they did prove useful in finding their way back to the settled area. Progress was slowed by the need to stop frequently for water and replenish food supplies.

Edain sat in the bow revising her maps as they flew over the landscape. She became aware of Fey watching her. "What is it?"

"How'd you manage to get the better of that Mechanic bloke who had the Lightning? I knew you weren't such a helpless molly."

Edain looked at her father who gave her a nod. "Daddy taught me how to shoot."

"I'm sure I taught you more than that."

Edain put down her map book. "And how to fence, how to ride and how to fly."

"I knew you was better than you gave the idea of. I hadn't ever killed a bloke until I shot the man on the Lightning, and that was in a desperate moment. Was it hard to kill the cove?"

"It wasn't terribly difficult. I didn't know who was in the airship initially, not until I saw the Order's flag. He flew in a search pattern, most likely looking for you and Rosalyn and Daddy. I kept him in sight and stalked him, knowing he would ground for water. He was stooped over a water hole when I came upon him."

"So you shot him in the back?"

"I tried to but he heard me when I drew close. I need to learn to be quieter, like the blacks; they can be very quiet. The man started to turn. I shot him in the side of the head."

Rosalyn, listening to the conversation from the helm, switched off the engine. "You tried to shoot a man in the back? Cecilia, that is terrible."

"Please, you can call me Edain."

"It makes you a murderess. And I can see you have no remorse."

Igneous interrupted. "The man Edain killed, the one piloting the Lightning, I saw him in Bathurst. He tortured and killed your Guardian."

"What? How do you know?" Rosalyn felt faint and held onto the wheel for support.

"Reverend Flynn, I came upon him at the scene. The wretched scoundrel almost took my life."

Rosalyn reached for the kettle. "I need a cup of tea."

Edain stood up. "Here, let me do that. You look quite pale."

Fey took out her pipe and tobacco and after packing it handed the tobacco to Igneous. "Go easy with that, it's the last of my Alabama smoke." She lit the pipe. "That cove who killed the Guardian must have been the same bloke who sliced the parson in Sydney."

Edain turned to her. "Oh, heavens no, Fey. That was me, too. I was quite proud of that."

Rosalyn and Fey stared at her speechless. Igneous packed his pipe. After a long silence, Rosalyn found her voice again. "You murdered a parson of my Church, and yet you stand there so boldly making tea. You can get off my vessel right now."

"No, I won't be disembarking. We're too high anyway."

"Why did you kill him?" asked Fey.

Edain poured the tea. "He was a spy working for the Divine Order of Mechanics."

Rosalyn sank to her knees. "I don't believe it."

Igneous took a pull on his pipe. "I think their plan was to kill your Guardian and the Mechanic assassin was to take his place. He would have been flying with you, Reverend Flynn, and if he found you to be of no use you would have been thrown overboard from a great height, or met some other bloody fate."

Rosalyn gave a small nod as she took the teacup Edain offered her. Fey, with pipe in mouth, took the wheel. "You're quite the blade girl. Who else have you done away with, Ses—that is, Edain?" asked Fey.

"Only the geologist. And I've only used the blade once. Daddy taught me to be flexible in my approach and use whatever works best for the situation."

"What geologist?" asked Rosalyn.

"Do you remember the one who kindly fell off the cliff so I could take his place on the expedition?"

"I remember you telling me. You didn't push him, did you?"

"Of course. I had to make it look like an accident."

"Cecilia, how could you?"

"It's Edain, and it was ever so easy. A middle-aged man wanting to impress a pretty young woman will go out of his way to make a fool of himself, if need be. Or go out of his way to pick that pretty little flower she found so delightful, growing out at the edge of the cliff. He only needed a tiny nudge."

Rosalyn's hand shook, spilling her tea. "Edain, you can't kill people just because you want their place in an expedition. And remorse? You show none."

"Reverend Flynn, the Royal Scientific Society for the Exploration of the Antipodes cancelled their expedition. With their geologist dead and their stores burned, their planned expedition was abandoned—Edain was never part of it and it was I who asked Edain to take care of the geologist."

"You? You're her father. Why?"

"The geologist was also a member of the Divine Order of Mechanics. He simply had to go, and I needed Edain in Sydney to help take care of things."

Fey grinned. "Love your style, Edain."

Rosalyn turned to her. "You don't approve of all this killing do you?"

"Yeah, got three of those Mechanic bastards, she did. And because she did, you're still alive and have your airship."

Rosalyn stared into the bottom of her cup, swishing the tea leaves. "I cannot find an argument, but I can't help thinking it's all so terribly wrong. I suppose you befriended me to find passage on my airship."

"Yes. I even had a man pretend to try to steal your luggage so I could ingratiate myself with you as someone you could trust."

"But... who was the man I saw, the one the luggage thief went to after we came on board?"

"I suppose that was me," said Igneous, knocking his pipe clean on the skyrail. "I needed to be sure Edain boarded the Iris safely. I sailed a few days later."

"I need another cup of tea. Do we have any rum? Put some rum in it, or gin. I don't care, anything." Rosalyn sat pondering for some minutes. She took the cup from Edain's hand. "And my room at the school? It was ransacked. Was that you?"

Igneous crouched down next to her and stroked his sideburns. "No. Do you remember the young chap who drove you to the school?"

"The boy? Timmy I think."

"Tommy. He works for me. He did it."

"But why?"

"Reverend Flynn, there's a lot at stake here. As I'm sure you're now aware, nobody is who they seem to be, me especially. Sometimes I don't know who I am, myself. We knew you were being sent out as a Missionary for the Church of the Sun Cog but we didn't know if there was more to it than that. It was unusual for a Missionary to be given an airship and that aroused our suspicions."

"I was, I am, only a Missionary. Nothing more."

"We had no way of knowing it. We wanted to see your Orders and any other documents you might have possessed. Your Church has been infiltrated by the Divine Order of Mechanics. We thought you might be one of them."

Rosalyn directed her attention to Edain. "And yet even when you knew I wasn't, you failed to tell me who you were."

"You didn't need to know. What you don't know you can't tell. Secrecy to me is like a forest of shadows—something I can hide in."

Rosalyn swallowed her tea and handed the cup back to Edain. "More—and more gin this time, less tea." She took the cup. "And what was it about Lord Spotswood? Why masquerade as his child when he had a son?"

"Sloppy work on my part, I'm afraid. Next time I'll do more research on my background story. This is the first time I've done this sort of work."

"You're bloody good at it, Edain. You take to it like Roz does with flying."

Rosalyn's eyes, staring blankly at the deck, were wet with tears.

"I'm sure it will all sit with you in time, Reverend. You've been given so much to think about. You've come a long way." Igneous stared out into the sky. "Time and distance, time and space. All in good time."

"Stay on track, Iggy. You've been focussed like an archer, don't let it slide."

"Daddy can be incredibly focussed at times. It's when his passion rises."

"It's been a bit of a stretch for me, too." Fey fumbled for her tobacco. "Edain, could you be a good molly and fix me a cup of tea, plenty of gin, hold the tea."

29

Rebels

Below and to the south, a cluster of lights could be seen. Edain checked the location against her map and declared the lights to be those of Bathurst. Continuing east, they sailed over the top of the ranges, turning south as the first line of morning sunlight touched the cloud tops. The clouds drifted past them, sometimes shrouding them completely. The air grew chilly and they huddled close to the engine for warmth. Rosalyn maintained a high altitude, keeping to the cloud cover. On the occasions the clouds parted, a view presented itself, stretching out to the east, all the way to the shimmering expanse of the Pacific Ocean. There, at the edge of it, lay Sydney.

The time of day wasn't favourable for a stealthy entrance into Sydney's air space. Rosalyn continued south and found one of the steep, secluded valleys of the Blue Mountains. With great care she brought the Lightning down into the gorge. Rugged cliffs loomed above them and a hundred feet below a sea of green treetops concealed the valley floor. The richness of the greenery provided a refreshing contrast after their time out west in the dry country. With nowhere to ground, Rosalyn kept the *Lightning* above the trees, the engine running. Constant watch had to be kept lest they drift into the side of the cliff or descend too low and become entangled in the trees.

"Fey, what approach do we make?" Rosalyn asked.

"Take it in low towards the coast and come up from the south. I'll show you where to drop me off and I'll meet you back at the same spot."

"I'm going with you."

"There's no need. I'll go alone. It could be dangerous."

"That's why I'm going with you. We have two other pilots on board and they're both more skilled than I am."

Fey considered this and nodded. "You'll have to wear something different. Going in there in your Church togs is going to draw attention, like if you were blowing a trumpet. Some of the coves I want to deal with might shy away from you, too."

"I don't have any other clothes."

"Settled then. You'll have to stay."

"You can borrow mine, we're about the same size."

Rosalyn looked at Edain and back to Fey. "Settled. I'm coming."

When night approached Igneous took the wheel and they headed east along the valley. Staying at a low altitude after leaving the mountains and picking up a favourable breeze, Igneous cut the engine and sailed by wind. Fey spotted a clearing in a thickly wooded area, created by a grand, old eucalypt which had fallen in a storm. Igneous grounded the *Lightning* next to the tree.

"Four days, Edain. Don't go wandering off again." Rosalyn inhaled as Edain finished lacing Rosalyn's corset.

"There, nice and tight. And don't worry, we'll be here. Are you sure this place is a safe haven?"

"Yeah," said Fey. "We're a good way south of Sydney now, and no one should be out this way. The trees are higher than the Lightning so you're unlikely to be spotted from a distance. Stay put and we'll be back."

"Will you need weapons?"

"I'll take a pistol. Roz can cloak herself in prayers to her Sun God."

Rosalyn slapped Fey on the shoulder. "Pig. I'm taking one, too."

Rosalyn and Fey disappeared into the trees. It was well into the day when they reached the outskirts of Sydney Town. Overhead, the red shape of the *Eyrie* hovered. Fey led the way through the laneways and brought them to The Rocks. Walking casually through the streets and alleys, the children and dogs took little notice of them. Fey was about to turn up one of the side paths when, from a doorway, a hand grabbed her arm and dragged her inside. Rosalyn spun around, startled by Fey's sudden exit from the street. She too, was grabbed and pulled in.

"Shhh! No noise."

A young fellow, dressed in a style similar to Fey's, with a black and yellow waistcoat and blue-striped shirt stood in front of them. A frown creased his brow.

"Scamper! What's your game?"

"I didn't think I'd see you back 'ere, Fey. Who's the mollisher yer got with yer?"

"She's my mate Roz. She's square."

Scamper moved closer to Roz, his nose inches from her face. He made a point of sniffing her. "She looks a bit queer of place. I ain't seen 'er around. Where did yer find 'er?"

"I said she's square. Why the hard patter?"

"Things 'ave changed a bit since you nash'd. Snitches and spies everywhere."

"I give you my word, she's square."

"If yer say so, Fey. Where yer been?"

"Long story. What's been on the go in the camp here?"

"Things went rocky when that airship came back. Queer things were 'appenin' before then but that airship turned the screws hard."

"What sort of queer things?"

"A lot of flash coves comin' ashore pretendin' as settlers. We suspicioned somethin' not right about them."

"I know about the men coming here. I was working that but I never learned who the coves were. Some of them were for the shipyard at Black Wattle Bay."

"They were Redbacks. When that airship came back the Redbacks took the town."

"Redbacks?"

"That's what we call 'em—Mechanical Order coves. The bastards 'id about like spiders in an out 'ouse and pounced when we wasn't expectin'. And there's that uniform they wears, black with red cuffs, collars and trousers."

"So what happened?" asked Rosalyn.

"Gettin' to that so 'ang onto yer snatch, love. The Bennelong was back in the sky when the Eyrie returned. It was bloody frightful. Most of Sydney saw it; I saw it with me own daylights. The Eyrie came up out of the west and of course the whole bloody town turned out to see it. It's a flash airship that one. So we was lookin' at it when this queer blue light blazed from it. The light 'it the Bennelong, and another and another. We could 'ear the men screamin' from 'ere." Scamper's voice shook. "The boat started to fall apart, men were fallin' from it. You could see the fires fallin' from its engine as it broke up. Most of it landed up 'ere around the observatory. The balloon drifted and when it lost its lift it come down in the 'arbour."

Scamper took a swig of something from a bottle and passed it to Rosalyn. Rosalyn looked to Fey, who nodded. "Ah yer slavey 'ey? I'm in the picture now."

"She isn't my slavey."

"Yeah, what yer say, Fey, I don't care, I know's yer a Tom. Goin' on, some of us went up there to the 'ill. It was a bloody shocker, Fey. There were bodies lyin' about, some of them broken from the fall, but others, they were missin' their bones. Brain boxes gone, nothin' there. Like body snatchers 'ad taken the bones right out of 'em."

Scamper took the bottle from Fey and had another good helping. "The whole town went 'ush. I never 'eard it so quiet after the Bennelong went down. Next thing shoutin' and shots firin' sounded from all over Sydney. The soldiers turned out and the cannons of the forts turned on the Eyrie. Didn't do much bloody good; the

Eyrie was out of reach and they fired that thing down 'ere."

Fey took the bottle from Scamper's shaking hand. "Don't want you spilling it."

Scamper appeared not to notice, his gaze flitting between Fey and Rosalyn. "I saw a soldier next to me get 'it amidships. 'is musket barrel turned to smoke and powder, 'is brass buttons clouds of yellow dust. Jesus and Mary, 'is chest caved in, like an empty sack, but no stuffin'. It was bloody awful, Fey. The poor bloke, 'e fell to the ground, 'is eyes lookin' at me like 'e was beggin' for somethin' and the poor feller in shock. I ain't seen nothin' like it. I could see is 'eart still beatin' under 'is skin like it were in a sack, and then 'e died."

"Could you not help him?"

"What could I do, Roz? Build 'im a new rib cage? I was bloody 'elpless."

"What happened next?"

"The soldiers who 'ad been trying to form up, they scattered. Too big a target, you see? And they were scared. We all was. I pissed me pants when that soldier next to me went limp. I ain't red-faced when I say it. Piss ran right down me legs into me boots. That weapon, it's a terrible bloody thing. Straight from 'ell itself. That's when the Redbacks came in. All those coves we 'ad lit comin' into Sydney were Redbacks. They put on those uniforms like I said before, and formed up. The garrison bein' dispersed didn't put up much of a scrap."

"What about the forts? Their artillery would have destroyed the Order's infantry."

"The thing on the Eyrie took out the guns and the gunners that weren't 'it, they ran. Governor Gipps 'ad no choice but to surrender."

"What about our lot?"

"We're stayin' on the low. Best to wait and see what 'appens. Muvver England ain't goin' to take this but it will be months before they gets word of what 'appened and send anyone 'ere."

Rosalyn's brow creased, her eyes narrowed and she turned to Fey. "What does he mean, 'our lot'?"

"Er, yeah, I was going to get to that."

"She don't know?"

"What don't I know?"

"Nothing much to it. We don't like the way things work here in the colony and we were going to ask the Governor to make some changes."

"There's more to it than that, Fey Grey. Tell me."

"You want it in an oyster shell?"

"Yes, Fey."

"We were going to seize the colony for ourselves."

"You what?" Rosalyn almost shouted the question out.

"I thought yer said she's square?"

"She is, she just don't know she's with us yet."

"Fey, I am not with you!" Rosalyn stamped her foot, her fists clenched. "You're talking treason. Are you telling me you were going to revolt against the crown?"

Fey stared at the floor, drawing an imaginary circle on it with the toe of her boot. "Yeah, that's what we was planning but now the Order has queered the pitch."

"They'll hang you. Fey, you must be mad. What are you thinking! They'd never allow you to get away with it."

"The Americans did."

"That was different. There were more of them and well organised, and they had France beside them. How on earth do you suppose you could take on the might of Britain and win?"

"We have our plans. Our people are armed and we're organised, too."

"I don't believe it." Rosalyn snatched the bottle from Fey's hand, sank to the floor and drank deeply.

"It's true. We have men and women all over Sydney and around who are prepared to rise up and take it. Most of the convicts will join us."

"I mean, I can't believe you never told me. We even kissed!"

"Yeah, she is yer slavey." Scamper reached down and took the bottle back.

"I am not her slave! And I am not part of your silly scheme to get yourselves killed. There will be order in the world and you have a part in it but it is not this part."

"You know what, Roz, bugger your order. Bugger your Church and bugger England."

"Fey! That's it. I'm going." Rosalyn stood and moved towards the door. Scamper moved quicker, blocking her exit.

"What are you doing? Let me go."

"Sorry love, can't 'ave yer goin' out there in that state. You'll give the game away."

"Fey?"

"He's right. You'll draw attention or give us up. Can't have that."

"Give you up? To them? What sort of person must you think I am?"

"You're a Church girl. You've got a clockwork machine where your brain should be. It's being wound up by them that put themselves over us—just like the rest of them. Not an independent thought in you, is there?" Rosalyn stared at Fey, lost for words. "We've been weeks out there." Fey continued. "Did you learn nothing'?"

The old floorboards creaked as Rosalyn sank back down onto them. She spoke quietly. "What was I supposed to learn?"

"That we've got minds of our own. You see that Mechanical Order you hate so much? An Order which seeks to steal away our freedom? Your Church is a milder form of that same slavery."

"And yet it's not the Church you rebel against."

"The government is the bloody same. When will the word of folk like me and Scamper ever carry the same weight as the men of money and titles?"

"There are opportunities, Fey."

"Bugger your opportunities, we want freedom—and we're going to have it."

Rosalyn looked up at the bottle in Scamper's hand. He passed it to her and she leaned back against the rough stone wall, taking a huge mouthful. Drops of rum trickled down her chin. She didn't pass the bottle back. The room stayed silent, Fey and Scamper watching Rosalyn as she stared vacantly at the wall opposite. "I suppose I didn't like the Church much anyway. Really I wanted to be an airship pilot. That's freedom, up there in the skies, flying."

Fey grinned. "And you are a pilot, Roz. You're a bloody good one. You've even got your own airship."

"You've got an airship?" Scamper looked at her in surprise. "We'd 'eard rumours of another in the colony."

"We have it hooked in the bush. We came into Sydney for some parts."

"Is it broken? In any case, it's going to be no match for the Eyrie with that weapon they 'ave." Fey and Rosalyn looked at each other. "What? What did I miss? I saw that look."

Rosalyn shrugged. "Tell him."

"The weapon on the Eyrie—we have one too, but we need parts to get it working proper."

Scamper looked at Fey wide-eyed. "You on the square?"

"Yeah, I'm on the square."

"Fey, we can bring down the Eyrie and take Sydney."

"It's not that simple," said Rosalyn. "Even with the parts, the weapon we have doesn't have the same range. We'd have to get in close without it seeing us."

"But you've got one. It changes the game. I'll 'ave to call a meetin'. What do yer need?"

"I need to go home and check on Mother first." Scamper turned away. "What?" Fey asked.

Scamper faced her, staring her straight in the eye. "I'm sorry, Fey, she copped it. So sorry. It only 'appened yesterday."

"What happened? Was she poorly?"

"No, she was in 'igh spirits. Then the Redbacks came lookin' for yer."

"Looking for me?"

"Yeah, they came to yer digs and was trying to push inside. Old Mother Mary put a wail on 'em and one of the bastards done 'er 'ead in with 'is musket butt. She died a few hours later."

Fey felt her legs give out, the blood drained from her face. She sank to the floor beside Rosalyn, taking the bottle from her. "They bloody killed her? The mongrels, they're going to pay for that."

"Bloody right, Fey. Yer can't go 'ome though, they 'ave the place watched."

"What do they want me for?" Fey's voice was trembling. A tear rolled down her cheek.

"Somethin' to do with the Missionary and another mollisher yer took to Moreton Bay with yer." Scamper turned to Rosalyn. "From the speakin' you must be the Missionary but yer don't look like one."

"Yes. I'm the Missionary," said Rosalyn quietly.

"Where's the other one?"

"She's with the Lightning, our airship." Rosalyn put her arm around Fey's shoulders. Fey rested her head and cried. Scamper sat on a stool by the window and busied himself with the process of packing and lighting a pipe. Rosalyn watched him as she cradled the sobbing Fey in her arms. The light drifted lazily through the window picking up specks of dust and illuminating the dark green glass of a bottle resting on the window ledge.

Fey's crying stopped and she sat upright, wiping her eyes with her sleeve. Her voice shook as she spoke. "Scamper, we need to get those parts, and a few tools."

"We'll 'ave to go over to see One 'ole. 'e's got connections at the mill. They might 'ave somethin' over there. We'll 'ave to be careful on the street; the Order don't like currency and they stop and 'arrass. I'll nobble Crayfish and 'e can get the youngs to light the way. Wait 'ere." Scamper disappeared, closing the creaking door behind him.

Rosalyn stood, taking Fey by the arm, drawing her to her feet. Slipping her arms around Fey's body she pulled her close. Fey began to speak. Before she could utter a sound Rosalyn's kiss sealed her lips and they stood in the room holding each other, neither wanting to end the embrace. Scamper returned too soon. Still in each other's arms, they turned to him as he entered the room.

"'ate to interrupt, ladies, but we 'ave to foot it. The youngs are lightin' out and we need to be with 'em."

Scamper opened the door and looked both ways. "It's clear. Come." Down the lane a young boy winked at them and started walking up another street. Rosalyn recognised him as the lad who had been selling papers the day she arrived in Sydney. As they walked, Scamper explained how the younger currency lads and lasses arranged themselves along streets singly or in twos and threes, giving signals to warn of a dangerous street or a safe one. They kept mobile, using different routes to stay ahead of the people being guided, always managing to look innocuous and innocent. To the children it was a game. The person or people being guided were the cargo and the goal was to get the cargo to the port without being discovered. In this way they arrived at the cottage of One Hole Bill.

Inside, they found several other people sitting around a table, two of them strangers to Fey. Fey once again found herself explaining the presence of Rosalyn. One Hole Bill outlined the situation to them. "The Order got reports of an airship seen over the Blue Mountains. They've got people out looking and from what we've learned, you, the Missionary and that bug woman are connected with it. They suspect you're in Sydney and they're hunting for your airship."

Fey described the weapon and the parts they needed. This caused something of a commotion. "Calm seas, lads and lasses." One Hole waved his hands in the air. "You'll bring attention with the noise. Fey, If you're square we have an opportunity."

"I'm square. I helped build it and I've seen it work. We have to connect it to the engine to get steam into it if we want to give it any sort of range. I can give you a list of the things we need but we need them hasty. We have to get back to the Lightning in short time, more so if the Order is out looking for it."

"We need to get a plan together to coordinate with your airship. Taking down the Eyrie is one thing but we still need to take the town back."

"If we can get the soldiers released and armed we're assured of success," said a well-spoken man, sitting at the end of the table.

"Who are you?" asked Fey.

"Captain Hallett of the 50th regiment. This here is Sergeant Hopson."

"I'm familiar with Sergeant Hopson. He taught me how to shoot on the ship coming out." Rosalyn turned to Sergeant Hopson. "I didn't see you sitting there in the corner. How is it you're in Sydney?"

"I was tasked as an escort for a convict group who got their tickets of leave. The fighting broke out the day after I arrived."

Fey ignored the exchange and looked at One Hole. "You brought the military in? They're the bloody enemy!"

"Things have changed, Fey. We have a common enemy now; we need to work together." One Hole paused. "We did a deal, Fey."

"You what? We said no deals. We had it planned."

"Most of what we want, we'll get. It's the best way, Fey. No one gets hurt."

Fey glared at him. "What sort of deal?"

"Transportation will finish and all convicts serving sentence for property crime and absconding will be given conditional pardons."

Fey quietened down and leaned with her back to the wall. "I suppose you're on the point, but I can't see how the Governor can put his word on an end to transportation. That has to come from England. Besides, there're other things afoot. New South Wales is about to become the prize ring in a bigger game. We could never hold it against what would come."

"Whatever do you mean?" asked Captain Hallett.

"The thing that powers the weapon—it's a stone called Aqua Glass. It can be found in the interior. We can't let the Order have control of it."

The room fell silent.

"Fey, we will have all the convicts with us and many of the colonial-born. We can take back Sydney with them."

"They're still untrained and largely unarmed, Mr One Hole. If you go against the Redbacks with pikes you'll have a repeat of the Irish rebellion at Castle Hill. We need to get my soldiers out and seize the weapons," said Captain Hallett.

"You can argue about it later. We need the parts to finish the weapon so we can return to the Lightning," said Rosalyn.

One Hole nodded and had one of the women present memorise the required items and go to the mill. The discussion resumed as to the best course of action, the consensus being that the release of the soldiers and weapons was the highest priority.

"We need to know when the Eyrie comes to hook for supplies. If we bring the Lightning in when the Eyrie is grounded we may have a better chance," Rosalyn said.

All eyes turned to Rosalyn and Captain Hallett explained to her, "It doesn't. There's another airship, a small resupply vessel that the Order revealed when the Eyrie returned to Sydney. They use it to shuttle supplies to the Eyrie and change crew. We don't think the Eyrie intends grounding at all."

Rosalyn and Fey exchanged glances and Rosalyn spoke again. "It will be a hard task to take down the Eyrie in an outright duel."

"We won't be able to do anything on the ground until the Eyrie is down," said Captain Hallett.

"Not so. We can work at night when the Eyrie can't see us. We can be in position and when we see the Lightning strike we'll move into action," said One Hole.

Captain Hallett nodded at him. "There's the curfew. We'll have to be careful."

"Fey, how long do you think it will take you to be ready once you have the things you need?"

"It should only take us a few hours to get the steam piped to the weapon. If we had our things today we could be back at the Lightning late tonight. Tomorrow evening we could come in and destroy the Eyrie. Can you have everything ready by then?"

One Hole nodded. "We can do that. We'll have to be bloody careful; the Order is on the alert due to the suspicion your airship is in the area."

Running footsteps could be heard on the veranda. A young girl burst into the room in a breathless state. "Redbacks are in the street."

Everyone in the room froze. A man looked out the window. "They're coming all right, in strength. They look determined."

"They might not be coming here but we can't take chances. You two," One Hole indicated Fey and Rosalyn. "You go with Scamper and the Captain. The rest of you, you know what to do. Smartly now, currency."

Fey and Rosalyn followed Captain Hallett and Scamper out the back door into a yard which they exited via a gate into a laneway. Shouts and shots came from further along. Bullets struck the fencing and walls. Fey and the captain turned and fired as one. Gunshots echoed across the laneway and clouds of smoke filled the air. A ball found its mark; a Redback fell screaming, clutching his face. More shots came their way as they reloaded. Scamper fired and at the same instant a ball hit Captain Hallett. He twisted, falling heavily on the rocky road.

Fey stooped, trying to help him up. Scamper clutched her by the arm and dragged her away. Their path took them along the bottom of a low cliff. A young lad appeared before them, guiding them into a gap where a set of rough stairs had been cut into the rock. More shots were fired and Fey fired back, ducking into cover and following her companions up the narrow flight of stone stairs. They emerged in a rough laneway. The lad led them between the houses and shanties and by a roundabout route they came again to Scamper's lodgings. "We're goin' to 'ave to get you away from 'ere. They'll 'ave men all over this place soon and no tellin' what's 'appened to One 'ole."

"We can't leave without the parts."

"I can organise it. Remember the place we 'ad the fight with the cove down on Parramatta Road? I'll take you down there tonight and you can wait. We'll bring what you need to you. Now we're goin' to 'ave to 'ide you and the place for that is right 'ere." Scamper tapped his foot on the floor boards and bent to lift up a section of them. Underneath lay a shallow crawl space in which sat a bottle of rum.

"There's not much room. We can't fit in there." Fey moved back from the hole.

"You're right. That's why we've got this." Scamper removed the bottle and fished around in the dirt with his hands. With a grunt he pulled up another panel of boards exposing a deeper hole. "That's the spot. It won't be at all comfy like, but you can lie in it. It's only until dark and I'll fetch you out again."

"That's worse; it's like a coffin. I'm not good in small spaces." Fey clenched her fist.

"I'll be beside you," said Rosalyn. "Come, I'll hold your hand." Fey didn't move. Rosalyn worked her fingers between Fey's. "It's this or take our chances on the street."

"You won't make it on the street. They'll 'ave people everywhere and it's not me they're lookin' for. You can take some bread down there and there's some grog in the 'ole. Don't drink it all, that's me livin'. I'll get yer some water. If you need to empty yourselves you best go now and 'urry. The Redbacks will be 'ere before too long."

"How are we going to breath down there?" asked Rosalyn.

"There's a pipe goes through to the earth bank beside the 'ouse. It looks like a drain but it isn't. That's where the air gets in. If you keep your heads up that end you'll be right, and keep your voices down, don't even talk if you can 'elp it. Anyone passin' could 'ear you through the pipe."

30

THE CONFESSIONAL

Rosalyn climbed into the hole, holding out her hand to help Fey down. Scamper passed them the bread and water and put the board back, spreading dirt over the top to conceal it. Inside the hole, a single, horizontal shaft of light from the pipe gave scant illumination in the darkness.

Fey's grip on Rosalyn's hand tightened to the point it became painful.

"Fey?" Rosalyn pressed her body to Fey's. Fey was shaking. She didn't reply.

"Fey, what's wrong? Speak to me." Extracting her hand from Fey's she ran her palm over Fey's cheek, feeling tears.

Fey pushed her hand away. "Don't touch me!"

Rosalyn pulled away. "What is it? Have I done something wrong?" She felt Fey's hand reach once more for her own, softer this time, weak.

Fey rolled onto her side, facing Rosalyn, her face bathed in the soft light from the pipe. She whispered, "Sorry, Roz."

"Please tell me what it is."

Fey closed her eyes, breathing deeply. "The worst thing that happened to me..." She opened her eyes.

"You don't have to tell me if it's too much."

Fey continued. "I was only young, not even a woman, living with my Mum. She got drunk at every chance and was always short of money. She brought a bloke in to live with us—bastard of a man. I got told I was in the way. Both of them would slap me around. Then my Mum got this idea in her head to lock me in a cupboard." Fey reached for one of Scamper's bottles and removed the cork. Her hand shook, spilling red wine down her chin. She placed the bottle to her mouth, taking a good swig.

"I never came out of that cupboard, not unless it was for a man."

"I don't understand."

"She was selling me, Roz. My Mum was selling me to men. Some of them were filthy creatures, even the ones in the flashest of togs. They'd take me on that filthy bed, or the table. When they were done with me I was shoved back in the cupboard. If I cried they'd open the door and beat me. I always had bruises."

"Fey, that's a terrible thing. For how long did they keep you?"

"I don't know. Maybe a month, maybe six." Fey drank heavily from the bottle. "One time this bloke used me and left. Mum and her bloke had passed out drunk on the veranda. I wasn't going back in that damned cupboard. I wasn't." Fey started crying again. Through the tears she continued. "I took all the money I could find and bolted. I lit out for Parramatta, a town further along. I never got there."

"What happened?"

"A cart came by, driven by a woman. I had me suspicions at first. She saw the wretched state of me—skinny, filthy, in rags. She took me up into the cart and gave me food. The first decent food I'd had for God knows how long. She was kind to me. Stroked my hair and wrapped her shawl around me. We went to her farm. Her husband had died the year before. I stayed there, helping out. She taught me how to sew and cook and read."

"Mother Mary," said Rosalyn.

"Yes. Mother Mary." Fey's tears stopped and she allowed Rosalyn to hold her. After being in the hole for so long they could see clearly even with the small amount of light. "There you have it, Roz. The worst thing that ever happened to me."

Rosalyn pressed herself to Fey. They lay together without speaking, Fey calm now, her body no longer trembling.

"We should put our minds to what's in front of us," said Fey, reaching for the bread.

"We should," said Rosalyn, taking a chunk of the bread Fey passed her. "Is there anything else you need to tell me."

"What do you mean?"

"This revolution you were organising. Do you think that might have been something I needed to know?"

"I didn't think you needed to know at all. Besides, I didn't know if I could trust you, being a Missionary of the Church of the Sun Cog and all. That's all about obedience."

"There's nothing wrong with obedience."

"I'd prefer to think for myself."

"Are you saying I don't ?"

"That's what I'm saying. You live the way you do because that's how you've been trained to live."

"I can think for myself." Rosalyn's voice carried a touch of indignation.

"I haven't seen a sign of that."

"No? What about this?" Rosalyn pulled Fey roughly to her, grabbing her by the hair at the back of her head, kissing her deeply before angrily thrusting her away again. "Do you think the Church taught me that?"

"If they did you've got a convert." They both giggled and settled into each other's embrace.

"I've thought for myself once before, too," whispered Rosalyn.

"That's twice. You're very bold."

"I'd slap you if we weren't so confined."

"I'll try to hold my tongue."

"That will take some work. Do you want to hear what I have to say or not?"

"Of course I do. I want to know all about you."

Rosalyn took a deep breath and continued. "I didn't want to join the Church. Mother wanted me to marry; she had someone picked out for me. Father backed her but only because mother was so adamant I marry, have children and be a dutiful wife."

"I can't imagine that suiting you, Roz."

"Neither could I. I wanted to fly airships but with the cost of lessons and me being a woman it was out of the question."

"Other women fly airships; I've read about them in the papers."

"Yes, a few have been lucky enough, or perhaps had fathers rich enough. At the time I was neither rich nor lucky. I was sitting on a river bank alone, feeling miserable and sorry for myself as I couldn't see a way out of that horrible fate. And then a woman came by, a clergywoman from the Enlightenment Church. Seeing my state she sat with me. I told her my troubles and she told me all about her Church and its attitudes to women, the training and being sent to other cities—countries even—to spread the word of our Enlightening God."

Fey handed her the wine bottle. "Have a swig, the subject just got dry."

Rosalyn ignored the comment and drank the wine, handing the bottle back to Fey. "I jumped at the chance. It was a lifeline to escape from marital servitude, but when I heard I was being sent to the Antipodes I felt like crying. I'd wanted to go to a big city— London or somewhere in Europe—away from my family—much as I love them. And then I was told I was being given an airship and trained to fly. The thing I desired most had come to pass."

"You got lucky there, Roz, and I'm real happy for you. You make a bloody good pilot too. I told you that."

"I've had good fortune but now we're lying in this... this coffin while being hunted by heartless killers."

"Yeah, and the bastards will pay for what they did to Mother Mary."

"I'm so sorry you lost her. She sounds like the most caring, loving woman."

"I wasn't the only one she looked after. Mother Mary taught reading and writing to a tribe of other currency kids. She took us all under her wing. She sold her farm not long after I met her and we moved back to Sydney. My Mum found out I was here but Mother Mary knew a few people—she was respected. Mum got warned off."

"So who was Mother Mary?"

"She came here as a convict. She was once a fine lady back in England, with servants and all. I don't know what she did to get sent out; she never said. I know she could have gone back after her seven years were up but she didn't. After the farm, back here in Sydney, she cared for the children of convicts, bringing us up as proper as she could. She was a real mother to me—and to a lot of others, too."

"Where's your first mother now?"

"She's here, in Sydney. She'll be in a shanty living with some rogue, both of them drunk."

"Do you see her?"

"Sometimes. I don't hate her or nothing. I call in on her from time to time but it's hard to see her like that. It was prison broke her and she never came right, I don't think she ever will." Fey's voice trembled. Rosalyn squeezed her hand. "I don't want to be a cog in your society, Roz. And I'm sorry I didn't tell you about our plans to take the colony. We want liberty is all—no machine, no cogs, just simple folk living simple lives, none above the rest." Rosalyn nested her head on Fey's shoulder and nodded.

Without speaking, they lay unburdened and relaxed. Loud voices came through the pipe from the street. From above them came the muffled sounds of booted feet on the wooden floor. The sounds died away. The light from the pipe faded, the evening leaving them in total blackness. "I don't think he's coming back, Roz. Something must have happened," said Fey. She pushed on the wood above her.

Together, they lifted the lid and slid it across, a trickle of loose, dry dirt covering them. With the second trapdoor opened they climbed out onto the floor of the empty room. Fey replaced the lids on the holes and they sat in the gloom listening for any sound. Shouting came from the distance but they couldn't make out what it was about. The veranda floorboards creaked and they readied their weapons. The handle turned, the door slowly opened. The silhouetted person was short and a voice came whispering, "Anyone 'ere?"

"Gumnuts, is that your voice?"

"Yeah, Fey. I come to get you."

"Where's Scamper?"

"'e's gone. 'as some business."

"Do you know where we're going?"

"Yeah, got a route an all. We better be quick or the sun will be up before we get there."

31

DUEL

Gumnuts led them through dark shadows and alleys. Patrols roamed the streets and spies and informers lurked in the darkness. A shot fired somewhere in the distance set dogs barking. Gumnuts led them out through the southern side of the town. "I 'ave to leave you 'ere, Fey. I'm goin' back. You 'ave to go on to get to your spot. Stay off the road and listen for someone in a cart, whistlin' 'Convict's Lament'."

It took another hour for Fey to find the place. Hidden by a stand of eucalypts near the road, they lay down to rest. A kookaburra sat in a tree above them, its loud, laughing call heralding the coming day. The cart's wheels crunched their way along the dirt road. The kookaburra fell silent and a man started singing, "One Sunday morning as I went walking, by Brisbane's waters I chanced to stray, I heard a convict, his fate bewailing, as on the sunny river bank he lay."

Fey stood and stepped into the road. "If you're going to warble, try to keep the tune."

"Hullo, Fey. Me singing is fine—it's your ears that are off key."

Fey grinned and shook the man's hand. "Have you got something for me?"

"I have, and you'd best take it quickly now and be on your way."

Fey beckoned Rosalyn from her hiding place and the man passed them the items, handing Fey a firkin. "You'll find your parts and tools in that—there's a false bottom. And you," he said, turning to Rosalyn. "Take this from me now. This length of timber is hollow, mind, but heavy. Inside is your brass pipe. Good luck and a good day to you both."

Rosalyn looked overhead. The *Eyrie* hovered menacingly over Sydney, its spying eyes turned away from them. They trekked south, avoiding the tracks, farms and shanties. In the late afternoon they emerged exhausted into the clearing, happy to see the *Lightning* again. Captain Hivetree and Edain were nowhere to be seen. A search of the area revealed nothing. "Do you think Edain has turned away from us?"

"I can't see it, Roz. I think she's on the square, same with Iggy. Something else has queered things. Look—Iggy's left his goggles here. We can't wait for them—we need to get started. They'll turn up."

Fey opened the firkin and with an axe, broke the wooden beam to extract the pipe. Fey studied the tools, pipe and the weapon.

"Can you make it work?"

"Yeah, Iggy explained it all to me as we were building it. We have to punch a hole in the side of the steam engine and run the pipe from it to the weapon. There're a few other little bits have to go on it to give it a flexibility. I'll start now."

"I'll keep a watch out for the others. Let me know if you need anything." Rosalyn lit the fire for the boiler and sat down on the fallen tree, staring into the bush and up at the sky. An ominous, dark cloudbank behind the Blue Mountains gave her cause to frown.

Fey laboured into the failing light and continued by lantern. Worn out and triumphant, she sat back on the skyrail. "It's done."

Rosalyn kissed her. "We'd best unhook."

"We're going in now?"

"We have to. I can only suppose Edain and Captain Hivetree

wandered off and got lost. We can't delay; your friends in Sydney are being rounded up and every hour makes them weaker. We have a colony to save." Rosalyn instructed Fey to unhook and douse the lantern.

The *Lightning* rose smoothly. Fey checked the weapon, fussing over its position at the front of the engine. Rosalyn took them to a high altitude, steering to the northwest. The wind picked up and it slowed the already sluggish craft even further. "Are you going to be able to work it in this weather?"

Rosalyn's jaw was set as firmly as her hands on the wheel. "Yes. When I get the Lightning turned we'll have the wind behind us and we can speed in on it. Can you see any sign of the Eyrie?"

Fey moved to the starboard side, scanning the sky for the other airship. "Over there. I see its lights about three hundred feet below us and further east."

"What's its heading?"

"Looks to be moving into the west and dropping altitude."

The wind grew stronger, Rosalyn squinting to keep it out of her eyes. Fey picked up Igneous's goggles and strapped them to Rosalyn's head.

"Are we directly west of the Eyrie?"

Fey looked over the side again. "Yes, it's battling the wind and moving slowly."

"It's trying to find shelter from the storm." Rosalyn had to shout to make herself heard.

"Storm?" Fey looked around as a flash of lightning illuminated a billowing cloud from within. "You can't fly in that!"

"Hold onto something, I'm bringing her around and we're going down." The *Lightning* banked and Rosalyn cut the blue aether. "Get the sails out."

Fey wound the handles, the wind caught the fabric and the airship accelerated. "The Eyrie is in front of us and below, heading our way."

"See to your gun." A loud clap of thunder boomed out across the mountains behind them and the first drops of rain splattered onto the airship.

Fey connected the pipe to the weapon, turned a valve and let the blue aether charge the device. "I don't know what the range is with this thing, Roz. I think two hundred yards will do it. If we wait too long they'll spot us."

"Wait until we're closer. If we fire and miss they'll be onto us." Rosalyn struggled with the wheel, trying to prevent the *Lightning* from being blown sideways.

Fey could see two of the crew on watch at the bow of the *Eyrie*, silhouetted by a lantern behind them. Another burst of lightning lit the sky, revealing the *Lightning* to the *Eyrie*'s lookout. One of the men turned and the other bent over a swivel gun. Fey aimed the weapon at the man at the gun. Squeezing the trigger, the weapon gave out a sharp, loud crack like a branch breaking. A pale blue light shot out of the muzzle. She watched as it connected with its target, bursting in a shower of powder and sparks. Both men collapsed and the gun fell from its mount.

Even over the storm they could hear shouting from the *Eyrie* and the shrill blowing of a whistle. Fey held onto the weapon. "Come on, come on, charge up," Fey urged it. Rosalyn had them down now at the same altitude as the *Eyrie*. Fey fired along its deck from bow to stern. The blue light burst along it and men cursed and screamed. Sir Rothwell could be heard yelling as the *Lightning* closed the distance.

As they drew close another swivel gun fired, the ball cracking into the hull of the *Lightning*, shattering planking and sending up splinters of wood. Fey moved back from the broken bow as a flash of blue light from the *Eyrie*'s own gun hit the *Lightning*. The light flashed past Fey and Rosalyn and burst on the cabin in the back. Pieces of timber dropped from the airship. The rain began pouring down, coming in almost horizontally with the wind.

On the ground below, people rushed from their houses, eyes focussed on the strange display of lights in the stormy sky. A cacophony of whistle blowing, cheering and shouting started up. Under the cover of the storm, and with their airship battling overhead, the rebels seized their chance. The Currency Rebellion had begun.

The starboard sail of the *Lightning* smashed into the bow of the *Eyrie*, the canvas and wood ripping and breaking. The combination of strong wind and the collision rocked the *Eyrie* and it listed heavily to port. The broken bow of the *Lightning* swung against the side of the enemy airship, the impact throwing the crew off their feet. Rosalyn gripped the wheel, trying desperately to get them away from the *Eyrie* as they passed it. The sail remained snagged on the *Eyrie*'s bow.

With the broken bow of the *Lightning* grinding against the side of the *Eyrie*, one of the enemy crew saw an opportunity. He climbed out of the *Eyrie*, sword in hand, his eyes fixed on Fey. Fey fired. The blue light exploded on the man's chest. His ribcage and spine dissolved, and unsupported, his head and shoulders fell forward. In his last moment he tried to turn, toppled, and fell over the side, plunging into the darkness without a sound.

The *Eyrie*'s gunner swung his weapon towards Rosalyn who watched the fight even as she struggled to control the airship. She threw herself backwards as the light impacted on the underside of the balloon. Rosalyn scrambled back into position.

The *Lightning*, tangled with the side of the *Eyrie*, caused the *Eyrie* to swing sideways to the storm. Shots fired from the *Eyrie*'s deck splintered into the wood around Fey. Rosalyn gave the balloon a burst of ascension. The airship rose against the side of its opponent.

Over the cracks of thunder, the sounds of the engines, the screeching propeller of the *Lightning* and the gunshots, Sir Rothwell could be heard shouting orders. The *Eyrie*'s bow turned back into the storm and gained altitude. Rosalyn tried desperately to create some distance from the enemy airship but the *Lightning* remained snared by the broken wing. The airship listed to starboard.

Fey fired down onto the *Eyrie*'s deck and had no idea what she hit. Blue light splashed onto it and men cried out in the darkness. Another burst of light spurted from the *Eyrie's* gun. It hit somewhere beneath the boat and Rosalyn lost propulsion. The iron shaft of the propeller disintegrated, and with nothing to hold it the propeller dropped from the airship.

With no propulsion, a snared and broken wing, Rosalyn lost control of the *Lightning*. Shots fired from the crew on the *Eyrie* smashed into the skyrail. Gusts of wind pushed the *Lightning* hard against the other vessel and both airships rocked and shuddered. Rosalyn clutched the wheel, hanging on tight. The impact threw Fey off her feet, her weapon's recharging pipe torn from the engine. Blue aether billowed out of the hole.

The *Eyrie* continued rising, pushing the *Lightning* up and to the side. Fey clambered back into position and aimed the weapon, firing its last charge. It struck a man in the head as he raised his weapon. The man's head, now without a skull, collapsed and he dropped to the deck, clutching his sagging face in his dying moment. Musket balls continued to slam into the *Lightning's* skyrail. Another bolt of light hit the stern cabin, sending more pieces of planking earthward.

Fey fired her pistols at the enemy crewmen as they threw hooks onto the *Lightning's* netting. A swaying of the airships saved Fey from obliteration as a shot of blue light burst on the underside of the balloon. Bolts of the balloon's support bracket disintegrated and the balloon twisted out of its housing.

Ignoring the rounds whistling by her head, Fey picked up the carbine and shot the enemy gunner before he could fire again. The fighting devolved into a duel with pistols, muskets and carbines. Fey and Rosalyn dropped to the deck as wood cracked and smashed under the sporadic fire from the enemy. Sir Rothwell's voice came to them across the gap. "Give it up, Reverend. You're beaten and you know it."

"Bugger you, Rothwell, you bloody bastard!" Rosalyn shouted back.

Fey stared at her in the gloom. "That was religious."

Rosalyn grinned and shrugged. Another volley of shots struck the *Lightning*. The women reloaded, struggling to keep their powder dry.

The voice of Sir Rothwell came to them again. "Prepare to be boarded. We won't be taking prisoners."

Fey and Rosalyn rose up together, fired off their weapons and sank back to the deck to reload. They heard Sir Rothwell shout out, "Behind!" There came another cracking of musketry, but the rounds were not directed at them. Peering above the skyrail, in the flashing of the muzzle fire, another airship could be seen on the other side of the *Eyrie*.

Rosalyn sprang up from the deck, grabbed one of the ropes hooking the *Lightning* and without heed of the danger, swung herself on to the *Eyrie*. A crewman, freshly reloaded, started raising his musket to fire. Rosalyn, only a few feet from the man, stepped forward and shot him in the chest. Blood sprayed her face, mixing with the rain water.

Fey, on seeing Rosalyn's action, followed her across to the *Eyrie*. The gunfire had stopped and the few survivors raised their arms. Armed currency men had boarded the *Eyrie* from the other airship. Rosalyn and Fey saw Sir Rothwell, exiting his cabin, and advanced on him. "It's over, Rothwell. You're our prisoner." Rosalyn's voice was calm and steady.

"Do you really think I'll let myself be taken by a couple of damned girls?"

"You have been."

Rothwell backed against the skyrail, looked at them, smiled and let himself fall. Rosalyn rushed to the rail. Rothwell didn't plummet but floated down to the darkness below.

Fey had come up beside her. "How'd he manage that?"

A woman's voice came from behind them. "It's a new machine; it allows one to float for a few seconds. If you're not close enough to the ground you fall." The voice belonged to Edain.

"Ses!"

"Edain!" Rosalyn wrapped her arms around Edain, hugging her closely.

"Sorry we had to leave the Lightning back there in the forest; there were Order men close by and we had to lead them away. It was quite a chase."

"Where is your father?"

Edain nodded in the direction of the other ship. "Daddy's the only one mad and skilled enough to fly an airship in a storm." She paused. "And you too, I see."

"Edain, how did you get another airship?"

"I'll tell you the details when this is over. In a nutshell, after we led the Order men away from the Lightning we evaded them, reaching Sydney. We learned another airship was here. It's the Eyrie's supply ship, apparently. We had the idea of stealing it only to find some of the colonials had the same notion. We joined forces and were about to seize it when the battle broke out in the skies above. That provided a timely diversion."

The Eyrie, now without a crew, had begun to swing wildly. Igneous disengaged, taking his airship to the safety of the ground. Rosalyn moved to the helm. "I have to get control of this airship. Edain, Fey, cut the Lightning free."

The women found axes and hacked at the ropes and canvas holding the Lightning to the Eyrie. With the lines cut, the wind took hold of the battered airship and swept it off into the eastern sky. Unencumbered, Rosalyn found the Eyrie manageable—even with the dying storm still tossing it around. Fey came and stood at Rosalyn's side. "Are you all right?"

"I've never felt more alive." Rosalyn's eyes were wild, her wet hair stuck in strands across her blood-streaked face. Her gaze fixed on the bow, she swung the airship around to bring it back over Sydney.

"You're bleeding."

"Not my blood. Stop talking and get to the weapon. We're going in to battle."

Fey, ignoring the dead crew of the Eyrie, took a position at the gun. The workings were similar to the weapon Igneous had put together out in the desert and Fey had no trouble in figuring out its operation. With the prisoners secured, the few currency men on board were taken in charge by Edain who put them to use working the sails.

Flashes of musketry in the barracks area showed the *Eyrie's* new crew where the fighting was most intense. A company of the Mechanical Order, barricaded in one of the buildings, held off the irregular forces of the Currency League. Rosalyn kept the *Eyrie* in a static position giving Fey the best possible angle of attack.

Fey fired, the blue light flashed through the dawn and splashed against one of the windows. For an instant, the fighting stopped. A fierce shout went up from the colonials as a second shot struck a door. The hinges turned to powder and it fell from its position. After several more shots at the barracks from Fey's weapon, the currency company rushed the main building. The fighting was brief. The defending men of the Divine Order of Mechanics, thoroughly demoralised by their own weapon being used against them, threw down their arms.

Down towards Bennelong Point, officers of the 50th Regiment were rallying their men for an assault on Fort Macquarie. Rosalyn brought the *Eyrie* around, hovering near the fort. Artillery fire kept the 50th at bay. Fey fired, hitting one of the cannons in the middle. The tip of its barrel fell to the ground, the crew recoiling in shock. The men of the 50th, heartened by the sight, gave a loud cheer and swarmed into the fort. The artillerymen ceded the fight.

For the next hour sporadic firing continued throughout Sydney as pockets of stragglers tried vainly to hold out. A silence settled over the town and Rosalyn grounded the *Eyrie* in the barracks square. Igneous, who had watched the progress of the battle, flew the supply ship over and grounded next to the *Eyrie*. The Sydneysiders—merchants, traders, ticket-of-leave men and women, seamen, householders and currency kids—came crowding around them, shouting and cheering at the focus of their liberation. Rosalyn managed to make her voice heard and a guard was put on the airships. Scamper came out of the crowd to join them.

"Greetin's, Fey. Good ter see yer."

"Scamper! I thought we'd lost you when you didn't come and get us out of that bloody hole."

"Sorry, Fey, 'ad to scarper. Things were tight."

"Where'd you go?"

Scamper took out his tobacco and offered a pinch to Fey, who accepted. "Kept on the run until I saw the sky light up. I knew it was you and yer slavey." Fey looked at Rosalyn who was talking to Igneous and Edain. She glanced over, smiled and went back to her conversation. Scamper lit his pipe and continued. "I joined in with the barracks push. I tell yer, Fey, that was a fight to live for. Can yer believe it? We got them Fey. We took the town."

"Rothwell escaped. He has to be found. And we have to set up the council before the military takes control."

"We 'ave an agreement, Fey, remember?"

"I don't reckon on them being square. Once they have control we'll have bugger all chance of getting it back." Rosalyn turned to them. "Fey, don't you think the military are better suited to restoring order?"

"Roz, they might be, but they'll be restoring their order. We live here—we know what we want and we don't want it like it was. Convicts or not, people aren't slaves. Things have to change."

Scamper nodded. "We want change. We want a share in governin' and that 'as to be done by the people. But, Fey, the military already agreed. Let's see if they're stickin' to the deal. We need to find One 'ole and get the council at a point."

"Where's the Governor? Has he been freed yet?"

"'e was under 'ouse arrest. I suppose 'e's freed now. The soldier's will be gettin' their dung in a tidy pile so I expect we'll see 'em and the Governor in a few ticks."

The rain had stopped and the morning sun's reflections sparkled off the puddles. One Hole arrived at the crowded Barracks Square followed by an entourage of men and women. Governor Gipps joined them, marching in with the triumphant men of the 50th, their colours flying and drums beating. The leaders of the Currency League, Governor Gipps and his officers, filed into the mess hall for their meeting. Rosalyn accompanied Fey. The room was alive with the murmurings of the attendees. Governor Gipps banged a pewter mug on the table for attention. "I understand there is in existence a colonial militia calling itself 'New Currency'."

One Hole spoke. "The Currency League, Governor."

"I'm also of the understanding that this militia was formed before these rascals of the Mechanical Order took Sydney, and this same militia was intending to take Sydney for itself."

"There might be some truth in it."

"Who are you?"

"One Hole, they call me. My name is Begley, Bill Begley. I'm the speaker for the Currency Council."

"Council?"

"Yes Governor, we formed a council to run our affairs."

"Your council is void. Your militia will disband."

"I beg to differ, Governor. We made an agreement with some of your officers while you were enjoying your own company under the guard of the Redbacks."

"Redbacks?"

One of the officers standing behind the Governor leaned over to him. "What the colonials call the soldiers of the Divine Order of Mechanics." The Governor nodded.

"We agreed to certain terms and conditions under which we'd continue to accept your authority."

"Any agreements made by my officers have no authority from me and are therefore null and void. Order will be restored as it was before."

The Currency League members in attendance muttered and Fey whispered to Rosalyn, "I told you we couldn't trust them."

"Governor, you were imprisoned and I believe the officers we spoke with were the highest ranking representatives at liberty. I would also like to remind you that you—and Sydney—were liberated only because the militia were in a position to oppose those who took it. We have no intention of disbanding and we will not accept the casting aside of our agreement with your officers. You might also think on this. Whatever powers that terrible weapon on the airship out there comes from the interior of this land. The knowledge of it can't be kept secret and there're going to be a lot of interested parties in Europe and elsewhere who will want to get hold of it. The defences here will need to be strengthened. Do you really want a war with us when we could be working together to common purpose?"

Governor Gipps stared at One Hole. The room waited for his response. He rubbed his chin. "I will ignore the threat of insurrection, Mr Begley. We'll have a short recess for tea while I discuss this with my officers."

Half an hour later they were seated back at the tables. The room filled up with pipe smoke. "Mister Begley, you and all your council could be hanged for treason." The room remained quiet and Governor Gipps continued. "But you won't be and nor will I agree to your demand to free any convicts." The currency men and women murmured angrily. The Governor raised his hand for silence. "However, those who have committed property offences under five pounds of value will be given all the privileges of free men except one: They will not leave the colony until their sentences have expired." He sat back as the voices of discontent abated.

"What about the council we want?"

"I agree to the forming of councils representing the interests of former convicts, free settlers and farmers. I will also include a council of the leading businesses. The councils will be advisory only but your voices will be heard."

One Hole nodded. "And the militia?"

"The militia will be allowed to stand. We will even provide them with uniforms but they must swear an oath of allegiance to the crown." This led to renewed discussion between the colonials, the result being a general nodding of heads in agreement.

"Good," said the Governor. "I will write in my report to England that the colonials formed a militia in secret to overthrow the Divine Order of Mechanics, and that you are all to be commended for your quick thinking and valour. In regard to your final demand I will also be recommending the transportation of convicts cease and to encourage the sending of more free settlers. Now, I have the British flag here and I expect, before you leave this room, you will take the oath of loyalty."

One Hole took a deep breath. "Agreed."

After Fey swore her allegiance, she and Rosalyn left the meeting and walked out to the barracks square. "That wasn't so bad was it, Fey?"

Fey sighed deeply. "It was like passing under the yoke, but I can live with it. What are Ses and Iggy up to?"

"Do you mean Edain?"

"Yeah, I meant Edain."

A heavy guard surrounded the airships. Many of the Sydney residents had returned to their homes or to the taverns. A small crowd who had no compelling reasons to be anywhere else, lingered, kept back from the airships by the soldiers. Only a handful of people were allowed close. Those included Rosalyn, Fey, Edain and Igneous.

"We're going back into the desert," said Edain quietly to Rosalyn and Fey.

"For Watson and Geoffrey?"

"Yes, for them, and to look at the area where I found the Green Wave."

"May I see it again?"

Edain removed the book from her satchel and handed it to Rosalyn. "It's a strange looking butterfly."

"Stranger than you think. I examined it closely through my sunglass. The tiny scales of the butterfly's wings are shedded and new ones grow."

"So what?" said Fey. "Dogs shed fur and it grows back."

"On the scales are minute parasites. I have a theory that the Aqua Glass grows either from the parasites or the shedded scales."

"So..." Rosalyn pondered. "You could breed the Green Wave and create more Aqua Glass."

"Yes. We need to find more of these butterflies."

Fey leaned against the side of the *Eyrie*'s supply airship. "I suppose you're taking this one."

"Yes, I suppose we are," said Igneous.

"You'll want to leave quietly and leave soon. I can see the military taking control of this one, too."

"They can have it when we return."

Fey packed her pipe. "If you're coming back you could call this airship Boomerang."

"What's a boomerang?" asked Rosalyn.

"It's a throwing stick the blacks use for hunting and fighting. Some of the sticks are made to return to the thrower. See, told you I could speak the language." Fey gave Edain a wink.

Edain rolled her eyes. "The Boomerang it is."

"When are you leaving?" asked Rosalyn.

Igneous stroked his sideburns. "We have to get provisions on-board, fuel and water, that sort of thing."

"I'll take care of it for you." Fey beckoned to a couple of currency lads from the crowd and spoke with them. The currency lads returned within the hour with half a dozen extra hands, carrying the supplies. The military guards questioned the activity and Captain Hivetree assured them it was an authorised rescue mission for a pair of stranded scientists. He climbed aboard and started the engine.

"Will you be here when we return, Rosalyn?" asked Edain.

"I don't know. My Church Mission was to find Doctor Phatts, locate a site for a Missionary station and bring Enlightenment to the heathens. I found the Doctor and a good site, but I think I might keep it to myself. I'll stay in Sydney and mind the Church here until I receive instructions from London."

"I'll be here," said Fey. "You call in and see me when you get back, and bring Iggy with you."

"Of course, Fey. You're my favourite colonial." Edain grinned and gave Fey a hug before turning to Rosalyn and doing the same. "It's been a pleasure flying with you, Captain Flynn."

"Captain Flynn?"

Edain stood back, her hands on Rosalyn's shoulders. "Yes, Captain Flynn. You make a far better airship pilot than you do a Missionary."

"Yeah, she's right, Roz."

"Apart from not doing any Mission work or returning with Doctor Phatts—and losing my airship—I thought I did a good job following my Mission Orders."

"See? You did a much better job of flying."

Igneous climbed out of the *Boomerang* and took Edain by the hand. "I do hate to interrupt your affectionate farewells but we really must get aloft before these military chaps dampen our endeavours. Good luck to you both, goodbye, God bless and all that, and remember, not a word about who I am. I do hate attention."

Fey and Rosalyn stood together watching as Edain and her father boarded the *Boomerang*. Edain pulled the hooks in and Igneous opened the injector. The *Boomerang* swayed, left the ground and rose above the barracks square. The small crowd cheered for no other reason than the excitement of seeing an airship rising into the sky.

In the evening most of Sydney celebrated the overthrow of the Mechanical Order and the restoration of the colonial government. Soldiers searched the town for Sir Rothwell but found nothing other than the device he'd used when he dropped from the *Eyrie*. Fey and Rosalyn didn't join the celebrations, instead slipping quietly away to sit on the veranda of Mother Mary's cottage. They watched the sun set, their fingertips linked loosely between them.

"Do you think you'll stay in Sydney, Roz?"

Rosalyn took a long pull from the bottle they were sharing. "I expect I'll hear from the Church soon. They said they were sending more clergy out and I suspect there'll be someone coming with authority to give me direction."

"You'll be here for a few weeks yet." Fey pulled on her pipe and watched the evening sky behind the Blue Mountains turn red.

"What will you do?" asked Rosalyn. "Are you going to go back to your old work of waiting for the ships to come in and guiding the new settlers?"

"I don't think so. I'll find some other line of work. Plenty of opportunities here for an enterprising colonial."

They both looked up, startled. A figure came rushing around the corner of the house. Before they realised who it was, the man raised a pistol and fired. Rosalyn clutched her chest and fell forward onto the floorboards with a thud.

"You're next, currency scum." Sir Rothwell raised another pistol. Fey sprang at him before he could fire, twisting his hand. The shot exploded under Sir Rothwell's chin, blowing out the top of his head. Before Sir Rothwell's body had hit the ground, Fey had turned back to Rosalyn. Her breathing had stopped and her blood flooded across the dry, grey planks of the veranda.

Fey left her and dashed into the cottage, pulling from her sack the Aqua Glass she had hidden for herself. Arranging a few pieces in a circle, she stepped out to where Rosalyn lay, and waited.

Fey and Rosalyn sat on the veranda of Mother Mary's cottage watching the sun set, their fingertips linked loosely between them. Rosalyn, puzzled, felt her chest. Fey ducked inside the cottage and took up her pistol. She returned to the veranda and said to Rosalyn, "This isn't ending here." She stepped around the corner of the cottage and raised her pistol at the figure standing there. Sir Rothwell, bewildered, started to raise his weapon. "Bit of a setback for you this." Fey fired, putting a neat round hole in Sir Rothwell's forehead. He dropped to the ground, raising a small dust cloud and his rich, red blood flooded across the dry, brown earth.

32

FAREWELL TO OLD ENGLAND FOREVER

The parson's house was much as she'd last seen it when he'd been found dead on the floor. The kitchen had been thoroughly cleaned but all the kitchenware was missing. Rosalyn purchased another kettle and new china and set about packing the parson's personal belongings. It felt disturbing to her to be sleeping in his bed so she chose instead to sleep on the couch in the drawing room. The paper boy came by, as she'd instructed him. She sat on the porch reading the news and sipping her tea.

After a cursory glance at the shipping intelligence she turned the page and scanned through the column headlines. One of them caught her eye: Gravitationally Ignorant Brass—Success Claimed. She browsed past it. The news of the crushing of the rebellion interested her most. Her eyes narrowed as she read:

'Messrs Barton and Flint of the Barton and Flint shipyard on Black Wattle Bay, have pleaded before a Judge their innocence of any knowledge of, or part in the insurrection of Sir Rothwell Blaze of the Divine Order of Mechanics. It should be noted that the Barton and Flint shipyard is owned by the Divine Order of Mechanics and the airship which wreaked such destruction on our peaceful colony was built in great secrecy in those same yards.

The two gentleman are the directors of the shipyard and furthermore both gentleman admit freely to being members of the Mechanical Order. In their defence they produced, as witness, a Sergeant Hopson, who led a detachment of soldiers to the shipyard during the recent battle and found the two gentleman under lock and key. A Redback soldier guarding the building was shot dead as he attempted to flee. Messrs Barton and Flint further claim the Divine Order of Mechanics had no knowledge of Sir Rothwell's treasonous activities and he acted of his own accord.

The gentlemen further insist the Eyrie is the property of the Divine Order of Mechanics and should be released to them forthwith. The Judge questioned them on their secrecy and of the presence of the weapon on board the Eyrie. The gentlemen answered that they had wished their expedition secret as they were looking for the Aqua Glass and had every right to retain their confidences when engaged on such an expensive search. The machine was included in the hope of being tested if Aqua Glass were found. Messrs Barton and Flint further claimed they were ignorant of the machine being a weapon as it was intended for the peaceful purpose of mining.

The Judge ruled that Sir Rothwell acted of his own accord and had deceived even members of his own expedition. However, the Judge also ruled that as the Divine Order of Mechanics had created the situation Sir Rothwell exploited then the Order be held somewhat responsible for compensation and damages to those who lost property in the insurrection. The Eyrie is to be made forfeit and sold at auction along with the shipyards. As there is much ill feeling against the Divine Order of Mechanics, the Judge also instructed that for their safety, the two gentleman must leave the colony on the first available vessel.

Sir Rothwell Blaze escaped the frightful battle in the sky but found justice when he was shot dead as he tried to take the life of the Reverend Missionary Rosalyn Flynn of the Church of the Sun Cog. We are pleased to report that Reverend Flynn, who played such a valiant and vital part in the liberation of our fair town, escaped harm and is now in occupation of the Sun Cog Parsonage and is holding services at the Church.'

Rosalyn let out a sigh and stared over at the Church. Every seat would be filled when she held the service, but it would be to see her rather than listen to her teachings of the Church's doctrines. The tea leaves floated in the bottom of her cup. She swished them around wondering how anyone could possibly know the future from them. As she stood to take her cup inside, a carriage drew up in front of the Church and a passenger alighted. She looked strangely familiar. The new arrival didn't notice Rosalyn at first; her eyes were fixed on the Church itself. She gazed around, saw Rosalyn standing on the veranda, gave a wave and walked over to her.

"This is unexpected," said Rosalyn.

"It is. I thought you would be out on the frontier," said Constance.

"Change of plans. I returned early."

"So I see." Constance pursed her lips and stared out towards the harbour.

"You must have had a change of plans also. Did London not suit you?"

Constance turned to Rosalyn. "I'm to take up a position at a new Church we're building at Bathurst."

Rosalyn noticed Constance's eyes growing teary and the trembling in her voice. "Perhaps you should come inside. We'll have a cup of tea."

The women settled in the drawing room. Constance's hand shook as she raised her teacup from the saucer, spilling a small amount of tea.

"What is it, Constance?"

Constance set the cup down and sighed deeply. "I suppose you'll hear of it anyway so you may as well hear it from me." She paused and took out a silk handkerchief with which she dabbed her eyes.

"When I arrived in London I had cause for celebration. I fear I drank too much and... and the short of it is that one of our Church elders took advantage of me. The indiscretion was witnessed." Constance started crying and buried her face in her hands. "I've made an awful mess of it."

Rosalyn set down her cup and wrapped an arm around Constance's shoulder. "I'm sorry that happened to you."

The woman's crying ceased and she wiped away her tears. "You're not going to gloat at my misfortune?"

"No. Why would I?"

Constance ignored the question. "If the Church wasn't in such need of people I would have been dismissed. Daddy gave me no support at all. He said I was a disgrace and he agreed to sending me to the colony. The elder was allowed to remain in London. It's so unfair."

"A lot of things are unfair. If we can't change things we have to make the best of them. I'm sure when you get used to it you'll find it quite refreshing here in New South Wales. I suppose you heard the news?"

"I heard about an insurrection which was quickly put down."

"Yes, that's it in a nutshell."

"So why are you in Sydney? Aren't you supposed to be out looking for Doctor Phatts?"

"I thought that was a secret. In any case I found him."

Constance leaned back. "That's wonderful. So he's back in Sydney now?"

"No, he chose not to return."

A quizzical look crossed Constance's features. "Odd. Why was that?"

"He's quite happy where he is. I returned to Sydney and with my Mission complete I decided to take up Reverend Barnes' position and wait for word from the Church. You did hear about the murder of Reverend Barnes didn't you?"

"A newspaper boy told me. It's such a terrible thing. As for your instructions, I did come bearing them." Constance reached into her satchel and handed Rosalyn an envelope. "I can tell you what it says. I was to inform you that if you had found Doctor Phatts you are to return to England immediately to report in person."

"Return to England. I see."

"I have in my party three more members of the clergy and a Guardian. In addition to the Church at Bathurst we'll be opening a second Church in Sydney. We expect there'll be many more throughout the colonies within the year. We live in exciting times, Rosalyn."

"Indeed we do. I suppose I'd best book a passage to England and start my packing."

"If you need assistance..."

"That's fine, Constance, and please, do make yourself at home."

Rosalyn left her trunk at the parsonage to be picked up by a porter and went in search of Fey. Her walk took her by the barracks. The guards recognised her and let her enter. She wandered around the *Eyrie*, trailing her fingers over the planking. A smile formed on her lips as she remembered the thrill of commanding the vessel and the exhilaration of boarding it while so high above the earth. She wondered who would be lucky enough to command the vessel. Continuing on, she found Fey's whereabouts by interrogating the young currency lads and lasses she came upon.

The tavern was mostly empty and Fey sat in a corner, her face illuminated by a shaft of light coming through the panelled window. A couple of men were in her company. They all looked at Rosalyn as she entered. "Conspiring again, Fey?"

Fey grinned. "Yeah, Sydney failed so we thought we might crack New Zealand." Fey noticed Rosalyn's forlorn look. "What's the ail?"

Rosalyn glanced at the two men and back to Fey, who addressed the men. "We'll continue this later."

The women walked in silence to Mother Mary's cottage and sat on the bench on the veranda. "I've been ordered back to England." Fey didn't make any response. "I'm supposed to leave when I can book a passage."

"I heard there were more of your cog turners in town off today's ship. They brought the instruction?"

Rosalyn nodded. "Do you have any gin?"

Fey went inside the cottage, returning shortly with a bottle and two pewter cups. "Are you going?"

"Yes." Rosalyn sighed. "I lost the Lightning. I don't suppose I'll have the opportunity to fly again."

"Is it the thought of being stuck on the ground that's got you under?"

"Not just that." Rosalyn looked at Fey and her eyes were wet with tears.

"You have to do what's right for you, Roz, but you got to know I'd love to have you stay in town."

"My family is in England. I have a place with the Church."

"You have a place here, too."

"Don't make this hard for me."

"It's hard for me too, Roz."

"I have to go home."

"You don't have to do anything."

"Don't fight me on this, Fey."

"I'm not fighting you—you're fighting yourself." Fey swallowed her gin and poured another serve.

Rosalyn made no reply and stared at the road, cupping her drink in both hands. A tear rolled down her cheek. "I'm going home, Fey."

Fey nodded without looking at her. "So this is farewell." Fey stood. "I won't see your ship off but I'll arrange for someone to take your baggage. You got baggage don't you?"

"Yeah," said Rosalyn, trying to smile. "I got baggage."

"You take care, Roz."

Rosalyn put her cup down and reached out for Fey's hand, stood, and hugged her. They held each other tightly. "It was an honour to fly with you, Captain Flynn."

Rosalyn arrived at the Central Office of the Enlightenment Church. Word of her arrival had preceded her and she was ushered into an expensively furnished meeting room where a fuss was made of her by the Church Council.

"You did well under the circumstances, Reverend Flynn. The Church attaches no blame to your failure to retrieve Doctor Phatts. It's obvious the man has become seriously deranged. The Royal Scientific Society will mount its own rescue mission."

"I don't think he wants rescuing."

The Cog Bishop ignored her. "From your account of their lives, the heathen should be easy to win over. Civilisation has much to offer them and they'll no doubt welcome a change of diet from kangaroo, grass seeds and grubs."

"Did you read the bit of my report saying they're quite happy?"

"You only saw the local picture. We see the big one. After reading your report, a new, better equipped Mission is currently being organised. Now, as for you, you may choose your post. Would you like Paris?"

Rosalyn's gaze drifted from the Cog Bishop to a crow outside the window. As she looked at it the bird launched itself into the air. Rosalyn quietly answered, "No."

"No? Where then?"

"I'm leaving the Church. I've realised it's not my calling."

"You've had a trying time for one so young. Perhaps you should take some time to consider. You need a period of rest and reflection."

"Yes, perhaps I do. I need to spend some time with my family."

"Before you do, your attendance is required for a presentation."

The coach picked up Rosalyn the following morning and with some of the Council in escort, delivered her to Buckingham Palace. The presentation of the Queen's Cross, a new award for outstanding service to the crown, was mercifully brief and attended with little fanfare. Queen Victoria was smaller than Rosalyn had expected. In her mind royalty were imposing and regal in appearance.

"Come, walk with me," said the Queen. Together and without company they walked through the corridors. "You've had quite a time in New South Wales. Tell me, how is Captain Hivetree?"

Rosalyn turned to the Queen in surprise. There'd been no public mention of Captain Hivetree being in the colony and only a handful of people had known he was there.

"He's well, Ma'am. How did you know he was in New South Wales?"

"I sent him. What's he doing with himself now?"

They stopped walking. "He went with a companion to retrieve a couple of members of the party who had to be left behind in the desert."

"I'm assuming the companion to be his daughter. How is Edain?"

"She's well also." Rosalyn paused as she tried to gather her thoughts. "Ma'am, may I ask a question?"

"Please do."

"Why did you send Captain Hivetree to the colony? What's the connection."

The Queen took Rosalyn's hands and looked at her in earnest. "He is someone I can trust. Can I trust you too, Reverend Flynn?"

"Of course."

"Then tell me of this Divine Order of Mechanics. You were a prisoner on the Eyrie. Do you think the villain, Rothwell Blaze, acted independently or do you think the Order was behind it."

"Ma'am, I was quite shocked to learn of the judge's acceptance that the Order was innocent of any wrongdoing. That wasn't my impression at all."

"Quite right. They are strong and certainly we know those members who are public but many of them are not known to us. Until we do know we cannot act lest we trigger the very event we hope to avoid."

"What is that, Ma'am?"

"A rebellion here in England—an overthrow of the state."

"Do you think that might happen?"

"Yes. We do have one or two people of our own in the Mechanical Order, and it is through their enterprise that we learned of some of their plans in the colony. Captain Hivetree was most suited for the task of learning what was afoot. He insisted on taking Edain and we relented."

"Ma'am, when you say 'we', do you mean the royal 'we' or do you refer to others?"

"There is a small union of people working at undoing the Mechanical Order and exposing their nest. There is something else— you found the Aqua Glass—did Captain Hivetree carry out any experiment after it was found?"

"Experiment? He shot a lizard, a frightfully big lizard; Varanus Rex Gilroy if I remember its scientific name correctly."

"Nothing else?"

Rosalyn stared thoughtfully at the plush carpet, "Yes, yes there was. We tested the Aqua Glass under moonlight and..." Rosalyn looked around to ensure that no other ears were listening. "...and we experienced a small Setback, an Ante Vidoram, but it was local."

"Are you certain of that?"

"Yes, Ma'am." Rosalyn related the true details of Rothwell's death at the hands of Fey.

"You died?" The Queen raised her eyebrows.

"Yes, Ma'am, and no one else knew of the Setback, or experienced one when we created the first Setback in the desert ruins."

The Queen walked to the window and looked out. "Captain Hivetree was right. Do you know what this means?"

"Yes, Ma'am. A central tenet of the teachings of the Enlightenment Church has been proved not to be the work of God but the work of people."

"People? Perhaps. I'm sure the Church can find a way to incorporate this new knowledge into its teachings. After all, it leaves in place our understanding of our free will."

"Yes, Ma'am. I'm sure the Church will survive it—if the knowledge ever becomes public."

"It will be a matter of time," said the Queen.

"Very witty, Ma'am."

Queen Victoria smiled. "Would you like to join our Union and work with us against the Mechanical Order?"

"Why, yes, Ma'am, it would be an honour. In truth I've been thinking of leaving the Church but I don't know what course I would then follow."

"I would like you to leave it and return to Sydney. That town is going to be the locus of attention, drawing people from all over the world. You can use the prestige you've gained from liberating the town to increase your social standing and become successful—and act as our eyes and ears in the colony. Does that suit you?"

Rosalyn disembarked. She made straight away for the young lad selling newspapers. "Good afternoon. Do you know Miss Fey Grey?"

"Yeah, everyone knows Fey."

"Do you know where I might find her?"

"Yeah."

"Are you going to tell me?"

"Are you goin' to buy a paper?" Rosalyn smiled and bought a copy. "She's in the cemetery."

Rosalyn's mouth dropped open, her hand curled into a fist around the newspaper. "How?"

"She walked there."

"What do you mean?"

The boy looked at her like she was simple. "She ain't dead or nuffin'. She took some flowers up. Wasn't long ago—you can catch 'er if you walk quick."

Rosalyn breathed a sigh of relief and asked the lad for directions.

It was a long walk to the cemetery and she had to search the rows of headstones. She saw a well-dressed man in a suit and approached him to ask if he might have seen Fey. The man knelt by a large grave marker. Hearing her approach, he stood and turned.

"Fey!"

Fey grinned. "Roz. I didn't think you'd come back."

"I couldn't stay away."

"Edain said you'd come back. I wanted to believe her."

"Well, here I am."

Fey looked from her to the grave. "I was putting some flowers there for Mother Mary."

"That's quite a head stone."

"I wanted her to have a fitting memorial."

"And your mother?"

"Still a drunk, but she gets sober now and then. That's something."

"And you? Look at you, so smartly dressed—and still mannish. What are you doing for employment?"

Fey looked Rosalyn in the eye. It had been nine months since they'd last seen each other. She moved impulsively towards Rosalyn who, surprised, stepped back. Fey faltered, took Rosalyn's hand and looked away. "Come, I'll show you." She led her through the streets of Sydney and they stopped along Pitt Street.

Rosalyn stared at the shop they were standing outside and read aloud the words on the window. "'Burke's Gentlemen's Outfitters'. You're a shop assistant?"

"Across the road, Roz."

Rosalyn turned and looked. A large yellow sign above the shop presented the title in bold, black letters, 'Colonial Airship Company', arching above a silhouette of an airship and below that, 'New South Wales'. "You work there?"

"Yeah, come and have a squiz." They crossed the street and the young man at the desk greeted them politely. Fey, still holding Rosalyn's hand, led her along a short corridor into a spacious room.

The walls were covered with airship designs and an airship model hung from the ceiling. An oak desk sat on the other side of the room and on it rested a small sign: 'Fey Grey, Proprietor'.

"You own the company?" asked Rosalyn in surprise.

"Yeah, Roz, I own it."

"Fey, that's wonderful." Rosalyn's gaze drifted around the room and back to Fey. "Do you have any airships?"

"I have two being built and several in the design stage. I only own the one as yet. I bought the Eyrie."

"Using the gold you found?"

"That and a piece of Aqua Glass I sold. Worth more than diamonds that stuff."

"And your business is doing well?"

"So well, Roz, that I need a partner. I've been holding the position open." Fey, who was still holding Rosalyn's hand, turned to her, taking her other hand. This time Rosalyn made no move to step back and leaned forward into Fey, her arms sliding around her neck. The kiss was long and soft. "Welcome home, Roz."

ACKNOWLEDGEMENTS

This book, my first novel, was four years in the making. Periods of inspired activity were interspersed with long stretches of disinterest, procrastination and 'why am I doing this?' Somehow I managed to get the work finished albeit with some help along the way.

First and foremost in the list is my Mum whose support and encouragement kept me going. She even read the manuscript and said nice things about it whilst claiming an unbiased opinion.

A couple of my brothers rendered assistance. Allan helped enormously with his dedicated readings of the story followed by detailed feedback, and Russell came to my aid with the formatting. It was with Russell that my imagination was honed in my formative years creating comics and artwork together.

Others who aided me in this project in one way or another were Jessica, Kelly, Kate, Shirley and Jason. Of indirect assistance were steampunks everywhere. You inspired me with your gadgetry and artistry in every creative field, from costume to music.

Lastly I'd like to thank Argo, who insisted I take breaks from writing to enjoy the sunshine and play Frisbee.

www.ingramcontent.com/pod-product-compliance
Lightning Source LLC
Chambersburg PA
CBHW030343120726
47901CB00007B/1890